STORIES OF MEN

Also Available in Prometheus's Literary Classics Series

Henry Adams
Esther

Aristophanes
Assembly of Women (Ecclesiazusae)

Anton Chekov
Stories of Women

Kate Chopin
The Awakening

Stephen Crane
Maggie: A Girl of the Streets

Nathaniel Hawthorne
The Scarlet Letter

Henry James
The Turn of the Screw and *The Lesson of the Master*

Sinclair Lewis
Main Street

Herman Melville
The Confidence Man

John Neal
Rachel Dyer

Mark Twain
The Mysterious Stranger

Walt Whitman
Leaves of Grass

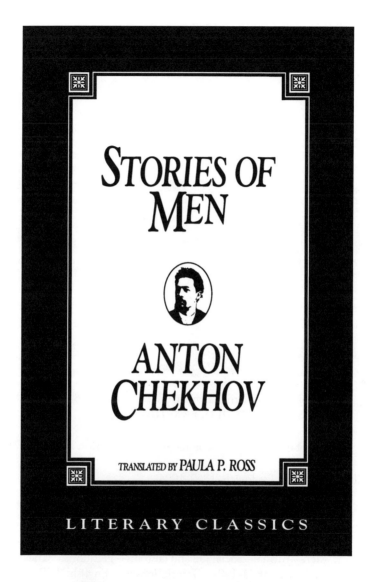

STORIES OF MEN

ANTON CHEKHOV

TRANSLATED BY PAULA P. ROSS

LITERARY CLASSICS

 **Prometheus Books**

59 John Glenn Drive
Amherst, New York 14228-2197

Published 1997 by Prometheus Books

59 John Glenn Drive, Amherst, New York 14228–2197,
716–691–0133. FAX: 716–691–0137.

Library of Congress Cataloging-in-Publication Data

Chekhov, Anton Pavlovich, 1860–1904.
    [Short stories. English. Selections]
    Stories of men / Anton Chekhov; translated by Paula P. Ross.
        p.   cm. — (Literary classics)
    ISBN 1–57392–135–1 (pbk. : alk. paper)
    1. Men—Russia—Social life and customs—Fiction. 2. Chekhov,
Anton Pavlovich, 1860–1904—Translations into English. I. Ross,
Paula P., 1921–   . II. Title. III. Series: Literary classics (Amherst,
N.Y.)
PG3456.A15R67   1997
891.73'3—dc21   96–38096
                                                                      CIP

Printed in the United States of America on acid-free paper.

"The bitter truth is better than a beautiful lie."

—old Russian saying

PAULA P. ROSS's interest in Russian literature began as an undergraduate in the 1940s. She has taught economics and sociology at Cedar Crest College, Chestnut Hill College, Drexel University, and Western Michigan University.

ANTON PAVLOVICH CHEKHOV was born on January 17, 1860, in Taganrog, a port on the Sea of Azov. His father, a small shopkeeper, had been born a serf, but his grandfather had saved enough money to buy freedom for himself and his sons.

Chekhov had four brothers and one sister, and their needs were a primary concern for him during his entire life. The family rived in a miserable neighborhood and their one-story house had a shop in the front and a tavern in the basement. The tyrannical father did not spare the boys in any way, and Anton was an often-flogged little garbage man and bartender.

In a letter to one of his brothers, Chekhov later wrote:

> I beg you to remember that despotism and lies destroyed your mother's youth. Despotism and lies have spoiled our youth to such a degree that it is loathsome and terrible to recall it. Remember the fear and revulsion we felt every time Father threw his indignant and furious tantrums at the dinner table because the soup was too salty, reviling and insulting our mother as if she were a dim-witted imbecile.

At age sixteen, Chekhov was left to fend for himself when his father moved the family to Moscow in order to escape debtor's prison. Anton remained in Taganrog where he was in school on a scholarship. Away from his father, his true nature blossomed and replaced misery with a youthful exuberance to which was added a passion for the theater and music.

After finishing school in Taganrog, Chekhov went to Moscow, where he studied medicine at the University on scholarship. To help with his family's finances, he started publishing articles, tales, jokes, and anecdotes. By the time that he earned his medical degree in 1884, his main interest was writing. His medical practice furnished him with constant contact with uninhibited human beings who in their weakened states provided him with an infinite amount of material—and skepticism. He wrote that medicine was his "legal wife" and that literature was his "mistress."

Chekhov's literary reputation grew with the publication of his collection *Motley Stories* (1886). In 1888 he was awarded the Pushkin Prize for another collection, *In the Twilight*. This, and publication of his story "The Steppe" (1888), established him as one of Russia's leading writers.

All of Chekhov's writing reflects the man himself. From age fourteen, when he had his first attack of pleurisy, until his death, he was often desperately ill. He understood the importance of what he called "life's trifles" and rarely neglected these in his writing. In the conduct of his life he was the epitome of all that was kind, generous, witty, and humane, and he was an inveterate optimist. On his deathbed, he wrote: "life and people are becoming better and better, wiser and more honorable. . . ." But he did not believe in shifting responsibility for one's behavior to circumstances and society. The human being, he intensely believed, was perfectly competent to judge right from wrong. This did not make him popular with the future socialist revolutionaries, and adverse criticisms of his work were at times purely political.

Chekhov has been known best in the English-speaking world for his plays, which he wrote in the last years of his life: *The Seagull* (1896), *Uncle Vanya* (1897), *The Three Sisters* (1901), and *The Cherry Orchard* (1904). His stories, however, were greatly admired from the beginning and were translated into many European languages soon after publication in Russia.

In 1901 Chekhov married the actress Olga Knipper, who played leading roles in several of his plays that were staged by the Moscow Art Theater. He died of tuberculosis on July 2, 1904, at a German health resort in Badenweiler.

CONTENTS

INTRODUCTION

In one of his notebooks Anton Chekhov wrote: "How pleasant it is to respect people! When I see books, I am not concerned with how the authors loved or played cards. I see only their marvelous works." When his editor, V. A. Tihonov, requested a biographical essay, his response dated February 22, 1892, was as follows:

> You need my biography? Here it is. I was born in Taganrog in 1860. In 1879 I graduated from the Taganrog high school. In 1884 I completed my medical training at the University of Moscow. In 1888 I received the Pushkin Prize. In 1890 I traveled to Sakhalin across Siberia and returned by sea. In 1891 I travelled to Europe where I drank wonderful wine and ate oysters. In 1892 I caroused with V. A. Tihonov on my name-day. In 1879 I began to write for *Strekoza*.* Collections of my works are: *Motley Tales, In the Twilight, Tales, Gloomy People*, and the narrative *Duel*. I sinfully but only moderately, worked on something dramatic. I've been translated into many foreign languages. The Germans translated

---

Dragonfly

me some time ago. The Czechs, the Serbs, also do a good job. And the French aren't above borrowing. I was introduced to the secrets of love when I was thirteen years old. With friends as with doctors, and in the same way with literary writers, I have excellent relations. I'm a bachelor. I would like to receive a pension. I'm busy being a doctor, and as much as possible, in the summers I act as a medical expert in postmortems but not in the last two or three years. I consider Tolstoy the greatest writer and Zadharin the greatest doctor.

But this is all nonsense. Print it if you want. If there aren't enough facts, add whatever you want, but be poetic.

After this was written there were more works of prose and the highly acclaimed plays that are still being performed. He married Olga Knipper, a talented actress, in a small church in Moscow in 1901 and it was a love match. Olga suffered a miscarriage and there were no living children from the union. Chekhov died in 1904 in Badenweiler, Germany, where he and Olga had gone for his health on the advice of his doctors.

It should be added that his life was full of snags and ironies, but the greatest irony occurred after his death. His body was shipped to Moscow in a railroad refrigerator car marked "Fresh Oysters." His funeral was attended by a hundred or so "lovers" of his writings, but while following the body to the cemetery on July 9, 1904, the conversations and decorum of the followers were so irreverent that the great baritone, Chaliapin, wept and cursed, and in despair remarked to Maxim Gorky who was walking along with him: "And for these miserable people he lived and worked!"

It is with these thoughts in mind, and how time and circumstances can change a man, that the stories in this collection were selected. They reflect Chekhov's own life from the budding of his masculinity to his imminent death. As Carl Sandburg once said, life is like an onion, you peel off one layer at a time and sometimes you weep. Such are these tales.

Why begin with "Volodya"? It is that first layer of life that not only will tear at the heart, but will speak truths that for some readers will be unbearable. Isn't it enough that adolescence is often a hell that has to be conquered without this kind of graphic torture? Volodya is young and at the brink of a new, independent life, but he makes the irreversible mistake that is a parent's nightmare. When this story was written, Moscow and St. Petersburg had had a spate of teenage suicides. It is Chekhov's answer to the question, Why? As a physician he was convinced that everything is causally motivated and determined. What one "hides" is the key. If you are going to seek the ultimate cause of a phenomenon, you cannot be kind.

But youth is not just about self-inflicted tragedy, loneliness, and danger. It is also full of comedy and inordinate vanity, as well as idiocy and self-knowledge, so there are such stories as "Lost Opportunity," "A Confession," "The Proud Man," "A Nasty Story," and "The Guardian." "The Guardian" is artistic game-playing and the winner is youth.

The early stories were written under pseudonyms for so-called comic magazines: A. Chekhonte, Ulysses, Prosaic Poet, Man Without Spleen, and others. He called these miniature tales *smelts* as one tale paid for a meal of smelts. Are they to be judged as "literature"? I think not. But even the most immature ones pursue the truth and are capable of nudging the reader. Very early in Chekhov's writing career an envious critic called him a "talented swine." Was this praise or insult? Read "The Critic." Literary censorship was inhibiting in that gutter language could not be printed even if the character's speech was full of any variety of obscenities. Still, there was a considerable amount of freedom and a writer's originality was not seriously hampered.

"Animate Merchandise" retains its integrity throughout because of Chekhov's uncanny ability to have the characters tell how they spent their lives, what their shortcomings were, their dreams, their desires, and all this without resorting to hyperbole or titillations. Don't judge these people, says Chekhov. Money may be the root of all evil but hunger, whether it be for love or material things, is human.

Who is corruptible? Everyone, as shown in "The Daddy," "The Chameleon," "In Disguise," "The Winning Lottery Ticket," "Chronicle of a Commercial Enterprise," and "At a Country Estate." Some individuals are only humorous, others are pathetic, vicious, ambiguous, ironic. "Nameless" is a masterpiece of dissolution that borders on farce. Not only is the reader given philosophical sustenance but he is entertained.

Just as loneliness cripples youth, servility, despotism, inflexibility, maliciousness, and prejudice have much to do with aging. The most savage work is "Rothchild's Violin." Why do people spend their lives doing the unnecessary and vile when there is so much going for them? The behavior of a talented but ignorant casket carpenter and musician is unjust and stingy, directed by deep-rooted lies planted by prejudices. The magic and solace of music cannot counteract his basic ignorance and greed. It is not until death beckons him and music redeems him that he realizes the foolishness and meanness of his way of life.

In "A Man Bound by a Cocoon" Chekhov takes you to another world, one that should be intelligent, humane, and just, but the trap of conformity is so powerful that freedom and truth rarely surface. The cowardice and fear that consume the teacher of Greek dominate not only him, but his colleagues. And yet the reader knows instinctively that he should pity this man, not malign him. You know that this man is not one-dimensional. Where does the guilt lie?

As man matures he loses much of the fear which pervades his youth, but not all of it. What we don't understand frightens us. Do we have a choice to fight or fly when the fear is extreme? "Fear," "It Was She!" and "The Preliminary Examination" are cavalier and amusing. But how is the hero of "Verochka" defined? Is it fear or is it his work that has defined him? Is he just a numbers cruncher or more complicated, undefined like the mist that peters out like "fireworks" when a personal decision is to be made? Who knows? asks Chekhov. A well-educated, talented doctor can suffer from lack of decisiveness and fear of public opinion as in "An Abominable Irony."

"The Wager" is one of the few stories that Chekhov has written that borders on being a political statement. He considered himself apolitical and would probably deny this. It begins with a superficial discussion of capital punishment and life imprisonment between a wealthy older man and a young intellectual. The question remains unresolved by either the wisdom of age or the imagination of youth. In this tale time changes the men and the circumstances for both good and evil. A gamble is a gamble, and the outcome is not a predictable mathematical probability. Was it worth it?

Chekhov was only forty-four when he died after years of poor health but great accomplishments. He knew university life from personal experience and knew the restlessness of the 1880s in czarist Russia. He was keenly aware of the impossibility of instructing anyone as to how to conduct his life or to be honest with oneself. "What is to be done?" was a popular question of the time and Chekhov was profoundly Russian. "A Tedious Tale" is a review of the good but imperfect life of a dying doctor-professor who accepts the imminence of his death, but finds there is no contentment in past achievements, only the bitter acceptance of the truth that we all die alone. Time drags for the doctor. His knowledge only brings death nearer but time is recalcitrant. He suffers from insomnia: it is somehow shameful for him to be awake when he should be sleeping, and he is ashamed of being ashamed. His mind is intact but his emotions are dulled. He notes that he was becoming petty and commonplace, that he has given up the struggle for life and thereby has given up living. He did not want to be remembered for his accomplishments, but for himself and as a loved human being. Finally, he is appalled by his indifference to what is going on around him. His beloved ward, Katya, lets him know that he is not seeing things more clearly as he approaches death but has simply become a malicious grumbler!

About Chekhov himself Maxim Gorky has written: "Detesting all that was vulgar and unclean, he described the seamy side of life in the lofty language of the poet with the gentle smile of the humorist, and the bitter inner reproach beneath the polished surface of his stories is scarcely notable." The stories are truly "emotion recollected in tranquility." To add to this would only be superfluous.

Paula P. Ross

VOLODYA

On one of those summer Sunday evenings, about five o'clock, Volodya, a bored seventeen-year-old youth, unattractive and painfully shy, sat in the arbor of the Shumikins' summer cottage. His unhappy thoughts ran along three directions. The first turned around the fact that on the next day, Monday, he was to take a mathematics examination. He knew that if he did not pass the written test tomorrow, he would not be able to go on to the next level. He had already been in the sixth class for two years and had only made a 2¾ grade in algebra. The second thought concerned his presence at the Shumikins, who were wealthy and pretentious people trying to be aristocrats. It was a persistent source of distress to his self-respect. It seemed to him that Madame Shumikin and her nieces considered him and his *maman** poor relations and spongers, and that they did not respect his mother and found her laughable. On the terrace he had overheard Madame Shumikin say to her cousin, Anna Fedorovna, that his *maman* constantly tried to appear younger than she was, primped,

*"mama" or "mother"

never paid up when she lost, and had a weakness for others' boots and snuff.

Volodya begged his *maman* every day not to go to the Shumikins. He described to her how disgraceful their situation as guests was, insisted, made nasty remarks, but she was a light-headed, pampered woman who had squandered two estates—hers and her husband's. She always hung around what she felt was high society. She did not understand what he was saying, and Volodya was forced to take her to the hated summer home once or twice a week.

The third thought troubling him was that he was continually agitated by a strange, unpleasant feeling which was absolutely new to him. . . . It seemed to him that he was in love with the Shumikin's guest and niece, Anna Fedorovna. She was a lively, vociferous, and easily amused young lady, thirty years old, healthy, vigorous, rosy, with round shoulders, a round wide chin, and a perpetual smile on her subtle lips. She was neither a beauty nor young—Volodya knew this very well, but for some reason he could not refrain from thinking about her. He could not keep from looking at her when she was playing croquet and shrugged her round shoulders or moved her smooth back, or when after a long bout of laughter she rushed up the steps, out of breath, dropped into an armchair, tightly closed her eyes, and gave the appearance that her chest was tight and she was suffocating. She was married. Her husband, a robust man who was an architect, came once a week to the summer home, had a good night's sleep, and then returned to the city. An inexplicable feeling against this man arose in Volodya and for no reason at all he disliked him and was happy every time he left for the city.

It was at this time as he sat in the arbor and thought of tomorrow's exam, and of his *maman* who was an object of derision, that he had a strong desire to see Nyuta (as the Shumikins called Anna Fedorovna), to hear her laugh, the rustle of her skirt. . . . This desire had no similarity to the feeling evoked by a poetic love which was familiar to him from novels and of which he dreamed every night when he lay down in his bed. It was strange, incomprehensible. He felt ashamed and afraid as if it were something bad and smutty, which was involuntary and which he found difficult to subdue. . . .

It's not love, he told himself. You don't fall in love with a thirty-year-old married woman. . . . It's simply some kind of hanky-panky. . . . Yes, it's hanky-panky. . . .

He thought about this hanky-panky, remembered his unconquerable shyness, thought about his adolescent beard, his freckles, his narrow eyes, and imagined himself beside Nyuta—and this match appeared impossible to him. Then he hastily imagined himself as handsome, bold, sharp, dressed in the latest style. . . .

Just as his dreaming was in full swing and he bent over with his eyes staring at the ground while sitting in a dark corner of the arbor, he heard light footsteps. Someone was sauntering up the path. The footsteps soon stopped and a white figure stepped into the opening.

"Is someone in here?" asked a feminine voice.

Volodya recognized the voice, was startled, and raised his head.

"Who's in here?" asked Nyuta upon entering the arbor. "Oh, is it you, Volodya? What are you doing here? Thinking? And how is it possible always to think, to think, to think. . . . It's enough to make you lose your mind!"

The embarrassed Volodya rose and glanced at Nyuta. She had just returned from the bathhouse. On her shoulders hung a sheet and a turkish towel. Her wet hair emerged from under a white silk kerchief and clung to her forehead. The damp, cool fragrance of the bathhouse and of almond soap enveloped her. Her breathing came in gasps from her rapid walking. The top button of her blouse was open and the youth could see her neck and bosom.

"Why are you so silent?" asked Nyuta, looking Volodya over. "It's vulgar not to respond when a lady addresses you. However, what a lummox you are, Volodya! You are always sitting, not uttering a word, thinking, like some kind of philosopher. There isn't any life or fire in you! Truly, you are unpleasant. . . . At your age you should live, jump around, chatter, court women, fall in love. . . ."

Volodya stared at the sheet which was held by a white, soft hand, and contemplated. . . .

"You are silent!" exclaimed the astonished Nyuta. "That's really strange. . . . Look here, be a man! Well, at least smile! Phooey, you nasty philosopher!" she ridiculed him. "Volodya, you know why you're such an oaf? Because you don't run after women. Why don't you court women? It's true there aren't any eligible young girls here, but there's nothing to keep you from pursuing ladies! Why, for example, don't you court me?"

Volodya listened, and hesitating in a serious, strained way, scratched his temples.

"To be silent and to love solitariness is only for very proud people," continued Nyuta, taking his hand away from his temples. "You are proud, Volodya. Why are you looking sideways? Let me see your face! That's better, lummox!"

Volodya decided to say something. Wanting to smile, he pulled at his lower lip, blinked his eyes, and again raised his hand to his temples.

"I . . . I love you!" he declared.

Nyuta raised her eyebrows in faked astonishment and began to laugh.

"What's this I hear?!" she sang out like an opera singer when she hears something terrifying. "How? What did you say? Repeat it, repeat it . . ."

"I . . . I love you!" repeated Volodya.

And, so without any participation of his free will, understanding nothing and without thought, he took a half-step toward Nyuta and took hold of her arms above her wrists. His eyes became misty and teary, and the whole world became a large turkish towel from which emitted the fragrance of the bathhouse.

"Bravo, bravo!" he heard exclaimed, followed by a merry laugh. "Why are you silent? I want you to speak! Well?"

Seeing that there was no objection to taking hold of her arms, Volodya glanced at Nyuta's laughing face, and clumsily and uncomfortably held her waist and then wrapped both his arms around her back. She put both her arms behind her neck, displaying the dimples on her elbows, straightened her hair under her kerchief, and said in a serene voice:

"It's necessary, Volodya, to be nimble, loving, sweet—and this happens only when you're under the influence of feminine company. However, you still have an unpleasant . . . angry face. You must express yourself, laugh. . . . Yes, Volodya, don't be a surly man. You are young and have time to philosophize later in life. So, release me and I'll leave. Take your hands off!"

She easily freed herself and humming something, walked out of the arbor. Volodya was left alone. He straightened his hair, smiled, paced the arbor several times, sat down on a bench, and smiled again. He was unbearably ashamed, so much so that he was surprised that a person's shame could be so great and stinging. He smiled from shame, whispered a few irrational words, and gesticulated.

He was ashamed of his adolescent behavior, ashamed of his shyness, but most important, that he had dared to hold a respectable married lady by the waist. He had no right to do so, not at his age, not because of his external qualities, nor his social position.

He jumped up, stepped out of the arbor, and, glancing all around, walked toward the part of the garden that was farthest from the house.

Ugh, I've got to get away from her as soon as possible! he thought, grasping his head. God, the sooner the better!

The train which Volodya and his mother had to take left at 8:40. There were still three hours before the train would leave, but he would have been happy to go to the station immediately, not waiting for his *maman*.

At eight o'clock he approached the house. His whole demeanor was that of decisiveness: What would be would be! He had decided, no matter what, to be bold, to come straight to the point, and to speak in a loud voice.

He walked across the terrace, into the large hall, and then into the drawing room and stopped there to take a breath. He could hear sounds from the neighboring dining room where they were drinking tea. Madame Shumikin, his *maman*, and Nyuta were talking and laughing about something.

Volodya overheard them.

"I assure you!" said Nyuta. "I couldn't believe my eyes!

When he stood up and told me he loved me, and even put his arms about my waist, I didn't recognize him. And really, he had finesse! When he said he loved me, his face reflected something savage, like that of a Circassian."

"You don't say!" gasped his *maman*, going into fits of laughter. "Really! How he reminds me of his father!"

Volodya quickly walked out into the fresh air.

How can they say such things out loud! His thoughts tortured him and throwing up his hands, he looked with horror up at the sky. They talk heartlessly. . . . And my *maman* was laughing . . . my *maman*! God, why did you give me such a mother? Why?

No matter what would happen, he had to return to the house. He walked up and down the path several times, calmed down a little, and entered the house. "Why didn't you come in time for tea?" Madame Shumikin asked him sternly.

"Excuse me . . . it's time for us to leave," he mumbled, not raising his eyes. "*Maman*, it's already eight o'clock!"

"Go by yourself, my dear," said his mother languidly. "I'm going to spend the night with Lili. Farewell, my dear. . . . Let me give you my blessing. . . ."

She made the sign of the cross over her son and then turning to Nyuta said in French:

"He resembles Lermontov* a little . . . doesn't he?"

As if stunned, and not looking at anyone, Volodya left the dining room. Ten minutes later he was marching on the road to the railroad station, and was exhilarated because he could do this. Fear had left him, there was no need for shame, and he moved lightly and freely.

Half a verst† from the station he sat down on a boulder by the road and began to look at the sun, more than half of which was concealed behind the embankment. Lamps had already been lit at the station and one green lamp flashed, but no train was yet to be seen. Volodya found it pleasant to sit there, not

---

*Mikhail Lermontov (1814–1841), a Romantic poet and novelist, considered second only to Pushkin

†A verst is approximately two-thirds of a mile.

moving, and listen to the gradual rise of evening sounds. The semidarkness of the arbor, the footsteps, the scent of the bathhouse, the laughter, and the waistline—all this offered his imagination a startling enlightenment and none of it any longer was frightening and meaningful as previously. . . .

It's nothing. . . . She didn't pull my hands away and laughed when I held her waist, he thought. That means she liked it. If she were repelled she would have become angry . . .

And now Volodya became annoyed with himself; that he hadn't been bold enough in the arbor. He became sorry that he was leaving in such a tizzy, and was convinced that if the opportunity recurred, he would be bolder and see things more clearly.

For the circumstance to repeat itself would not be difficult. The Shumikins took long walks after dining. If Volodya took a walk with Nyuta in the dark garden, well—there's the circumstance!

I'll go back, he thought, and take the morning train tomorrow. . . . I'll say I missed the evening train.

So he went back. . . . Madame Shumikin, his *maman*, Nyuta, and one of the nieces were sitting on the terrace and playing vint.* When Volodya lied to them, saying that he missed the train, they were concerned that he shouldn't miss the train tomorrow and be late for his exam. They advised him to get up early. While they were playing cards, he sat nearby, greedily looking Nyuta over and waiting. . . . He had a plan ready: he would go up to Nyuta at dusk, take her by the arm, then embrace her; it wouldn't be necessary to say anything for they would both understand without superfluous conversation.

However, the ladies did not go for a walk after dinner, but continued to play cards. They played until midnight and then separated to go to bed.

It's all so stupid! thought the irritated Volodya while lying in his bed. Well so what, tomorrow's another day. . . . Once again in the arbor tomorrow. Never mind. . . .

But sleep escaped him and he sat up in his bed with his arms wrapped around his knees and ruminated. Thoughts about

---

*a precursor to bridge, like the English whist

the exam were annoying. He had already decided that he'd fail and the failure wouldn't be devastating. On the contrary, it would be to the good, even very good. Tomorrow he would be free, like a bird. He would dress with care, would smoke with a casual air, court Nyuta when convenient. He would no longer be a high-school boy but a "young man." Finally, a decision about his career and the future was clear: Volodya would become self-employed as a telegrapher, and later work in a pharmacy and become a pharmacist. . . . Unimportant jobs? Almost two hours had passed and he still sat and thought. . . .

It was after two o'clock in the morning and beginning to get light. His door quietly creaked and his *maman* entered the room.

"You aren't sleeping?" she asked and yawned. "Son, son, I'll only be a minute. I need to get some medicine. . . ."

"What did you come for?"

"Poor Lili is having spasms again. Son, my dear child, you have an exam tomorrow. . . ."

She took a bottle from a small chest, went to the window, read the label, and left.

"Marya Leontyevna, these are not the right drops!" Volodya heard a feminine voice exclaim a minute later. "This is landish* and Lili is begging for morphine. Is your son sleeping? Ask him to look for it. . . ."

It was Nyuta's voice. Volodya shivered. He quickly pulled on his trousers, threw a coat over his shoulders, and went to the door.

"Do you understand? Bring morphine!" informed Nyuta in a whisper. "It'll probably be written in Latin. Wake Volodya. He'll find it. . . ."

His *maman* opened the door and Volodya saw Nyuta. She wore the same blouse in which she went to the bathhouse. Her hair was loose, falling over her shoulders, her face was sleepy, appearing dusky in the dim light. . . .

"There, Volodya is not sleeping . . . ," she said. "Volodya find, dear man, the morphine in the small chest! It's prescribed for Lili. . . . She always has something wrong with her."

---

*tranquilizing drops drawn from the lily-of-the-valley blossom

His *maman* mumbled something, yawned, and left.

"Go look for it," declared Nyuta. "Why are you standing there?"

Volodya went to the small chest, squatted, and began to check the medicinal labels on the bottles and pills. His hands were shaking, and his chest and stomach felt as if his insides were being overrun by chilling waves. The smell of ether, carbolic acid, and a variety of medicinal chemicals, which for no reason he picked up with his trembling hands and caused to spill, dulled him and made his head spin.

It seems *maman* has left, he thought. That's good . . . very good. . . .

"Will you hurry?" asked Nyuta in a drawl.

"One moment. . . . This here appears to be morphine . . . ," said Volodya, having read on a label 'morph———.' "Here it is!"

Nyuta stood in the doorway so that one leg was in the corridor and the other in his room. She was straightening her hair, which was difficult to straighten—it was so very, very thick and long!—and was absentmindedly looking at Volodya. In the loose blouse, sleepy-looking, with her hair down, in the weak light which came into the room from the white sky, still not brightened by the sun, she appeared fascinating, voluptuous, to Volodya. . . . Charmed, his whole body trembling and with the happy recollection that he had embraced this beautiful body in the arbor, he handed her the drops and said:

"What a . . . you are . . ."

"What?"

She came into the room.

"What?" she asked, smiling.

He remained silent and stared at her, then, as in the arbor, he took hold of her arms. . . . But she only stared at him, smiled, and waited: What would be the next move?

"I love you , . . ," he whispered.

She stopped smiling, thought it over, and said:

"Wait, it seems someone is coming. Ugh, really, I think its the schoolboys!" she remarked in a low voice, going to the door and looking out into the corridor. "No, there isn't anyone. . . ."

She returned. . . .

After this it seemed to Volodya that the room, Nyuta, daylight, and he himself all blended into one intense, new feeling,
which was not the happiness for which one could give one's life
or submit to eternal torture, but that which occurred in an
instant and suddenly disappeared completely. Volodya saw only
a full, unattractive face distorted by a vile expression, and he
felt repelled by what had occurred.

"In any case, I must leave," said Nyuta, looking with disgust
at Volodya. "What an unpleasant, pitiful . . . fie, ugly duckling!"

Now her long hair, loose shirt, her footsteps, her voice, all
seemed hideous to Volodya!

A nasty interlude . . . , he thought after she left. Really,
I'm vile. . . . Everything is vile.

Outside the sun was rising, the birds were singing noisily.
The gardener could be heard walking in the garden, and how
his wheelbarrow creaked. . . . A little later the mooing of the
cows could be heard, and the sounds of shepherds' shouts. The
sunshine and the sounds told him that out there in the world
was an unsullied existence, elegant and poetic. But where? No
one had ever spoken to Volodya about these things, neither his
maman nor all the people with whom he had contact.

When the butler came to awaken him in time for the
morning train, he made believe he couldn't be awakened. . . .

Let him and all the others go to hell! he thought.

He got out of bed at eleven o'clock. Combing his hair in
front of a mirror and examining his unattractive, pale face from
a sleepless night, he thought:

Perfectly true . . . an ugly duckling.

When his *maman* saw him and was horrified that he was
not taking the exam, Volodya said:

"I overslept, *maman*. . . . Don't upset yourself. I'll get a medical excuse."

Madame Shumikin and Nyuta slept until one o'clock.
Volodya heard the reverberation as Madame Shumikin opened
her window, how in her husky voice Nyuta answered her as she
burst out laughing. He saw how the door from the drawing
room opened, and the string of nieces and hangers-on (in the

last group was his *maman*), how Nyuta's washed, laughing face flashed by, and along with her face the dark brows and beard of the just-arrived architect.

Nyuta wore the Ukrainian national dress which did not become her and made her appear heavy; the architect cracked jokes crudely and stupidly; the cutlets that were served for lunch had too much onion—such were Volodya's perceptions. It also seemed to him that Nyuta deliberately laughed raucously and looked in his direction in order to let him know that the memory of the night did not in any way disturb her, and that she did not acknowledge the presence of the ugly duckling at the table.

At four o'clock Volodya was on his way to the railroad station with his *maman*. The nasty memory, the sleepless night, the imminent expulsion from the school, the pricking of his conscience—all now aroused in him a ponderous, somber anger. He looked at his *maman's* slender profile, at her little nose, at the raincoat she was wearing which was given to her by Nyuta, and he muttered:

"Why do you powder your face? It's not seemly at your age! You primp, don't pay your debts, use others' snuff . . . it's reprehensible! I don't love you. . . . I don't love you!"

He continued to berate her while her eyes expressed fear, and she threw up her hands and in a frightened whisper said:

"What are you saying, my dear? My God, the coachman will hear you! Be quiet or the coachman will hear you! He hears everything!"

"I don't love you . . . I don't love you!" he continued spasmodically. "Don't wear that raincoat. Do you hear? I'll tear it to pieces. . . ."

"Pull yourself together, my child!" cried the *maman*. "The coachman will hear you!"

"And what happened to my father's estate? What did you do with your money? You've squandered everything! I'm not ashamed of my poverty but I'm ashamed that you are my mother. . . . Whenever my friends ask about you, I blush."

There were two station stops to their town. Volodya, his whole body trembling, stood on the platform the entire time. He did not want to go into the coach since his despised mother sat there. He hated himself too, and the conductors, and the smoke from the stack, and the cold, to which he attributed his trembling. . . . And the heavier the weight upon his soul, the stronger was his feeling that somewhere in this world there were people whose lives were unsullied, prosperous, warm, graceful, full of love, caresses, happy, free, and easy. . . . He felt this and grieved so intensely that one passenger, looking directly into his face, asked:

"Really, do you have a toothache?"

In town Volodya and his *maman* lived with Marya Petrovna, a genteel lady who leased a large apartment and then rented part of it to others. His *maman* rented two rooms: in the one with windows where her bed was, hung two portraits in gold frames, but the other adjoining it was small and dark. This was Volodya's. In it was a couch upon which he slept, and besides this couch there was no other furniture. The room was taken up with wicker baskets full of clothing, hat boxes, and junk which the *maman* stored for some reason. Volodya prepared his schoolwork in his mother's room or in the "social room"—as a large room was called where all the lodgers could get together during meals and in the evening.

Upon returning home, he lay down on the couch and covered himself with a blanket to stop his body's shaking. The hat boxes, the baskets, and the junk reminded him that he didn't have his own room, a place of refuge, where he could hide from his *maman*, from her guests and the voices that carried from the so-called social room. His schoolbag and books thrown in the corner reminded him of the exam he had not taken. . . . For some reason, at the same time, he thought of Menton where, when he was seven years old, he had lived with his late father. He also remembered Biarritz and two English girls with whom he ran on the sand. . . . He wanted to recall the color of the sky and the ocean, the height of the waves, and his mood at that time, but he found it impossible. The English girls flashed in his imagination as if alive, but all the rest was confused, disorderly, blurry. . . .

It must be cold in here, thought Volodya. He got up, put on his overcoat, and went to the social room.

Tea was being drunk in the social room. Three people were sitting near the samovar: his *maman*, the music teacher (a little old woman with a tortoiseshell pince-nez), and Avgustin Mihailich, who was an old, very obese Frenchman who worked in a perfume factory.

"Dunyash!" called out the Frenchman.

It appeared that the hostess had sent the maid somewhere.

"Oh, it's not important," declared the Frenchman, smiling broadly. "I'll go for the bread myself right now. It's nothing!"

He put down his strong, smelly cigar in a spot all could see, put on his hat, and went out.

When he left the *maman* began to tell the music teacher about her visit to the Shumikins and how hospitable they were.

"Lili Shumikin is really a relative . . . ," she told her. "Her late husband, General Shumikin, is a cousin of my husband's. By birth she is the Baroness Kolb. . . ."

"*Maman*, that's not true!" exclaimed the agitated Volodya. "Why are you lying?"

He knew very well that his *maman* spoke the truth. There wasn't a single lie in her account of the General Shumikin and the Baroness Kolb, but all the same he was convinced that she lied. He felt that her manner of speech, the expression of her face, her gaze, and her whole being were phony.

"You lie!" repeated Volodya and banged on the table with his fist so fiercely that all the dishes shook and his *maman's* tea splashed. "Why are you talking about the general and the baroness? It's all lies!"

The music teacher was taken aback and coughed into her handkerchief, made believe she was choking, and his *maman* began to weep.

Where shall I go? thought Volodya.

He had already been out on the street, and he was ashamed to go to his friends. Unintentionally, he again recalled the two English girls. . . . He paced the social room and then went to Avgustin Mihailich's room. The powerful odor of volatile oils and glycerine soap pervaded the room. On the table, on the windowsills, and even on the chairs were many small flasks, glasses, and goblets full of liquids in a variety of colors. Volodya picked up a newspaper from the table, opened it, and read the headline: "Figaro." . . . The paper gave off a strong, pleasant odor. Later he took a revolver out of the front desk drawer. . . .

In the adjacent room the music teacher was comforting his *maman*. "One must see the whole picture and not pay attention to him! He's still very young! At his age young people always allow themselves excesses. One must resign oneself to this."

"No, Yevgenya Andreevna, he's too spoiled!" said his *maman* in a singsong voice. "He needs someone older over him, and I'm weak and can't do anything with him. No, I'm unfortunate!"

Volodya put the muzzle of the gun in his mouth, groped around for the cock or the trigger, and squeezed it with his finger. . . . Then he groped around again for some kind of protuberance, and once more squeezed. Nothing happened. He took the muzzle out of his mouth, wiped it off with the bottom of his overcoat, and checked the lock. He had never before had a gun in his hands. . . .

"Seems that this needs to be lifted . . . ," he surmised. "Yes, that must be so. . . ."

Avgustin Mihailich had returned to the social room and, laughing boisterously, began to give an account of something that had happened. Volodya once again put the muzzle in his mouth, held it with his teeth, and squeezed the trigger. A shot rang out. . . . Something struck the back of Volodya's neck with terrible force and he fell on the table, his face landing on the flasks and goblets. Thereupon he saw his dead father in his high hat with its wide black ribbon that he had worn in Menton at the funeral of a lady; his father suddenly embraced him with both arms and together they ran into some kind of very dark, deep abyss.

The whole picture then became distorted and vanished.

1887

LOST OPPORTUNITY:
A VAUDEVILLIAN SCENE

I have a terrible desire to weep! If I could wail, it seems that I would feel better.

It was a marvelous evening. I put my best clothes on, combed my hair carefully, sprayed myself with cologne, and like a Don Juan wended my way to her home. She is living at their summer cottage in Sokolnik. She is young, beautiful, has a dowry of thirty thousand rubles, is educated, and, like a kitten, loves me, a writer.

After arriving in Sokolnik, I found her sitting on her favorite bench under tall, elegant fir trees. Seeing me, she quickly got up and, beaming, came to meet me.

"How cruel you are!" she accosted me. "How could you be so late? You know how dull it is without you! What a tease you are!"

I kissed her lovely little hand and, trembling, walked with her to the bench. I quivered, ached, and felt that my heart was inflamed and close to bursting. My pulse was running wild.

And it was no wonder! I had come to settle my fate ultimately. It was my neck, as they say, or nothing. . . . Everything hung on what happened this evening.

The weather was miraculous, but it meant nothing to me. I didn't even hear the first nightingale over our heads—in spite

of the fact one is obligated to listen to the nightingales even
when having a not-so-important rendezvous.

"Why are you silent?" she asked, looking directly at me.

"It's like this. . . . Such a marvelous night. . . . Your *maman*
is well?"

"She is well."

"Hm . . . it's so. . . . I, you see, Varvara Petrovna, want to
talk to you. . . . That's the only reason I drove here. . . . I've
been silent, wordless, but now . . . I'm your obedient servant!
I'm in no state to be reticent."

Varya lowered her head and with shaking, tiny fingers tore
the petals from a flower. She knew what it was I wanted to say.
I kept silent for a moment and then continued:

"Why am I silent? Neither taciturn, nor timid, sooner or
later, I'll get the nerve . . . come to my senses and speak. . . .
You, it's possible, will be hurt. . . . It's possible you won't understand, but . . . what can be done?"

I shut up. It was necessary to compose what I would say next.

"So speak!" her eyes protested. "Procrastinator! Why are
you tormenting me?"

"You, of course, have long ago guessed," I continued, hesitating for a moment, "why I've come here every day to be with
you and been an eyesore to you. Haven't you guessed? You,
most likely, with your astuteness, have guessed for a long time
the feeling which . . . (pause) Varvara Petrovna!"

Varya lowered her head even more. Her tiny fingers began
to dance.

"Varvara Petrovna!"

"Well?"

"I . . . What can I say?! Even without words it's compre-
hensible. . . . I love you, that's all. . . . What more needs to be
said? (Pause) I love you to distraction! I love you, as. . . . In one
word, gather all the sentimental novels in the whole world,
read all that is in them about the revelation of love, the vows,
the sacrifices, and . . . you will discover that, which . . . is now
within my breast, that . . . Varvara Petrovna! (Pause) Varvara
Petrovna! Why are you so silent?"

"What do you want me to say?"

"Is it possible . . . is it not?"

Varya raised her head and smiled.

Oh, the hell with it! I thought. She smiled, moved her lips, and almost audibly said, "Why not?"

I desperately grasped her hand, desperately kissed it, violently grasped the other hand. . . . She's brave! While I carried on with her hands, she laid her little head on my breast, so that I, for the first time, knew how luxurious was her marvelous hair.

I kissed her head and the warmth of my breast felt as if a samovar had been placed in it. Varya lifted her face, and there remained nothing left for me to do but kiss her lips.

And here, when Varya was finally in my arms; when I was assured in writing of thirty thousand rubles; when, in a word, I was assured of a beautiful wife, good money, and a fine career, the devil tugged at my tongue. . . .

I wanted to explain to my promised wife that I was a man of principle, and to show off a little. In truth, however, I myself didn't know what I wanted. . . . How awful it came out!

"Varvara Petrovna!" I began after the first kiss. "Before I take from you your word that you will become my wife, I consider it my holy duty, in order to avoid any misunderstanding, to tell you a few things. I will be brief. . . . Do you, Varvara Petrovna, know who and what I am? Yes, I'm an honorable man! I'm a hard worker! I . . . I'm proud! Moreover . . . I have a future. . . . But I'm poor. . . . I don't have anything."

"I know that," said Varya. "Happiness is not found in money."

"Yes. Who's talking about money? I . . . I'm proud of my poverty. The kopecks I receive for my literary efforts I wouldn't exchange for the thousands of rubles which . . . which . . ."

"That's understood. Well . . ."

"I'm accustomed to poverty. It doesn't mean anything to me. I can take a week of not eating. . . . But you! You! Is it true that you, who can't take two steps without hiring a cab, who puts on fresh clothes every day, throws money around, never having known need, you, for whom an unfashionable flower creates great unhappiness, is it true that you agree to give up earthly blessings for me? Hm . . ."

"I have money. I have a dowry!"

"A trifle! It would take but a few years to use up tens of thousands of rubles. . . . And then? Poverty? Tears? You must believe, my darling, in my experience! I know! I know what I'm talking about! In order to struggle with poverty you must have a strong will, a superhuman character!"

I'm really going overboard with this rigmarole! I thought as I continued:

"Think about it, Varvara Petrovna! Think about the step you are about to take! An irrevocable step! Do you have the strength—marry me, I don't have the strength to struggle—refuse me! Oh! It's better that I lose you than . . . than you should lose your peace. The hundred rubles which I earn monthly for my writing is nothing! It isn't enough! Think it over before it's too late!"

I jumped up.

"Think about it! Where there is weakness—there are tears, reproaches, premature gray hair. . . . I'm forewarning you because I'm an honorable person. Do you consider yourself strong enough to share a life with me that from your objective view has no resemblance to the life you now live, which is foreign to you?"

"I have a dowry!"

"How much? Twenty, thirty thousand rubles! Ha—ha! A million? And for all that, would I permit myself to consider it mine? No! Never! I have my pride!"

I strutted around the bench several times. Varya was reflective. I crowed. When others became meditative, this meant to me that I was held in esteem.

"That's it, life with me and deprivation, or life without me and wealth. . . . Choose. . . . Do you have the strength? Does my Varya have the strength?"

I spoke in this fashion for a very long time. Unwittingly, I was carried away. As I spoke, at the same time I felt myself split in two. One half of me was carried away with what I was saying, and the other half was dreaming: "Wait a bit, little mother! We can live on your thirty thousand in a way that we won't feel the heat! It'll make do for a long time!"

Varya listened, listened. . . . Finally she got up and extended her hand to me.

"I'm grateful to you!" she said with a voice which made me

tremble and stare into her eyes. In her eyes and on her cheeks tears glistened. . . .

"I'm grateful to you! You've laid out very well what were revelations to me. . . . I can't be your future wife. . . . I can't. . . . I'm not a match for you. . . ."

And she sobbed. I had made a fool of myself. . . . I'm always flustered when I see crying women, and in this case, more so. While I thought about what to do, she stopped sobbing and wiped her tears.

"You are right," she said. "If I married you, I would be deceiving you. I could not be your wife. I'm a rich woman, not your future wife. I ride in carriages. I eat delicacies and the finest food. I never have cabbage and other soups for dinner. I'm even constantly embarrassed by my mother. . . . I can't do without wealth! I can't go on foot. . . . I'd get tired. . . . And clothing. . . . I'd have to sew my own clothing. . . . No! Farewell!"

Making a tragic gesture with her hand, for no reason at all, she cried out:

"I'm unworthy of you! Farewell!"

After this pronouncement, she turned and went home. And I? I stood dumbfounded, semiconscious, followed her with my eyes, and felt that the earth was rocking under me. When I recovered and recalled where I was, and what grandiloquent nonsense my tongue had uttered, I howled. Her trail had already disappeared when I wanted to scream after her: "Come back!"

Disgraced, having nothing for my pains, I left. There was no tram at the gate. I had no money for a cab. I had to walk home.

Three days later I went back to Sokolnik. They told me at the cottage that Varya was ailing with something and her father was taking her to Petersburg to her grandmother. I didn't get to talk to her at all. . . .

Now I'm lying on my bed, biting the pillow, and banging the back of my head. I am sick at heart. . . . Reader, how can such things be straightened out? How can I take back my words? What can I say or write to her? It boggles the mind! The opportunity was lost—and how stupidly it was lost!

1882

A Confession: Would It Be Olya, Zhenya, or Zoya? (A Letter)

You, *ma chère*, my dear, never-to-be-forgotten friend, in your sweet letter ask me, among other things, why up to this time I have not married, despite my thirty-nine years?

My dear! I love family life with all my heart and have not married only because mischievous fate has not provided the opportunity for me to marry. I braced myself to be married at least fifteen times and was not married because everything on this earth, and especially in my life, is subordinate to circumstances, and all depends on that! Circumstance—is a despot. I'll cite a few occasions, thanks to which I, up to this time, lead my life in contemptible solitude. . . .

Opportunity Number 1

It was a delightful June morning, the sky was cloudless, and as clear as Prussian blue. The sun played on the river and its rays slid over the damp grass. It seemed that the river and the verdant growth were showered by precious diamonds. The birds sang as if they had sheet music before them. . . . We strolled

along a small path covered by yellow sand, and with happy
bosoms breathed in the aroma of the June morning. The trees
looked down upon us indulgently, whispered something to us
that had to be very beautiful, very tender. . . . Olya Gryzdovski's
hand (she's the one who is now the wife of your district's supervisor) rested on my arm, and her little finger trembled on my
thumb. . . . Her cheeks were hot, and her eyes. . . . O *ma chère*,
they were fantastic eyes! Such charm, integrity, innocence,
gaiety, childish naivete shone in those blue eyes! I was in love
with her fair braids and the tiny footprints her diminutive feet
left on the sand. . . .

"I have dedicated my life, Olga Maximova, to science," I
whispered, fearing that her little finger would slip from my
thumb. "I expect my future will be in a professorial chair. . . .
There are questions bothering me . . . scientific. . . . The life
will be hard-working, full of concern, on a high level . . . such
as . . . well, in a word, I'm going to be a professor. . . . I'm an
honorable man, Olga Maximova. . . . I'm not rich, but . . . I
need a woman's friendship, which by its presence . . . (Olya
became embarrassed and lowered her eyes; her little finger
shook) which by her presence. . . . Olya! Look at the sky! It's
pure . . . so is my life pure in that way, boundless. . . ."

My tongue had not succeeded in extricating itself from
saying this rot when Olya lifted her head, pulled her arm away
from me, and clapped her hands. Coming toward us was a goose
and her goslings. Olya ran toward the geese, laughing her bell-
like laugh, and stretched her tiny hands toward them. . . . Oh,
what charming tiny hands, *ma chère*!

"Tyer . . . tyer . . . tyer . . . ," hissed the geese, lifting their
necks and looking askance at Olya.

"Goosie, goosie, goosie!" cried out Olya, stretching her
hand toward one of the goslings.

The gosling was wiser than his years. He ran from Olya's
hand to his father, a very large and foolish-looking gander,
and, from all appearances, complained to him. The gander
spread wide his wings. The crazy Olya went after another
gosling. This time something terrible happened. The gander
pressed his neck to the ground, and, hissing like a snake, men-

acingly waddled toward Olya. Olya shrieked and ran back. The
gander came after her. Olya looked back, shrieked louder, and
grew pale. Her beautiful feminine face showed fear and revulsion. It looked as if all hell had let loose and was after her.
I rushed to help her and hit the gander on the head with
my cane. The vile gander had succeeded in grabbing a corner
of her gown. Olya, her eyes huge, with a distorted face, her
whole body quivering, fell against my breast. . . .
"What a little coward you are!" I said.
"Kill that gander!" she exclaimed, and began to cry. . . .
There was so much that was not naive, not childish, but
idiotic in that frightened little face! I can't tolerate, *ma chère*,
faintheartedness! I can't envision being married to a fainthearted, cowardly woman!
The gander spoiled everything. . . . Having calmed Olya, I
went home, and that fainthearted, idiotic little face was fixed in
my mind. . . . Olya had lost all her charm for me. I rejected her.

Opportunity Number 2

You, of course, my dear friend, know that I am a writer. The
gods lit in me the holy fire, and if I don't take the pen in hand,
I feel guilty. I'm Appolonius's priest. . . . Every heartbeat, every
breath I take, in short—I have given my entire self to the
Muse's altar. Take from me my pen—and I will die. You laugh,
you don't believe it. . . . I swear that it is so!
But you, of course, know, *ma chère*, that this earth's globe is
not a good place for art. The earth is huge and plentiful, but
there is no room for the life of a writer. A writer—he's forever
an orphan, a scapegoat, a defenseless child. . . . I divide humanity into two parts: the writers and the envious. The first write
and the second die from envy and place all kinds of filth in the
path of the first. I've been ruined, am being ruined, and will be
ruined by the envious. They have marred my life. They have
taken into their hands the reins of government relating to the
writer's business, call themselves editors and publishers, and try
with all their might to ruin our brotherhood. Damn them!!

Listen. . . .

At one time I courted Zhenya Pshikov. You, of course, will recall this sweet, dark-haired, dreamy child. . . . She's now married to your neighbor, Karl Ivanovich Vantsye (apropos: in German *Vantsye* means . . . *flea*. Don't tell this to Zhenya, she would be offended). Zhenya loved the writer in me. She believed in my vocation as intensely as I. She lived with the same hopes as I. But she was young! She could not yet understand the aforementioned division of mankind into two parts! She did not believe it, and one marvelous day . . . we were annihilated.

I was living at the Pshikovs' cottage. They considered me a future son-in-law, and Zhenya's betrothed. I wrote—she read. What a critic, *ma chère*. She was honest, like Aristides, and stern as Cato. I dedicated my works to her. She was especially struck by one of these works. Zhenya wanted to see it in print. I sent it to one of the humorous journals. I sent it in the first of July and expected a reply in two weeks. The fifteenth of July arrived. Zhenya and I received the expected reply. We hurriedly opened it and read it at the mailbox. She first flushed, then blanched. The letter in the box was addressed to me as follows: "Shlyendov Village. G. M. B——y. You don't have a drop of talent. What a hell of a pile of rubbish! Don't waste a stamp and leave us in peace. Involve yourself in something else."

Well, this is stupid. . . . It's obvious right away that fools wrote this.

"Hmmmmm . . . ," uttered Zhenya.

"Wh-at scoun-n-drels!!!" I grumbled. "How do you like that? And you, Evgenia Markovna, will you now stop liking my work?"

Zhenya thought a moment and yawned.

"What about it?" she said. "It could be that you have no talent! They know better than we do. Last year Fedor Fedosevich fished with me all summer and all you do is write. . . . How boring! . . ."

How do you like that? And that, after sleepless nights spent together over writing and reading! After making mutual sacrifices to the Muses. . . . How come?

Zhenya cooled toward my writing and then toward me. We parted. It had to be. . . .

Opportunity Number 3

You, my never-to-be-forgotten friend, know, of course, that I
intensely love music. Music is my passion, my essence. . . . The
names Mozart, Beethoven, Chopin, Mendelssohn, Gounod are
not the names of people, but of giants! I love classical music. I
reject operettas just as I reject vaudeville. I'm one of the constant frequenters of the opera. Hochlov, Kochetova, Bartsal,
Ysatov, Karcov . . . amazing people! How I regret that I'm not
acquainted with these singers! If I were acquainted with them,
I would unburden my heart before them in gratitude. Last winter I went especially often to the opera. I didn't go alone but
with the Pepsinov family. It's too bad that you don't know this
nice family! The Pepsinovs get a loge for the season every winter. They are completely devoted to music. . . . Colonel Pepsinov's daughter, Zoya, is the beauty of this fine family. What a
lass she is, my dear! Her rosy lips are sufficient to drive a person like me out of my mind! She's elegant, beautiful, smart. . . .
I loved her. . . . I was wildly in love, passionately, terribly! My
blood boiled when I sat next to her. You are smiling, *ma chère*.
. . . Smile! The strange love of a writer is unfamiliar to you. . . .
The love of a writer—it's Etna plus Vesuvius. Zoya loved me.
Her eyes always rested on my eyes, which were constantly fixed
on her eyes. . . . We were happy. . . . The wedding was only
one step away. . . .

But we lost our life.

Faust was being performed. *Faust*, my dear, was composed
by Gounod, and Gounod is one of the greatest composers. On
the way to the theater I had decided to declare my love to Zoya
during the first act, which I don't understand. . . . The great
Gounod did a bad job with the first act!

The performance began. Zoya and I were alone in the foyer.
She sat close by me, and trembled from expectation and happiness, mechanically playing with her fan. By evening lighting,
ma chère, she was magnificent, incredibly beautiful!

"The overture" (I was going to declare my love) "has made
me think about some things, Zoya Yegorovna. . . . So many

feelings, so many. . . . You listen and you yearn . . . yearn for something like that and listen. . . ."

I hiccuped and continued:

"It's something so special. One hungers for something unearthly. . . . Love? Passion? Yes, it must be . . . love. . . . (I hiccuped.) Yes, love. . . ."

Zoya smiled, became disconcerted, and fiercely waved her fan. I hiccuped. I can't stand hiccups!

"Zoya Yegorovna! Tell me, I beg you! Do you know such a feeling? (I hiccuped) Zoya Yegorovna! I'm waiting for an answer!"

"I . . . I . . . don't understand you. . . ."

"Hiccups have overcome me. . . . It'll pass. . . . I'm speaking of that all-embracing feeling, which. . . . What the dickens!"

"Take a drink of water!"

I'll tell her and then go to the buffet, I thought, and continued: "I'll make it brief. Zoya Yegorovna . . . you, of course, have already been aware . . ."

I hiccuped and in annoyance bit my tongue.

"You, of course, have noticed (I hiccuped). . . . You have known me now for almost a year. . . . Hm. . . . I'm an honorable man, Zoya Yegorovna! I'm a worker. It's true I'm not rich, but . . ."

I hiccuped and jumped up.

"Take a drink of water!" advised Zoya.

I took several steps around the divan, pressed on my throat with a finger, and hiccuped again. *Ma chère*, I was in a most fearful situation! Zoya got up and headed for the loge. I went after her. Opening the door to the loge for her, I hiccuped again, and then hurried to the bar. I drank five glasses of water, and it seemed that the hiccuping had let up somewhat. I smoked a cigarette and returned to the loge. Zoya's brother got up and gave me the seat next to Zoya. I sat down and immediately . . . hiccuped. Five minutes passed—I hiccuped, hiccuped in a peculiar way with a wheeze. I got up and stood by the door of the loge. It is better, *ma chère*, to hiccup by the door than into the ears of one's beloved! I hiccuped again. A schoolboy in the neighboring loge looked at me and laughed loudly. . . .

With what delight he, the rascal, laughed! With what delight I would have yanked out with its roots the ear of this callow young scoundrel! He is laughing at the same time that the magnificent *Faust* is being sung on the stage! Blasphemy! No, *ma chère*, when we were children, we were much better behaved. Cursing this lousy schoolboy, I hiccuped again. . . . In all the neighboring loges there was laughter.

"Bis!" hissed the schoolboy.

"What the deuce!" muttered Colonel Pepsinov into my ear. "You should have done your hiccuping at home, Sir!"

Zoya blushed. I hiccuped again and, furiously with fists clenched, I rushed out of the loge. I began to walk about the corridor. I walk, I walk, I walk—and all the time I'm hiccuping. What I didn't eat, what I didn't drink! At the beginning of the fourth act, I didn't give a hang and went home. When I arrived at home, as if in spite, I stopped hiccuping. . . . I struck the back of my head and exclaimed:

"Hiccup now! Now you can hiccup, you laughingstock of a suitor! No, you're not a laughingstock! You didn't hoot at yourself, but . . . made an ass of yourself!"

The next day I went, as usual, to the Pepsinovs. Zoya did not come out to dinner and sent a message to me that she was ill and could not see me, and Pepsinov made a speech about how some young people don't know how to conduct themselves courteously in society. . . . Blockhead! He isn't aware that the organs causing hiccups are not controlled by a voluntary stimulus. Stimulus, *ma chère*, means motive force.

"Would you give your daughter, if you had one," Pepsinov addressed me after dinner, "to a man who allows himself to belch in the presence of other people? Well? What do you say?"

"I would give her . . . ," I muttered.

"It's hopeless!"

I had lost Zoya. She was unable to forgive my hiccuping. I was crushed.

Do you want me to tell you about the other twelve cases?

I would declare them, but . . . enough! There are lines across my brow, I shed tears, and my liver is agitated. . . .

There's something fatal in the fate of those of us who belong to the brotherhood of writers! Allow me, *ma chère*, to wish you all the best! I press your hand and send regards to your Paul. I heard that he is a good husband and a good father. . . . He is praiseworthy! It's only too bad that he's a hard drinker (that is not a rebuke, *ma chère*!). Be in good health, *ma chère*, be happy, and do not forget that I'm your most humble servant.

Makar Baldastov*

---

*"Dunderhead"

THE PROUD MAN

This happened at the wedding of the son of the merchant, Sinerilov.

The best man, Nedorezov,* a tall young man with bulging eyes and short hair, wearing a frock coat with protruding lapels, stood with a group of gentlemen and was declaring:

"A woman must be beautiful, but a man can get around without being handsome. A man needs brains and education to carry weight, and handsomeness for him—isn't worth a fig! If your brain is uneducated and you're incompetent, then you're not worth a kopeck, even though you're superhandsome. . . . Yes . . . I don't like handsome men! Phooey!"

"You say that because you're not handsome. Take a look through the door into the other room at the man sitting over there! He's really handsome! All eyes are on him! Take a look! He's loaded with charm! Who is he?"

The best man looked into the other room and laughed derisively. There, slouching in an armchair, was a handsome, dark-eyed man with brown hair. With legs crossed, and fiddling

---

*Like Dickens, Chekhov played with names. This young man is still "unfinished" or "not fully cut."

with his watch chain, he was squinting his eyes, and with an air of self-esteem was looking over the guests. A scornful smile played on his lips.

"He's nothing special!" said the best man. "So-so. Even ugly, you could say. The face even looks a little stupid. . . . The Adam's apple on his throat is two arshins."*

"All the same, he's attractive!"

"In your opinion he's handsome, but in mine, he isn't. But even if he were handsome, if he's uneducated, he's dull. Who is he?"

"We don't know. . . . He has to be from other than the commercial clique."

"Hm . . . I'm ready to bet he's not very bright. . . . He's dangling his legs. . . . He rubs you the wrong way! I'll find out presently what kind of a bird he is . . . how smart he is. Right now."

The best man cleared his throat and boldly entered the other room. Stopping in front of the dark-haired man, he coughed, hesitated, and then began:

"How do you do?"

The dark-haired man looked at the best man and laughed.

"So . . . so . . . ," he answered reluctantly.

"Why so-and-so? Mustn't one must always be progressing?"

"Why must one progress?"

"That's the way it is. Everything is progressing now. Take electricity, and the telegraph, all kinds of phonographs and telephones. Yes, sir! Let's take the word *progress*, by way of illustration. . . . What does the word designate? Well, it designates that everything must move forward. So, you too are going forward. . . ."

"Where, for example, am I now going?" The dark-haired man laughed.

"There are many places to go. If there's a desire . . . there are many places. . . . So, for example, I want to go to the bar. . . . Would you like to? When you meet for the first time, a cognac helps. . . . Yes? To exchange ideas . . ."

"Please," agreed the dark-haired man.

The best man and the dark-haired man made their way to

---

*An arshin is a Russian and Turkish unit of measurement equal to 70 cm.

the bar. A waiter with short hair, in a frock coat, and with a stained white tie, poured two glasses of cognac. The best man and the dark-haired man drank up.

"Fine cognac," commented the best man, "but there are more important topics. . . . Let's drink a glass of red wine to our acquaintance. . . ."

They each downed a glass of red wine.

"Now-ow we are acquaintances," said the best man, mispronouncing *now* and wiping his lips, "and, it can be said, drank together. . . ."

"Not *now-ow* but *now*," corrected the dark-haired man. "You still don't know how to speak correctly, but you're wanting to instruct about telephones. If I were in your place and was so uneducated, I'd keep quiet, and not put myself to shame. . . . Ha!"

"What's so funny?" asked the insulted best man. "I used *now-ow* for a laugh, for a joke. . . . You needn't be so nasty! It may be attractive to young girls, but I don't like it. . . . Who are you? Where do you come from?"

"It's none of your business. . . ."

"What's your rank? Your name?"

"It's none of your business. . . . I'm not such a fool as to let everyone I meet know my rank. . . . I'm arrogant enough that I'm not willing to open up to you. I don't pay much attention to the likes of you. . . ."

"You don't say. . . . Hm. . . . So you won't tell me your name?"

"I don't wish to. . . . If you tell everybody your name, that is to introduce yourself, there won't be an end to what's said. . . . I'm a very proud man, and for me you are on the same level as the waiter . . . an ignorant person!"

"You don't say. . . . What's your birthright? Well, it appears that we'll presently find out what kind of an artist you will be."

The best man lifted his chin and pointed it toward the groom who was sitting with his bride, and, red as a lobster, winked. . . .

"Nikisha!" the best man called to the groom, nodding his head toward the dark-haired man. "What's this artist's name?"

The groom shook his head.

"I don't know," he said. "I don't know him. I suppose my father invited him. Ask him."

"Your father is in the study, dead drunk . . . snoring like a rabid beast." He then turned to the bride, "You don't know him either?"

The bride said she didn't know the dark-haired man. The best man shrugged his shoulders and began to question the other guests. The guests revealed that this was the first time in their lives that they had seen the dark-haired man.

"He's a party-crasher," decided the best man. "He's here without an invitation and walks around as if he belongs. All right! We'll show him *now-ow!*"

The best man approached the dark-haired man, and putting his hands on his hips, asked:

"Do you have an invitation? Please show me your invitation."

"I'm a very proud man and needn't show my invitation to just anyone. Leave me alone. . . . Why are you pestering me?"

"It follows then that you don't have an invitation. If you don't have an invitation, you're a party-crasher. It's now obvious where you're coming from and what your title is. . . . I now-ow. . . . that is, now know what kind of operator you are. . . . You're a party crasher—and that's all."

"If an intelligent man would be so rude to me, I'd give it to him in his ugly mug, but you, stupid, are not responsible for anything."

The best man scurried around the room and collected six of his friends and along with them approached the dark-haired man.

"If you please, dear sir, let me see your invitation!" he declared.

"I don't wish to. Leave me alone. . . . At the moment I don't wish to . . ."

"You don't wish to show your invitation? Does that mean you have entered without an invitation? By whose permission? You're a party-crasher, is that it? Please leave! If you please! You're welcome! We'll show you the steps. . . ."

The best man and his friends took hold of the dark-haired man's arms and led him to the outside door. The guests were very noisy. The dark-haired man loudly blasted their vulgarity and declared his own self-esteem.

"If you please! You're welcome, handsome man!" muttered

the solemn best man, while leading the dark-haired man to the door. "I know you, you dandies!"

At the door they pulled on his coat, put on his hat, and gave his back a good shove. The best man giggled from satisfaction and poked the back of his neck with his signet ring. The dark-haired man reeled, fell on his back, and slid down the steps.

"Farewell! Regards down there!" gloated the best man.

The dark-haired man picked himself up, brushed off his coat, and, lifting his head, said:

"The stupid act stupidly. I have self-respect and do not lower myself before you, but let my coachman tell you who I am. Come here, please! Grigory!" he called out toward the street.

The guests came downstairs. Within a minute a coachman entered the driveway.

"Grigory," the dark-haired man addressed him. "Who am I?"

"My master—Semyon Panteleich."

"And what is my rank and how did I get this rank?"

"You're an honorable citizen, and you earned this rank with your learning. . . ."

"Where am I located and what service do I perform?"

"You serve at the factory of the merchant Podschekin, as a mechanical engineer, and your salary is stated as three thousand. . . ."

"Now, do you understand? That for my invitation! I was invited to the wedding by the father of the groom, the merchant Sinerilov, who apparently is drunk now. . . ."

"My dear fellow! My good man!" exclaimed the best man. "Why didn't you say so sooner?"

"I'm a proud man. I have self-respect. . . . Farewell!"

"No, no, stay. . . . My fault, brother! Turn back, Semyon Panteleich! It's obvious now that you are such a person. . . . Let's drink to your learning . . . to ideas . . ."

The proud man frowned and came upstairs. Within a few minutes he was standing at the bar drinking cognac.

"Without pride you can't exist in this world," he revealed. "I won't give in to anyone ever! Not to anyone! I know my worth. However, that's incomprehensible to you, ignoramuses!"

1884

VEROCHKA

Ivan Alexeich Ognev* recalls how on that August evening the glass door opened with a tinkling sound, when he stepped onto the terrace. He had on a light, very loose shirt and a straw hat with a wide brim. The hat was the same one which now lies along with his high boots in the dust under the bed. In one hand he held a large bundle of books and a packet of notepaper, and in the other, a walking stick.

Behind the door, lighting his way with a lamp, stood his host, Kuznetsov. Kuznetsov was a bald old man with a long gray beard wearing a white-as-snow pique jacket. The old man was smiling genially and nodding his head.

"Farewell, grandfather!" Ognev called out to him.

Kuznetsov put the lamp down on a little table and walked onto the terrace. Two long narrow shadows fluttered across the steps toward the blooming flowerbed, swung around, and settled on the trunks of the linden trees.

"Farewell and thanks again, dear man!" said Ivan Alexeich. "Thank you for your cordiality, for your kindness, for your love.

---

*Chekhov's ironic humor in naming the hero "Red-hot"

. . . I will remember your hospitality forever. You are fine, and your little daughter is fine, and everything in your household is good, happy, cordial. . . . It was so wonderful being a guest here that I don't even know how to express it!"

From an excess of feeling and under the influence of the liquor he had drunk, Ognev spoke in a singsong seminarian manner, and was so emotional that he not only expressed his feelings with words, but just as much with blinking his eyes and with the twitching of his shoulders. Kuznetsov, also having had a bit too much to drink, was moved, came up to the young man and exchanged cordial kisses with him.

"I've gotten so used to being at your home, that I feel like a stool pigeon!" continued Ognev. "I wended my way to your place almost every day, every once in a while I spent the night, and drank so much that now I'm embarrassed to recall it. But most important of all, I want to thank you, Gavril Petrovich, for your cooperation and help. Without you, I and my statistical work would have puttered on 'til October. I will note this in my acknowledgments: 'I wish to express my indebtedness and thanks to the president of the N——ski district council, Kuznetsov, for his very kind assistance.' The statistics are going to have a brilliant future! I bow deeply to Vera Gavrilovna, and to the doctors, to the two investigators, and to your secretary, I will never forget their help! And now, grandfather, let us embrace one another and kiss for the last time."

The relaxed Ognev exchanged kisses with the old man again and started down the steps. On the last step he turned around and asked:

"Will we meet again?"

"God knows!" answered the old man. "Probably never!"

"Yes, that's true! You couldn't be lured to Petersburg by the finest of pastries, but I might at some time fall into this district. Well, now, farewell!"

"Why don't you leave your books here?" Kuznetsov called out to him. "Why should you drag such heavy stuff with you? I'll send a messenger with them to you tomorrow."

But Ognev was no longer listening and made a hasty retreat from the house. Warmed by the wine, his spirit was cheerful, lighthearted, and glowing, and a little sad. . . . As he walked along he thought of how often when you meet fine people it is sad that nothing more comes of the acquaintance than memories. That was how you felt when cranes flash across the horizon and a breeze carries their sorrowful, rhapsodical cries, but within a minute, as if from some kind of covetousness, you don't peer into the blue remoteness and you see not a single dot or hear a single sound—it's just in this way that people's faces and words flash through our lives and then become buried in our past, leaving behind nothing more than insignificant traces of memory. Having lived in the N——ski district since spring and having been hosted by the cordial Kuznetsov almost every day, Ivan Alexeich felt like a relative with the old man, with his daughter, with the servants. He knew every detail of the house: its pleasant terrace, every turn of the paths, the silhouettes of the trees over the kitchen and the bathhouse. But when he left the gate behind him, all this would be but a memory and its reality would be lost for him, and as a year or two passed, all these lovely pictures would grow dim in his consciousness and become equal to the fruits of the imagination and fantasy.

Nothing is more important in life than people! thought the overwrought Ognev, striding down the path toward the gate. Nothing!

It was still and warm in the garden. The air was fragrant with the scent of mignonette, of tobacco and heliotrope which had not yet succeeded in shedding their blossoms on the flowerbeds. The spaces between the bushes and the trunks of the trees were full of a gentle mist, not dense, and pierced throughout by the moonlight; there were clumps of mist resembling apparitions, silent but easily seen, in a single file, one after the other across the paths. The scene would remain in Ognev's memory for a long time. The moon stood high above the garden, and somewhere in the east beneath it rose luminous abutments. It seemed that the whole world consisted only of dark silhouettes and roaming white shadows. Almost for the first time in his life, observing the mist on this moonlit August evening, Ognev thought that he was not looking at a natural phenomenon but at an ornamentation, as when fireworks, intended to light up the garden with the white light of a Bengalian compound, imperfectly settle under the bushes, and along with their flashes release a white smoke into the atmosphere.

When Ognev reached the garden gate, a dark shadow came out of the lower front garden and came to meet him.

"Vera Gavrilovna!" he exclaimed with delight. "You are here? I searched and searched for you to say goodbye. . . . Farewell, I'm leaving!"

"So soon? It's not even eleven o'clock."

"No, it's time to leave! I have to walk five versts and pack. I must get up early tomorrow. . . ."

Kuznetsov's daughter, Vera, stood before Ognev. She was about twenty-one. She usually dressed carelessly, and was somewhat melancholy but interesting. Young women who dream a great deal, spend a lot of time reading and lying around, act languidly in everything they do, and appear bored and spiritless generally dress carelessly. For those whom nature has favored with good looks, this easy carelessness in dress is especially charming. At least Ognev, remembering pretty Verochka afterward, could not picture her without a loose blouse that was crumpled around the waist in thick folds, with no relation to her figure, and curls that protruded from her high hairdress onto her forehead. A red shawl with shaggy fringes, and tied any old way, drooped dejectedly on Verochka's shoulders like a flag when there is no breeze. During the day it lay rumpled in the entry among the men's hats, or even in the dining room on the chest where the impudent old cat slept. From this shawl and from the folds of the blouse, there exuded an air of easy freedom, a solitariness, and a good nature. It may be that since Ognev found her attractive he read into every button and turn of speech something warm, cozy, naive. It was something so fine and poetic that women who are insincere and cold, devoid of beautiful feelings, do not have.

Verochka had a good figure, a perfect profile, and lovely curly hair. To Ognev, who in his lifetime had not seen many women, she appeared a beauty.

"I must leave!" he said to her, parting with her at the gate. "Remember only good things about me! Thank you for everything!"

With the same singsong seminarian tone with which he had earlier conversed with the old man, with the same grimacing and shrugging of his shoulders, he began to thank Vera for her hospitality, kindness, and cheerfulness.

"I wrote about you to my mother in every letter," he said. "If everyone were like you and your father, it wouldn't just be existence in the world, but living in a land of milk and honey. Everyone in your home is extraordinary! Everyone is simple, heartwarming, and sincere."

"Where are you going from here?" asked Vera.

"I shall first go to my mother's in Orel, remain there possibly for a week or two, and then—on to Petersburg and work."

"After that?"

"After that? I'll work all winter and in the spring I'll go somewhere to another district to collect data. Well now, be happy, live to be a hundred . . . don't think badly of me. We may not meet again."

Ognev leaned over and kissed little Vera's hand. After an emotional silence, he straightened his billowing shirt, took a better grasp of the rope tying his books together, hesitated, and then said:

"It's become fairly cloudy!"

"Yes. You haven't forgotten anything?"

"Why? It doesn't appear so . . ."

Ognev stood silently for several seconds and then clumsily turned toward the gate and walked out of the garden.

"Wait, I'll accompany you up to our forest," declared Vera, walking after him.

They walked along the road. The trees no longer screened the wide expanse above, and the heavens and the remote land could be seen. As if covered by a veil, all of nature concealed itself by a filmy, lusterless smoke through which her beauty peeked out. The mist, which was thicker and whiter, lay unequally around the bushes, and where the soil was turned over or scattered in clumps over the road, clung to the ground as if it were trying to hide itself from the surrounding area. Penetrating the haze, the whole road to the forest was visible with its dark ditches alongside. Small shrubs that grew in the ditches disturbed

the wandering of the clumps of mist. The darkening strip of the
Kuznetsovs' forest was visible about half a verst from the gate.

*Why has she come with me? Really , I'm just going to have
to walk her back!* thought Ognev, but glancing at Vera's profile,
he indulgently smiled and said:

"I hate to leave such fine weather! The evening is genuinely romantic, with the moon, with the silence, and with all
its details. Do you know what, Vera Gavrilovna? I've been on
this earth for twenty-nine years, but there's never been any
romance in my life. In my whole life there hasn't been even
one romantic episode; anything like a rendezvous, sighs along
secret paths, and kisses I only know by hearsay. It's abnormal!
In town when you're sitting in your hotel room, you don't
notice this deprivation, but here in the fresh air, it becomes
deeply felt. . . . How vexing it is!"

"Why are you this way?"

"I don't know. Perhaps I haven't been anywhere, and it could
be that I just haven't met the kind of woman who. . . . However,
I don't know many people and I really haven't been around."

The young people walked silently for about three hundred
steps. Ognev glanced at Verochka's uncovered head and her
shawl, and his soul became full with memories, one after the
other, of the spring and summer days. It was a time, when far
from his Petersburg room, he reveled affectionately in good
people, nature, and rewarding work. He did not note how day-
break changed into evening, or how in turn the song of the
nightingales, then the quails, and a little later the crows pre-
dicted the end of summer. . . . Time passed unnoticed, which
meant that life was good and easy. . . . He began to speak aloud
of his memories and of how he was not eager, as a poor man
unaccustomed to traffic and people, to travel at the end of April
to the N——ski district, where he had expected to be bored and
lonely and indifferent about the data he was to collect, which
in his opinion, now would have an obvious place in the center
of his research. Arriving on that April morning in the district's
little town of N——, he had been put up at the local inn run by
the Old Believer Ryabukin, where for twenty kopecks a night he
was given a bright and clean room with the condition that he

would not smoke inside, and if he did want to smoke to go out on the street to do so. After having rested, he found out that in the district lived the chief of land management, and unhesitantly went on foot immediately to see Gavril Petrovich. He had to cover four versts of lush meadows and young bushes. Beneath the clouds the air was filled with the silver sounds of tremulous larks, and above the green fields, the crows, sturdy and asserting their high rank, rose up waving their wings.

Lord, thought Ognev in amazement, is the air here like this or is it just today, for my sake?

Expecting a dry, businesslike reception, he went to Kuznetsov gingerly, disconcerted and bashfully tugging on his beard. The old man frowned at first and could not understand how the young man and his collection of statistics could be good for land management. However, when it was made clear to him what the data was about and where it would be collected, Gavril Petrovich brightened, smiled, and with childlike curiosity began to go over Ognev's notebooks. . . . In the evening of the same day, Ivan Alexeich was having dinner at the Kuznetsovs' and soon had too much to drink of the strong liquor. Looking at the peaceful faces and indolent movements of his new acquaintances, his whole being felt a sweet, dreamy laziness such as one experiences when one needs to sleep, to stretch, to smile. And the new acquaintances looked at him kindly and asked if his father and mother were still alive, how much did he earn a month, did he often go to the theater. . . .

Ognev recalled his travels through the rural districts, the picnics, the fishing, the trip with everyone to the Maiden's Nunnery to visit the mother superior, Marvya, who gave all the guests a beaded purse; recalled the warm-hearted, never-ending, purely Russian arguments, with the disputants sputtering and banging fists on the table, not understanding and interrupting each other, not even noticing that they were constantly contradicting themselves or changing the subject, but after two or three hours would laugh and say:

"What the hell were we arguing about? We began about health and ended with peace!"

"Do you remember when you and I and the doctor were riding horseback to Shestov?" asked Ivan Alexeich of Vera as they approached the forest. "Later on we met a *yurodivy*.* I gave him a five-kopeck coin and he blessed me three times and threw the coin into the bushes. Lord, I'm taking away with me so many impressions that if it were possible to compress them into a solid nugget, I'd have a fine gold ingot! I don't understand why wise and sensitive people stay in crowded capital cities and not live here. Really, is it that on the Neva River in large damp houses there is more space and truth than here? Really, my furnished rooms—the building from top to bottom full of artists, scholars, and journalists—seem to exist because of a deep-rooted falsehood."

Twenty steps from the forest there was across the road a small narrow bridge with posts on its corners. This bridge acted as a way station for the Kuznetsovs and their guests when taking evening strolls. From this spot you could, if you wished, hear forest echoes and could see how the road disappeared into the dark opening of the forest.

"So, we've come to the bridge!" stated Ognev. "You have to go back at this point. . . ."

Vera stopped and took a deep breath.

"Let's sit down," she said, sitting down on one of the posts. "Before one leaves when one is saying goodbye, it's customary to sit together for a bit."

Ognev made a place for himself near her on his books and continued to talk. She was breathing rapidly as if from the strain of the walk, and was not looking at Ivan Alexeich but somewhere sideways so that he could not see her face.

"What if in about ten years we meet," he said, "what will we be like then? You will already be a respectable mother of a family, and I, an author of some kind of a respectable, useless, statistical abstract, thick as forty thousand other abstracts. We will meet and reflect on old times. . . . We now feel genuinely, we are filled with emotion, but then, when we meet, we will have forgotten the day, the month, or even the year when we saw each other for the last time on this little bridge. You, I think, will have changed. . . . Look here, will you change?"

_____

*a Russian homeless man considered one of God's fools

Vera sighed and turned her face to him.

"What?" she asked.

"I asked you just now. . . ."

"Excuse me, I wasn't listening to what you were saying."

It was only then that Ognev noted a change in Vera. She was pale, panting, and the unevenness of her breathing made her hands and her lips tremble, and not just one curl as usual broke loose upon her forehead, but two. . . . It was obvious that she was avoiding looking at him directly, and was trying to mask her agitation by straightening her collar, acting as if it were cutting into her neck, and transferring her shawl from one shoulder to the other. . . .

"It seems that you are cold," remarked Ognev. "Sitting outside when it is damp is not healthy. Allow me to accompany you back to the house."

Vera remained silent.

"What is the matter?" Ivan Alexeich smiled. "You are silent and don't answer me. Are you sick or angry? What is it?"

Vera pressed a palm firmly to her cheek, turned toward Ognev, and abruptly pulled it away.

"It's a terrible situation . . . ," she whispered with a very pained look. "It's terrible!"

"What's so terrible?" asked Ognev, shrugging his shoulders and not hiding his amazement. "What's the matter?"

Continuing to breathe rapidly and with her shoulders shaking, Vera turned her back to him and stared at the sky for a minute and then said:

"I need to speak with you, Ivan Alexeich. . . ."

"At your service."

"It's possible it will seem strange to you. . . . You might be amazed but it's all the same to me. . . ."

Ognev shrugged his shoulders again and prepared to listen.

"It's that . . . ," began Verochka, lowering her head and fiddling with the fringe of her shawl. "You see, I want to . . . want to tell you. . . . It will seem strange to you and . . . stupid, but I . . . I'm at a loss."

Vera's words became muddled and suddenly she broke into tears. The pathetic young girl covered her face with her kerchief, bent lower still, and bitterly sobbed. Ivan Alexeich was confused, hemmed and hawed, was dumbfounded, and, not knowing what to say or to do, hopelessly looked around. He was unaccustomed to crying and tears clouded his own eyes. "Now, enough of this!" he mumbled out of consternation. "Vera Gavrilovna, what is it you want to ask? Dear child, are you . . . are you in pain? Has someone insulted you? Tell me. It's possible I can . . . be able to help. . . ."

While trying to calm her, he allowed himself to withdraw her hands from her face. She smiled at him through her tears and declared:

"I . . . I love you!"

These words, simple and ordinary, were expressed in unequivocally human language, but Ognev, extremely embarrassed, turned away from Vera, got up, and, following the feeling of embarrassment, he became alarmed.

The sad, warm, and sentimental mood that had overcome him from the farewells and the drinks suddenly disappeared and was replaced by a sharp, unpleasant feeling of awkwardness. As if his spirit had somersaulted, he looked askance at Vera, and now she, after revealing her love for him, had cast off the inaccessibility that women are accused of, seemed to him immature, simpler, and more vague.

What's this all about? he thought, horrified by his reaction. But, really, how do I feel about her . . . do I love her or not? What a problem!

And she, when she had finally spoken what was the most important and difficult, now breathed easily and freely. She, too, got up and, looking directly at Ivan Alexeich, began to speak rapidly, unrestrained and passionate.

Just as a person who is unexpectedly frightened cannot later remember the order in which the sounds came that stunned him during a catastrophe, in just this way Ognev could not recall Vera's words or phrases. His memories were only of her speech, and of the effect her words had on him. He recalled how, as if smothered, his voice was a bit hoarse from emotion, and with unusual dissonance and passionate intonations. Crying, laughing, sparkling teardrops on her lashes, she told him that from the first day she met him, she was struck by his originality, wisdom, elegant intelligent eyes, his work, and the way he conducted his life, and that she loved him passionately, madly, and deeply. She told him that when during the summer it happened that she left the garden to go into the house and saw his billowing shirt in the entryway, or heard his voice in the distance, her heart froze from the anticipation of happiness. Even his dry jokes made her giggle, in every figure in his notebook she saw something unusually wise and grand, and even his walking stick was for her an example of marvelous wood.

And the forest, the clumps of mist, the dark ditches along the side of the road seemed silenced listening to her. But in Ognev's soul something happened that was undesirable and strange. . . . Having revealed her love, Vera was fascinatingly lovely, she spoke eloquently and warmly; but, as he would have wished, he did not experience joy, nor was he glad to be alive, but only had a feeling of compassion for Vera, pain and regret that a fine human being was suffering because of him. God knows, was it his book knowledge that told him, or his compelling habit of objectivity—which so often confuses people's lives—that Vera's ecstasy and suffering seemed to him sick, insincere, but at the same time he was perturbed by a feeling that whispered to him that what he had seen and heard from the standpoint of natural and personal happiness was more sincere than any data, books, truisms. . . . And he was angry with himself, and reproached himself, although he had no comprehension of what he was guilty.

To compound the awkwardness, he couldn't decide what to say, but it was necessary to say something. To tell her straightforwardly "I don't love you" was impossible for him. But he couldn't say yes either because it would compromise him, and in his heart there wasn't even a spark. . . .

He kept quiet and she continued saying that there could be no greater happiness for her than to be with him, to follow him at once if he wanted it, wherever he desired, to be his wife and helper, and if he went away from her, she would die from anguish. . . .

"I can't be left here!" she said, wringing her hands. "I'm sick of my home, of this forest, and of this air. I can't bear the everlasting peacefulness and useless life; I can't bear our uninvolved and bland people, who all resemble each other like drops of water! They're all genuine and well-meaning because they're well-fed, never suffer, never struggle. . . . But I want to be part of a larger, more raw existence where there is suffering, where one is made tough by troubles and necessity. . . ."

And this seemed to him as sick and insidious. When Vera finished, he still didn't know what to say, and it was impossible to say nothing, and so he mumbled:

"I, Vera Gavrilovna, am very obliged to you, although I feel I haven't done anything to deserve such . . . from you . . . feelings. Secondly, as an honorable man, I must say that . . . happiness is based on a balance. That is to say, when both parties . . . love equally. . . ."

But Ognev instantly felt ashamed of his mumbling and shut up. He felt that his face, as he spoke, looked stupid, guilty, flat, and that it was tense and strained. . . . Vera probably read the truth on his face, because she abruptly became grave, blanched, and hung her head.

"You must forgive me," muttered Ognev, not being able to keep quiet. "I respect you so much that . . . it hurts!"

Vera turned sharply and speedily went back toward the garden. Ognev followed her.

"No, you needn't come!" cried Vera, waving him away. "Don't come. I want to go alone. . . ."

"No, all the same . . . I must accompany you."

Regardless of what Ognev said, to the very last words, it was all repulsive and lifeless. The guilt feelings rose in him with every step. He grew angry, clenched his fists, and swore at his coldness and ignorance in the conduct of himself with women. Trying to arouse himself, he looked at Verochka's beautiful figure, at her long braid and footprints left on the dusty road by her tiny feet, but all this was only touching and did not upset his soul.

Ah, it's not possible to force love! he convinced himself, and at the same time thought: When will I love willingly? I'm almost thirty years old! I've never met a finer woman than Vera, and may never meet one. . . . Oh, it's a dog's old age! To be old at thirty!

Vera walked faster and faster in front of him, not turning around and with her head hanging. He surmised that grief had shrunken her, that her shoulders had become narrower. . . .

I can imagine what is happening to her being at this time! he thought, looking at her back. Most likely it's so ashamed and hurt that she wants to die! Lord, there's so much in this life that's poetic, thoughtful, that it could move a stone, but I . . . I'm stupid and callous!

At the gate Vera cast a cursory glance at him and, bent, wrapped in her shawl, walking at a fast pace, went down the path.

Ivan Alexeich remained alone. Turning back toward the forest, he walked slowly, and now and again turned around to look at the gate. His whole body appeared to reflect that he didn't believe himself. He sought Verochka's footprints on the road and could not believe that a young girl who had appealed to him so much, just when she told him of her love, he had clumsily rejected her! For the first time in his life he had had the opportunity to know by experience how little depends upon one's own goodwill, and to experience the emotional state of a proper and warm-hearted person, and against one's own volition to inflict undeserved pain upon those close to one.

His conscience bothered him, and when he could no longer see Vera, it seemed to him that he had lost something very dear and close, which he would never find again. He felt that along with Vera, part of his youth had slipped away, and those minutes which he had so fruitlessly outlived would never be repeated.

Reaching the little bridge, he stopped and fell into deep thought. He wanted to find a reason for his coldness. It was clear to him that it was something in him and not in her. He sincerely admitted to himself that it was not a rational coldness that intelligent people so often have, it was not the coldness of a self-centered fool. Was it simply a lack of character and inability to perceive profound beauty and to age prematurely, or was it from the acquisition of an education and the chaotic struggle for a livelihood and living in rented rooms without a family?

From the little bridge he slowly, as if unwillingly, entered the forest. Here, where the thick dark shadows were covered at random with penetrating patches from the rays of moonlight, his thoughts dominated his being and he intensely wanted to retrieve what he had just lost.

And Ivan Alexeich recalled that he had again turned back. Congratulating himself for his recollections, he reminisced that he had forced himself to imagine Vera's appearance, and had rapidly walked back to the garden. On the road and in the garden, as if cleansed, the mist was gone and the bright moon shone down. Only in the east was it overcast and hazy. . . . Ognev recalled his cautious steps, the dark window, the thick fragrance of the heliotrope and mignonette. The dog, Karo, recognized him and waved his tail in friendship, came up to him and muzzled his hand. . . . The dog was the only living creature who saw how he walked around the house several times, and stood under Vera's dark window, and then, giving it up as a bad job, gave a deep sigh and left the garden.

Within an hour he was in the small town. He was exhausted, broken up, his body stooped, and his face hot when he reached the inn and knocked. Somewhere in the town a half-awake dog barked, and as if in answer to his knock, church bell sounds were rung out on a cast iron plank. . . .

"Gadding about at night . . . ," grumbled the Old Believer who ran the inn, as he opened the gate for him. He wore a long feminine nightshirt. "You'd be better off praying than gadding about."

In his room, Ivan Alexeich fell on the bed and stared at the fire for a long time, then shook his head, got up, and began to pack. . . .

1887

A NASTY STORY: SOMETHING LIKE A ROMANCE

Winter activities were still going on.

There was a ball. The music was loud, the candelabras were lit, the smart young men were cheerful and made the young ladies' lives delightful. There was dancing in the ballrooms, card-playing in the reception rooms, drinking in the barroom, and desperate declarations of love in the library.

Lelya Aslovskaya, a curvaceous, pink-cheeked blonde with large blue eyes, long hair, and a passport showing she was twenty-six years old, was angry with everyone. Angry at all society and herself, she sat alone and fumed. She was sick at heart. The fact was that men conducted themselves toward her like swine. In the last two years especially, their conduct was reprehensible. She had noticed that they had stopped paying attention to her. It was with an air of reluctance that they danced with her. Moreover, the rascals walked past her—didn't even look at her, as if she were no longer a beauty. If one of them did look at her, somehow inadvertently, by chance, it was not with admiration, not even licentiously, but the way he looks at a rich tart or a roast before dinner.

And, besides, in past years . . .

It's this way every evening, at every ball! thought Lelya

angrily, biting her lips. I know why they aren't paying any attention to me, I know! They're getting back at me because I scorned them! Well . . . well, when will it all end with a husband? Will I ever marry? Time doesn't stand still, it waits for no one! What scoundrels you are!

On the evening we're writing about, fate decided to have some pity upon Lelya. When Lieutenant Nabridlov, drunk as a lord, instead of dancing the promised third quadrille with her, walked by her and stupidly smacked his lips demonstrating his complete disdain for her, she couldn't take it. . . . Her anger reached a peak. Her blue eyes filled with moisture, her lips trembled. The tears were ready to flow. . . . In order not to show the ignoramuses her tears, she turned toward the misted windows, and—oh wondrous moment, it's you!—in one of the windows she saw a magnificent youth who couldn't take his eyes away from her. The young man made a touching picture, immediately piercing her very heart. He appeared—chic, eyes full of love, wonder, questions, answers; his face melancholy. Lelya became animated instantly. She assumed an appropriate pose and properly returned his attention. It followed that the youth was not casting his eyes randomly, not so-so, but not taking his eyes away from her, was feasting his eyes and was thrilled.

Oh God! thought Lelya. If only someone would think of introducing him! He's a new, uncorrupted young man! He noticed me immediately!

Shortly afterward the youth turned, walked around the halls and began to join the men.

He wants to get acquainted! He's asking to be introduced! thought the transported Lelya.

It was really so. In about ten minutes an amateur actor with a clean-shaven, devil-may-care appearance heeded the plea of the youth and, vigorously shuffling his feet, introduced him to Lelya. The youth proved to be one of our "set," an obsessed, talented artist whose name was Nogtev. Nogtev—is about twenty-four years old, has brown hair, intensely sad eyes, a beautiful mustache, and pale cheeks. He never paints anything but he is an artist. He has long hair, a small pointed imperial beard, a gold palette on his watch-chain and gold palettes on his studs, gloves to his elbows, and incredible high heels. He's a nice guy but stupid as a goose. His father is honorable, as is his mother, and he has a rich grandmother. He's a bachelor.

He timidly held Lelya's hand, timidly sat down, and after being seated, began to devour Lelya with his enormous eyes. He began to speak slowly and timidly. Lelya chattered while he only said: "Yes . . . no . . . I, you know," hardly breathing, answered her absentmindedly, and in his confusion continually rubbed his (his, not Lelya's) left eye. Lelya warmly applauded. She decided that the artist was captivated, and was exultant.

On the day following the ball Lelya was sitting by the window in her room feeling jubilant and looking out upon the street. In front of her window on the street Nogtev was rambling back and forth. Nogtev rambled and cast glances up at her window. He looked as if he were getting ready to die: sorrowfully, languorously, endearingly, passionately. On the next day—the same thing. On the following day it rained, and he was not there. (Someone had convinced Nogtev that an umbrella wouldn't complement the scene.) A day later it was arranged that he should appear at Lelya's parents' home for a visit. The acquaintance was to be tied with a Gordian knot: tied so that it would be impossible to untie it.

Within about four weeks there was to be another ball. (The show begins.)

Nogtev stood by a door, his shoulders leaning against the door frame, and devoured Lelya with his eyes. Lelya, wanting to make him jealous, flirted with Lieutenant Nabridlov, who was drunk, but not dead drunk, but, almost, just about there.

Her daddy came alongside Nogtev.

"Do you draw anything?" asked the daddy. "You are a professional artist?"

"Yes."

"Tsk. . . . It's a good business. . . . God given, God given. . . . hm . . . Such a talent is truly God given. Tsk. . . . We all have our unique talents. . . ."

The daddy was silent for a moment and then continued:

"So, my young friend, that's what you do. As a matter of

fact . . . you can draw everything. Come to our country estate in the spring. There are very remarkable places there! The sights, I assure you, are exciting! Such rock formations artists have not had the occasion to paint. We'll be very happy to have you come. Our little daughter has . . . become such . . . friends with you. . . . Eh . . . hem . . . hm. . . . Young people, young people! Heh . . . eh . . . eh. . . ."

The artist bowed, and on the first of May this year, along with his baggage, wended his way to the Aslovski estate. His baggage consisted of an unneeded case with paints, a piqué waistcoat, an empty cigar case, and two shirts. He was received with open arms. He was given two rooms for his use, two lackeys, a horse, and they would have given him anything he wished if only he would give them hope. He took advantage of his new situation splendidly. He had a terrific appetite, drank a great deal, slept long hours, was carried away by the natural setting, and never took his eyes off Lelya. Lelya was ecstatic. *He* was her intimate, he was young, handsome, was like a slave . . . so in love! Like a quail, he just didn't know how to approach her but watched her from afar, from behind the curtains, or from behind the bushes.

A timorous lover! thought Lelya with a deep sigh. . . .

On one marvelous morning her daddy and Nogtev were sitting on a garden bench and conversing. The daddy was exclaiming about the charm of his familial happiness, and Nogtev listened patiently while he sought Lelya's body with his eyes.

"You're an only son?" asked the daddy, among other things.

"No . . . I have a brother, Ivan. . . . A fine fellow! A charming man! You aren't acquainted with him?"

"I haven't had the pleasure. . . ."

"Too bad that you don't know him. He's such a card, you know, a jovial guy, a big-hearted person! He's all bound up in literature. The publishers are all asking for his material. He works for *Jokes*. It's unfortunate that you aren't acquainted with him. He would be happy to know you. . . . That's true! If you wish, I'll write to him and ask him to come here? Yes? Really and truly? It'd be lots of fun!"

The daddy's heart felt as if it had been caught in a door

jamb at this proposal, but—what's to be done?—courtesy demanded saying: "My pleasure!"

Nogtev jumped at the sign of approval of his proposal and quickly wrote an invitation to his brother.

Brother Ivan wasn't slow in showing up. Not only did he arrive, but he brought with him a friend, one Lieutenant Nabridlov, and an enormous, toothless old dog named Turk. He explained that he brought them with him in order to discourage highway robbers from overtaking him, and so that he'd have someone to have a drink with. Three rooms were set aside for him, two lackeys, and one horse for the two of them.

"You, dear hosts," said Ivan, "don't bother yourselves about us! We won't trouble you! We don't need feather beds, nor sauces, not pianos—we don't need anything! But if in your generosity you want to provide us with some beer and vodka, well . . . that's another matter!"

If you can picture for yourself a huge, thirty-year-old, mouthy fellow in a canvas shirt, with a shaggy beard, swollen eyes, and with his tie askew, you'll relieve me of describing Ivan further. He was one of the world's most intolerable characters.

When he was sober, he was still tolerable: he lay in bed and was quiet. He was unbearable when drunk, like a burr on bare skin. When drunk he talked incessantly, using foul language, and not restraining himself in the presence of women and children. He spoke of lice, fleas, underwear, and the devil knows what else. Other subjects, or newer ones, were beyond his ability. Daddy, Mommy, and Lelya were at a loss and blushed when Ivan, sitting at the dinner table, began to crack his jokes.

Unfortunately, he was never sober during all the time he stayed at the Aslovski estate. Even Nabridlov, a small, diminutive lieutenant, tried with all his ability to behave like Ivan.

"We're not artists!" he exclaimed. "What do we need art for? We're muzhiks*!"

Ivan and Nabridlov at the first chance took off for the manager's quarters because they found the mansion of the nobility stifling. The manager was not adverse to having a

---

*"peasants"

drink with what he considered upper-class individuals. After
this they took off their frock coats and paraded around the
courtyard and the garden without them. Lelya also came upon
the brother and his friend dishabille in the garden where they
were lying under a tree. The brother and the lieutenant drank,
ate, fed the dog pastry, made jokes about the hosts, chased the
cooks around the yard, bathed noisily, slept like the dead, and
praised fate, which had chanced to bring them to this place
where they could live so well.

"You listen to me!" said Ivan to the artist, winking his
drunken eyes in Lelya's direction. "If you'd marry her . . . oh,
the hell with you! We won't interfere. You began it and you
know best. You're very welcome! We're nobility. . . . We wish
you luck!"

"We won't discourage you!" corroborated Nabridlov. "It
would be swinish of us."

Nogtev shrugged his shoulders and focused his greedy eyes
on Lelya.

When things are too calm, it gets boring and you yearn for
a storm. When you're sitting peacefully on top, it gets boring
and you need to create some havoc. When Lelya got bored
with bashful love, she began to get annoyed. Timorous love—
it's a cock-and-bull story for nightingales. To her great distress,
the artist was as bashful in June as he was in May. At the mansion they were sewing the trousseau. Day and night the daddy
thought about the loan necessary for the wedding. Not only
this, but their relations did not develop in the traditional manner. Lelya had the artist go fishing with her all day long. But
this didn't help. He stood alongside her with a fishing line, was
silent, hesitated when speaking to her, devoured her with his
eyes—and that's all. Not a single, terribly sweet word! Not a
single revelation of love.

"Call me . . . ," the daddy once said to him. "Call me. . . .
Excuse me for addressing you by the familiar 'you' . . . I like you,
you know. . . . Call me 'Dad.' . . . I would like that."

The artist foolishly began to call the daddy "Dad," but this
didn't help either. As before, he was mute, when to speak out
against the gods for giving man only one tongue and not ten

would have been appropriate. Ivan and Nabridlov caught on to Nogtev quickly.

"We see what you're up to!" they muttered. "You're not feasting on the harvest yourself, but you won't let anybody else have it! What a swine! Gobble it, blockhead, as long as there's a piece in your mouth! If you don't want it, we'll take it! That's that!"

But all things come to an end on this earth. There'll be an end to this story, too. The end, too, came to this unorthodox relationship between the artist and Lelya.

The plot of this romance was revealed in the middle of June.

It was a quiet evening. The air was fragrant. The nightingale was singing its heart out. The trees were whispering. The atmosphere as expressed by eloquent Russian novelists was heavy with sweet bliss. . . . The moon, of course, was also shining. Only needed to complete the heavenly mirage was a fata morgana to stand behind the bushes and read his captivating poetry for all to hear.

Lelya, wrapped in a shawl, was sitting on a bench, deep in thought, looking through the trees at the stream.

Am I really so unapproachable? she thought. In her imagination she saw herself as majestic, proud, haughty. . . . Her thoughts were interrupted by the approach of her daddy.

"So—what's happening?" asked the daddy. "Nothing changed?"

"Still the same."

"Hm. . . . Hell. . . . When will this all end? As you know, good heavens, feeding these freeloaders is costing money! Fifty rubles a month! That's not chicken feed! Just for that dog's biscuits it's thirty kopecks a day! If he's wooing you, so let him woo, but if not, so the hell with him, and his brother and his dog! Has he at least said something? Has he spoken to you at all? Has he expressed his desire?"

"No. He, Daddy, is too bashful!"

"Bashful. . . . I know such bashfulness! Your eyes will be opened. Wait here, I'll send him to you in a little while. Come to a conclusion with him! Don't fool around. . . . Time's up. Allow me, for God's sake, to say. . . . You're not getting any younger. . . . No doubt you know all the tricks!"

The father disappeared. In ten minutes, shyly wending his way through the lilac bushes, the artist appeared.

"You wanted to see me?" he asked Lelya.

"Yes, I did. Come here! You didn't have to rush! Do sit down!"

The artist quietly came toward Lelya and quietly sat down on the edge of the bench.

How handsome he is in the dark! thought Lelya, and, turning toward him, she said:

"Tell me something! Why are you so secretive, Fedor Pantelayich? Why are you always so silent? Why don't you open up your heart to me? What have I done to deserve such distrust? It's true, I'm offended. . . . You'd think we weren't friends. . . . Won't you begin to speak?"

The artist coughed, gasped, and said:

"I have a great deal I must tell you, a very great deal!"

"What is stopping you from doing it?"

"I'm afraid I might insult you, Yelena Timofeyevna. You won't be insulted?"

Lelya giggled.

The moment of truth has arrived! she thought. How he's trembling! How he's trembling! Has he been caught, poor dear?

Lelya herself was shaking in her shoes. She was enveloped by such gentleness as every romantic novelist prattles about.

In a few minutes the revelation, the kisses, the vows, will begin. . . . Ah! . . . She gave herself up to dreaming, and in order to put a little oil in the fire, she touched the artist with her warm, naked elbow.

"Well? Why so hesitant?" she asked. "I'm not such a touch-me-not as you think. . . . (Pause.) Do speak! . . . (Pause.) Don't be so reticent!"

"Well you see. . . . I, Yelena Timofeyevna, love nothing in life more than painting . . . art, that is to say. Comrades have found that I have talent and that I can become a pretty good artist. . . ."

"Oh, that's for sure. *Sans doute!**"

---

*"Without a doubt!"

"Well yes. . . . That's so. . . . I love my own work. . . . It means. . . . I prefer genre painting, Yelena Timofeyevna! Art. . . . Art, you know . . . is a wonderful mystery!"

"Yes, a rare mystery!" said Lelya, and having encouraged the snake to uncoil, huddled under her shawl and partially closed her eyes. (Young women know little about the details of lovemaking, and are brave where passion is concerned!)

"I, you know," continued Nogtev, cracking his white fingers, "I've been getting ready to speak to you for a long time, but always . . . I was afraid. I thought you'd get angry. . . . But you, if you understand me, well . . . you won't be angry. You also love art!"

"Oh . . . well yes. . . . So what! Art is art!"

"Yelena Timofeyevna! You know why I'm here? Can't you guess?"

Lelya was extremely confused, and, as if involuntarily, placed her hand on his elbow. . . .

"It's true," continued Nogtev hesitantly, "among artists there are swine. . . . It's true. . . . They don't give a fig for feminine modesty. . . . But I really . . . I really am not like that! I have sensitive feelings. Feminine modesty is such . . . such modesty, it's impossible to neglect!"

Why is he telling me this? thought Lelya and hid her elbows in her shawl.

"I'm not like those. . . . Woman for me—is sacred! You have nothing to fear. . . . I'm not like that, I don't permit myself to be up to such rubbish. . . . Yelena Timofeyevna! Will you permit it? But hear me out, I, really, am sincere that it is not for myself but for art's sake! I have art as my highest goal, and not the satisfaction of animal instincts!"

Nogtev grasped her hand. She leaned slightly in his direction.

"Yelena Timofeyevna! My angel! My happiness!"

"W . . . well?"

"May I ask you?"

Lelya giggled. Her lips were already in position for the first kiss.

"May I ask you? I beg you! For God's sake, for art! I am so

taken with you, so taken with you! You are the one, the one who I just need! The devil with the others! Yelena Timofeyevna! My dear friend! Will you be my . . ."

Lelya leaned over, ready to fall into his arms. Her heart stood still.

"Will you be my . . ."

The artist grasped her other hand. She modestly tilted her little head toward his shoulder. Tears of happiness rested on her eye lashes . . .

"My darling! Will you be my . . . model!"

Lelya raised her head.

"What?!"

"Will you be my nude model!"

Lelya arose.

"How? Who?"

"My model. . . . Will you!"

"Hm. . . . That's all?"

"You would oblige me exceedingly! You will give me the possibility of painting a picture, and . . . what a picture!"

Lelya's face grew pale. The tears brought on by love suddenly turned into tears of despair, anger, and other virulent feelings.

"So that's it . . . what?" she exclaimed, her whole body trembling.

Poor artist! A bright red glow reddened one of his white cheeks when the sound of a slap on the face could be heard, blending with its own echo in the dark garden. Nogtev rubbed his cheek and became numb. He was stunned. He felt that he was being swallowed by the whole universe. . . . Flashes of lightning darted before his eyes.

Lelya, trembling, pale as death, a little mad, stepped forward and staggered a little. It was as if she had been run over by the wheels of a carriage. Exerting all her strength, she pulled herself together, and with uneven, painful steps walked toward the house. Her legs were giving way under her, sparks were shooting from her eyes, her hands reached toward her hair with the obvious intention of pulling it. . . .

It was only a few yards to the house when once more something happened to make her face turn white. In her path, near the arbor, covered with wild grapes, stood, with wide-open arms, the drunken, heavy-faced Ivan, uncombed and with an unbuttoned jacket. He stared at Lelya's face, sardonically smirked, and defiled the air with a Mephistophelian "ha-ha." He grabbed Lelya's hand.

"Get out!" railed Lelya and pulled her hand away. . . .

What a nasty story!

1882

A NERVOUS BREAKDOWN

I

Mayer, a medical student, and Ribnikov, a student in a
Moscow school of sculpture and architecture, came one
evening to their friend Vasilyev, a law student, and proposed
that he go with them to a certain red-light district. Vasilyev at
first refused but later got dressed and went with them.

He knew about prostitutes only by hearsay and from books,
and had never been in a house of prostitution. He knew there
were such immoral women who under the pressure of disastrous
circumstances—environment, poor upbringing, poverty, and
similar forces—are compelled to sell their bodies for money.
They knew nothing about pure love, had no children, and
were not protected by the law. Mothers and sisters shed tears
over them as if they were dead, moral instruction denounces
them as evil, and men speak to them with contemptuous famil-
iarity. In spite of all this, they do not lose sight of the fact that
they were born in the image of God. They recognize that they
are sinners and hope to be saved. The means of salvation are
available to them in many ways. It's true, society does not for-

give people their past, but for God, the holy Mary Magdalene is not considered beneath other saints.

When Vasilyev recognized a prostitute on the street either by her dress or her manners, or saw her portrayed in one of the comic journals, he always remembered a particular story he had once read: In this story a young man, pure and unselfish, fell in love with a prostitute and proposed to her. She, however, considering herself unworthy of such happiness, poisoned herself.

Vasilyev lived on one of those side streets off Tverski Boulevard. It was about eleven o'clock when he left with his friends. The first snow had just fallen and all of nature was under its spell. The air smelled of snow; underfoot the snow crackled; the ground, the roofs, the trees, the benches on the boulevard—all were soft, white, young. Outside all had changed from the day before; the lamps were brighter, the air was transparent, the carriages made less noise, and in one's heart, along with this fresh, light frosty air, there arose feelings similar to the white, new, fluffy snow.

"Don't know what has brought me to these dismal shores," sang the medical student in his pleasant tenor voice. "I'm being led by an unknown force . . ."

"Behold the mill . . . ," joined in the artist. "It's in ruins . . ."

"Behold the mill. . . . It's in ruins," repeated the medical student, raising his brows and sorrowfully shaking his head.

He was silent for a moment, wiped his brow, remembered the words, and then sang so loudly and so well that passersby turned and stared at him:

"There was a time when I was free,
In her own sweet way my love met me."

The three young men entered a restaurant and, without removing their coats, drank two shots of vodka at the bar. Before drinking his second glass, Vasilyev noticed a piece of cork in his drink, lifted the glass before his eyes, stared at it for some time with his nearsighted eyes, and frowned. The medical student misunderstood and said:

"So, what are you staring at? Please, no philosophizing! The vodka is here in order to be drunk, the sturgeon to be eaten, women—in order to be with them, snow—in order to walk over it. Live like a human being for at least one evening!"

"Okay. It's nothing . . . ," Vasilyev said, laughing. "Have I refused?"

The vodka warmed his chest. He looked fondly at his friends, admired them, and envied them. How intact and smooth everything was in the minds and hearts of these healthy, strong, boisterous men who took everything in stride! They sing, passionately love the theater, paint, have a lot to say, and drink and don't have a headache the next morning; they're even poetic and dissipated, tender and impertinent; they even know how to work, can be outraged and laugh spontaneously, and talk nonsense; they are warm, honorable, selfless, and as human beings no worse than he, Vasilyev, who watches his every step and every word, is nervous, cautious, and is ready to treat the smallest gaffe as if it were of great importance. He wanted to live at least for one evening like his friends, unwind, be out of control. Did he like to drink vodka? He was going to drink, even though tomorrow his head would be splitting from pain. They were taking him to women? He was going willingly. He was going to laugh, to act like a fool, answer frivolously to the remarks of passersby. . . .

He walked out of the restaurant laughing. His friends pleased him—one of them was wearing a wide, wrinkled hat with a pretense of artistic disarray, the other wore a sealskin cap—not a poor student but with the pretense of being part of student Bohemia. The snow pleased him, the pale lamplight; the sharp, dirty paths made by the pedestrians after the first snow. The atmosphere pleased him, especially the clear, tender, naive, somewhat virginal tone which could be observed only twice a year: when everything was covered by snow and in the spring on those bright days or moonlit nights when the ice was breaking up on the river.

"Don't know what has brought me to these dismal shores," he started to sing loudly, "I'm being led by an unknown force . . ."

For some reason this motif never left the tongues of Vasilyev and his friends during the whole distance they covered. All three sang mechanically and completely out of time with each other.

Vasilyev's imagination was picturing how when in ten minutes he and his friends would knock on a door; how through dark corridors and dark rooms they would steal toward the women; how he, making use of the darkness, would strike a match and see a long-suffering face and a guilty smile. The unknown blonde or brunette would probably be with her hair down and in a white nightgown. She would be frightened by the light, be terribly embarrassed, and would say: "For God's sake, what are you doing? Put the light out!" It was all terrifying, but curious and new.

II

The friends turned from Trubnaya Square to Grachevka and soon reached the sidestreet which Vasilyev only knew by hearsay. Seeing the two rows of houses with brightly lit windows and with wide-open doors, and hearing the merry music of pianos and violins—sounds which came from all the doors and blended into a strange hodgepodge, resembling the tuning up of what in the darkness might have been an unseen orchestra on the roofs—Vasilyev was surprised and said:

"What a lot of houses!"

"This is nothing!" said the medical student. "In London there are ten times more. They have around a hundred thousand such women there."

The cabmen were sitting on their coach boxes as peacefully and indifferently as they did on other streets. On the sidewalks pedestrians walked as they do on all streets. No one appeared hurried, no one hid his face behind his umbrella, no one shook his head reproachfully. . . . And in their indifference, in the noisy tangle of pianos and violins, in the bright windows, in the wide-open doors, something candid, naked, daring, and swinging could be felt. No doubt it was just as merry and loud in the time of the slave markets, and the faces and the gait of the people reflected the same kind of indifference.

"Let's start with the very first one," suggested the artist.

The friends entered a narrow corridor, lit by a reflecting

lamp. When they opened the door, a man in a black frock coat with an unshaven lackey's face and sleepy eyes lazily arose from a yellow divan. It smelled like a laundry and, besides that, of vinegar. From the foyer a door led to a brightly lit room. The medical student and the artist stood in the doorway stretching their necks in unison and looking over the room.

"Bonsoir, signori, Rigoletto-Hugenotti-Traviata!" began the artist, bowing theatrically.

"Havana-tarakano-pistoleto!" said the medical student, pressing his cap against his chest and bowing deeply.

Vasilyev stood behind them. He also wanted to bow theatrically and to say something stupid, but he could only smile, feel awkward, feel something like shame, and wait impatiently for what was to come next.

A small blonde about seventeen or eighteen appeared, her hair cropped, and in a short blue dress with a white metal ornament hanging on her breast.

"Why are you standing in the doorway?" she asked. "Take your coats off and come into the drawing room."

The medical student and the artist continued to jabber in Italian while entering the drawing room. Vasilyev indecisively followed them.

"Gentlemen, remove your coats!" commanded the flunkey. "You can't enter as you are."

Besides the blonde there was another woman in the drawing room who was very tall and heavy with a foreign face and with exposed arms. She was sitting by the piano and laying out cards on her lap for a game of patience. She paid no attention to the "guests."

"Where are the other ladies?" asked the medical student.

"They're having tea," said the blonde. "Stepan," she called out. "Go tell the ladies that students have arrived!"

Soon a third young woman came into the drawing room. She had on a bright dress with blue stripes. Her face was crudely and heavily made-up, her forehead was hidden behind hair, her eyes did not blink and appeared frightened. As soon as she entered, she began to sing something in a strong, vulgar contralto. After her came a fourth young woman and then a fifth. . . .

In all this Vasilyev did not see anything novel or curious. It seemed to him that this drawing room, the piano, the mirror with its cheap gold frame, the aglet, the dress with blue stripes, and the dull, blank faces he had seen somewhere before and not just once. There was not even a hint, however, of the darkness, silence, secrecy, guilty smiles that he had expected to meet and which had troubled him.

All was ordinary, prosaic, and uninteresting. Only one thing slightly peaked his curiosity—the terrible, as if on purpose, tastelessness of the cornices, of the dirty pictures, in the dresses and the aglet. In this tastelessness there was something characteristic and quirky.

How pathetic and stupid it all is! thought Vasilyev. What is there in all this rubbish which I'm looking at now that can seduce a normal person, awake in him the desire to commit an awful sin—to buy for a ruble a living being? I can understand illicit love when there are sparks, beauty, grace, passion, good taste, but not what's here! What's here that's worth sinning for? However . . . I mustn't think about it!

"You, with the beard, buy me some port!" the blonde addressed him.

Vasilyev was instantly confused.

"With pleasure . . . ," he said, bowing politely. "But excuse me, Miss, I . . . I can't drink with you. I don't drink!"

About five minutes later the friends entered another whorehouse.

"Well, why did you order the port?" remarked the angry medical student. "What a millionaire! You threw six rubles to the wind for no reason at all!"

"If she wanted it, why not treat her?" answered Vasilyev, justifying his action.

"You treated the boss, not her. They're instructed by the boss to ask guests to treat them because they make money that way."

"Behold the mill . . . ," sang the artist. "It's in ruins . . ."

Entering the next house, the friends only stood in the foyer and did not enter the drawing room. As in the first house, a figure in a frock coat with a sleepy lackey's face arose from the divan in the foyer. Looking at this flunkey, at his face and wrinkled frock coat, Vasilyev thought: "How much does an ordinary simple Russian have to endure before destiny casts him here as a lackey? Where was he earlier and what did he do? What awaits him? Is he married?" And so involuntarily in every house Vasilyev directed his attention first to the lackey. In one of the houses, it seemed to him that it was the fourth, the lackey was short, frail, lifeless, with a watch-chain on his vest. He was reading the newspaper, *Leaflet*, and paid no attention to the incomers. Observing his face, Vasilyev for some reason thought that such a person could steal, kill, and commit perjury. But nonetheless the face was interesting: a high forehead, gray eyes, a flat nose, small, tight lips, a blunt expression which at the same time was brazen like that of a young hunting dog when it's chasing a rabbit. Vasilyev thought that he would like to touch this flunkey's hair: Would it be coarse or soft? Like the dog's, it would be coarse.

III

The artist, after drinking two glasses of port, appeared suddenly to have become tipsy and became unnaturally lively.

"Let's go to another house!" he commanded, waving his arms. "I will lead you to the best!"

Having brought his friends to this house, which in his opinion was the best, he revealed a genuine wish to dance a quadrille. The medical student complained that the musicians would have to be paid, but agreed to be his vis-à-vis. They began to dance.

The best house was as repugnant as the worst. There were the same mirrors and pictures here, the same kind of hairdos and apparel. Looking over the furniture and the costumes, Vasilyev now understood that it wasn't just tastelessness but what one could call the style of the red-light district, and which could not be found anywhere else—something complete in its scandalousness which was not thoughtless, but which had been developed over time. After he had been in eight houses, he was no longer surprised by the color of the dresses, nor the long trains on them, nor the bright ribbons, nor the sailor suits, nor the thick, violet rouge on the cheeks. He understood that this conformity was necessary, for if only one of the women would dress as women normally did, or if on the walls decent gravures were hung, the whole district would suffer from this respectable tone.

How clumsily they sell themselves! he thought. Is it that they cannot conceive that vice is only fascinating when it is made beautiful and conceals itself, when it wears the veil of virtue? Modest dark dresses, pale faces, sad smiles, and dim light are more enticing than this crude trumpery. It's stupid! If they cannot understand this, the guests should teach them. . . .

A young woman in a Polish national dress with white fur trimming came up to him and sat down beside him.

"You charming brunette, why aren't you dancing?" she asked. "Why are you so bored?"

"Because it is boring here."

"Treat me to some Lafitte. Then it won't be boring."

Vasilyev did not answer at once, but then asked her:

"What time do you go to bed?"

"At six in the morning."

"And when do you get up?"

"Sometimes at two and sometimes at three o'clock."

"And when you get up, what do you do?"

"We drink coffee, and at seven o'clock we have dinner."

"And what do you have for dinner?"

"Usually . . . cabbage or some other kind of soup, beefsteak, and dessert. Our madam takes good care of her girls. Why are you asking me these things?"

"So we can have a conversation."

Vasilyev wanted to speak with her about other things. He felt a strong desire to know where she came from; were her parents alive, and did they know she was here; how she had fallen to this level into this whorehouse; if she were happy and content or was she sad and depressed by dismal thoughts; did she hope that there might be a time when she could leave this present situation. . . . But he could in no way think of how to start and in what form to put the questions so as not to appear indiscreet. He mulled this over and then asked her:

"How old are you?"

"Eighty," she joked, looking and laughing at the gyrations the dancing artist was executing with his hands and feet.

Suddenly she burst into a peal of laughter and then shouted some shameful comment so that all could hear. Vasilyev was appalled and not knowing how to react, forced a smile. He was the only one who smiled. All the rest—his friends, the musicians, and the women—didn't even look at his neighbor and acted as if they hadn't heard.

"Treat me to Lafitte!" she demanded again.

Vasilyev felt repelled by her white fur trimming, and by her voice, and walked away from her. The atmosphere seemed close and hot to him and his heart beat slowly, but forcefully, like a hammer: one!-two!-three!

Taking hold of the artist's sleeve, he said, "Let's get out of here!"

"Wait a bit, 'til we finish."

While the artist and the medical student finished the quadrille, Vasilyev, in order not to look at the women, looked over the musicians. At the piano was a good-looking old man wearing glasses and resembling Marshal Bazyen; on the violin—a young man with a light-brown beard, and dressed fashionably. The young man's face was neither stupid nor dissipated, but on the contrary, was intelligent-looking, young and fresh. He was dressed fastidiously and tastefully, and played with feeling. Vasilyev gave himself an assignment: How did he and this pleasant, respectable-looking old man find themselves here? Why aren't they ashamed of being here? What are they thinking about when they look at these women?

If at the piano and on the violin you had shabby, hungry, drunken, morose people with dissipated or blank faces, then their presence, perhaps, could be understood. Now Vasilyev understood nothing. He recalled the story of the fallen woman that had been read to him, and he now found that this humane picture with the guilty smile had nothing in common with what he now observed. It appeared to him that in these women he saw something else, an absolutely different world, foreign to him and incomprehensible. If he had seen this scene in a theater or read about it in a book, he would not have believed it. . . .

The woman with the white trimming again began to laugh and loudly shout repulsive words. A feeling of disgust overwhelmed him, he reddened and walked out.

"Wait, we're coming!" shouted the artist to him.

IV

"I just had a conversation with my damsel while we danced," recounted the medical student when the three of them were out on the street. "The conversation concerned her first love. He, the hero—was some kind of bookkeeper from Smolensk with a wife and five children. She was seventeen years old and was living with her mother and father. Her father sold soap and candles."

"How did he capture her heart?" asked Vasilyev.

"By buying her fifty rubles' worth of underwear. Who the hell knows!"

He was able to get his lady to talk about her romance, thought Vasilyev about the medical student. But I don't know how. . . .

"Gentlemen, I'm going home!" he declared.

"Why?"

"Because I don't know how to behave here. So I'm bored and repelled. What fun is there here? If, at least, there were people here, but these are savages and animals. I'm leaving. Do as you wish."

"Now, now, Grisha, Grigorii, dear friend . . . ," said the artist in a tearful voice, hugging Vasilyev. "Let's go! Just one more house, and let them drop dead. . . . Please! Grigoriants!"

They talked Vasilyev into it and ascended a stairway. In the carpet, in the gilded railings, in the servant opening the door, and in the panel decorating the foyer, it could be sensed that here too was the same style of the district but improved, more impressive.

"Honestly, I'm going home!" said Vasilyev while taking off his coat. "Now, now, dear fellow . . . ," said the artist, kissing his neck. "Don't be so capricious. . . . Gri-Gri, be a pal! We came together, so let's leave together. Don't be some kind of a brute, really."

"I'll wait for you on the street. Really and truly, it makes me sick!"

"Well, well, Grisha. . . . It's ugly but you must see it! Understand? Observe!"

"It's necessary to be objective about what's going on," the medical student remarked seriously.

Vasilyev went into the drawing room and sat down. There were many other guests besides him and his friends: two infantry officers, a gray and bald gentleman with gold-rimmed glasses, two beardless students from the local college, and a very drunk man who looked like an actor. All the girls were busy with these men and paid no attention to Vasilyev. Only one of them, dressed like Aida, gave him a sidelong glance, smiled, and remarked, yawning:

"A dark handsome one has arrived. . . ."

Vasilyev's heart began to pound and his face burned. He was ashamed before the other guests for his presence there, and felt dirty and miserable. He was tortured by the thought that he, a decent and affectionate person (which he had considered himself up to this time), hated these women and felt no sympathy for them, only revulsion. He wasn't sorry for these women, nor for the musicians, nor for the flunkies.

It's because I'm not trying to understand them, he thought. They all appear more like animals than human beings, but all the same, they are human beings and they have souls. One must try to understand them and then judge. . . .

"Grisha, don't leave, wait for us!" called out the artist and then disappeared.

The medical student soon disappeared too.

Yes, it's necessary to try to understand, but I can't . . . , Vasilyev continued to think.

So he began to stare at the faces of all the women and to look for a guilty smile. But—either he did not know how to read their expressions, or not one of these women felt any guilt —on every face he only saw a vacant expression of common-place, vulgar tediousness and satisfaction. Stupid eyes, stupid smiles, grating stupid voices, brazen movements—and nothing else. Apparently, in all their pasts was a romance with a book-keeper and underwear bought for fifty rubles, but now there was nothing more pleasant than a cup of coffee, a dinner of three different dishes, wine, quadrilles, and sleeping 'til two o'clock in the afternoon. . . .

Not finding even one guilty smile, Vasilyev began to seek at least one intelligent face. His attention was drawn to one pale, a little sleepy, exhausted face. It was an older brunette, dressed in an outfit sprinkled with sparkles. She was sitting in an armchair, staring at the floor, and seemed to be deep in thought. Vasilyev walked around and, as if accidentally, sat down beside her.

I have to begin with something trite, he thought, and then gradually move on to something serious.

"What a fine outfit you have on!" he said and touched the fringes with his finger.

"So what . . . ," she said listlessly.

"What province are you from?"

"Me? From far away . . . from Chernigovska."

"That's a nice district. It's lovely there."

"It's nice when you're not there."

Too bad that I'm not good at describing nature, thought Vasilyev. It might be possible to touch her with a description of the natural beauty of the district. She must love it because she was born there.

"Are you bored here?" he asked.

"It's no secret. It's boring."

"Why don't you leave if you're bored?"

"Where can I go? To beg for charity?"

"It's better to ask for charity than to live here."

"How do you know? Have you ever begged?"

"I begged when I couldn't pay for my lessons. You don't have to be a beggar, however, to understand begging. A beggar, no matter what, is free, and you are a slave."

The brunette stretched and signaled with her sleepy eyes to the lackey who was carrying glasses and seltzer water on a tray.

"Treat me to port," she said and yawned once more.

Port . . . , thought Vasilyev. And what if right now your brother or your mother entered? What would you say? What would they say? I can imagine there would be port then too. . . .

Suddenly loud sobbing was heard. From a neighboring room, where the lackey took the seltzer water, a fair-haired man with a red face and angry eyes came dashing out. Behind him came the tall, heavy madam who with a piercing voice screamed:

"No one has given you the right to slap the girls! We have more important clients than you, and they don't dare! You lousy phony!"

Hubbub arose. Vasilyev was frightened and blanched. In the neighboring room loud sobbing continued and the unfeigned sound was that of a truly abused human being. He then appreciated the human nature of the residents, and that they as human beings could be hurt, suffer, cry, ask for help. . . . The painful hatred and disgust he had felt gave way to an acute feeling of pity and anger at the offender. He dashed into the room from which the crying came. Through the rows of bottles standing on a marble-topped table, he discerned a suffering face wet with tears, stretched his hands out to this face, and started to walk toward the table, but almost immediately stepped back in surprise. The tear-stained woman was drunk.

Making his way through the noisy crowd which had gathered around the blond man, he lost heart, became a coward like a young boy. It seemed to him that this incomprehensible world was pursuing him, beating him, showering him with foul language. . . . He pulled his coat from the hanger and ran out down the stairs.

V

Leaning on the fence around the house, he waited for his friends to come out. The dissonant sounds of the pianos and violins were at once merry, bold, outrageous, and sad, and muddled round in some kind of chaos, and, as before, sounded in the dark as if an orchestra on the rooftops was tuning up. If one glanced upward into the darkness, the entire black background was sprinkled with white moving specks. It was the falling snow. Dropping on him, it was caught in the light, lazily swirling in the air like down, and even more lazily dropping on the ground. Light snowflakes swirled around Vasilyev and clung to his beard, his eyelashes, his eyebrows. . . . The cabdrivers, the horses, and the pedestrians were white.

How can snow fall on this alley? thought Vasilyev. These are damned houses!

His legs were collapsing from exhaustion after dashing down the stairs; he was gasping for breath as if he had been climbing a mountain; his heart was beating so hard that he could hear it. He was tormented by the desire to get away from this alley and go home, but he had an even stronger desire to wait for his friends and unmask his heartache.

There was a great deal he didn't understand in the whorehouses; the lost souls of the women remained as illusive to him as before, but it was clear to him that things were much worse than he could have imagined. If the guilty woman who poisoned herself was called fallen, it was difficult to find an appropriate name for all those who were dancing now to the ringing chaos and spoke in long, vulgar sentences. They were not on the road to ruin, they were already ruined.

Vice exists, he thought, but not with the recognition of guilt, nor with the desire to be redeemed. They are sold and bought, drowning in sin and abominations, but like sheep, they are dense, indifferent, and ignorant. My God, my God!

It was also clear to him that all that is known as human dignity, personality, likeness unto God was being fundamentally defiled; "dead drunk" as the alcoholic would say, and that the district and the obtuse women were not the only guilty ones.

A group of students, white from the snow, passed by him, carrying on merrily and laughing boisterously. One of them, a tall, thin fellow, stopped and, staring at Vasilyev, said in a loud drunken voice:

"One of ours! Have you had too much to drink, brother? Aha-ha, brother! It's nothing, take a walk! Go ahead! Don't be so doleful, old man!"

He took hold of Vasilyev by the shoulders and pressed his cheek with its wet and cold mustache, slipped, staggered, and, waving both hands, called out:

"Careful! Don't fall!"

And, starting to laugh, he hurried to catch up with his friends.

Above all the noise, the voice of the artist was heard:

"Don't you dare to strike a woman! I won't permit it, damn you! You're all scoundrels!"

The medical student showed up at the doorway. He looked all around and seeing Vasilyev, said in an agitated voice:

"You here? Listen, I swear you can't go anywhere peacefully with Yegor! I can't understand him! He's begun a riot! Do you hear it? Yegor!" he shouted into the doorway. "Yegor!"

"I won't allow you to strike women!" the strident voice of the artist could be heard.

Something heavy and cumbersome rolled down the steps. It was the artist rolling down head over heels. He, it was obvious, had been thrown out.

He picked himself up from the ground, dusted off his hat, and with an angry, indignant face shook his fist upward and shouted:

"Villains! Fleecers! Vampires! I won't allow you to beat women! To beat a weak, drunken woman! Oh, you . . ."

"Yegor. . . . Now, now, Yegor . . . ," the medical student began to implore him. "I give you my word of honor I'll never go out with you again. Word of honor!"

The artist gradually calmed down and the friends started homeward.

"Don't know what has brought me to these dismal shores," sang the medical student. "I'm being led by an unknown force. . . ."

"Behold the mill . . . ," chimed in the artist a bit later. "It's already in ruins. What a snowfall, Holy Mother! Grisha, why did you leave? You're a coward, an old woman, and nothing more."

Vasilyev walked behind his friends, looked at their backs, and thought:

There are two choices: Either we only imagine that prostitution is evil and we overstate it, or if, as a matter of fact, prostitution is as evil as we think it is, these dear friends of mine are like the slaveowners, conquerors, and murderers as the populations of Syria and Cairo are described in *Niva*. They are now singing, laughing, arguing, reasonably, but really aren't they exploiting hunger, ignorance, and stupidity? They—I was an onlooker. What is there here of their humanity, their medicine, their art? The science, art, and the high-mindedness of these murderers reminds me of a piece of suet in an anecdote. Two highwaymen in the forest cut a beggar's throat. They began to share his clothing and found a piece of pig suet in a bag. "How lucky," said one of them, "let's eat." "You can't say that, how can we?" questioned his horrified partner. "Have you forgotten it's Wednesday?" So they didn't eat. They had cut a man's throat, but left the forest with the conviction intact that they had not broken the proscribed fast. Just as these men, having bought women, leave and consider themselves artist and scientist. . . ."

"Listen to me!" he declared angrily and pointedly to his friends. "Why do you come here? Is it that . . . is it that you have no comprehension of how terrible it is? Your medical training tells you that every one of these women will die before her time from tuberculosis or some ailment that is preventable. Your art tells you that her morality dies even earlier. Every one of them dies from the fact that in her lifetime on the average she takes on about five hundred men. Every one of these five hundred men kill her. Included in the five hundred are—you two! Now, if both of you in your lifetime visit this place and similar ones two hundred and fifty times each, you are both guilty of murdering a woman! Is it possible you don't understand this? Is it possible that you don't think it's terrible? For a group of two, three, five men to kill one stupid, hungry woman! My God, isn't that dreadful?"

"I knew how it would end," said the artist, frowning. "We shouldn't have gone with this blockhead, this dumb cluck! You think that great ideas are mulling around in your head? No,

the devil knows what, but not ideas! You look at me now with
hatred and disgust, but in my opinion, it would be better if
you'd set up twenty more such houses than to look like that at
me. There's more vice in your eyes than in all those houses!
Come on, Volodya, the hell with him! He's an idiot, a blockhead, and nothing more. . . ."

"We human beings kill each other in reciprocity," said the
medical student. "It is, of course, immoral, but philosophy is of
no use here. So long!"

The friends said good-bye and parted at Trubnaya Square.
When left alone Vasilyev walked rapidly along the boulevard.
He was afraid of the dark, and of the snow, which was falling
in large flakes upon the ground and it seemed that it wanted to
cover the whole world; the lights from the lamps were frightening, too, as they flickered weakly through the clouds of snow.
His spirit was seized by an uncontrollable, fainthearted fear.
When he met other pedestrians he timidly shunned them. It
seemed to him that on every side women were staring at him,
only women. . . .

I'm starting to crack up, he thought. I'm having a nervous
breakdown. . . .

VI

At home he lay on his bed, his whole body trembling, and he
exclaimed:

"They're alive! They're alive! My god, they're alive!"

He tried in every possible way to clarify his fantasies, imag-
ining himself the brother of a prostitute, then the father of the
one with the painted cheeks, and these thoughts created terror
in him.

It appeared to him for some reason that he had to settle the
question quickly no matter what the cost, that it was not someone else's concern but his very own. He pulled himself together
with great effort, fought his despair, and sitting on the bed
holding his head with his hands, tried to decide: How to save
all these women he had seen that day? The logical method to

resolve problems used by all educated individuals was one he knew well. And even though he was extremely agitated he held strictly to the method. In his mind he reviewed the history of the question, its literature, and after three o'clock he paced the room and tried to recall all the experiments that would be practical at present for the salvation of the women. He had many acquaintances and friends who lived in the rooming houses. . . . Among them were many honorable and selfless men. Some of them had tried to save such women. . . .

All of these attempts, thought Vasilyev, can be separated into three groups. The first bought her out of the den of inequity, rented her a room, bought her a sewing machine, and she became a seamstress. While a student, having been her patron, whether she liked it or not, he considered her his and made her his mistress. When he received his degree he turned her over to some other decent man as if she were a thing. And the fallen woman remains a fallen woman. The second bought her out, also rented a room for her, bought the inevitable sewing machine, taught her to be literate, to listen to sermons, and to read books. The woman lived in this way and earned her living sewing. While it was new and interesting, this was her life. But later, becoming bored, she began to surreptitiously receive men or even ran back to where it was possible to sleep to three o'clock, have coffee, and dine well. The third, the most passionate and altruistic, were more daring and took a more positive step. They married her. But when the impudent, dissipated, or dull, half-dead creature became a wife, a housekeeper, and later a mother, there was a complete reversal from top to bottom of her life and worldview, to the extent that in the wife and mother it would be difficult to recognize the former fallen woman. Yes, marriage is better than, I'm sorry to say, remaining single.

"But that's impossible!" Vasilyev said aloud and threw himself on the bed. "I couldn't marry one of them! You'd have to be a saint to do that and not be repelled by dislike or not feel disgust. But suppose that I, the medical student and the artist, subdued our instincts and married whores. What would be the result? What kind of outcome? While that would be a solution here in Moscow, some Smolensk bookkeeper will corrupt another set and this set will stream up to Moscow from Sarat, Nizhni-Novgorod, Warsaw . . . to fill vacancies there. And what do you do with the hundred thousand whores in London? Where do you put the ones from Hamburg?"

The lamp, whose kerosene had burned out, began to smoke. Vasilyev did not notice it. Once again he began to pace and continued to concentrate on the same subject. He now placed the question to himself differently: What needs to be done to eliminate the demand for prostitutes? What is necessary in order to convince men who buy and kill these women of the immorality of their slaveholding role and to frighten them. These men had to be redeemed.

It's obvious that science and art can do nothing . . . , thought Vasilyev. There's only one way out—the Scriptures and conversation.

So he began to dream how tomorrow evening he would stand on the corner of the red-light district and say to every passerby:

"Where are you going? You must have the fear of God!"

He would turn to the indifferent cabdrivers and say:

"Why are you standing here? Why aren't you bothered and indignant? Do you really believe in God and know what is sinful, what do you go to hell for? Why do you keep quiet? It's true they are strangers to you, but they, too, have fathers and brothers just as you do. . . ."

Vasilyev had once been told by one of his acquaintances that he was talented. There are literary talents, theatrical talents, artistic talents, but that he had a special talent—*humanitarian*. He possessed a gentle, splendid sensitivity to pain other than his own. Like a fine actor who assumes the actions and voice of someone else, Vasilyev could sense in his soul someone else's pain. When he saw tears, he would cry too; if he were around someone in pain, he, too, became a patient and groaned with pain; if he saw violence, it seemed to him that he was the victim and became cowardly, and like a little boy, ran in fear for help. The pain of others upsets him, excites him, and drives him into a frenzy, and so on.

If his friends were right—I don't know but what Vasilyev was going through when he thought the question was resolved was equivalent to inspiration. He cried, laughed, spoke aloud the words which he would say tomorrow, felt intense love for those who would listen to him and stand on the corner with him in order to preach; he would write letters, make vows to himself. . . . All this did resemble ecstatic inspiration and therefore did not last long. Vasilyev soon grew tired. The massive numbers of prostitutes from London, Hamburg, and Warsaw crushed him, as mountains crush land. In the face of this mass, he was subdued and became flustered. He remembered that he had no talent for words, that he was cowardly and fainthearted, that unconcerned people really had no desire to either hear or understand what he had to say. He was only a third-year law student, a shy and unassuming person, and a true missionary does not limit himself to preaching but acts.

When it became light and carriages could be heard on the street, Vasilyev lay motionless on the divan and focused on one spot. He no longer thought about the women, or the men, or the conversions. His attention was completely absorbed by the spiritual pain that was torturing him. It was a pressing pain, without a purpose, indeterminate, resembling anguish and extreme terror and despair. He could not place the source of it. Was it in his chest under his heart? It was impossible to equate it with anything. Previously he had had a severe toothache, he had had pleurisy and neuralgia, but in comparison with this spiritual agony it had been nothing. This agony made life unbearable. His dissertation, an excellent piece of work, was already written; people he was fond of, the redemption of the fallen women—all which only yesterday he had either loved or been indifferent about—now in recollection irritated him as much as the noise of the carriages, the dashing about in the hallways, the daylight. . . . If at this time he had seen the performance of a great act of charity or one of outrageous violence, both actions would have gotten the same response from him. Of all the thoughts muddling around in his head only two did not disturb him: One, that at any moment he had the power to kill himself, and the other, that this anguish would not last more than three days. The latter he knew from experience.

After having lain for a while, he got up, and wringing his hands, began to pace the room, not in the usual fashion but along the four walls. He glanced cursorily at himself in the mirror. His face was pale; his cheeks were pinched; his temples sunken; his eyes were bigger, darker, motionless, as if someone else's, and expressed unbearable spiritual agony.

In the afternoon the artist knocked on the door.

"Grigori, are you in?" he asked.

Not getting an answer, he stood for a moment, and answered himself in Ukrainian:

"He's not in. Must have gone to the university cafeteria, poor fellow."

So he left. Vasilyev lay on the bed, and hiding his head in the pillow, his agony caused him to begin crying, and the more abundant the tears, the greater became his soul's anguish. As it grew dark, he thought of the torturous night which awaited him and a terrible sense of despair overcame him. He quickly dressed, rushed out of his room leaving his door wide-open, and without any kind of rhyme or reason went out on to the street. Not asking himself where he was going, he walked rapidly along Sadovaya Street.

As yesterday, snow was falling, but it was melting. Thrusting his hands in his sleeves, shivering, frightened by the tramping of the horses and the sound of their bells and by the passersby, Vasilyev went from Sadovaya Street to the Suhareva Tower, then to the Red Gates, and from there turned on to Basmanaya. He entered a tavern and drank a large glass of vodka, but it gave him no relief. Reaching Razgulyaya he turned right and walked on side streets over which he had never been in his whole life. He reached the old bridge where the Yauza roared and from which could be seen long rows of lights in the windows of the Red Barracks. In order to ease his spiritual agony with some new sensation or a different pain, not knowing what to do, crying and trembling, Vasilyev opened his coat and shirt and exposed his naked chest to the damp snow and the wind. But even this did not alleviate his agony. Then he leaned over the railing of the bridge and looked down on the black, turbulent Yauza and he wanted to plunge in headfirst, not because of a loathing of life and desire to commit suicide, but in order to injure himself and for one pain to displace the other. But the black water, the dark, deserted shores covered with snow, were fearful. He shuddered and went further. He passed the Red Barracks, turned back and found himself in some kind of grove, and from the grove went back to the bridge. . . .

No, I must go home, go home! he thought. At home, it seems, it's a little better. . . .

And he went back. Returning home, he took off his wet coat and cap, paced along the walls, and untiringly walked until morning.

VII

When the artist and the medical student came to his quarters the next morning, he was in a torn shirt, his hands were bitten, and he was thrashing around the room and groaning agonizingly.

"For God's sake!" he sobbed, seeing his buddies. "Take me wherever you want, do what you can with me, but, for God's sake, don't waste time saving me! I'm going to kill myself!"

The artist blanched and lost his head. The medical student also almost broke into tears, but, believing that a medical professional under all circumstances is obligated to keep his cool and be composed, said coldly:

"You're having an attack of nerves. It's nothing. We'll go immediately to a doctor.

"Wherever you want to, only, for God's sake, quickly!"

"Don't work yourself up. You have to exert control over yourself."

With shaking hands the artist and the medical student dressed Vasilyev and led him out to the street.

"Mihail Sergeyich has wanted to meet you for a long time," said the medical student while they were on the way to the doctor. "He's a great guy and is an expert in his field. He got his degree in '82 and already has a large practice. He's friendly with students."

"Faster, faster . . . ," pressed Vasilyev.

Mihail Sergeyich, a stocky, fair-haired doctor, met the friends courteously, was composed, coolly professional, and smiled amiably.

"I have already heard of your illness from Mayer and Ribnikov," he said. "I'm happy to be of service to you. So? Please take a seat . . ."

He had Vasilyev sit in a large armchair near a table and offered him a cigarette from a case.

"Well, sir?" he began, stroking his knees. "Let's get to work. . . . How old are you?"

He asked questions which the medical student answered. He asked whether Vasilyev's father had ever been ill from anything exceptional, was he a heavy drinker, was he known for his cruelty or any kind of abnormality. He asked the same questions about Vasilyev's grandfather, his mother, his sisters and brothers. Hearing that his mother had an excellent voice and at times acted in the theater, he abruptly became more alert and asked:

"Excuse me, but do you recall if your mother had a passionate attachment to the theater?"

About twenty minutes passed. Vasilyev became annoyed that the doctor was stroking his knees and kept talking about one and the same thing.

"As far as I can understand your questions, Doctor," he said, "you want to know whether or not my illness has a genetic basis. It is not genetic."

The doctor persisted in questioning him. When he was younger did Vasilyev have any kind of secret vices, head injuries, passions, strangeness, exceptional predilections? Half of the questions were those which any conscientious doctor usually asked and could remain unanswered without any effect on the patient's treatment, but the faces of Mihail Sergeyich, the artist, and the medical student looked as if all would be lost if Vasilyev didn't answer one question. The doctor recorded his answers in a notebook. Being informed that Vasilyev had a degree in the natural sciences and was now in law school, he pondered. . . .

"He wrote an excellent thesis last year . . . ," said the medical student.

"Excuse me, but don't interrupt me. You're interfering with

my concentration," said the doctor, smiling wryly. "Yes, of course, it plays a role in anamnesis. Intense mental struggle, overwork. . . . Yes, yes. . . . Do you drink vodka?" he addressed Vasilyev.

"Rarely."

Twenty more minutes passed. The medical student began to give his opinion of more recent reasons for the attack and told how three days ago he, the artist, and Vasilyev went to the red-light district.

The callous, restrained, cold tone in which his buddies and the doctor discussed the women and the unfortunate district seemed to Vasilyev the height of grotesqueness. . . .

Controlling himself in order not to be rude, he asked: "Doctor, tell me only one thing, is prostitution evil or not?"

"Dear man, who disputes that?" said the doctor with an expression that he had already made that decision long ago. "Who disputes that?"

"You are a psychiatrist?" Vasilyev rudely asked.

"Yes, I'm a psychiatrist."

"It's possible all of you are right!" declared Vasilyev, getting up and starting to walk about the room. "It's possible! But it's amazing to me! I've studied two disciplines—it's considered an accomplishment. Because I wrote a thesis which in three years will be discarded and forgotten, I am highly acclaimed. But because I cannot speak as cold-bloodedly about prostitution as I can about these chairs, I'm considered sick, called insane, deplored!"

Vasilyev was overcome with an unbearable sorrow for himself, for his comrades, for all those he had seen three days ago, and for the doctor. He started to sob and fell into the armchair.

His friends looked questioningly at the doctor. He, giving the appearance that he understood exceedingly well the tears and the despair, as a specialist in this area, went up to Vasilyev and quietly gave him a drink with some medicine, and when Vasilyev had calmed down, undressed him and checked the sensitivity of his skin, the reflexes of his knees, and so forth.

And Vasilyev felt better. When he left the doctor's office, he had already begun to feel ashamed, the carriage noises did not disturb him, and the heaviness in his heart lightened, as if it were melting away. He had two prescriptions in his hands: one was for a bromide and the other for morphine. . . . These remedies he was already acquainted with!

He stood on the street a bit longer, and then parting with his comrades, languidly moved toward the university.

1889

THE GUARDIAN

I overcame my reticence and entered the office of General Shmigalov. The general was sitting at a table and laying out cards for a game of solitaire called "Ladies' Whims." "What can I do for you, my fine fellow?" he asked me courteously, and nodded toward an armchair.

"I've come to you, your honor, on business," I said, sitting down, and for some reason began to button my jacket. "I've come to you on private—not official business. I came to ask for the hand of your niece, Varvara Maximova."

The general slowly turned toward me, looked me over attentively, and let the cards fall on the floor. His lips quivered for a long time, and then he exclaimed:

"You . . . what? . . . Are you out of your mind? Are you out of your mind, I ask you? You . . . you dare?" he sputtered, his face becoming purple. "You dare, you kid, you're still wet behind the ears! You dare to joke with me . . . you beggar. . . ."

And stamping his foot, Shmigalov screamed so loudly that even the glasses shook:

"Stand up!! You have forgotten to whom you are speaking!

Please get up and remove yourself from my sight! Please leave! Out!"

"But I wish to be married, your excellency!"

"You can get married somewhere else, but not in my house! You haven't matured enough for my niece, you beggar! You're not a match for her! Neither your fortune nor your social standing give you the right to make such a . . . proposal! From you it's impudence! I beg you, boy, I beg you not to aggravate me any more!"

"Hm. . . . You've already gotten rid of five suitors by this means . . . but you won't succeed with this sixth one. I know the reason for these rejections. That's it . . . your excellency . . . I give you my honorable and noble word that upon marrying Vara, I will not ask for a kopeck from you of the money which you have squandered as Vara's guardian. I give you my word of honor!"

"Repeat what you have just said!" declared the general in an unnatural, cracking voice, bending and coming toward me at a trot, like an excited gander. "Repeat it! Repeat it, you scoundrel!"

I repeated it. The general became crimson and nervously moved about.

"That would be the last straw!" he rattled, shifting around and lifting his arms high. "It's too much to take, that my subordinates come to me with terrible, indelible insults in my own home! Dear God, what have I come to! I . . . feel faint!"

"But I assure you, your excellency! I don't want a kopeck from you, nor do I hint with even a word, that you dissipated Vara's money because of your weak character! And, I will see to it that Vara will do the same! My word of honor! Why are you still getting so agitated, beating your breast? I'm not going to take you to the court!"

"This kid, this greenhorn . . . this beggar . . . dares to say such vileness to my face! Please leave, young man, and don't forget that I'll never forget it! You have insulted me appallingly! However . . . I'll forgive you! You have spoken these loathsome words because you are thoughtless, stupid. . . . Ah, please keep your fingers off my table, and the hell with you! Don't touch the cards! Leave, I'm busy!"

"I'm not touching anything! What are you contriving? I give you my word of honor, General! I give you my word, there won't be even a hint! I won't allow Vara to demand anything from you! What else do you want? What a queer fish you are, really. . . . You squandered the ten thousand left her by her father. . . . Well, what of it? Ten thousand isn't a lot of money . . . it can be pardoned."

"I didn't squander anything. . . . yes, sir! I'll show you right now! Immediately . . . I'll show you!"

With shaking hands, the general removed a box from the table, took out of it a bundle of some kind of paper money, and red as a crab, began to count it. He counted for a long time, slowly and pointlessly. The poor devil was terrible agitated and confused. Fortunately for him, the butler entered the office and announced that dinner was being served.

"Good . . . I'll show you after dinner!" mumbled the general, putting the paper currency away. "Once and for all . . . to avoid gossip. . . . Let's have dinner first . . . you will see! Somehow, forgive him Lord . . . a youth who was played for a sucker, still playing with balls . . . he 's still wet behind the ears. . . . Let's have dinner! After dinner . . . I'll show you. . . ."

We proceeded to the dining room. During the first and second courses the general appeared angry and depressed. He salted his soup frenetically, rumbled like distant thunder, and noisily moved around on his chair.

"Why are you so cross today?" Vara asked him. "I don't like you when you behave that way . . . really. . . ."

"How dare you say that you don't like me!" the general snapped at her.

By the third and last course, Shmigalov began to heave deep sighs of relief and his eyes blinked. Then a crestfallen look of defeat spread over his face. . . . He started to appear unhappy, offended! Large beads of perspiration formed on his brow and nose. When dinner was over he invited me into his office.

"My dear fellow!" he began, not looking at me and taking hold of the lapel of my dress jacket. "You can have Vara, I agree. . . . You're a fine, good person. . . . I'm in agreement. . . . My blessings upon you . . . upon both of you, my angels. . . . You must forgive me for chiding you before dinner. . . . I was angry. . . . It was really because of my love for her . . . fatherly love. . . . But one thing. . . . I did not spend ten thousand rubles but . . . sixteen. In one night I lost those which her Aunt Natalia left her . . . gambled away. . . . Let's drink to much happiness . . . clink our champagne glasses. . . . Have you forgiven me?"

And the general, fixing his gray eyes upon me, at once appearing ready to burst into tears and at the same time to appear triumphant. I forgave him the additional six thousand and married Vara.

All good stories end with a wedding!

1883

THE CONVERSATION

Individuals of both sexes sitting in comfortable armchairs, eating fruit, and having nothing else to do, were inveighing against doctors. They decided that if there were no doctors in the world, it would be marvelous. At least people wouldn't be sick and dying so often.

"However, ladies and gentlemen, sometimes . . . however . . . ," finally remarked a small, classy blonde while eating a pear and blushing. "Sometimes doctors are useful. . . . You can't deny their usefulness under certain circumstances: in family life, for example. Picture for yourself that the wife. . . . My husband isn't around here, is he?"

The blonde cast her eyes over the conversationists and, convinced that her husband was not in the vicinity, continued:

"Picture to yourself, that the wife, for some reason, was unable, did not wish to, let us propose that . . . her husband exercise his marital rights. . . . Picture that she can't, simply . . . love her husband because . . . in short, she has given herself to someone else . . . a person she loves. Well, what would you tell her to do? She goes to a doctor and asks him to . . . find a reason. . . . The doctor approaches the husband and tells him that if . . . in plain

Russian, you understand what I mean. The writer Pisyemski writes somewhere about this kind of situation. . . . The doctor goes to the husband and in the name of his wife's health, orders him to give up his rights as husband. . . . *Vous comprenez?*"

"I don't have anything against doctors," noted an old man, a bureaucrat, who was sitting nearby. "They are the kindest, and I can say truly, the wisest people! If you care to think about it they are our benefactors. You can judge for yourselves, dear ladies. . . . You here, Madame, have spoken about a wife's duties, and I will tell you about our responsibilities. We, too, really love peace of mind and our heartfelt desire is for everything to be congenial. I know what my duties are, but if, I propose, you need that which is above the call of duty, excuse me, that, too, will be taken care of. We, too, value our peace. . . .

"Do you know our chief? A sensitive man! Greathearted! His sins, it can be said, are emotional! In order not to offend you, he offers his hand, asks about your family . . . a supervisor who conducts himself on an equal plane with you. He tells great jokes, witty remarks, anecdotes. . . . He's like a father and that's the long and short of it. But, about three times a year in this wonderful person a cataclysm occurs. He changes! He really becomes another personality and . . . God forbid this should happen to you! At this time he loves to carry out some reforms. . . . This is his thing, his vision as the socialists say. And when— about three times a year this happens to him—and he begins to carry out his desired reforms, at this time he is unapproachable! He becomes something like a tiger or a lion! He walks around red-faced, sweaty, trembling, and complaining that he has no workers. At this time we walk around pale and . . . are frightened to death. He orders us to work late at night; we write, we run, dig into the archives, the reference books . . . and God forbid if this angry Tartar doesn't get what he wants. You'd be better off in hell. A few days ago he cried, that no one understands him, that he has no reliable workers. . . . He cried! Is it a pleasant sight to see an important man cry?"

The old man stopped talking and turned his back so as not to show the tears that were glistening in his eyes.

"Why is a doctor needed?" asked the blonde.

"Ah, the reason is. . . . Stop to think. . . . If as soon as we would notice that this kind of upheaval is beginning, we could go immediately to a doctor: 'Ivan Matveich, dear man! You are our benefactor, our father, help us! You are our only hope! Do us a godlike favor, send him abroad! It's impossible for us to live with him. . . .' Well the doctor is a well-known seasoned man. . . . It's common knowledge that there had been a time when he himself had been treated as a subordinate, but had also tasted all kinds of sweetness. He goes to our man and examines him. . . . 'The liver,' he says, 'is not what it should be. Something is not right with it, your excellency. . . . It would be beneficial if,' he says, 'if you went abroad to profit from the waters. . . .' So, frightening him about his liver. It's well known that he is a person who is overanxious about his health and afraid of being sick. . . . Abroad he goes immediately and the reforms—amazingly disappear! So there!"

"Well, assume that you're a juror," began the merchant: "to whom can you go, if . . ."

After the merchant, an elderly lady began to tell that only a short while ago her son had very nearly not gone to do his military service.

So they all began to praise doctors. They declared that one could not do without doctors, that if there were no doctors on this earth it would be terrible. Finally, they decided that if there were no doctors, people would suffer and die far more often.

1883

THE DADDY

Slim like a Holland herring, the Mommy entered the study of the fat, round like a beetle Daddy, and coughed. When she entered, the maid jumped up from the lap of the Daddy and slipped behind a curtain. The Mommy didn't even blink an eye nor pay the slightest heed, since she had already become accustomed to this little weakness of the Daddy and looked upon it from the point of view of the wise wife, who understood her sophisticated husband.

"Daddy-O," she said, as she sat down on his lap. "I came, my own darling, to get advice from you. Wipe your lips, I want to kiss you."

The Daddy blinked and wiped his lips with his sleeve.

"What's your problem?" he asked.

"Well it's, little Daddy. . . . What are we to do with our son?"

"What do you mean?"

"You don't know? My God! All of you fathers are so carefree! It's awful! Daddy-O, even if you don't want to act like a father, finally . . . you won't be able to be a husband!"

"You're repeating yourself! I've heard this a thousand times already!"

The Daddy made an impatient move, and the Mommy almost fell from his lap.

"You men are all the same. You don't want to hear the truth."

"Did you come to talk about the truth or about our son?"

"Now, now, I won't. . . . Daddy-O, our son has again brought home a poor report card from school."

"Well, so what?"

"So what? You know he won't be allowed to take the finals! He won't be passed to the fourth level!"

"So he won't be passed . . . big deal. If he weren't spoiled at home, he'd probably study more."

"But, little Daddy, he's fifteen! At fifteen, can he remain in the third level? That worthless mathematics teacher gave him a two again. . . . Well, what does that look like to you?"

"It looks like he needs a thrashing."

The Mommy ran her little finger over the Daddy's lips, and in her opinion, wrinkled her little brow coquettishly.

"No, little Daddy, don't talk about punishment to me. . . . Our son is innocent. . . . The teacher has it in for him. . . . Our son belittles himself. He's so advanced that it can't be true that he doesn't know some dumb arithmetic. He knows everything superbly. I'm convinced of that!"

"He's a charlatan and that's that! If he were spoiled less and studied more. . . . Get off my lap and sit on a chair. . . . I don't think it's appropriate for you to sit on my lap."

The Mommy hopped off the Daddy's lap and it seemed to her that she moved as gracefully as a swan to an armchair.

"Lord, how unfeeling you are!" she whispered, sitting down and closing her eyes. "No, it can't be that you don't love your son! Our son is so good, so smart, so handsome. . . . They have it in for him! No, he can't be made to repeat the year. I won't permit it!"

"You'll permit it as long as the good-for-nothing is a lousy student. . . . Oh, you, you mothers! . . . So, go with God, I have work to do. . . ."

The Daddy turned to his desk, leaned over some papers, and out of the corner of his eye, like a dog at a plate that wasn't his, glanced at the curtain.

"Little Daddy, I won't leave. . . . I won't leave! I can see that I'm creating a problem for you, but be patient. . . . Little Daddy, you have to go to the mathematics teacher and order him to give our son a good grade. . . . You must tell him that our son knows his mathematics excellently, but that he has a weak constitution, and because of that he can't please everybody. You've got to twist the teacher's arm. Can a young man be left behind in the third level? You can do it, Daddy! Picture to yourself how our son would look like a pariah if Sofia Nikolaevna found out!"

"That's all very flattering, but I won't go! I have no time to go."

"You have to go, little Daddy!"

"I won't go. . . . That's final. . . . Now, go with God, darling. . . . I have work to do. . . ."

"You'll go!"

The Mommy got up and raised her voice.

"I won't go!"

"You'll go!" screamed the Mommy. "And if you don't have any sympathy for your only son, then . . ."

The Mommy shrieked and with the gesture of an infuriated tragedian pointed to the curtain. . . . The Daddy became confused and was taken aback, and out of the blue, came out with some kind of protest and took off his frock coat. . . . He always forgot himself and became a perfect imbecile when the Mommy let him know she knew what was behind the curtain. He gave in.

They called for the son and asked for a statement from him. Sonny boy got angry, frowned, scowled, and said that he knew more math than the teacher himself and it wasn't his fault that the only high school students that are given a five are the wealthy and the apple-polishers. He burst into tears and gave the address of the math teacher with minute detail. The Daddy shaved, combed his few hairs, dressed elegantly, and went off "out of pity for his only son."

With his customary pomposity the Daddy entered the math teacher's home without being announced. You only see and hear things that you wouldn't if you were announced! He heard how the mathematics teacher said to his wife: "You're too expensive for me, Ariadna! . . . You don't know when to curb your caprices!" He saw how the teacher's wife threw herself around the teacher's neck and exclaimed: "Forgive me! I am worth little to you but I value you more than anything!" The Daddy saw that the teacher's wife was a good-looker, but if she weren't so well dressed, she would have been less attractive.

"Hello!" he called out, scraping his feet and casually approaching the pair. The teacher was confused for a minute and his wife gasped and slipped away like lightning into another room.

"Excuse me," began the Daddy with a smile. "It may be that I'm . . . that I'm disturbing you. . . . I understand this very well. . . . How do you do? May I have the honor to introduce myself. . . . I'm not exactly a stranger, as you can see. . . . I'm an old campaigner, too. . . . Ha-ha-ha! Don't be embarrassed!"

Exhibiting the least possible bit of courtesy, the teacher smiled and politely indicated a seat. The Daddy turned smartly on one leg and sat down.

"I," he continued, pointing to his gold watch, "came to speak with you. . . . Hm—and. . . . You, of course, must forgive me. . . . I admit I'm no expert about education. Putting it simply, you know what a tough road it is. . . . Ha-ha-ha! You're a university graduate?"

"Yes."

"That's so! . . . Well, yes. . . . It's warm today. . . . You, Ivan Fedorich, gave a grade to my sonny. Hm. . . . Yes. . . . But that's nothing, really. . . . What one deserves . . . give it to him— what one gets is also a lesson—a lesson. . . . He-he-he! . . . But you know, it's unpleasant. Does my son really understand mathematics that poorly?"

"What can I say? It's not that he isn't capable of knowing it; he just doesn't apply himself. Yes, he knows very little."

"Why does he know very little?"

The teacher's eyes opened wide.

"Why?" he asked. "He doesn't know anything because he doesn't apply himself."

"For pity's sake, Ivan Fedorich! My son applies himself

superbly! I work with him myself. . . . He burns the midnight oil. . . . He knows everything extremely well. . . . So, he's a clown. . . . But that's youth. . . . Who of us hasn't been young? I'm not disturbing you?"

"Have some pity on me, what do you want? . . . I'm even very grateful to you. . . . You fathers so rarely come to us pedagogues. . . . However, it does indicate how much confidence you have in us; that's the most important thing—this confidence."

"Goes without saying. . . . It's important—not to interfere. . . . Does that mean that my son will not be passed to the fourth class?"

"Yes. You know it's not just in mathematics he's deserved a two?"

"It's possible. I'll have to go to the others, too. Well, how about mathematics?. . . . H-h-h-he!. . . . You'll correct the grade?"

"I can't!" The teacher smiled. "I can't! . . . I wanted your son to pass, I tried with all my might, but your son would not apply himself and only spoke nonsense. . . . I had unpleasant encounters with him several times."

"He's y-young. . . . What can be done? At least change his grade to a three!"

"I can't!"

"Well, that's fiddlesticks! What are you telling me? As if I didn't know . . . what's possible and what's impossible. It's possible, Ivan Fedorich!"

"I can't! What would the other students getting a grade of two say? It would be unjust. No matter how hard it is for you to believe. Really and truly, I can't!"

The Daddy winked an eye.

"You can, Ivan Fedorich! Ivan Fedorich! Let's not waste time discussing it! It's not the kind of business that we have to spend hours chattering nonsense. . . . Tell me, in your opinion as a learned person, what you consider justice? We both know the nature of your justice. He-he-he! Let's use straight talk, Ivan Fedorich, without quibbling! You simply decided to give him a two. . . . What kind of justice is that?"

The teacher's eyes opened wider and . . . that's all; and why he wasn't insulted remains for me an eternal mystery, a secret held in the teacher's heart.

"Unintentional," continued the Daddy, "you expected guests.
. . . Ha-he-ha-he!. . . . So what? If you please! . . . I'm in agreement. . . . He's been given a grade—given a grade. . . . I understand how things operate, as you can see. . . . Things don't change
much . . . all the same, you know. . . . Hm, yes . . . old ways are
best, the most useful. . . . When you're rich you can be happy."

The Daddy took out his wallet and pressed a twenty-five
ruble note into the teacher's hand.

"Please!"

The teacher flushed, moved, and . . . that's all. Why he
didn't show the Daddy the door—The teacher's soul remains
an eternal secret to me . . .

"You," continued the Daddy, "don't be embarrassed. . . . I
really understand. . . . He who says he wouldn't be on the take—
takes. Everybody is on the take these days. It's impossible, my
good man, not to take. . . . You just aren't used to it yet? Please!"

"No, for God's sake . . ."

"Too little? Well, I can't offer more. . . . Won't you take it?"

"Have some sympathy for me! . . ."

"As you wish. . . . Well, do change the two!. . . . Not for
me, but for his mother. . . . You must know how tearful she is.
. . . Heart palpitation and other things. . . ."

"I have complete sympathy for your wife, but I can't!"

"If my son isn't passed to the fourth class, then. . . . what
will happen?. . . . M-m-yes. . . . No, you will pass him!"

"I would be happy to, but I can't. . . . Would you like a cigarette?"

Thanks very much . . . it won't interfere with the exchange. . . . What's your rank?"

"Titular.* . . . However, my official job is in the Eight Class.
Kgm! . . ."

"That's-sss. . . . Well, we can agree . . . with one stroke of
the pen, yes? It'll occur? He-he! . . ."

"I can't, even if you kill me, I can't!"

The Daddy hesitated briefly, but then once again pressured
the teacher. The attack continued for a very long time. The

---

*lowest rank in tsarist Russia

teacher repeated his immutable "I can't." Finally the Daddy besieged the teacher and became more unbearable. He started to thrust kisses upon him, begged that *he* be given a mathematics exam by the teacher, told some risque anecdotes, and became familiar. It sickened the teacher.

"Vanya, it's time for you to leave!" called the teacher's wife from the other room. That Daddy got the drift and barred the door with his broad body. The teacher lost his patience and began to whimper. In the end he had what he considered a brilliant solution.

"This is what," he said to the Daddy. "I'll give your son a passing grade if my colleagues also pass him in their subjects."

"Honestly?"

"Yes, I'll change his grade if they do."

"Done! Let's shake on it! You're not just a man, but— smart! I'll tell them that you've already changed his grade. Your wench will love you! A bottle of champagne on me! When can I have it sent to you?"

"Right now."

"So, it's understood that we're friends now? Will you pay us a friendly visit?"

"With pleasure. Be well!"

"Au revoir! He-he-he-hmi! . . . Ah, young man, young man! . . . Farewell! . . . Shall I give your regards to your colleagues? I'll do so. My most polite compliments to your wife. . . . Do visit us!"

The Daddy shuffled his feet, put on his hat, and vanished into thin air.

Nice guy, thought the teacher, his eyes following the retreating Daddy. Nice guy! He says what he thinks. He's straightforward and just as he appears. . . . I like such people!

That evening at home the Mommy sat on the Daddy's lap again (and after her sat the maid). The Daddy reassured her that "our son" would pass and that you don't prevail upon educated people as much with money as with pleasantries and taking them by the throat in a civilized manner.

1880

ANIMATE MERCHANDISE

I

Groholski embraced Liza, kissed all her little fingers with their bitten pink nails, and sat her down on the couch which was upholstered in cheap velvet. Liza crossed her legs, put her hands under her head, and lay still.

Groholski sat alongside on a stool and leaned toward her. He held her whole figure in the scope of his sight.

How lovely she appeared to him with the rays of the setting sun shining upon her!

The setting sun, golden with a slightly purple overcast, made the whole scene visible from the window.

The living room was brightly lit but not enough to allow a clear picture. The room and Liza, too, for a brief moment were gilded. . . .

Groholski was enamored. God knows, Liza was not a beauty. True, her small, feline face, with its hazel eyes and turned-up nose, fresh and piquant, her thin curly hair—black like soot—and her small, graceful body, ascetic and proper, was like the body of an electric eel, but, on the whole. . . . However,

113

I admit, she wasn't my type. Groholski, spoiled by women, and in and out of love a hundred times, saw her as a beauty. He loved her, and love is blind and always sees the object of its love as an ideal beauty.

"Listen," he began, looking directly into her eyes. "I came to talk about something with you, my sweet. Love can't tolerate uncertainty, indecision. . . . You know we have an ambiguous relationship. . . . I spoke to you yesterday, Liza. . . . Let's try today to answer the question raised yesterday. Well, let's decide. . . . What's to be done?"

Liza yawned, knit her brow, and removed her right hand from behind her head.

"What's to be done?" she repeated after Groholski in a barely audible tone of voice.

"Well, yes, what's to be done? Your wise little head must settle this. I love you and a person in love can't do anything right. He is primarily an egoist. I don't know how to deal with your husband. In my mind I could tear him to pieces when I think that he loves you too. And, to make another point, you love me. . . . A necessary condition for love is complete freedom. . . . Are you really free? Doesn't the thought that this man is eternally a thorn in your soul torment you? A man whom you don't love, and possibly, it wouldn't be unnatural, that you hate. . . . That's the second point. . . . The third . . . what's the third point? Oh, yes. . . . We're deceiving him, and that . . . is dishonorable. Honesty above all, Liza. Let's cast away lying!"

"Well, what's to be done?"

"You can guess. . . . I must, I'm obliged to, tell him about our ties and we must leave him and be free. These two things must be achieved as soon as possible. . . . For example, this evening you must tell him. . . . It's time to end it. . . . Aren't you sick of making love on the sly?"

"Tell him? Tell Vanya?"

"Of course!"

"That's impossible! I told you that yesterday, *Michel*, that's impossible!"

"Why?"

"He would be hurt, start shouting, do all different kinds of nasty things. . . . Really, don't you know what he's like? Lord preserve us! It's not necessary to tell him! What an idea!" Groholski brushed his hand across his brow and took a deep breath.

"Yes," he said. "More than anything else he will be hurt . . . I am depriving him of his happiness. Does he love you?"

"He loves me. Very much."

"That makes it even more difficult! It's hard to know where to begin. To keep it from him—it's vile. To tell him—is to kill him. . . . What the devil! But, what shall we do?"

Groholski pondered this. His pale face was gloomy.

"We can go on as we've been doing," said Liza. "If he wants to know, he can find out for himself."

"But really that's . . . that's sinful too and. . . . Ultimately you are mine and no one has a right to think that you belong to anyone other than me! You're mine! I won't step aside for any- one! I'm sorry for him, God sees how sorry I am, Liza! But . . . but what's to be done at last? Isn't it true that you don't love him? Why are you going to pine away with him? He must be told! We'll tell him and leave for my place. You are my wife, not his. Let him know. Somehow he'll get over it. . . . He's not the first to go through this, nor will he be the last. . . . Do you want to escape? Well? Speak quickly! Do you want to run away?"

Liza stood up and with pleading eyes looked at Groholski.

"To run away?"

"Well, yes. . . . To my estate . . . then to the Crimea. . . . We'll write him a letter. . . . We could leave tonight. There's a train at half-past one. Yes? Is it settled?"

Liza lazily scratched the bridge of her nose and thought it over.

"All right," she said and . . . began to cry.

Red spots rose on her cheeks, her eyes became swollen, and tears streamed down her little feline face. . . .

"What's the matter?" asked the alarmed Groholski. "Liza! What is it? Well? Why are you crying? You must see how it is! Well, what of it? Darling! Mommy!"

Liza stretched her arms out toward Groholski and hung on to his neck. You could hear her sobs.

"I'm sorry for him . . . ," mumbled Liza. "Oh, how sorry I am for him!"

"Who?"

"Va . . . Vanya. . . ."

"And I'm not sorry for him? But what's to be done? We are the cause of his suffering. . . . He will suffer, curse. . . . But are we guilty because we love each other?"

Having said this, Groholski jumped away from Liza as if stung, and sat down in the armchair. Liza flitted from his neck and quickly, without batting an eye, dropped onto the couch. They both reddened painfully, dropped their eyes, and coughed.

A tall, broad-shouldered young man about thirty years old, wearing an official's uniform, had entered the living room. His entrance had been unnoticed. Only the noise of the chair, which had been caught in the door, gave the lovers the knowledge that he was there and made them turn around. It was the husband.

They had turned around too late. The husband saw how Groholski had held Liza around the waist, and saw how Liza had hung on Groholski's white, aristocratic neck.

He saw! both Liza and Groholski thought at the same time, trying to conceal their guilty hands and disconcerted eyes. . . .

The ruddy face of the dumbfounded husband had paled. For three minutes there was a drawn-out torturous, strange, soul-searing silence. Oh, what three minutes! Groholski remembers them to this day.

The first one to move and break the silence was the husband. He began to walk toward Groholski with an inexplicable grimace on his face, resembling a smile, and offered him his hand. Groholski barely shook his soft, moist hand and flinched as if he had taken hold of a cold frog.

"Greetings," he mumbled.

"How do you do?" responded the husband. His hoarse voice was barely audible. He sat down opposite Groholski and then straightened the back of his collar. . . .

An anguished silence arose once again . . . but this silence had more meaning. . . . The first paroxysms, the most difficult and nondescript had passed.

The only thing that remained now was for one of the two to retreat and look for matches, or some other kind of triviality. They both had a powerful urge to leave. They sat staring at each other, pulling on their beards, seeking in their agitated brains a way out of this mortifying position. They were both perspiring. Their suffering was intolerable, and both were devoured by hate. Both wanted to lay their hands on each other, but . . . how to do it, and who was to be the first? If only *she* would leave!

"I saw you yesterday at a party," mumbled Bugrov (that was the husband's name).

"I was there . . . was. . . . Did you dance?"

"Hm . . . yes. With that . . . with the younger Lyukotska . . . dancing was difficult. . . . She can't dance. She's a master chatterer. (Pause) She chatters incessantly."

"Yes . . . it was boring. I saw you too. . . ."

Groholski inadvertently glanced at Bugrov. . . . His eyes met with the wandering glance of the deceived husband, and he could not bear it. He stood up quickly, shook Bugrov's hand, excused himself to her, grabbed his hat; his back cringing, he went to the door. It seemed to him that a thousand eyes were on his back. He felt just as an actor feels when he's hissed off the stage, backing into the curtain, or as a fop feels who has been slapped and led away by the police. . . .

As soon as Groholski's steps could no longer be heard, and the door to the entrance was shut, Bugrov jumped up and after circling the room several times, walked over to his wife. The feline little face scrunched up and blinked its eyes, as if it expected to be slapped. His face pale and distorted, her husband came up to her, stepped on her gown, knocked her knees with his knees, and shook her head and shoulders.

"If you're such trash," he said with a dull, weeping voice, "if you let him in here again only once, I'll fix you. . . . He shouldn't dare take one step in here! I'll kill him! Do you understand? A-a-a—You worthless trash! You're trembling! Loath . . . some!" Bugrov took hold of her elbows, shook her, and flung her like a rubber ball toward the window.

"Trash! Whore! You have no shame!"

She ran to the window, barely touching the floor with her
feet, and grabbed hold of the drapes.

"Silence!" screamed her husband, going up to her, his eyes
flashing, his feet stamping.

She kept quiet. She stared at the ceiling and sobbed, and
had on her face the expression of a naughty little girl who was
about to be punished.

"So that's what you're like? Yes? With a womanizer? Nice
going! And before the altar? Who was it? Swore to be a good
wife and mother! Shut up!" And he struck her attractive delicate back.

"Shut up! Trash! Or I'll give it to you even worse! If that
scoundrel dares show up here once more, if I catch you only
once again. . . . Pay attention!! If I see you with that lout, I'll.
. . . Don't ask for mercy! Even if I have to be sent to Siberia, I'll
kill you! And him! Nothing will stop me! Leave! I can't bear
the sight of you!"

Bugrov wiped his eyes and his brow with his sleeve and
stomped around the room. Liza, sobbing louder and louder, her
shoulders twitching, and with her turned-up nose, looked like
a piece of lace on the curtains.

"You're a harlot!" screamed the husband. "Your head is full
of crazy nonsense! So he comes here all the time! I, brother,
and you, Lizaveta, that . . . that's not the point! I don't want a
seducer in my house! I won't have it! If you want to conduct
yourself in this way. . . . It stinks! There's no place for you in my
home! March, if . . . you're a loose woman, debauched . . .

"Drive out such dandies from your head! It's all folly! Don't
let it happen again! We can still talk about it! Love your husband! You were given to your husband to love only your husband! That's it! Isn't one enough for you? Leave while. . . .
T . . . tormentors!"

Bugrov remained silent for a moment and then shrieked:

"Leave, I say! Go to the nursery! What are you howling for?
You're guilty and you're howling! So that's the way it is! Last
year you hung around with Peter Tochkov, and now with that,
Lord forgive you, you've hung onto a devil. . . . Phew! It's time
one learned what you're really like! A wife! A mother! The

amusement disappeared last year, but now the diversion has
gone too far. . . . Phew!"

Bugrov grunted loudly and the air became filled with the
scent of sherry. He had just returned from dining out and was
slightly tipsy. . . .

"Aren't you aware of your responsibilities? No! . . . You'll
have to be taught! You're still wet behind the ears! You're a
trollop like your mother. . . . Howl! That's right! Howl!"

Bugrov went to his wife and pulled the drapes out of her hands.

"Don't stand by the window. . . . People will see how you're
howling. . . . Don't let this happen again. You'll go from
embraces to poverty. . . . You'll put your foot in your mouth. Do
you think I'd find it pleasant to have horns growing out of my
head? That's what will happen if you carry on with these bums.
. . . Well, enough. . . . You do this another time . . . it won't be
like this. . . . I really, Liza. . . . Give it up . . ."

Bugrov stopped to take a breath and the vapors of sherry
covered Liza.

"You're young, stupid, don't know the score. . . . I'm often
not at home. . . . Well, they take advantage of this. You have to
be smart, discriminating! They seduce you. Anyhow, I won't
tolerate it any longer. . . . I've had it. . . . Absolutely! If you'd be
dying, I wouldn't repent. For being deceived I . . . I, little
mother, am ready to do everything. I can beat you mercilessly
and . . . drive you away. I could send you to your lout." Bugrov
then wiped the wet, tearstained face of the unfaithful Liza with
his huge meaty palm (*horribile dictu**). He treated his twenty-
year-old wife like a small child!

"Well, enough of this. . . . I forgive you, but don't let it happen again. God forbid! I've forgiven five times but not the sixth.
It's like God's word. For such things even God won't forgive."

Bugrov leaned over and stretched his shining lips toward
Liza's little head.

But he didn't succeed in kissing it. . . .

In the foyer, the dining room, the hallway, and the drawing
room the doors slammed, and into the drawing room, like a

*horrible to relate

whirlwind, ran Groholski. He was pale and unsteady. He waved and crushed his expensive cap. His frock coat dangled behind him as if it were on a hanger. He personified someone who was dangerously feverish. Upon seeing him, Bugrov left his wife and began to look out the other window. Groholski ran up to him and, moving his hands as if all was hopeless, breathing heavily, and not looking at anyone, spoke in a tremulous voice:

"Ivan Petrovich! Let's stop performing this comedy before each other. Enough of this attempt at deceiving each other! Enough! I've had it! You do what you want to, but I've had it. It's finally become low and repulsive! It's disgusting! Understand me, it's disgusting!"

Groholski gulped and took a deep breath.

"It's not according to my principles. And you're an honorable man. I love her! I love her more than anything on earth! You have seen us and . . . I'm obliged to tell you!"

What shall I say to him? thought Ivan Petrovich.

"This must end! This farce can't go on! It must be settled somehow." Groholski took a deep breath and continued:

"I can't live without her. She feels the same way. You're an educated man and you can understand that under such conditions your family life cannot continue. This woman is no longer yours. So, but. . . . In a word, I beg you to look at this situation from an indulgent, humane point of view. Ivan Petrovich! Accept at least that I love her, love her more than myself, more than anything in the world, and to resist this love would take greater strength than I have."

"And she?" Bugrov asked in a gloomy, somewhat mocking voice.

"Ask her! Well now, ask her! To live with someone you don't love, to live with you while loving someone else, really that . . . that . . . means to suffer!"

"And she?" repeated Bugrov, but no longer in a mocking voice.

"She . . . she loves me! We love each other. . . . Ivan Petrovich! Kill us, despise us, persecute us, do whatever you wish . . . but we are no longer able to hide our love from you! We're both here! Judge us as severely as a man must whom we. . . . Fate has denied you happiness!"

Bugrov got red as a boiled crab and gave Liza a glance. His eyes blinked. His fingers, lips, and eyelids trembled. Poor man! Liza's teary eyes told him that Groholski was right and that this was serious business. . . .

"Well, what of it?" muttered Bugrov. "If you. . . . In these times, it's the same all over. . . ."

"God sees," Groholski wheezed in a high tenor voice, "that we know how you feel! Do you think we're unaware of your position, that we're insensitive? I know the suffering I've inflicted upon you. God sees everything! But try to be indulgent! I beg you! We aren't guilty of sin! Love is not a sin. It isn't subject to a free will. . . . Give her to me, Ivan Petrovich! Release her to me! Take what you want from me for causing you pain, take my livelihood, but give me Liza! I'm prepared for everything. . . . So, tell me, what can I do, at least in part, in exchange for her? In reciprocity for imposing this misfortune upon you I can give you another kind of good fortune! I can, Ivan Petrovich! I will agree to anything! It would be vile on my part to leave without giving you some satisfaction. . . . I understand your feelings at this moment."

Bugrov waved his hand as if he were saying "Leave for God's sake!" His eyes had begun to become clouded with what looked like treacherous moisture. . . . It could be seen shortly what a crybaby he was.

"I know how you feel, Ivan Petrovich! I will give you other good fortune, such as you haven't experienced. What do you want? I'm a rich man, I'm the son of an influential man. . . . You want something? Well, what do you want?"

Bugrov's heart began to beat rapidly. . . . He held onto the window's drapes with both hands.

"Do you want . . . fifty thousand? Ivan Petrovich, I beg you. . . . It's not a bribe, not a purchase. . . . I only want to smooth over a little bit, in my way, the sacrifice which your incalculable loss entails. . . . Do you want a hundred thousand? I'm ready to give you that! Do you want a hundred thousand?"

My God! Two enormous hammers beat upon the perspiring temples of the unfortunate Ivan Petrovich. . . . The resonant bells of a Russian troika rang in his ears. . . .

"Accept from me this sacrifice!" continued Groholski. "I beg you! You will lift a weight from my conscience. I'm asking you for a favor!"

My God! The window through which Bugrov's moist eyes stared was sprinkled by a May shower, and a smart four-seat carriage rolled by on the road. The horses were dashing, fierce, glossy, and smart. Sitting on the carriage were people with contented faces, wearing straw hats and holding long fishing rods and fishnets. A high school boy in a white peaked hat held onto a hunting rifle. They were on their way to a summer cottage and to fish, hunt, and drink their tea outside in the fresh air. They were going to those heavenly places where he had once upon a time run barefoot over the fields, forests, and shores. He was then a sunburned little Bugrov, only the son of a village deacon, but a thousand times happier than now. How hellish was this cuckolded May! How fortunate were those who could take off their heavy uniforms, sit in a carriage, and cross the fields where the quails squawked and the air was filed with the fragrance of fresh hay.

Bugrov's heart skipped a beat from a pleasant, cooling sensation. . . . A hundred thousand! Together with the carriage all his old dreams appeared which he had entertained while conducting his dull life as a bureaucrat sitting in his provincial office, or in his own puny study. . . . The deep river with its fish; an expansive garden with its narrow paths, spouting springs, its shadows, flowers, bowers; a luxurious cottage with terraces and towers, with an aeolian harp and silver bells. . . . (He knew about aeolian harps from German novels.) The blue sky was cloud-free and the fragrant, clean, transparent air reminded him of his barefoot, hungry, and oppressed childhood . . . when he had to get up at five in the morning and to lie down at nine in the evening! A life where one fished during the day, hunted, carried on conversations with the peasants. . . . Wonderful!

"Ivan Petrovich! Don't torture me! Do you want the hundred thousand?"

"Hm. . . . A hundred and fifty thousand!" barked Bugrov in an undertone, sounding like a hoarse bull. . . . He barked and bent over, as if ashamed of his words and awaited an answer. . . .

"It's settled," said Groholski. "We're agreed! I'm grateful to you, Ivan Petrovich. . . . I will proceed immediately. . . . I won't keep you waiting. . . ."

Groholski jumped up, put on his hat, and walking backward, hurried out of the drawing room.

Bugrov held onto the drapes more tightly. . . . He was ashamed. . . . But the attractive glittering hopes had buried themselves between his throbbing temples and made his soul base and dull. He was rich!

Liza understood nothing and feared that he would leave the window and hurl her aside. Her whole body shaking, she slipped through the half-open door. She went into the nursery, lay down, and curled up on the nanny's bed. Her body shook feverishly.

Bugrov remained alone. The room began to suffocate him. He opened the window. What a pleasant breeze fanned his face and neck! One could breathe wonderfully in such air and could relax on the pillows in the carriages. . . . There, far from the city, surrounded by trees and cottages, the air would be even fresher. . . . Bugrov even began to smile, dreaming about the air that would envelop him when he would go out on the terrace of his cottage to enjoy the scene. . . . He dreamt for a long time. . . . The sun set and he was still standing and dreaming, using all his power of mind to cast out any thought of Liza which had persisted to pursue him in his dreaming.

"I've brought it, Ivan Petrovich!" Groholski whispered in his ear, having returned to the room. "I've brought it. . . . You've got it. . . . In this packet here is forty thousand rubles. With this document here you can receive twenty thousand on the day after tomorrow at Valentinov. . . . And here's a promissory note . . . a check . . . for the rest in a few days. . . . My steward will deliver it to you."

Groholski, all worked up, flushed, and with his arms and legs in constant motion, placed before Bugrov the pile of documents and the packet. It was a big pile of many colors and variety. Bugrov in all his life had never seen such an accumulation! He spread out his fat fingers and without looking at Groholski began to pick up the packet and the documents. . . .

After putting down his money, Groholski began to tramp around the room looking for his bought and sold Dulcinea.*

Bugrov filled his pockets and his wallet and hid the other documents in the desk. He then drank half a carafe of water and darted out into the street.

"Cabby!" he cried out in an agitated voice.

He arrived at the entrance to the Hotel Paris at 12:30 at night. He entered noisily and went up the stairs and knocked at Groholski's door. A servant admitted him. Groholski was packing his things into a suitcase. Liza sat nearby at a table, trying on some bracelets. They both were frightened by Bugrov's entrance. It appeared to them that Bugrov had come for Liza and was returning the money which had not been taken from conviction, but in the heat of the moment. But Bugrov had not come for Liza. Ashamed of his new jacket and feeling terribly awkward in it, he bowed and remained in the doorway as if he were a lackey . . . the new jacket was ravishing. Bugrov was unrecognizable in it. His whole outfit was spic-and-span, brand new, from French knit, in the latest style, and closely fitted his huge figure. Up to this time the only thing he had worn had been an ordinary uniform. And he had on half-boots with brilliant buckles. He stood, ashamed of his new jacket, and covered with his right hand the ornaments for which he had paid three hundred rubles an hour ago.

"I came about another thing . . . ," he began. "There's more to discuss than money. I won't give up Mishytka. . . ."

"Who's Mishytka?" asked Groholski.

"My son."

Groholski and Liza exchanged glances. Liza's eyes grew wide, her cheeks reddened, and her lips began to throb. . . .

"All right," she said. . . .

She thought of Mishytka's warm little bed. It would be cruel to exchange this warm little bed for a cold hotel couch, and she was in agreement with Bugrov.

"I will come to see him," she said.

Bugrov bowed, left, and victoriously ran down the stairway, and with his expensive new cane slashed the air.

---

*idealized sweetheart

"Home!" he ordered the coachman. "I want to leave at five o'clock tomorrow morning. . . . Come for me at that time. If I'm asleep, wake me up. I want to leave town. . . ."

II

It was a fantastic autumn evening. The sun, which was fringed by a golden background and slightly covered by purple, stood above the western horizon ready to descend to distant burial grounds. Shadows and half-shadows had already vanished from gardens and the air had become damp, but the tops of the trees were still playfully gilded. . . . It was warm. Rain had fallen a little while ago and had freshened air which was already fresh, transparent and aromatic without this.

I'm not describing the capital's August, which is cloudy, tearful and dark, and has unbearably damp dawns. Lord preserve me from those! I am not describing the northern cruel August. I ask the reader to relocate in the Crimea on one of its shores close to Fodociya, at that particular place where the cottage of one of my heroes stands. It's a nice clean cottage surrounded by flowers and pruned bushes. Behind it, about a hundred feet away, there is a fruit orchard which is turning blue in which the cottage residents stroll. . . . Groholski pays a big price for this cottage: a thousand rubles a year, it seems . . . the cottage isn't worth this, but it is nice. . . . It is tall, graceful, with exceptionally good walls and very graceful railings; it is delicate, charming, painted light blue, with awnings all around, portieres and drapes. It reminded me of a good-looking, gentle bread-and-butter miss.*

On the evening being described, Groholski and Liza were sitting on the terrace of this cottage. Groholski was reading the *New Times* and was drinking milk from a green mug. On the table before him was a siphon bottle with seltzer water. Liza was sitting on a soft armchair that was far away from the table. With her elbows leaning on the railing and supporting her little face on her fists, she was looking at the cottage *vis-à-*

---

*school girl

vis. * . . . The sun was flickering across the windows of this cottage. The rays from the hot panes blinded her. . . . The front yard and the few trees around the cottage faced the endless blue sea with its billows and white sails. . . . How lovely it was! Groholski was reading a satire written by Neznakomets† and after every ten lines or so would cast his blue eyes upon Liza's back. . . . The former passionate, overwhelming love still shone in these eyes. . . . He was infinitely happy, despite his fancied catarrh of the lungs. . . . Liza felt his eyes on her back and thought of the brilliant future of Mishytka; and she was very much at peace and her spirit was revived. . . .

It wasn't the sea that held her attention or the blinding caused by the sun's rays on the windows of the cottage *vis-à-vis*, but the string of wagons that were coming up to the cottage one after another.

The wagons were loaded with furniture and a variety of household utensils. Liza saw how the wicker gates and the large glass doors were opened, and the seemingly endless squabbles the carter had about the furniture. They carried the larger armchairs and the couch, that were covered in dark red velvet, through the opened doorway, then the tables for the hallway, the drawing room and the dining room, and a large double bed and a child's bed. . . . They also carried in something huge, carefully tied up in quilted matting and very heavy. . . .

It's a piano, thought Liza and her heart skipped a beat.

She loved to listen to piano playing and had not heard any for a long time. They didn't have a single musical instrument at the cottage. Groholski and she were only music lovers and played no instruments.

After the piano they carried in many boxes and packages on which was written "Handle With Care." They were boxes with mirrors and china.

A splendid luxurious carriage came through the gates and two white horses resembling swans were led in.

My God! What wealth! thought Liza, and was reminded of

---

*directly opposite
†"Stranger"

the aging pony bought for her by Groholski for only one hundred rubles, because he didn't care for riding horses. Her pony compared with these swanlike horses seemed like a bedbug to her. Groholski was afraid of galloping and purposely bought Liza a poor horse that could not gallop.

What wealth! Liza thought and whispered, looking at the noisy coachman.

The sun was hiding behind the mounds, the air had lost its clarity and dryness, but the unloading of furniture continued. Finally, it became too dark to do this, and Groholski had to stop reading the newspaper, but Liza looked and looked.

"Shall we have the lamp lit?" asked Groholski, who was afraid that a fly might fall into his milk and would be swallowed by him in the dark. "Liza! Shall we have the lamp lit? Or shall we sit in the dark, my angel?"

Liza did not answer. She was engrossed with the chariot which had been driven up to the gates of the cottage vis-à-vis theirs. What a fine little horse pulled this chariot! It was not large but of an average size and graceful. . . . In the chariot sat a gentleman wearing a top hat. On his knees sat a three-year-old child dangling his little hands. The child appeared to be a boy. . . . He was dangling his little hands and shrieking with delight. . . .

Liza suddenly let out a cry, got up, and leaned forward with her whole body.

"What's the matter?" asked Groholski.

"Nothing. . . . I was. . . . It seemed to me. . . ."

A tall broad-shouldered man wearing a top hat hopped out of the chariot, took the little boy by the hand, and gaily hurried toward the glass doorway. The doors were opened with fanfare and they disappeared into the unlit cottage rooms.

Two toadies stepped up to the little coach and courteously led it through the gates. The lights were soon lit in the cottage vis-à-vis and the clatter of dishes, knives, and forks could be heard. The gentleman in the high hat had sat down to dine and judging from the prolonged tinkling sound of dinnerware, he ate leisurely. To Liza it smelled like cabbage soup and chicken and roast duck. After dinner the sound of erratic piano playing filled the air. It was evident that the gentleman in the high hat was entertaining the child and was allowing him to bang on the keys.

Groholski came up to Liza and put his arm around her waist.

"What magnificent weather!" he exclaimed. "What marvelous air! Do you feel it? I, Liza, am very happy . . . very, very happy. My happiness is so great that I'm even afraid it might be destroyed. But to be destroyed, usually requires important reasons. . . . But you know what, Liza? Despite how happy I am, I'm not absolutely . . . content. . . . I'm tortured by a single persistent thought. . . . Tortured terribly. . . . It doesn't give me any peace, day or night. . . ."

"What kind of thought?"

"What kind of thought? Terrible, dear heart. I'm tortured by the thought . . . of your husband. I've kept quiet up to this time, not wanting to worry. But I can't keep quiet any longer. . . . Where is he? What has become of him? Where has he gone with his money? It's terrible! His face is before me every night, haggard, suffering, pleading. . . . So, judge, my angel! We have really deprived him of his happiness! We've destroyed, shattered it! We have based our happiness on the ruination of his happiness. . . . Can the money which he, from the goodness of his heart accepted, make up for his loss of you? Did he love you very much?"

"Very much!"

"Well, you see! Either he's become a drunkard, or . . . I fear for him! Ah, how I fear for him! Wouldn't it be a good idea to write to him? He needs to be consoled. . . . Write him a kind word, really. . . ."

Groholski sighed deeply, shook his head, and, exhausted from the intensity of his single-mindedness, dropped into an armchair. Supporting his head on his fists, he began to think. Judging from his face, his soul was tormented. . . .

"I'm going to bed," said Liza. "It's time. . . ."

Liza went to her room, undressed, and tremulously got under the covers. She regularly went to bed at ten o'clock and got up at ten o'clock. She did not like to live like a sybarite.

Morpheus soon embraced her. She began dreaming and

continued to dream all night long. Her dreams were bewitching. . . . She dreamed of love affairs, stories she knew, Arabian tales. . . . The hero of these dreams was . . . the gentleman in the high hat who just that evening had caused her to exclaim in surprise.

The gentleman in the top hat seized her from Groholski, roared, beat both her and Groholski, brought the little boy under her window, told her he loved her, and took her for a drive in the chariot. . . . Oh, what dreams! In one night, with eyes closed and lying on one's back, it is possible to live a dozen happy years. . . . Liza in this night lived through a great deal and very happily, in spite of and even during, the beating. . . .

Awakening at eight o'clock, she hastily threw on her clothes, quickly combed her hair, and putting on her pointed Tatar shoes, she rushed headlong onto the terrace. Covering her eyes with one hand, and holding up her entangled gown with the other, she stared at the cottage *vis-à-vis*. . . . Her face began to glow.

She doubted no longer. It was he.

Beneath the terrace of the cottage *vis-à-vis*, in front of the glass doors, stood a table. On the table was a silver samovar at the head and a china service that sparkled and shimmered. At the table sat Ivan Petrovich. He held a silver saucer in his hand and drank tea. He drank greedily. This last could be noted because the swilling was so loud it could be heard by Liza. He wore a brown dressing gown with black flowers on it. Its enormous tassels fell to the floor. Liza had never seen her husband in a dressing gown, and especially in such an expensive one. . . . Mishytka sat on his knee and disturbed his tea drinking. He wiggled around and tried to take hold of his daddy's sleek lip. After swallowing several times, the daddy would lean over and kiss the top of his head. A gray cat was rubbing itself on one of the legs of the table, and raising its tail while mewing to be fed.

Liza hid behind the portiere and took in with her eyes her former family. Her delight in the scenes lit her face. . . .

"Mishel!" she whispered. "Misha! You're here, Misha! Darling! And how he loves Vanya! Lord!"

And Liza shook with laughter when Mishytka stirred his father's tea.

"And how Vanya loves Mishelya! My sweethearts!"

Ecstasy turned Liza's head and made her heart beat faster. She dropped into an armchair and began to cogitate her observations.

"How did they get to come here?!" she asked herself while blowing a kiss to Mishytka. "Who thought up the idea to bring them here? Lord! And does all this wealth really belong to him? Do those swanlike horses which were brought through the gates really belong to Ivan Petrovich? Oh!"

After drinking his tea, Ivan Petrovich went inside. Ten minutes later he came out on the porch and . . . startled Liza. He, as a young man only seven years ago had stopped being called Vanka and Vanyushka, had been ready to have his jaw displaced for twenty kopecks and to turn the house upside down. He was dressed in such incredible finery. He had on a wide-brimmed straw hat, astonishing splendid Wellington boots, and a pique vest. . . . A thousand large and small suns shone from his jewelry. He held his gloves and riding whip smartly in his right hand. . . .

There was some arrogance and pride in the bearing of his ponderous figure when he, with a graceful extension of his hand, ordered the lackey to get his horse.

He climbed importantly into the chariot and ordered that Mishytka and the fishing rods which had been leaning on the chariot be handed to him. Seating Mishytka beside him and placing his left arm around him, he took hold of the reins and they trotted off.

"Go-o-o-o!" shouted Mishytka.

Liza, not even conscious that she was doing it, waved her handkerchief sending them off. If she had looked into a mirror, she would have seen a flushed little face, laughing and crying at the same time. She was saddened because she was not sitting beside the exultant Mishytka, and that it was impossible *for some reason* to cover him with kisses.

For some reason! . . . The deuce take it all, you tender conscience!

"Grisha! Grisha!" Liza rushed into Groholski's bedroom and began awakening him. "Get up! They're here! Darling!"

"Who has arrived?" asked the half-asleep Groholski.

"Our family . . . Vanya and Misha. . . . They're here! In the cottage *vis-à-vis*. . . . I looked over there, and there they were. . . . They had tea. . . . And Misha too. . . . What an angel our Misha has become. If only you could have seen him! He's a mother's dream child!"

"Who? What are you saying? . . . Who has arrived? Where?"

"Vanya and Misha. . . . I was looking at the cottage *vis-à-vis* and there they are drinking tea. Misha knows how to drink his own tea already. . . . You saw what was delivered yesterday? They are the ones who arrived!"

Groholski frowned, wiped his brow, and blanched.

"He arrived? Your husband?" he asked.

"Yes. . . ."

"What for?"

"He's going to live here no doubt. They don't know we're here! If they knew they would have looked at our cottage. They were having tea and . . . paid no attention at all to our cottage. . . ."

"Where is he now? Good heavens, say something sensible! Well, where is he?"

"He went fishing with Misha . . . in the chariot. Did you see the horses yesterday? They were their horses . . . Vanya's. . . . Vanya rides on them. Do you know that, Grisha? We'll invite Misha over here. . . . We can invite him, can't we? He's such an attractive little boy! So marvelous!"

Groholski became lost in thought but Liza kept talking, talking. . . .

"It's an unexpected encounter," said Groholski after a long and, as usual, torturous reflection. "Well, who could have expected that we would meet here? So . . . that's how it is. . . . That's it. Fate found it convenient. I can imagine how awkward it will be for him when we meet!"

"Will we invite Misha?"

"We'll invite Misha. . . . It'll be awkward to have his father here. . . . Well, what will I say to him? What can we talk about? It will be awkward for both of us. . . . We don't have to meet. We will converse, if it's necessary, through our servants. . . . I

have, little Liza, a terrible headache. . . . My hands and feet
hurt. . . . I'm cracking up. Is my head hot?"

Liza felt his forehead with the palm of her hand and found
it hot.

"I had terrible dreams all night. . . . I'm going to stay in bed
today. . . . I'll have to take some quinine. Have my tea brought
here, little mother. . . ."

Groholski took the quinine and stayed in bed all day. He
drank hot water, groaned, changed his linen, complained, and
created a most trying atmosphere for all those around him. He
was unbearable when he imagined he had a cold. This situation
made it necessary for Liza to interrupt her curious observations
and leave the terrace for his room. At dinnertime she had to
apply a mustard plaster on him. All this would have been very
boring for my heroine, dear reader, if it weren't for the favors
provided by the cottage vis-à-vis. Liza spent most of the day
looking at this cottage and being transported with delight.

At ten o'clock Ivan Petrovich and Mishytka returned from
fishing and had breakfast. At two o'clock they had dinner and at
four o'clock went somewhere in the carriage. The white horses
shot out like lightning and carried them speedily away. At seven
o'clock mainly male guests arrived. On the terrace two tables of
cards were played until midnight. One of the men was a magnificent pianist. The guests played, drank, ate, and laughed. Ivan
Petrovich roared with laughter while telling an anecdote from his
Armenian experience. He spoke completely uninhibited in his
own inimitable way, so he could be heard all over. How jovial it
was! And Mishytka, too, stayed up till midnight with them.

Misha is full of fun and he doesn't cry, thought Liza. It
means he doesn't remember his mother. He's forgotten me!

And Liza became sick at heart. She cried all night long.
Her conscience began to goad her a little, and she was vexed
and depressed, and had a powerful desire to talk with Mishytka
and kiss him. . . . In the morning she got out of bed with a
headache and tear-swollen eyes. Groholski attributed these
tears on his behalf.

"Don't cry, darling!" he said to her. "I'm better today. . . .
My chest aches a little now and then but it's nothing."

When they drank tea, at the cottage *vis-à-vis* they break-fasted. Ivan Petrovich looked at his plate and saw nothing but a piece of goose which dripped with fat.

"I'm very pleased," whispered Groholski, glancing askance at Bugrov. "I'm very happy that he lives so well! His comfort-able circumstances have curtailed my concern. It's severed, Liza! Seeing him. . . . I don't have to talk with him now. . . . God be with him! Why disturb his peace?"

As if to offset Groholski's tranquility, dinner was not so untroubled. Namely, during dinner occurred the "awkward sit-uation" that Groholski greatly feared. When Groholski's favorite dish, partridges, was brought to the table, Liza suddenly became disconcerted and Groholski took to wiping his face with his napkin. On the terrace of the cottage *vis-à-vis* they saw Bugrov. He was standing, his hands holding onto the railing, and, with wide open eyes, was staring directly at them.

"Leave, Liza. . . . Leave . . . ," whispered Groholski. "He wants to have dinner with us! What guts, you . . ."

Bugrov continued to stare and then shouted. Groholski saw before him a very surprised face. . . .

"Is it really you?" called out Ivan Petrovich. "You?! You're here too? Greetings!"

Groholski moved his fingers from one shoulder to the other. It is said that when it is impossible to scream, the chest becomes weak. Liza's heart palpitated and her eyes became dim. . . . Bugrov rushed from his terrace, crossed the road, and within several seconds stood by the terrace where Groholski and Liza were dining. The partridges were wasted!

"Greetings," he stated, blushing and putting his huge hands in his pockets. "You're here? You're really here?"

"Yes, we too are here."

"How did you come to be here?"

"And how did you come to be here?"

"I? It's a long story! Don't let me disturb you, eat your dinner! I lived, as you know, up to this time . . . in the Orlovski province. . . . I rented an estate. A magnificent manor! Go on eating! I lived there to the end of May, but, gave it up now. . . . It's cold there, so a doctor in the Crimea recommended leaving. . . ."

"You have some kind of ailment?" asked Groholski.

"Well, yes. . . . It seems as if everything here . . . something is seething. . . ." And Ivan Petrovich, when he said "here," moved his hand from his neck to the middle of his stomach.

"So you are here too. . . . That's . . . that's . . . that's very nice. Have you been here long?"

"Since June."

"Well, and you, Liza, how are you? Are you well?"

"I'm fine," answered a disturbed Liza.

"Have you pined for Mishytka? Yes? He's here with me. . . . I'll send him right over with Nikofor. This is just great! Well, goodbye! I need to leave. . . . I became acquainted with Prince Ter-Gaimazov. He's a man with a soul even though he's an Armenian! There's a game of croquet going on at his place today. . . . I'm going to play. . . . Goodbye! The horses have been brought out. . . ."

Ivan Petrovich made a sharp turn, shook his head, and waving "adieu" hurried to his cottage.

"Unfortunate man!" said Groholski, following him with his eyes and sighing deeply.

"Why is he unfortunate?" asked Liza.

"To see you and not to have the right to call you his own!"

"Fool!" Liza dared to think. "Wimp!"

In the late afternoon Liza was hugging and kissing Mishytka whom Nikofor had brought over to the Groholski cottage. Mishytka cried at first but when he was given a cherry tart, he became friendly and smiled.

Groholski and Liza did not see Bugrov for three days. He was off somewhere and only spent the nights at home. On the fourth day he showed up at their cottage at dinnertime. . . . He extended both his hands and sat down at the table. . . . His face had a serious look.

"I'm here on business," he said. "Read this!" And he handed Groholski a letter.

"Read this! Read it out loud!"

Groholski read aloud the following:

"My kind and comforting, never-to-be-forgotten son, Ivan! I received your kind and courteous letter in which you invited your very old father to the Crimea with its excellent, mild weather to breathe the healthy air and to visit a land I've never seen. I'm replying to this letter of yours that as soon as I'm retired I will be with you, but not for long. My colleague, Father Gerasim, is an ailing, feeble man and cannot be left by himself for an extended time. I am deeply touched that you have not forgotten your parents, your father and mother. . . . With your generosity you rejuvenate your father and with your prayers you remember your mother; for that is the proper way. Meet me in Feodiciya. What kind of town is Feodiciya? It will be very nice to see. Your godmother who held you at the christening font is named Feodisiya. You write that God considered you worthy of winning two hundred thousand rubles. That seems seductive to me. But if the circumstances should occur that you will achieve a high-level rank, you will not stop working. Even the rich man finds it fitting to work. I give you my blessing always, today and forever. Andropov Ilya and Sergey send their regards. You could send them a ten-ruble note. They need it!

"Your loving father, Peter Bugrov, Priest."

Groholski read this letter aloud and together with Liza looked questioningly at Bugrov.

"You can see what the problem is . . . ," began Bugrov ingratiatingly. "I am begging you, Liza, that while he is here you don't show yourself to him and remain hidden. I wrote him that you were ill and have gone to be cured in the Caucasus. If you two should meet, then . . . you yourself know . . . it would be awkward. . . . Hm . . ."

"All right," said Liza.

It's possible, thought Groholski. If he is making a sacrifice, why shouldn't we?

"Please, if he should see you, it would be tragic. . . . He requires rigid moral behavior. He would damn at every opportunity. You, Liza, don't leave your apartment and that's all. . . . He won't stay long. Don't be upset. . . ."

Father Peter soon arrived. On one beautiful morning Ivan Petrovich came over and in a secretive tone sputtered:

"He's arrived! He's sleeping now! So, please, stay put!"

Liza settled herself within four walls. She didn't allow herself to go outside or on the terrace. She could only see the sky

from behind the windows' drapes. . . . To her grief, Ivan Petrovich's daddy was always out under the open sky and even slept
on the terrace. Father Peter was a small priest who usually wore
a brown cassock and a tall headpiece with a turned-up brim. He
slowly strolled around the cottages and looked with curiosity
through his antiquated glasses at what he called "unknown
lands." Ivan Petrovich accompanied him wearing the Stanislavski medal in his buttonhole. Ordinarily he didn't wear this
medal but he liked to kowtow before his father. When in the
presence of his father, he always put on the medal.

Liza was dying from boredom. Groholski suffered, too. He had
to take walks alone without his mate. He was on the verge of tears,
but . . . one had to submit to fate's dictates. In addition, Bugrov
would hurry over every morning and in a hoarse voice present
them a bulletin, of which they had no need, of the daily health of
the little Father Peter. He bored them with these bulletins.

"He slept extremely well last night!" he would inform
them. "Yesterday he was incensed that there were no pickles.
. . . He loves Mishytka. He's always stroking his head. . . ."

Finally after about two weeks, Father Peter walked about the
cottages for the last time, and to the great delight of Groholski
left, exceedingly satisfied with his visit. . . . Groholski and Liza
resumed their former way of life. Groholski again blessed his
good fortune. . . . But this happiness did not last. . . . Another
misfortune revealed itself, worse than that of Father Peter.

Ivan Petrovich began to drop in on them every day. Ivan
Petrovich, speaking candidly, was a fine fellow but crude. He
would arrive at dinnertime, dine with them, and stay late. This
might have been tolerated, but they had to buy vodka for him
to drink with his dinner, and Groholski could not tolerate this.
Bugrov would have about five drinks and talk incessantly
throughout the dinner. Even this wasn't that important. . . . He
would stay until two in the morning and not let them go to bed.
. . . And even more important, he permitted himself to talk
about things it would be better not to mention. . . . When two
o'clock was approaching and he had had his fill of vodka and
champagne, he would take Mishytka by the hand and, crying,
say to him in the presence of Groholski and Liza:

"Oh, my son! Mihail! What's it all about? Who's at fault? I
... I'm a scoundrel! I sold your mother! I sold her for thirty
pieces of silver. . . . Punish me, Lord! Mihail Ivanich! Little
piglet! Where is your mother? Pfft! You don't have one! She
was sold into slavery! Well, now what? I'm a scoundrel, that's
what. . . ."
These tears and words wrenched Groholski's soul. He
glanced timidly at the blanching Liza and wrung his hands.
"Go to bed, Ivan Petrovich!" he would say diffidently to him.
"I'm going. . . . Let's go, Mishytka! God will judge me! I
can't even think of sleeping when I know that my wife is a
slave. . . . But Groholski is not guilty. . . . It was my merchandise, his money. . . . The freeman has a free will, the redeemed
has paradise. . . ."
During the day Ivan Petrovich was no more tolerable. To
the great consternation of Groholski, he clung to Liza. He
went fishing with her, told her gossip, took walks with her.
And once even, taking advantage of the fact that Groholski
was indisposed with a cold, took her in his carriage. God knows
where, and didn't return until nightfall.
It's disgraceful! Inhumane! thought Groholski, biting his lips.
Groholski loved to kiss Liza constantly. He couldn't live
without these sickly-sweet kisses, but in the presence of Ivan
Petrovich it was somehow discommodious to be kissing. . . .
Torment! The poor man felt isolated. . . . But fate soon took
pity upon him. . . . Ivan Petrovich suddenly disappeared some-
where for a whole week. Some guests arrived and took him and
Mishytka away with them.
One beautiful spring morning Groholski came in from tak-
ing a walk in a merry mood and radiant.
"He's returned," he told Liza, rubbing his hands together.
. . . "I'm very glad he's returned. . . . Ha-ha-ha!"
"Why are you laughing?"
"He's brought some women with him. . . ."
"What kind of women?"
"I don't know. . . . It's right that he's brought some women.
. . . In fact, it's excellent. . . . He's still young and passionate. . . .
Come over here! Take a look. . . ."

Groholski led Liza out to the terrace and pointed to the cottage *vis-à-vis*. They both had a belly laugh. It was hilarious. On the terrace of the cottage *vis-à-vis* stood a smiling Ivan Petrovich. Down below the terrace stood two unknown brunettes and Mishytka. The dames were speaking in French and giggling.

"Frenchwomen," noted Groholski. "That one closest to us is not stupid. She's easy with the men but that is unimportant. . . . Even among such there are good women. . . . However, these . . . are bold."

What was so hilarious was that Ivan Petrovich had stretched his long arms down to where he could take hold of the shoulders of one of the Frenchwomen and, laughing, would lift and put her down on the terrace.

After lifting both of the dames, he picked up Mishytka. The dames ran back down and the lifting game was replayed. . . .

"Strong muscles!" muttered Groholski, watching the scene.

The game was repeated about six times. The dames were good-looking, and not in the least embarrassed when a strong wind swirled their skirts so that they were blown up. Groholski modestly lowered his eyes when, after reaching the balcony, the dames threw their legs over the railing. And Liza looked and laughed! What business was it of hers? She knew what men were like and since she was a lady she would have to be ashamed, but these dames!

In the evening Ivan Petrovich hurried over, and a little flustered, informed them that he was now a family man. . . .

"You mustn't think that these are loose women," he said. "It's true they're Frenchwomen, loud, and drink wine . . . that's well known! They're very educated! It can't be helped. . . . I was given them," added Ivan Petrovich, "by a prince. . . . Like a gift. . . . 'Take them . . . take them,' he said. You must become acquainted with this prince. A highly educated man! He writes all the time. . . . You know what their names are? One is called Fannie and the other Isabel. . . . Europe! Ha-ha-ha. . . . It's the West! Goodbye!"

Ivan Petrovich left Groholski and Liza in peace and stayed

with his dames. All day long from his cottage could be heard the sound of conversation, laughter, and the clatter of dishes. . . . The lights were kept lit until late at night. . . . Groholski was overjoyed. . . . After the long siege of torment he finally felt himself happy and content once more. Ivan Petrovich with his two women couldn't possibly be as content as he was with his one. . . . But—so what! Fate doesn't have a heart. It toys with the Groholskis, the Lizas, the Ivans, and the Mishytkas as if they were pawns. . . . Groholski once again lost his contentment. . . .

Once (after about a week and a half had gone by), Groholski, having overslept, went out on the terrace and saw a scene which startled him, perturbed him, and made him extremely indignant. Beneath the terrace of the cottage *vis-à-vis* stood the Frenchwomen and with them was . . . Liza. She was having a conversation with them, and with a side-glance at their cottage seemed to say: has this tyrant, this despot awakened? (Groholski told himself that that was what the glance meant.) Ivan Petrovich, standing on the terrace with his arms hanging, first lifted Isabel, than Fannie, and then . . . Liza. When he lifted Liza, Groholski could see that he pressed her to himself. . . . Liza also threw a leg over the railing. . . . Oh, these women! There isn't a single one who isn't wanton!

When Liza returned home from her husband's, it so happened that she tiptoed into the bedroom. Groholski, pale, with red spots on his cheeks, lay as if he had collapsed, and was groaning. Upon seeing Liza, he jumped out of bed and stomped around the room.

"So that's how it is?" he squealed in a high tenor tone. "So that's how it really is? I'm very grateful to you! It's insufferable, my dear madame! Immorality finally! Are you aware of that?"

Liza became pale and, of course, cried. Women when they feel they are falsely accused swear and cry, and when they know they are guilty they only cry.

"You've joined these harlots? Oho . . . that's . . . that's the lowest kind of indecency! They're mercenaries! Courtesans! And you an honorable woman have drifted to the same level as they? And that . . . that man! What more does he want? What more does he want from me? I don't understand him! I gave him half of my fortune, gave him more! You know that yourself! I gave him what I don't have. . . . Just about everything. . . . And he! I tolerated your addressing each other in personal terms, to which he has no right, tolerated your strolling together, kisses after dinner. . . . I bore it all, but this is too much! . . . Make your choice, it's me or him. . . . I've had it! The cup is full. . . . I've already suffered a great deal. . . . I'm going to talk to him right now . . . this very minute! When you get right down to it, he's nobody! You know who he is! Well, he's nothing. . . . His high opinion of himself is meaningless. . . ."

Groholski expressed still many more brave and venomous words, but never went "right now": cowardice and shame restrained him. He went to Ivan Petrovich three days later. . . .

Upon entering Ivan Petrovich's, his mouth fell open. The luxury and wealth with which Bugrov surrounded himself amazed him. The upholstery was all in velvet and the armchairs were frightfully expensive. . . . One even felt the need to be cautious upon entering. Groholski in his time had known many wealthy people, but he had never in his life seen such exorbitant extravagance. But what a mess he saw when he entered the main drawing room! The piano was covered with plates full of crumbs, on the piano stool was a glass, under a table was some kind of a basket with an ugly rag covering it. Nutshells were all over the window ledges. . . . When Groholski entered, Bugrov himself was disheveled. He was strutting around the room, flushed, uncombed, rumpled, and was talking to himself. . . . He was obviously extremely disturbed by something. On the divan in the room sat Mishytka, who was rending the air with piercing screams. . . .

"This is terrible, Grigory Vasilich!" exclaimed Bugrov upon seeing Groholski. "Such a mess, such a mess. . . . Please be seated. Please excuse my state of undress. . . . That's not worth discussing. . . . It's awful chaos! I don't know how people can live here! I don't understand it! Servants don't do their work, the climate is terrible, everything is expensive. . . . Shut up!" Bugrov shouted as he stopped before Mishytka. "Shut up! I'm talking to you! Monster! You won't be still?"

And Bugrov took hold of Mishytka's ear.

"This is intolerable, Ivan Petrovich!" exclaimed Groholski in a tearful voice. "How can you beat such a little child? It's true your class of people . . ."

"Let him stop howling. . . . Shut up! Or I'll flog you!"

"Don't cry, Misha, darling. . . . Daddy won't beat you anymore. Don't beat him, Ivan Petrovich! He's only a little child. . . . Now, now . . . would you like a little horse? I'll bring you a little horse. . . . Such as you, it's true . . . are hard-hearted. . . ."

Groholski kept quiet and then asked:

"And how are your dames, Ivan Petrovich?"

"No way. . . . Threw them out . . . without ceremony. I would have kept them, but it became objectionable: the boy was fighting with them . . . copying his father. . . . If I were alone that would be a different matter. What do I need them for? Phf. . . . What a comedy! I speak in Russian and they speak to me in French. . . . They're pigheaded and don't understand anything. . . ."

"I've come here on business, Ivan Petrovich, to talk over something. . . . Hm. . . . It won't take long . . . a few words. . . . Actually, I want to ask a favor of you."

"What kind?"

"Could you find it, Ivan Petrovich, possible to leave . . . here? We're very glad you're here, it's very pleasant but, you know, it's uncomfortable. . . . You know what I mean. It's somehow disconcerting. . . . These nontraditional arrangements . . . are always clumsy when there is contact. . . . Separating is desirable . . . even necessary. . . . Forgive me, but you yourself, of course, can understand that similar opportunities for living together lead to . . . reconsideration. . . . Not reconsideration, but revelation of feelings of discomfort."

"Yes . . . that's so. I've thought about this myself. Okay. I'll leave."

"We'll be very obliged to you. Believe me, Ivan Petrovich, our memories of you will be most flattering! The sacrifice, which . . ."

"All right. . . . Only, where can I get the money? Listen, buy this furniture from me! Would you do that? It'll be cheap.

... Eight thousand ... ten ... for the furniture, the carriage, the piano. ..."

"Agreed. ... I'll give you ten thousand! ..."

"That's excellent! I'll leave tomorrow. ... I'll go to Moscow. I can't live here anymore! Everything costs too much! Terribly high! Money is squandered. ... You can't take a step without spending a thousand. ... I can't afford this. I'm a family man. ... So, thank God, you'll buy the furniture from me. The money will come in handy for I'm just about bankrupt. ..."

Groholski got up, parted with Bugrov, and exultant, went home. In the evening he sent the ten thousand over to Bugrov.

Early in the morning on the next day, Bugrov and Mishytka were already in Feodisiya.

III

Several months went by. Spring came.

With the spring came bright, clear days when life was less distasteful and dull, and the earth was at its most handsome time. ... Warmth blew in from the sea and from the fields. ... New grass covered the ground and on the trees new leaves became green. Nature was reborn and appeared in a new dress. ...

It would seem that when nature is renewed, young, fresh, that in the human being would stir new hopes and desires. ... But it is difficult for man to be reborn.

Groholski lived in the same cottage as before. ... His hopes and desires were small, modest, concentrated completely upon the same Liza, and only upon her, not upon anything else! As before he could not take his eyes off her and regaled himself with the thought: How fortunate I am! The poor devil, as a matter of fact, believed he was terribly happy. Liza, as previously, sat on the terrace and tediously, inexplicably, stared at the cottage *vis-à-vis* and at the trees surrounding it through which the blue sea was visible. ... She kept even more silent than before, cried often, and now and then put mustard plasters on Groholski. However, one could congratulate her on something new. A worm had begun to tear at her insides. This worm—was yearning. Her yearning was intense; she yearned for her son, for her former way of life, for gaiety. The past life had not been especially gay, but all the same much merrier than the present. . . . Living with her husband she now and then went to the theater, to social affairs, associated with acquaintances. But here with Groholski? It was empty, still. . . . By her side was only one person, and that was it, with his ailments and continual sickly-sweet kisses, and resembling an old meek grandfather perpetually crying about how happy he was. Boring! There was no Mikaya Sergayich who liked to dance the mazurka with her, nor was there Spiridon Nikolaich, the son of the editor of the *Provincial News.* Spiridon Nikolaich was a marvelous poet and recited poetry. There was no table of hors d'oeuvres, nor guests, nor Gerasimova, the nanny who constantly scolded her for eating too many pastries. There wasn't anyone! It was a living death from yearning.

Groholski gloried in the solitariness, but . . . his exuberance was in vain. He paid for his egoism earlier than he should have. Early in May, when it seemed the air itself loved and pined from happiness, Groholski lost everything: the loved woman and . . .

Bugrov traveled to the Crimea at this time. He did not rent the cottage *vis-à-vis,* but dallied with Mishytka about the Crimean towns. He drank, ate, slept, and played cards in the towns. As to fishing, hunting, or the Frenchwomen, who, just between us, had robbed him not a little bit, he had lost all such inclinations. He lost weight, stopped looking genial and smiling broadly, and dressed only in sailcloth. Now and then he visited the Groholski cottage. He brought Liza pastries, candy, and fruit, and tried in his way to alleviate his depression. Groholski was not troubled by these visits, and all the more, since they were rare and short, and obviously gave pleasure to Mishytka, to whom one could no longer deprive of the right to meet with his mother. Bugrov would arrive, lay out his house gifts, say a few words and leave. And these few words would be to Groholski and not to Liza. . . . He said nothing to Liza. And Groholski was undisturbed. . . . But there is a Russian saying that it wouldn't have done any harm for Groholski to remember: "Don't be afraid of the dog that barks, but of the one that is silent." The saying is malicious, but in life it is sometimes enormously useful. . . .

Once, while strolling in the garden, Groholski heard the sound of two voices. One was a man's and the other a woman's. The first was Bugrov's and the second was Liza's. Groholski listened and the blood left his face and he looked like death itself. He softly stepped toward the conversationists and stood behind a lilac bush to observe and to listen. His hands and feet became like ice. A cold sweat arose on his brow. In order not to stagger or to fall, he took hold of the bush's branches. All was lost!

Bugrov was holding Liza around the waist and saying to her:

"My darling! What are we to do? With things as they were, God was satisfied. . . . I was a scoundrel. . . . I sold you. I was tempted by the tyrant's wealth, so that he would empty his pockets. . . . And what good came of this wealth? Only discontent and vainglory! Neither content, nor happiness, nor a rise in class. . . . I'm sitting, like a clumsy oaf, stuck in one place and can't take one step forward. . . . Have you heard? Andrushka Marzykin became a chief. . . . That idiot, Andrushka! And here I sit. . . . Lord, Lord! I'm deprived of you and of happiness. I'm a scoundrel! A lout! Do you think I'll go to hell on Judgment Day?"

"Let's leave here, Vanya!" cried Liza. "I'm dying from boredom here."

"It's impossible. . . . I accepted the money."

"So, give it back!"

"I'd be glad to, but . . . tprrr. . . . Not that easy, young filly! I've spent it all! We must resign ourselves, little mother. . . . God is punishing us. Me for my self-interest and you for your light-headedness. . . . So what of it? We will suffer torment. . . . It will be easier later."

And in this stream of religiosity Bugrov raised his eyes toward heaven.

"But I can't stay here! It's painfully depressing!"

"What's to be done? Do you think it isn't depressing for me? Is it merry for me without you? I'm pining away and I'm all dried up! My chest hurts! . . . You are my legal wife, part of my flesh . . . one flesh. . . . You must live and be patient! Well, but I . . . will go away to call upon . . ."

And leaning closer to Liza, Bugrov whispered, but so loudly that you could hear it several feet away:

"I will come at night to you, Lizanka. . . . Don't worry . . . I'm in Feodisiya, not far away. . . . I'll live near you while I still have some money . . . until the last kopeck has been spent! Eh-e-eh! What kind of life is this? Boredom, aching all over. . . . My chest hurts, my stomach hurts . . ."

Bugrov stopped talking. Now it was Liza's turn. . . . My God, how cruel this woman is! She began to cry, complain, list all the faults of her lover, her torments. . . . Groholski, upon hearing her, felt like a thief, a criminal, a destroyer. . . .

"He has worn me out!" Liza concluded. . . .

Kissing Liza goodbye and going out by the garden gate, Bugrov stumbled into Groholski who was standing at the gate waiting for him.

"Ivan Petrovich!" exclaimed Groholski in the voice of a dying man. "I heard and saw everything. . . . It's dishonorable on your part but I'm not blaming you. . . . You love her too. . . . But understand that she belongs to me! She's mine! I can't live without her! Why can't you understand this? All right, we'll accept the fact that you love her, that you are in pain, but didn't I pay you at least in part for your suffering? Go far away, for God's sake! Go far away, for God's sake! Leave here forever. I beg you! Anything else will kill me. . . ."

"I have no place to go," declared Bugrov in a muffled tone. . . .

"Hm. . . . You squandered everything already. . . . You're a dissipated man. . . . Well, all right. . . . Go to my estate in Chernigovski province. . . . Are you willing? I'll make a gift of it to you. . . . It's small, but very nice. . . . On my word of honor, it's very nice! . . ."

Bugrov smiled broadly. He immediately felt himself in seventh heaven.

"I'll make you a gift. . . . I'll write today to the steward and I'll send him confirmation of a completed deed of purchase. You can say everywhere that you've bought it. . . . Go! I beg you!"

"Okay . . . I'll go. I understand what you're saying."

"Let's go to the notary. . . . Now," declared the elated Groholski, and he went to order the harnessing of the horses.

On the next day in the evening, when Liza sat on the garden bench upon which she had usually had a rendezvous with Ivan Petrovich, Groholski came quietly up to her. He sat down beside her and took hold of her hand.

"Are you bored, Lizochka?" he said after a prolonged silence. "You're bored? Why don't we go somewhere? Why do we always stay at home? We must go places, have a good time, get acquainted. . . . Really, must we?"

"I don't need anything," answered pale and thin Liza, as she stared down the path over which Bugrov had been coming to meet her.

Groholski fell to thinking. He knew whom she was waiting for and whom she needed.

"Let's go into the house, Liza," he said. "It's damp out here. . . ."

"You go ahead. . . . I'll be in presently."

Groholski again became contemplative.

"You're expecting him?" he asked with a grimace on his face, as if his heart had been gripped by a pair of hot tongs.

"Yes. . . . I want to give him some stockings for Misha."

"He isn't coming."

"How do you know?"

"He's driven away. . . ."

Liza's eyes opened wide. . . .

"He's gone. . . . Gone to Chernigovski province. I gave him my estate. . . ."

Liza paled terribly, and in order not to fall, held on to Groholski's shoulders.

"I drove him to the boat . . . at three o'clock. . . ."

Liza suddenly grasped her head; she bolted away and dropped onto the bench, all her limbs trembling.

"Vanya!" she cried out. "Vanya! I'll go too, Vanya! . . . Darling!"

She had an attack of hysteria.

And from this evening up to July itself, in the garden in

which the cottagers strolled, there could be seen two shadows. The shadows walked from morning until night and put a damper upon the other cottagers. Behind Liza's shadow Groholski's shadow followed relentlessly. I'm calling them shadows, because they had both lost their former appearance.

They had both become thinner, paler, shrunken, and reminded one more of shadows than of living people. . . . They both were withering like the fleas in the classic tale of the Jews selling flea powder.

Liza ran away from Groholski early in July, leaving a note in which she wrote she was going to her "son" for a while. . . . For a while! She ran away at night when Groholski was sleeping. . . .

After reading the note, Groholski dawdled around the cottage like a mad man, not eating and not sleeping. In August he contracted a relapsing fever and in September went abroad. Abroad he drank too much. He thought he could find respite in wine and women. He squandered his wealth and, poor devil, could not get out of his head his beloved with her little feline face. . . . One doesn't die from happiness and one doesn't die from unhappiness. Groholski became gray, but he didn't die. He's still alive now. . . . He returned from abroad to see Liza "with his own eyes." Bugrov met him with open arms and insisted he be his guest for an unlimited time. He's at Bugrov's till this day.

※ ※ ※

Just this year I came to be passing by Groholevka, Bugrov's estate. I found the master and mistress having dinner. Ivan Petrovich was extremely delighted to see me and insisted upon regaling me. He had put on weight and had become a little paunchy. His face had gotten back its earlier fullness, and was shining and ruddy, and he wasn't at all bald yet. Liza had also put on weight. Her face had not remained thin and it was beginning to lose its feline look and alas! was getting leathery. Her cheeks were filling out from top to bottom and to the sides. The Bugrovs live very well. Everything is lush. They have many servants and a home filled with food. . . .

We conversed while we were having supper. I forgot that

Liza did not play, and asked that she play something for us on the piano.

"She doesn't play!" said Bugrov. "She's not a performer here. . . . Hey! Who's there? Ivan! Ask Gregory Vasilich to come here! What's he doing over there?" And turning to me Bugrov added: "The playboy will be here in a minute. . . . He plays the guitar. The piano is for Mishytka who is taking lessons. . . ."

Five minutes later Groholski entered, sleepy looking, uncombed, unshaved. . . . He came in, bowed to me, and sat down at a distance away.

"Well now, who goes to bed so early?" said Bugrov to him. "What a character you are, brother! Sleeping all the time, sleeping all the time . . . Sonya! So, play something cheerful for us. . . ."

Groholski tuned his guitar, plucked the strings, and sang: "Yesterday I expected my friend . . ."

I listened to the singing and observed Bugrov's well-fed body and thought: "What a despicable thug!" I wanted to cry. . . . Finishing the song, Groholski bowed to us and left. . . .

After he left, Bugrov turned to me and remarked: "What am I to do with him? He's a lot of trouble for me! During the day he spends all his time in deep thought, and at night he groans. He sleeps but continually groans and moans. . . . He has some kind of sickness. . . . What am I to do with him? My brain can't fathom him! He won't let us sleep. . . . I'm afraid he'll do himself in. I think it's bad for him to live here . . . but what's bad about it? He eats and drinks with us. . . . The only thing I don't give him is money. . . . Give it to him and he'll drink and squander it. . . . It's another menace I have hanging over my head! Lord, forgive me the sinner!"

I stayed overnight. When I awoke the next morning I heard Bugrov reading the riot act to someone in the next room:

"Give up this idiotic praying to God, for he is all-knowing. So, who makes the leaves turn green? Use your head! Consider! Why are you silent?"

"I . . . I . . . made a mistake . . . ," justified a hoarse tenor voice. . . .

The tenor voice belonged to Groholski. . . .

Groholski drove me to the railroad station.

"He's a despot, a tyrant," he whispered to me during the whole way. "He's a noble man but a tyrant! Neither his heart nor his brain have ever fully developed. . . . He worries me! If it weren't for his noble wife, I would have left long ago. . . . I'm sorry for her and can't leave. I have to be as patient as I can be with both of them."

Groholski sighed and continued:

"She's pregnant. . . . Did you notice? In truth, it's my child. . . . Mine. . . . She soon recognized her mistake and has shunned me since then. She can't stand him. . . ."

"You're a weakling!" I couldn't restrain myself from remarking to Groholski.

"Yes. I have no character. . . . That's true. I was born that way. Do you know how I got conceived? My late father greatly enslaved an official. It was fearful how he was enslaved! My father poisoned his life! So. . . . But my dead mother was compassionate, she came from the common people, a member of the middle class. . . . Out of pity she became intimate with this official. . . . So . . . that's how I came to be. . . . From an oppressed man. . . . Is there any source for character? Where would it come from? However, the second bell is ringing. . . . Farewell! Come again and don't tell Ivan Petrovich what I said about him!"

I shook hands with Groholski and jumped on the train. He bowed toward my passenger car and then headed for the water fount. Evidently he needed a drink. . . .

1882

OVERSPICED

The surveyor, Gleb Gavrilovich Smirnov, arrived at the Gnilushki railroad station. To get to his destination he had to go about thirty or forty versts with horses. (If the driver is not drunk and the horses are not worn out and emaciated, it wouldn't even be thirty versts, and if the driver wasn't drunk but the horses tired, it could be fifty versts.)

"Tell me, please, where I can hire postal horses?" the surveyor asked the station's gendarme.

"What kind? Postal horses? You won't even find a dog here for a hundred versts let alone postal horses. . . . Where do you want to go?"

"To Devkino, the estate of General Hahatova."

"Why not?" yawned the gendarme. "If you go behind the station you can sometimes find a muzhik who transports passengers."

The surveyor sighed and walked slowly to the back of the station. Here he found a tough-looking, tall muzhik, who was sullen, pockmarked, and dressed in a torn caftan and trousers.

"The devil knows what kind of a cart you have!" exclaimed the surveyor, wrinkling his face in disgust as he climbed into

150

the cart. "You can't distinguish between the rear and the front. . . ."

"What's there to know? Where the horse's tail is, that's the front, and where you sit yourself down, that's the rear. . . ."

The little horse was young, but scrawny, with her legs spread out and her ears bitten. When the driver whipped her to get started, she only shook her head, so he whipped her again, and the cart squeaked and shook as if it were feverish. After the third lash the cart lurched, and after the fourth it moved from the spot.

"Is this how we're going to move over the whole distance?" asked the surveyor, having been given a strong jolt and being amazed how Russian drivers can combine a quiet, at-snail's-pace ride with jolting that wrenches the soul.

"We'll g-et there!" reassured the driver. "The filly is young, smart. . . . Let her get running and you won't be able to stop her. . . . Bu-u-t, damn . . . you!" he yelled at the horse.

When the cart left the station, it was twilight. On the right of the surveyor stretched the dark, still plain, seeming endless and borderless. . . . If you ride across it you'll certainly come to the end of the world. On the horizon where it disappears and blends with the sky, the autumn sunset lazily settles. . . . On the left from the road, in the darkening atmosphere loomed some kind of mounds, neither last year's haystacks nor trees. What was before them the surveyor could not see: everything was hidden by the broad back of the driver. All was silent, cold, and frozen. . . .

How remote it is here! thought the surveyor, trying to cover his ears with his collar. Neither house nor home. It's dangerous—you could be attacked and robbed, nobody would know it, even if a cannon were shot. And the driver doesn't present much security. . . . What a broad back he has! All he has to do is move a finger to kill you! He has a beastly, suspicious-looking mug.

"Say, young man," asked the surveyor, "what's your name?"

"Me? Klim."

"Well, Klim, how do you feel driving in this area? Isn't it dangerous? You're not afraid of robbers?"

"No problem, God is merciful. . . . Who's around to rob us?"

"That's fine that there aren't any robbers around. . . . But just in case, I brought three revolvers with me," lied the surveyor. "As you know, you don't play games with a revolver. You could take on a dozen thieves."

It grew dark. The cart suddenly creaked and, as if it were reluctant to do so, turned left.

Where's he taking me? thought the surveyor. He was going straight ahead and then suddenly turns left. The scoundrel is taking us to some godforsaken place and . . . and . . . Something is about to happen!

"Listen," he addressed the driver. "So you say it's not dangerous here? Too bad. . . . I like to tangle with robbers. . . . I look like a skinny, sickly wimp, but I'm as strong as a bull. . . . Three thieves jumped me once. . . . What do you think happened? I socked one so hard that . . . that, you must know, he died. I saw to it that the other two were sentenced to hard labor in Siberia. I haven't the faintest idea where my strength comes from. . . . You take hold of a strong, tall man, like you, with one hand and . . . and it can kill him."

Klim looked around at the surveyor, blinked, and lashed the filly.

"Yes sir, buddy . . . ," continued the surveyor. "God help him who tries to tangle with me. Moreover, if the robber loses hands and legs, he still has to answer before the court. All the judges and district police know me. I'm a bureaucrat and a useful man. Where I'm going all the bosses know about it. . . . They'll look after me so that nothing untoward happens to me. Along the road behind the bushes are police and hundreds of stumbling blocks. . . . St . . . st . . . stop!" suddenly yelled the surveyor. "Where have you turned into? Where are you taking me?"

"Can't you see? It's the forest!"

No doubt, it's a forest . . . , thought the surveyor. And I was frightened! He's already noticed that I'm afraid. Why does he keep turning around and watching me? No doubt he's scheming about something. . . . Earlier he was moving so-so, dragging his feet, and now he's speeding ahead!

"Listen, Klim, why are you spurring the horse?"

"I'm not doing anything. She's speeding up by herself. Once she gets going it's hard to stop her. . . . She's not too happy with it herself that her legs react this way."

"You're lying, brother! I can see that you're lying! I'm simply advising you to slow down. Hold back your horse. . . . Do you hear! Hold her back!"

"Why?"

"Because . . . because four of my pals have left the station after us. They have to catch up with us. . . . They promised to catch up with us in this forest. . . . The ride will be more lively with them along. . . . They're healthy, sturdy guys. . . . all have pistols. . . . Why are you constantly looking around and act as if you're sitting on pins? What? No, brother. . . . . There's nothing to see on me . . . nothing interesting. . . . Only my revolvers. . . . If you want I'll take them out and show you . . . if you want."

The surveyor made believe that he was rummaging in his pockets, and then something unexpected happened, that which he could not have anticipated because of his own cowardice. Klim suddenly jumped out of the cart and raced into a grove on all fours.

"Help!" he shouted in a loud and frightened voice. "Help! Take everything, you devil, take the horse and the cart, only don't kill me! Help!"

You could hear the sound of running feet, the snapping of dry branches—and then nothing. . . . The surveyor had not expected this turn of events, stopped the horse, and then settled himself more comfortably on the cart and began to mull it over.

"He ran away. . . . The dunce got frightened. . . . Well, now what? It's impossible for me to go on alone because I don't know the road, and it might even be thought that I stole the horse from him. . . . What's to be done? Klim! Klim!"

"Klim," answered an echo.

Considering that he might have to spend the whole cold night in this dark forest, and to hear only wolves and the echo responding to the snorting of this emaciated little horse, the surveyor felt a jarring below his spine as if a cold rasp was working on it.

"Klimie!" he called out. "Dear man! Where are you, Klimie?"

The surveyor called for about two hours and only after he

became hoarse and resigned to having to spend the night in the forest, a little breeze carried someone's groan to his ears.

"Klim! Is that you, dear man? Let's get going!"

"Y . . . you'll kill me!"

"I was just joking, dear man! Strike me dead, Lord, if I weren't joking! I don't have any guns! I was lying out of fear! Be so kind, let's get going! I'm freezing!"

Klim, realizing correctly that a real robber would have left long ago with the horse and cart, stepped out of the forest and hesitatingly walked toward his passenger.

"So, why, silly, did you get frightened? I . . . I was joking, and you were frightened. . . . Get in!"

"God will be your judge, sir," muttered Klim, climbing into the cart. "If I had known, I wouldn't have driven you for a hundred rubles. I almost died from fright. . . ."

Klim lashed the filly. The cart shuddered. Klim lashed the filly once more and the cart lurched. After the fourth lash, as the cart began to move, the surveyor hid his ears in his collar and became thoughtful. The road and Klim no longer seemed dangerous.

1885

THE CHAMELEON

A police inspector, one Ochumelov,* in a new overcoat with a bundle in his hand, walks across the marketplace. A red-headed constable of lower rank trails behind him with a colander filled to the top with confiscated gooseberries. There is an ominous silence. . . . Not a soul is in the square. . . . The open doors of the shops and taverns look out cheerlessly on God's world like hungry jaws; there aren't even any beggars near them.

"That's for you, damn you. You want to bite?" Ochumelov hears out of the blue. "Lads, don't let her loose! Don't let it bite anyone else today. Hold her! Ah . . . a!"

A dog's whine is heard. Ochumelov looks in the direction of the whine and sees: out of the lumberyard of the merchant Pichugin, hopping on three legs and looking back, a dog is fleeing. A person in a starched calico shirt with an unbuttoned waistcoat is chasing her. Running after her and throwing himself forward, he falls on the ground and grabs the dog's hind legs. For a second time the dog's howl and a shout is heard:

---

*"Slightly mad"

"Don't let it loose!" Sleepy shopkeepers drift out of the shops, and soon a crowd, as if arisen from the earth, gathers around the lumberyard.

"It seems there's some trouble, your honor!" says the local policeman.

Ochumelov makes a half turn to the left and strides toward the gathering. By the gate to the lumberyard he sees the above-described person in the unbuttoned waistcoat who, raising his right hand in the air, is showing the crowd a bloody finger. On his half-drunken face, as if it were written there, can be seen: "The owner of this vicious hound will have to pay for this!" The finger itself has the mark of triumph. Ochumelov recognizes the person as the goldsmith Kryukin.* In the center of the crowd, her front paws spread out and her whole body trembling, on the ground sits the culprit of this chaos—a white borzoi puppy with a pointed mug and a yellow mark on her back. Fright and misery are expressed in her teary eyes.

"What are you all doing here?!" asks Ochumelov, elbowing his way into the crowd. "Why are you here? You, what happened to your finger? . . . Who was shouting?"

"I'm walking, your honor, minding my own business . . . ," begins Kryukin, coughing into his fists, "to get firewood with Mitri Mitrich—and suddenly this brute for no reason at all goes after my finger. . . . You must excuse me, but I'm a working man. My work doesn't pay much. I'll have to be compensated for this because—with this finger, I probably won't be able to get around. . . . You know, your honor, there's no law that one has to tolerate animals. . . . If we're all going to be bitten, it'd be better not to live on earth. . . ."

"Hm. . . . All right . . . ," says Ochumelov sternly, coughing and moving his eyebrows. "All right. . . . Whose dog is it? I won't let this be overlooked. I'll be severe. I'll show you, you who let your dogs run around freely. It's about time attention is directed toward such gentry who won't submit to county decrees! When I fine him, the scoundrel, he'll learn from me the cost of letting his animals run around!" He continues with

_____

*"Complainer," "Grunter"

another vulgar denunciation. "Yeldirin," the inspector addresses the local policeman, "find out whose dog it is and draw up a record of the proceedings! The dog needs to be exterminated. Immediately! She's obviously rabid. . . . Whose dog is it?"

"It seems like it's General Zhigalov's!" says someone in the crowd.

"General Zhigalov's? Hm. . . . Help me off with my overcoat, Yeldirin. . . . It's terribly hot! I suppose we must settle this before it rains. . . . However, there's one thing I don't understand. How could she bite you?" he asked, turning to Kryukin. "Can she reach your finger? She's small and you're so tall! It must be that you scratched your finger with a nail, and then it came into your head to get money from the owner. You. . . . It's well known how people like you operate! I know you, you wretches!"

"He, your honor, was putting a homemade cigarette to the puppy's snout for a laugh, and she not being stupid,—she nipped him. . . . He's an adult and should know better, your honor!"

"You're lying, you one-eyed bastard! You didn't see anything, so why are you making it up? The honorable gentry are smart and know who is lying and who is honest, as one is when before God. . . . And if I'm lying let the justice of the peace decide. He knows the law. . . . Today we're all equal. . . . My own brother serves in the military police. . . . If you want to know . . ."

"Silence!"

"No, it's not the general's . . . ," thoughtfully remarks the local policeman. "The general doesn't have this breed. His dogs are all more like setters. . . ."

"You know that for a fact?"

"Precisely, your honor. . . ."

"I also knew that. The general has expensive, pedigreed dogs, and this one. . . . Who the hell knows what it is! This dog doesn't look like anything, neither her coat, nor her shape. . . . And who wants to keep such a mutt?! Where are your brains? If such a dog was found in Petersburg or Moscow, you know what would happen to it? They wouldn't bother even to look at the law, but in a minute—it wouldn't be breathing! You, Kryukin, you have suffered and we won't leave it at that. . . . Somebody has to be taught a lesson! It's about time. . . ."

"It's possible that it is the general's . . . ," says the policeman, thinking out loud. "It's not written on his mug. . . . I saw such a dog in his courtyard last night."

"Of course. It's the general's!" says a voice from the crowd.

"Hm!. . . . Help me with my overcoat, brother Yeledrin. . . . The wind is beginning to blow. . . . It's getting cold. . . . Lead it to the general's and ask if it belongs there. Say that I found it and am returning it. . . . And tell them not to let her out on the street. . . . She might be an expensive breed, and some swine is going to put a lit cigarette to her nose. She'll soon be ruined. A dog—is a delicate creature. . . . And you, you blockhead, put your hand down! You don't have to keep showing your stupid finger! It's your own fault!"

"The general's cook is coming toward us. We'll ask him. . . . Hey, Prokor!"

"Come here, my fine fellow! Take a look at this dog. . . . Is it yours?"

"Some imagination! We've never had such a breed!"

"It's not necessary to ask anyone else," says Ochumelov. "She's a stray! We don't have to discuss it any further. . . . If I say it's a stray, that means it's a stray. . . . It's to be put away and that's all there is to it."

It's not ours," continues Prokor. "It's the general's brother's. He arrived the other day. We don't use borzois for hunting. The brother loves them. . . ."

"Has his brother really arrived? Vladimir Ivanich?" asks Ochumelov, and his whole face radiates with a benign smile. "You don't say! My God! And I wasn't aware of it! Is he going to stay a while?"

"A visit. . . ."

"You don't say! My God. . . . The brothers have missed each other. . . . And I didn't know it! So this is his little dog? I'm glad. . . . You take her. . . . She's a nice little pup. . . . A lively one. . . . Nipped this guy's finger! He-ha-ha! Now, now, why are you shivering? Rrr. . . . Rr. . . . Sweet little rascal. . . . What a fine pup. . . ."

Prokor calls the dog and leaves the lumberyard with her. . . . The crowd laughs at Kryukin.

"I'll take care of you yet!" Ochumelov growls at Kryukin, and bundling up in his overcoat continues on his way across the marketplace.

1884

FATTY AND SKINNY

Two friends met at a station of the Nicholayevska railway: one was heavyset and the other very thin. The heavyset one had just finished eating his dinner at the station's restaurant, and his lips were still covered with some butter and shone like ripe cherries. The scent of sherry and orange blossoms exuded from him. The thin one had just gotten off the train and was bent over with suitcases, bags, and cartons. He smelled from ham and coffee grounds. From behind his back a thin woman with a long chin peeped out—she was his wife, and with her stood a tall schoolboy with squinting eyes—he was his son.

"Porfirii!" exclaimed the heavyset one, upon seeing the thin one. "Is it really you? My dear fellow! Haven't seen you for a long time!"

"Good heavens!" exclaimed the surprised thin man. "Misha! My childhood friend! Where did you fall from?"

The friends exchanged the traditional three kisses and stared into each others' tear-filled eyes. They were both pleasantly stunned.

"My dear!" began the thin man after the kisses. "I never expected this! What a surprise! Well, take a good look at me!

160

Remember how handsome I was! Such a character and a dandy! Oh, you, good heavens! Well, what are you doing? Rich? Married? I'm married, as you can see. . . . This is my wife, Luisa, born Vantsenbach . . . a Lutheran. . . . And this is my son, Nafanail, a third-year student. This, Nafanya, is my friend from childhood! We were in high school together!"

Nafanail hesitated a bit and then took his cap off.

"We were in high school together!" continued the thin man. "Remember how they teased you? They teased you, calling you Gerostrat* because you burned the account book with a cigarette, and I was Efialt† because I liked to squeal. Ho-ho. . . . What children we were! Don't be afraid, Nafanya! Come a little closer. . . . And this is my wife, born Vantsenbach, a Lutheran."

Nafanail hesitated a little and then hid behind his father's back.

"So, how goes it with you, my friend?" asked the heavyset man, looking fervently at his friend. "Do you have a desk job? Have you risen up the ladder?"

"I do, dear fellow! I'm the provincial assessor now for the second year, and have the Stanislavski Order. The salary isn't great . . . but forget it! My wife gives music lessons, and in my free time I carve cigar cases from wood! I sell them for a ruble apiece. If someone takes ten or more, that one, of course, gets a discount. There's enough to live on somehow. I had a job in the department office, you know, but now I've been transferred here to be the supervisor of the branch because I have the know-how. . . . I'll be working here. Well, but how about you? You're probably a state councillor already? Yes?"

"No, dear fellow, I'm a bit higher than that," said the heavyset one. "I've already worked up to the secret service. . . . I have two stars."

The thin man suddenly blanched, froze, and his face

---

*the ancient Greek who burned down the temple of Artemis in Ephesus in order to win fame for himself

†the traitor who showed the Persians the path around the Greek army in the battle of Thermopylae

quickly screwed up on all sides with a very wide smile: It seemed that sparks flew from his face and eyes. He himself slithered down, hunched over, grew narrower. . . . His suitcases, bags, and boxes slithered down, seemed to contract. . . . The long chin of his wife became even longer. Nafanail straightened up and buttoned up all the buttons of his uniform.

"I, your honor. . . . Very pleasant to have met you! A friend, as it's said, of one's childhood, and all at once he's risen to such importance! Ts-ts-s."

"Well, enough of that!" said the frowning, heavyset man. "Why such a manner? We're friends from childhood—why do we need this courtesy according to rank!"

"For goodness sake. . . . That you, sir . . . ," giggled the servile thin man, slithering down even further. "Your gracious attention, your excellency, is like life-giving moisture. . . . This here, your excellency, is my son Nafanail . . . my wife Luisa, a Lutheran, as it were. . . ."

The heavyset man wanted to raise an objection to this obsequiousness, but on the face of the thin man was written such reverence, sweetness, and courteous servility that the privy councillor became nauseous. He moved away from the thin man, and in parting offered his hand.

The thin man grasped three fingers of his hand, bowed from the waist, and giggled nervously like a Chinese: "hi-hi-hi." The wife smiled. Nafanail clicked his heels together in salutation and dropped his cap. All three were gratifyingly wonder-stricken.

1883

A SET OF TWO IN ONE

Two-faced chameleons are not to be trusted! These days it's easier to lose your faith than to lose an old glove—and I've lost my faith!

It was evening. I was on a trolley. As a VIP it was not fitting for me to ride on a trolley, but on this occasion I had on a large fur coat and could bury myself in its sable collar. It is cheaper, too, as you know. . . . In spite of the late hour and the cold, the car was crowded. No one recognized me. The sable collar allowed me to be incognito. I rode, dozed, and looked over my fellow low-class passengers. . . .

No, it can't be him! I thought, looking at one short man in a coat made of rabbit fur. It can't be him! No, it's him! Ugh!

My thoughts fluctuated. I believed, and did not believe, my eyes. . . .

The man in the rabbit-fur coat strongly resembled Ivan Kapitonich, one of my office drudges. . . . Ivan Kapitonich was a small, dejected-looking, downtrodden creature, living for one reason only: in order to pick up dropped handkerchiefs and to congratulate others on holidays. He was young, but his back was curved like a bow, his knees were bent, his hands were dirty and hung down along the seams of his trousers. . . . His face looked as if it had been smashed in a door or like a wrung-out wet rag. It was bitter and pitiful, and when you looked at him, you felt like singing "Lychinysky"* and to whine. When I approach him he trembles, grows pale, and then flushes, as if I were going to eat him or cut his throat. When I correct him, he shivers and all his limbs shake.

I don't know of any one more submissive, reticent, and insignificant. I don't even know of an animal who would be meeker than he. . . .

The man in the rabbit-fur coat strongly reminded me of this Ivan Kapitonich: he resembled him perfectly! The only difference was that this man was not as bent, did not seem as dejected, and was free and easy in his carriage. What was more shocking than anything, he was talking politics with his neighbor. He could be heard throughout the train.

"Gambetta† has died!" he declared, turning around and waving his hands. "This plays into Bismarck's hands. Gambetta was crafty! He would have fought with the Germans and demanded compensation for losses, Ivan Matvyeich! That's because he was a genius! He was a Frenchman, but he had a Russian soul. What a talent!"

"What a piece of rubbish you are!" I said to myself.

When the conductor approached him for his ticket, he left Bismarck in peace and attacked the conductor.

"Why is it so dark in the trolley? Don't you have any lights? Why are you so inefficient? Someone should teach you a lesson! You'd be sacked outside our borders! The people aren't your servants, you're the people's servant! The devil with you! I can't understand what your supervisor sees!"

In the next minute he ordered all of us to move over.

"Move over! I'm speaking to you! Give the lady a seat! Be courteous! Conductor! Come here, conductor! You took her money, now provide her with a seat! Low-down behavior!"

"Smoking is not permitted!" shouted the conductor to him.

"Who says so? Who has the right? It's an infringement on

---

*a folk song bemoaning a birch splinter which won't provide light
†nineteenth-century French statesman

my freedom! I won't permit anyone to infringe upon my freedom! I'm a free human being!"

"What a piece of rubbish you are!" I repeated to myself. I looked at his ugly mug and couldn't believe my eyes. "No, it can't be him! It can't be! He doesn't even know such words as 'freedom' and 'Gambetta.' "

"Well, I declare. It's a great system!" he stated, throwing down his cigarette. "Try to live with such gentlemen! They're wild about form and the letter of the law! Bureaucrats, philistines! They're suffocating us!"

I couldn't restrain myself any longer and laughed aloud. Hearing my laugh, he stole a glance in my direction and his voice faltered. He had recognized my laugh and, possibly, recognized my coat. His back bent instantly, in a moment his face soured, his voice died out, his arms dropped to his trousers, his legs bent. Instantly, he was completely transformed! I no longer had any doubts that this was Ivan Kapitonich, my office wimp. He sat down and hid his nose in the rabbit fur.

I now looked at his face.

Is it possible, I thought, that this dejected, down-trodden little figure knows how to use such words as "philistine" and "freedom"? Oh? Really? Yes, he knows how. It's incredible but true. . . . What a piece of rubbish!

After this experience I believe what the wretched physiognomies of these chameleons tell me. I've lost my trust!

I don't believe anything anymore. I tell myself to knock it off. It's bad enough as it is.

1883

In Disguise

In the social club of Ch——, there was a charity ball or as it was called by the local ladies, the gala ball.

It was midnight. Intellectuals without masks were not dancing—there were five of them. They sat around the large table in the library with their noses and beards buried in newspapers, and were reading or dozing. As expressed by the local correspondent from the capital newspapers, they were very liberal gentlemen—"thinking men."

The sounds of the quadrille, "Vyushki," could be heard from the ballroom. Running past the doors, the butlers' heavy footsteps stomped and the dishes being brought in clattered. Only in the library itself was a heavy silence.

All of a sudden, a low, smothered voice was heard saying: "It seems that this will be a more satisfactory place!" It seemed, so to say, that it arose out of the hot air created by the dancing. "Put it down here! Put it here, lads!"

The door opened and a broad, thickset man, dressed in a coachman's costume, a hat with peacock feathers, and a mask, entered. Following him were two ladies also in masks, and a butler with a tray. On the tray was a round-bellied bottle with liqueur, three bottles of red wine, and several glasses.

"This way! It'll be cool in here," said the man. "Put the tray on the table. . . . Do sit down, mademoiselles! I want it to be like a ménage à trois!" he said in fractured French. "And you, gentlemen, buzz off . . . you're not needed here!"

The man staggered a little and with his hand shoved some journals off the table.

"Put it here! And you, gentlemen readers, buzz off. There's no room here for newspapers or for politics. . . . Chuck it!"

"I would beg you to be quiet," said one of the intellectuals, peering at the masked man through his glasses. "This is the library and not the bar. . . . This is not the place for drinking."

"Why not? Is the table rocky or the ceiling about to come down? That's funny! But. . . . There's no time for talk! Get rid of the newspapers. . . . You've read a little and that's enough for you. You're very smart already, and you're ruining your eyesight, but most important—I don't want you in here."

The butler placed the tray on the table, and throwing a napkin over his elbow, stood at the door. The ladies immediately took to the wine.

"What kind of smart people are there that prefer newspapers to these drinks," began the masked man wearing peacock feathers, pouring himself a liqueur. "In my opinion, you, honorable gentlemen, like newspapers because you don't have what it takes to drink. That's what I say! Ha-ha!. . . . They can read! Well, what is written there? You, sir, in the glasses! What kind of acts are you reading? Ha-ha! Well, throw it away! You'll get friendly! It's better to take a drink!"

The masked man in the peacock feathers arose and snatched the newspaper from the hands of the gentleman in the glasses. That gentleman paled, then flushed and in amazement looked at the other intellectuals, and they—at him.

"You forget yourself, dear sir!" he sputtered. "You're turning the library into a tavern, you permit yourself to ignore rank, snatch newspapers from people's hands! I will not permit it! You don't know who you're dealing with, dear sir! I am the director of the Zhestyakov Bank!"

"I wouldn't give a glob of spit to know who you are—Zhestyakov! And the same to your newspaper. . . ."

The masked man then picked up the newspaper and tore it into bits.

"Gentlemen, what's this all about?" muttered the stupefied Zhestyakov. "This is strange, it is . . . it is even supernatural. . . ."

"They're getting angry," laughingly remarked the masked man. "Fie on you, well, you, you're frightened! You're quaking with fear. That's it, honorable gentlemen! All joking aside, I don't want to converse with you . . . because I wish to be left alone with these mam'selles. I want it set up to my satisfaction, so I ask you not to protest and to leave. . . . Please! Mr. Belebykhin,* leave and join the other filthy dogs! Why are you screwing up your mug? I tell you get out or else! Get out! Step lively, look at the clock, exactly at one o'clock you'll get it in the neck!"

"How can this be?" asked Belebykhin, the treasurer of the orphans' court, his face flaming and shrugging his shoulders. . . . "I can't even understand. . . . How could such a boor crash in here and . . . what a to-do!"

"What impudent lout said that?" shouted the masked man with peacock feathers, becoming angry, and banging his fists on the table so that the glasses hopped on the tray. "Who do you think you're talking to? Do you think because I'm in disguise you can say anything to me? You're just a lot of hot air! Get out while I'm still talking! You, bank director, make yourself scarce for your good health! All of you leave, so there's not a one of you rascals left here! Leave! Join the other filthy dogs!"

"Well, we'll see immediately!" exclaimed Zhestyakov, whose eyes were even becoming moist with emotion. "I'll show you! Hey, you, call the captain on duty here!"

Within a minute a small, red-headed chief entered. He wore a blue ribbon on his lapel and was breathless from dancing.

"I'm asking you to leave!" he began. "This is not the place to drink! Please, in the bar!"

---

*"Paleface"

"Where did you spring from?" asked the man in the mask. "Indeed, did I call for you?"

"Please don't be familiar with me, and, if you please, leave!"

"It's like this, my dear fellow: I shall give you exactly one minute. . . . As you are the chief officer here, and an important individual, I ask you to take these artists by their arms and lead them out. My mam'selles don't like it if there are outsiders here. . . . They feel inhibited, and I want to get my money's worth, and have them in the nude."

"Obviously this petty tyrant doesn't understand that he's not sober!" shouted Zhestyakov. "Call Yevstrat Spiridonich here!"

"Yevstrat Spiridonich!" rang out through the club. "Where's Yevstrat Spiridonich?"

Yevstrat Spiridonich, an old man in a police uniform, soon appeared.

"I ask you to leave here!" he wheezed, opening his frightened eyes wide, his dyed mustache shaking.

"You see, he's scared!" cried the masked man and laughed from amusement. "Really and truly, he's scared! There's so much abject fear. Lord strike me dead! Mustache, like a cat's, eyes bulging. . . . Heh-heh-heh!"

"I beg you not to argue!" the quaking Yevstrat Spiridonich shouted with all his might. "Get out! I'll order you to be carried out!"

Ugly sounds arose from the library. Yevstrat Spiridonich, red as a crab, shouted, stamping his feet. Zhestyakov shouted. Belebykhin shouted. All the intellectuals shouted, but all the voices were shrouded by the low, thick, smothering basso of the man in the mask. Thanks to the general turmoil, the dancing was cut short and everyone headed for the library.

Yevstrat Spiridonich called all the police in the club for support, and sat down to write a report on the proceedings.

"Write, write," said the masked man, poking his finger at his pen to write. "Now what's going to happen to poor me? My poor little head! Why are you destroying me, poor little orphan that I am? Ha-ha! Well, why not? Is the report ready? Everything written up? Now, take a look! . . . One . . . two . . . three!! . . ."

The masked man stood up, stretched to his full height, and tore the mask from his face. Having uncovered his drunken face, and staring at everyone, admiring the effect produced, he fell into a chair and laughed uproariously. The impression he made was unusual. The intellectuals were taken aback and paled, several scratched the back of their necks. Yevstrat Spiridonich grunted, like a person who had inadvertently made a stupid mistake.

They all recognized the brawler as Petigorov,* a millionaire, a factory-owner, a gentleman by birth, and a citizen known for his scandalous behavior, philanthropy, and—how more than once it was said on the local society page—his love for enlightenment.

"Well now, will you leave or not?" asked Petigorov after a moment's silence.

The intellectuals were speechless, and not saying a word, walked out of the library on their tiptoes, and Petigorov closed the door after them.

"You really knew that it was Petigorov!" in the next minute croaked Yevstrat Spiridonich in an undertone, shaking the butler, who had carried the wine into the library, by the shoulders. "Why didn't you say something?"

"Nobody asked me!"

"Nobody asked you. . . . When I denounce you and put you in jail for a month then you'll know what 'nobody asked me' means! Get out! . . . And you, good gentlemen," turning to the intellectuals, "have caused a great ruckus! Couldn't you leave the library for at least ten minutes? So now straighten out this mess. Eh, gentlemen, gentlemen. . . . I really don't like them!"

The intellectuals walked despondently around the club, subdued, guilty, whispering, as though they had presentiments of something mischievous. . . . Their wives and daughters, having learned that Petigorov was "insulted" and angry, became hushed and started to get ready to go home. The dancing stopped.

———————————

*"Five Mountains"

Two hours later Petigorov came out of the library. He was dead drunk and staggered. Coming into the ballroom, he sat down by the orchestra and dozed as the music played; later his head dropped and he snored.

"Stop the music!" the club foreman ordered and waved the musicians away. "Sh-sh! . . . Yegor Nilich is sleeping. . . ."

"Would you like to order that you be driven home, Yegor Nilich?" asked Belebykhin, leaning close to the millionaire's ear.

Petigorov made with his lips exactly as if he wanted to blow a fly from his cheeks.

"Would you like to order that you be driven home," repeated Belebykhin, "or to say that your carriage be delivered?"

"What? Whose? You . . . what do you want?"

"To take you home. . . . It's time to go to bed. . . ."

"I want to—go home. . . . Ta-ake me!"

Belebykhin glowed with pleasure and began to help Petigorov up. The other intellectuals jumped to his side and, smiling pleasantly, lifted the gentleman-by-birth, citizen Petigorov, and carefully led him to his carriage.

"Only a talented artist could make fools of the whole assemblage," jovially remarked Zhestakov, helping him into the carriage. "I was literally stunned, Yegor Nilich! I'm still laughing. . . . Ha-ha. . . . We were boiling, making a big fuss! Ha-ha! Can you believe it? There hasn't been such a good comedy even in the theater. . . . Infinitely funny! I'll remember this unforgettable evening all of my life!"

After taking Petigorov to his carriage, the intellectuals were lighthearted and serene.

"He offered me his hand in parting," remarked the very satisfied Zhestyakov. "That means it was nothing and he's not angry."

"God willing!" sighed Yevstrat Spiridonich. "A scoundrel, a base human being, but really—a philanthropist! . . . Impossible!"

1884

THE VANDAL

A small, unusually emaciated muzhik is standing before a court investigator. He is wearing a crude, homemade, multicolored shirt and worn-out baggy trousers. His face is unshaven, his skin is coarse and full of pockmarks, and his eyes, barely visible because of his thick, overhanging eyebrows, have the appearance of sullen sternness. The hair on his head has not been combed for a long time and is a mass of knots, and gives him an appearance of cobweb-like obstinacy. He is barefoot.

"Denis Grigorev!" begins the investigator. "Come closer and answer my questions. On the seventh of July of this year the railroad watchman, Ivan Semyonov Akinfov, checking the rails in the morning, on the fourteenth section of the rails, caught you unscrewing a nut which rivets the rails to the ties. Here is the nut! . . . This is the nut he caught you with. Is this the way it occurred?"

"What?"

"Did all happen as described by Akinfov?"

"Of course, that was the way it was."

"Good. Now, why were you unscrewing the nut?"

"What?"

"You'd better chuck that 'what' and answer the question: Why were you unscrewing the nut?"

"If it wasn't needed, I wouldn't have been unscrewing it," answers Denis in a complaining tone, staring at the ceiling.

"What did you need this nut for?"

"The nut? We use them for sinkers."

"Who do you mean when you say 'we'?"

"We, the people. . . . The people who live in the village, Klimovka."

"Listen, brother, don't treat me like a fool and speak sense. You don't have to lie about a nut!"

"I haven't lied ever in my life, and here it seems I lie," muttered Denis, blinking his eyes. "But really, your honor, can one get along without a nut? If you have a minnow or a bug on the hook, how can it drop to the bottom without a sinker? They lie . . . ," Denis grinned. "Hell, you don't get any use out of a minnow that's swimming on top of the water! Perch, pike, burbot always swim on the bottom, and if any fish swim on the top only carp can catch it, and that rarely. . . . No carp live in our river. . . . This fish likes lots of room."

"Why are you telling me about carp?"

"What? You yourself asked me! Even the gentry in our village fish that way. Even the dumbest kid fishing doesn't try to get along without a sinker. Of course, if you don't understand this, you'll try to fish without a sinker. Nature's laws are not written for the stupid. . . ."

"Are you telling me you unscrewed the nut in order to use it for a sinker?"

"Of course. That and nothing more. It's not for playing bones!"

"But for a sinker you could use a piece of lead, a bullet . . . some kind of nail. . . ."

"You can't find a piece of lead on the road, you have to buy it, and a nail doesn't work. You can't find anything better than a nut. . . . It's heavy and has a hole in it."

"You're just pretending to be some kind of dummy! As if you were born yesterday, or just fell out of heaven. It can't be true that you're such a dunderhead that you don't understand what happens when you unscrew a nut on the rails? If the watchman hadn't observed this, the train could have been derailed, people would have been killed! You would have been guilty of murdering people!"

"Lord deliver me, your honor! Why do you say kill? Are we some kind of unbaptized pagans or evil people? Praise the Lord, good God, we've lived our whole life without killing anything, or even had thought of murder. Save and have mercy on me, Mother of God. . . . How can you say that!"

"And what causes train wrecks, would you say? You unscrew two or three nuts and a wreck occurs!"

Denis grins in disbelief and stares at the investigator with his eyes squinting.

"Well! For several years the whole village has been un-screwing nuts, and Lord protect us, these wrecks . . . people killed. . . . If I had taken out a rail I suppose, had put a log in the path, then, perhaps, the train would overturn, but this. . . . tpfy . . . ! A nut!"

"You know that the nuts hold the rails down to the ties!"

"We know that. . . . We don't unscrew all of them. . . . We leave some. . . . We use our heads when we take any. . . . We know what we're doing. . . ."

Denis yawns and makes the sign of the cross over his mouth.

"Last year a train left the rails," says the investigator. "Now it is understood why. . . ."

"What are you implying, please?"

"It is now apparent why the train left the tracks last year. . . . I can understand!"

"Our Lord knew what he was doing when he gave you edu-cated generous gentlemen the ability to understand. You can judge what the true situation is, but the watchman is a muzhik, who comprehends nothing, simply grabs you by the collar and drags you along. . . . You judge first and then drag! As the saying goes—a muzhik has a muzhik's brain. . . . You can also put down, your honor, that he hit me twice in the teeth and the chest."

"When they searched you, they found another nut. . . . Where did you unscrew that and when?"

"Are you talking about the nut that had lain under the red trunk?"

"I don't know where you had found it lying, only that it was found on you. Where did you unscrew it?"

"I didn't unscrew it. Ignashka, the son of one-eyed Semyon, gave it to me. As for the one under the trunk, Mitrofan and I unscrewed it from the sleighs left outside."

"Who is Mitrofan?"

"Mitrofan Petrovich. . . . Haven't you heard of him? He makes rakes and sells them to the gentry. He needs a lot of these nuts. For every rake he needs at least ten. . . ."

"Pay attention. . . . Statute 1081 dictates the penalties for deliberate destruction of the railroad which could cause the dangerous overturning of cars assuming that the guilty one knew that his action would cause disaster. . . . Do you understand? He knew! And it is impossible that you did not know what would follow your unscrewing nuts. . . . He was sentenced to hard labor in exile."

"Of course, you know better than us. . . . We're an unenlightened people who don't know the law. . . . What do we understand?"

"You understand everything! You are a liar, you are pretending ignorance!"

"Why lie? Ask in the village if you don't believe me. . . . Without sinkers you can only catch carp, and they're worse than gudgeon, which you can't even catch without sinkers."

"Tell us another carp story!" exclaims the investigator, smiling.

"We don't have carp. . . . We put out lines without sinkers to float on the water and catch butterflies. Carp are rare."

"Now, be quiet. . . ."

Silence descends. Denis waits, shifting his weight from one foot to the other, staring at the table covered with a green cloth, and squints as if he is looking at the sun and not at the cloth. The investigator writes rapidly.

"Can I leave?" asks Denis after some time elapses without anything being said.

"No. I must arrest you and send you to prison."

Denis stops squinting and raising his thick brows, questioningly looks at the official.

"How come to jail? Your honor! I can't. I have to go to the
market. I have to get three rubles for suet from Yegor. . . ."

"Be quiet, don't disturb me."

"To jail. . . . I'd go there if there was some reason for it, but
. . . I live a clean life . . . what for? I didn't steal, it seems, and
I didn't have a fight. . . . And if you think I didn't pay my taxes,
your honor, don't believe the village elder. Ask the village
council . . . the village elder is a bastard. . . ."·

"Silence!"

"I've kept my mouth shut . . . ," muttered Denis. "What
the village elder wrote down was wrong. I'll say this under oath
. . . I'm one of three brothers: Kyzma Grigorev, in this order,
Yegor Grigorev, and me, Denis Grigorev. . . ."

"You're disturbing me. . . . Hey, Semyon!" the investigator
calls out. "Take him away!"

"We're three brothers," mumbles Denis, as two strong sol-
diers take hold of him and lead him out of the chamber. "A
brother doesn't answer for his brothers' actions. . . . Kyzma
doesn't pay his taxes, and you, Denis, have to answer for it. . . .
Courts! If only the baron-general hadn't died, may he rest in
peace, he would show you judges. . . . You have to know the
facts to judge, not for nothing. . . . At least punish with lashes
according to the situation. . . ."

1885

THE WINNING
LOTTERY TICKET

Ivan Dmitrich, an average person, lived with his family on one thousand two hundred rubles per year and, very content with his circumstances, relaxed after dinner on the couch and began to read the newspaper.

"I forgot to look in the newspaper today," said his wife as she cleared the table. "Take a look and see if there's a list of lottery winners?"

"Yes, there is," answered Ivan Dmitrich. "Haven't you pawned your ticket?"

"No, on Tuesday I redeemed it."

"What's the number?"

"Serial number 9499. Ticket number 26."

Ivan Dmitrich was a skeptic about lottery luck and at another time wouldn't deem to look over the list of numbers drawn, but because he had nothing else to do at the moment, and—since he had the newspaper before him—he ran his finger down the serial numbers. And, as if precisely to ridicule his disbelief, no further than the second line from the top, the number 9499 sharply stood out. Not looking for the ticket number, not checking whether he saw correctly, he quickly dropped the paper onto his knees and, as if someone had splashed cold water on his abdomen, felt a pleasant coolness in the pit of his stomach; so ticklish, and terrible, and sweet!

"Masha, nine thousand four hundred ninety-nine is listed!" he exclaimed quietly.

His wife looked at his amazed, frightened face and realized he wasn't joking.

"Nine thousand four hundred ninety-nine?" she asked, her face growing pale, and dropping the folded cloth on the table.

"Yes, yes . . . I'm serious!"

"How about the ticket number?"

"Oh, yes! I still have to find the ticket number. However, wait . . . just a minute. But, what about it? All the same our serial number is here! All the same, do you understand? . . ."

Ivan Dmitrich, staring at his wife, had a wide, bewildered smile, like a young child who is shown a magnificent toy. For her, as for him, it was a pleasant feeling to have him read off only the serial number and not immediately to hurry to find the lucky ticket number. To be kept in suspense, to tantalize oneself with the hope of possible good fortune—that was sweet—creepy!

"We know our serial number has been selected," said Ivan Dmitrich after a long pause. "It means there is a probability that we have won. Only a probability, but it does exist!"

"Well, now take a look."

"Just wait. There's still time to be disappointed. It's on the second line from the top and this means that the amount to be won is 75,000 rubles. That's not money, that's capital! And if I look at the list right now, and there's—26! Well? Listen, what about it, if we really won?"

The couple began to laugh and looked at each other for a long time not uttering anything. The possibility of good luck overwhelmed them. They couldn't even dream of, say, what they needed 75,000 rubles for, what they could buy, where they would travel. They thought only of the numbers 9499 and 75,000; made them indelible in their imagination. Of the good luck itself, which was so imminent, they had no thought.

Ivan Dmitrich, holding the newspaper in his hands, paced

up and down the room several times, and only when he had calmed down from the first impression, began to dream a little. "What if we did win?" he said. "That would, you know, mean a new life, it would be catastrophic! It's your ticket, but if it were mine, before all else, of course, I would buy some property for about 25,000; 10,000 would go for those things you only buy once: new furniture . . . travel, pay off our debts, and so forth. The remaining 40,000 I would put in the bank and collect interest. . . ."

"I agree; property—that's good," said his wife, sitting down and dropping her hands into her lap.

"Somewhere in the Tulska or the Orlovska provinces. . . . At first, we wouldn't need a cottage, and also, however, there'd be some income."

Many scenes crowded his imagination, one after another, sweet, romantic, and in all these scenes he saw himself completely satisfied, without problems, healthy, and he felt himself become warm, even hot! He saw himself having eaten his favorite ice-cold soup, lying on his back on warm sand near his own stream, or in the garden under a lime tree. . . . It's hot. . . . His small son and daughter are crawling around nearby, digging in the sand or chasing gnats in the grass. He has sweet dreams, thinks of nothing, and with his whole being feels that he will never again have to go to work, not today, nor tomorrow, nor the day after tomorrow. When he is bored with lying around, he will go out where the mowing is going on, or to the forest for mushrooms, or even to look at the muzhiks fishing with nets. When the sun began to set, he would take a sheet, some soap, and head for the bathhouse, where he doesn't hurry to undress, gives his naked chest a good rubdown with his palms, and lies around in the water. In the water the small fish play around the clusters of soapsuds while the green water plants wave around. After bathing, tea with cream and rich cakes. . . . In the evening, a walk or playing cards with the neighbors.

"Yes, it's a good idea to buy an estate," says his wife, who is also dreaming, and by her face it is obvious that she is enthralled by her thoughts.

Ivan Dmitrich pictures for himself the fall with its rains,

with its cold nights, and with its Indian summer. This was the time to take longer walks in the flower garden, around the vegetable garden, on the banks of the river, so that one could be chilled by the brisk air, and then drink a large glass of vodka and eat a salted mushroom, or a dill pickle, and—then have another drink. The children rush in from the vegetable garden dragging carrots and radishes from which one can smell the fragrance of fresh soil. . . . After this you throw yourself down on the couch and indifferently scan an illustrated magazine, and then cover your face with it, unbutton your waistcoat, and give yourself to dreaming. . . .

When Indian summer is over—gloomy, rainy days. Rain falls day and night, the barren trees weep, and the wind is damp and cold. The dogs, the horses, the chickens—all are wet, cheerless, timid. There's no place to walk; it's impossible to get out of the house; the whole day is spent in pacing up and down and looking sadly at the cloudy windows. It's boring!

Ivan Dmitrich hesitated and looked at his wife.

"You know, Masha, I would like to travel abroad," he said.

And he began to think about how nice it would be to go abroad in the late fall, somewhere in the south of France, Italy . . . India!

"Certainly I would also like to travel abroad," said his wife. "However, take a look at the ticket number!"

"Take it easy! Wait a bit. . . ."

He walked about the room and continued to think about the possibilities. It came to his mind: What if his wife really went abroad with him? Travel alone or in the company of frivolous women without cares—one-night stands—was one thing, but traveling with those who are constantly thinking and talking only about the children, sighing, are fearful, and watch over every kopeck. Ivan Dmitrich pictured his wife in the train compartment with many baskets and bundles; she is sighing about something and complaining that she has a headache from the traveling, that too much money has been spent; that it would be necessary to rush out and get some water for tea at the station, for a sandwich or a drink of water. . . . She won't have a dinner because that would cost too much. . . .

You know she would keep account of every kopeck, he thought, glancing at his wife. It's her ticket and not mine! Why does she have to go abroad? What would she see there? She'd sit in the hotel room and wouldn't let me loose. . . . I know!

And for the first time in his life he turned his attention to the fact that his wife was aging, had gotten dull, had become permeated with the smell of the kitchen, while he was still young, healthy, virile, could marry again.

Of course, that's all nonsense and stupid, he thought, but . . . why should she go abroad? What does she understand? What if she did go? . . . I can imagine. . . . Really, whether it's Naples or Klin—it's all the same. She'd just mess things up for me. I would even be dependent upon her. I can imagine, as soon as she'd get the money, like a female, she'd immediately put it under lock and key. She'd hide it from me. She'd be generous with her relatives, but she'd add up every kopeck she gave me.

Ivan Dmitrich thought about this family. All the brothers sisters, aunts, uncles would come by when they heard of the winnings, would begin to pay homage, sweetly smile, be hypocritical. Such repulsive, wretched people! Give them something, and they'll beg for more; and if you refuse them—they'll curse you, spread scandal, wish you all kinds of misfortune.

Ivan Dmitrich thought of his relatives. Their faces upon which he had looked indifferently in the past now appeared repulsive to him—hateful.

They're such curs! he thought.

And his wife's face also seemed repulsive, hateful. In his heart anger boiled over against her and, gloating, he thought:

No point in thinking about the money because she's stingy. If she won, she'd only give me about a hundred rubles, and the rest—under lock and key.

He was already looking at his wife not with a smile, but with hate. She also was looking at him with hate and anger. She had had her optimistic dreams, her plans, her considerations; she understood perfectly what her husband was dreaming about. She knew who would be first to put his paw on her winnings.

It's nice to dream while someone else pays! said her eyes. No, you wouldn't dare!

Her husband understood her look: hate filled his heart, and in order to annoy his wife, spitefully, he quickly took a look at the fourth page of the paper and declared solemnly: "Serial number 9499, ticket number 46! Not 26!"

Hope and hate both disappeared at once, and at the same time it seemed to Ivan Dmitrich and his wife that their home was dark, small, and the ceiling too low; that their dinner, which they had eaten, was not satisfying, but only weighed down the stomach; and that the evening was long and tedious.

"Why the hell," said Ivan Dmitrich, beginning to carp, "no matter where you walk, there's trash underfoot, crumbs, some kind of shells. The rooms are never swept clean! The time will come when I'll leave, the devil will take me for good. I'll go and hang myself on the first aspen I meet."

1887

THE CARD GAME

On one ugly fall night Andrei Stepanovich Peresolin* was being driven home from the theater. He was deep in thought about the effect of morality plays if they were performed in the theaters. As they were passing the government building, he cast this thought aside, and looked at the windows of the building in which he, as expressed by poets and barge-shippers, was the captain at the helm. Two windows in the watchman's room were brightly lit.

Are they really involved in honest work at this time? thought Peresolin. There are four idiots employed there and they still aren't finished! I don't care that people will think that I won't even leave them alone at night. I'm going to speed them up. . . .

"Stop, Gyri!" he ordered the coachman.

Peresolin got out of his carriage and went inside the government building. The front door was locked, but the rear entrance, which had only one worn-out bolt, was wide-open. Peresolin entered the back door and in a few minutes was

---

*"Overreactor"

standing in the doorway of the watchman's room. Peresolin looked in the slightly open door and saw something unusual. By the light of two lamps, sitting at the table, which was strewn with large sheets of accounting paper, sat four clerks playing cards. With intensely concentrated, immobile faces, colored by the green light from the lampshades, they resembled gnomes from fairy tales or, God preserve us from such, counterfeiters. . . . The game gave them an even more inscrutable appearance. Judging from their manners and the card terms which they at times called out, they were playing the game of vint. However, from all that Peresolin heard, this game could not be called vint, or even a game of cards. It was something unheard of, stranger, and secretive. . . . Peresolin recognized the clerks Serafin Zvizdulin, Stepan Kulakevich, Yeremay Nedoyekov, and Ivan Pisulin.*

"Why did you lead that, you Dutch devil," exclaimed the angry Zvizdulin, making enraged eye contact with his partner. "How can that be? I had in my hand two Dorofeyev, Shepelev and his wife, and Stepka Yerlakov, and you lead a Kofeykin. We don't even have two! You, you cabbagehead, you should have led a Pogankin!"

"Well, and what would come of that?" snapped his partner. "I could have led with Pogankin, but in my hands was Ivan Andreyich Peresolin."

They've dragged in my name . . . , thought Peresolin, shrugging his shoulders. I'm baffled!

Pisulin dealt again, and the clerks continued:

"State bank. . . ."

"Double—Treasury Department. . . ."

"No trump. . . ."

"You have no trump? Hm! . . . Provincial Government—double. . . . To lose, so to lose, take it fool! I don't have a single Provincial Government left, so Public Education will get into trouble. I don't give a damn!"

"A small slam with Public Education!"

---

*Chekhov's cardplayers are "Noisemaker," "Feisty," "Undernourished," and "Squeaker."

"I don't get it!" whispered Peresolin.

"I lead with the State Councillor. . . . Vanya, drop a titled or a provincial."

"What do we need a titled one for? We'll get it with a Peresolin. . . ."

"We'll take your Peresolin by the teeth . . . we'll bite. . . . We have Ribnikov. You'll lose three tricks! Show your Madame Peresolin! She's no good to you, you rascal, hiding her in your cuff!"

They've brought my wife in . . . , mused Peresolin. What's it all about?

So, not wanting to be in the dark any longer, Peresolin opened the door and entered the guard room. If the devil himself with horns and a tail had appeared before the men, he would not have surprised or frightened them as much as the sight of their supervisor. If the executive who had died the year before appeared before them and addressed them in a loud voice, "Follow me, angels, to the place prepared for rascals," and blew his breath on them from his cold grave, they wouldn't have grown as pale as when they recognized Peresolin. Nedoyekov's nose began to bleed from fright; Kulakevich heard ringing in his right ear and had to loosen his tie. The clerks threw down their cards, stood up slowly, and, exchanging looks, all stared upon the floor. Silence reigned in the watchman's room. . . .

"You're recording the day's events in a fine way!" began Peresolin. "Now it's understandable why you seemed to like writing reports. . . . What are you doing?"

"Sir, we've only been taking a minute off," quietly answered Zvizdulin. "We were looking over the little cards. . . . Relaxing. . . ."

Peresolin walked over to the table and slowly shrugged his shoulders. There were no playing cards on the table, but ordinary photos, cut out from cardboard and pasted on playing cards. There were a great many of them. Looking them over, Peresolin recognized himself, his wife, many of his subordinates, acquaintances. . . .

"What nonsense. . . . What kind of game are you playing?"

"We didn't make it up, sir. . . . Lord preserve us. . . . We only copied. . . ."

"Zvizdulin, enlighten me! How is this game played? I saw and heard everything, how you beat me with Ribnikov. . . . Well, why are you hesitating? I'm not going to eat you! Tell me what it's all about!"

Zvizdulin held back for some time, having cold feet. Finally, when Peresolin began to get angry, snorting and flushing from impatience, he obeyed. Gathering the cards and shuffling them, he laid them out on the table and explained:

"Every picture, sir, and every card has a point to it. . . . has a meaning. As in the usual deck, there are fifty-two cards and four suits. The bureaucrats of the Treasury Department—are hearts; Provincial Administrators—are clubs; the members of the National Ministry of Education—are diamonds; the members of the State Bank are spades. So . . . the actual State Councillors are aces, the lower-level councillors are kings, the wives of those of the fourth and fifth rank are queens, colleagues of the councillors are jacks, those of the eighth rank are tens, and so on down the line. I, for example—here's my card—am a three, since I'm only a Provincial Secretary. . . ."

"You don't say. . . . I'm, as it were, an ace?"

"An ace of clubs, and her excellency—is the queen. . . ."

"Hm. . . . That's original. . . . So, let's play! I'll see what it's all about. . . ."

Peresolin took off his overcoat and, smiling warily, sat down at the table. The clerks also sat down as he had ordered and the game began . . .

When Nazar, the watchman, came into his room at seven o'clock in the morning, he was startled. The scene that met him, as he entered holding a broom to sweep it out, was so striking that he can't forget it even when he's dead drunk. Peresolin, pale, sleepy, and disheveled, stood before Nedoyekov, whom he had buttonholed, and was saying:

"You'd better understand that you wouldn't lead a Shepelev if you knew that in my hand I had myself and three others. Zvizdulin had Ribnikov and his wife, three high school teachers, and his wife. Nedoyekov had to have State Bank people and three small Provincial Government administrators. You should have led Krishkin! It doesn't matter that the Treasury was led! They're slick!"

"I, sir, led with a titular, because I thought that they had an Actual Councillor."

"Ah, dear fellow, that's not the way to figure it! That's no way to play! Only crude shoemakers play that way. Think about it! . . . When Kulakevich led with a low-level provincial bureaucrat you should have dropped Ivan Ivanovich Grenlandski, because you knew that he had Natalia Dmitrieva with two others of the same suit, with Yegor Yegorich, too. . . . You ruined everything! I'll show you right away. Sit down, gentlemen, let's play one more rubber!"

And, dismissing the startled Nazar, the bureaucrats sat down and resumed the game.

1884

AN ABOMINABLE IRONY

Grigory Ivanovich Ovchinnikov, the district physician, was a man about thirty-five years old. He was lean and sensitive, known to his colleagues for his collecting of medical statistics and intense involvement in what were known as "current problems." He was making his morning rounds in the hospital ward and, as usual, his assistant, Mihail Zaharovich, walked behind him. The assistant was an elderly man with a swollen face, greasy flat hair, and wearing an earring.

The doctor had hardly begun his rounds when he was annoyed by a frivolous circumstance that appeared very suspicious to him, namely, the assistant's vest kept puffing out in folds and sticking straight up despite the assistant's attempts to press it down and straighten it out. His shirt was wrinkled and it, too, was puffing out; his long black frock coat, his trousers, and even his tie had white fuzz on them here and there. . . . It was obvious that the assistant had slept in his clothes, and, judging from his appearance and his efforts to pull down his vest and straighten his tie, that the clothing was making him uncomfortable.

The physician gave him a good once-over and understood what was the matter. The assistant was not unsteady, answered

188

questions correctly, but his dull and morose face, his vacant eyes, the quivering of his neck and the tremor of his hands, his disorderly clothing, and, most important, the effort to exert control over himself and to cover up his condition, indicated that he had just gotten out of bed, had not had enough sleep, and had been drunk, dead drunk, the day before. . . . He was having a bad case of "the morning after," was suffering, and apparently was very disgruntled with himself.

The doctor did not like the assistant and for reasons of his own felt a strong desire to say to him: "I see that you're drunk!" He found the vest, the frock coat, the earring in his large ear offensive, but he restrained himself and asked in his usual soft and courteous voice:

"Has Gerasim been given milk?"

"He has been given it, sir . . . ," answered Mihail Zaharich also in a soft voice.

After speaking to Gerasim, the patient, the doctor looked at his chart to see what his temperature was, and reacted with another rush of antipathy, restrained himself in order to speak civilly, but did not succeed and asked rudely and brusquely:

"Why hasn't his temperature been recorded?"

"Not recorded, sir!" softly remarked Mihail Zaharich, looking at the chart, and when convinced that the temperature had not been recorded, he shrugged his shoulders in bewilderment and muttered: "I don't know how that happened, sir. It must be that Nadezhda Osipovna . . ."

"Last night's wasn't recorded either!" continued the doctor. "All you do is drink, the devil with you! You're drunk now, too, dead drunk! Where's Nadezhda Osipovna?"

The midwife, Nadezhda Osipovna, was not around although it was one of her duties to be present every morning to change bandages. The doctor looked around and found that the ward had not been cleaned up, that everything was scattered around, nothing that needed to be done was done. It was the same everywhere—messy, mussed, covered with fuzz like the aggravating vest of the assistant. He had the desire to pull off his white uniform, scream, give it all up, spit, and leave. But he controlled himself and continued the rounds.

The patient Gerasim was followed by a surgical patient with an inflammation of the cellular tissue over his whole right arm. It needed a new dressing. The doctor sat down on the stool before the patient and became involved in examining the arm.

They went to a name-day party yesterday, he thought, slowly taking off the bandage. Just wait, I'll give you a name-day party! On the other hand, what can I do? I can't do anything.

He felt about the swollen, inflamed, ulcerated arm and exclaimed:

"Scalpel!"

Mihail Zaharich, trying to show that he was standing on steady legs and able to do his job, pulled himself together and quickly handed him a scalpel.

"Not that one! Give me one of the new ones," remarked the doctor.

The assistant minced toward the stand upon which stood a container with bandages and began to quickly rummage in it. He whispered about something with the nurses, moved the container on the stand, rattled something around, dropped something, and the doctor sat, waiting, and felt his back bristling from the whispering and rattling.

"Why so slow?" he asked. "It must be that you've left it downstairs. . . ."

The assistant hurried toward him and handed him two scalpels, but in the process unguardedly breathed in the doctor's direction.

"Not these!" spat out the disgruntled doctor. "I told you in plain Russian, hand me one of the new ones. It would be better if you'd move away and sober up. You smell like a saloon! You're irresponsible!"

"What kind of knife do you still need?" asked the shook-up assistant, slowly shrugging his shoulders.

He was vexed with himself and ashamed that the patients and nurses were staring at him, so in order not to appear guilty, he forced a laugh and repeated:

"What kind of knife do you still need?"

The doctor felt tears in his eyes and shaking fingers. He controlled himself and repeated in a quivering voice:

"Go sober up! I don't want to talk to a drunk. . . ."

"You can only order me out for dereliction of duty," continued the assistant, "and if I, let us assume, have a drink, no one has the right to deny me this. Ain't I here to serve you? What else do you want! Ain't I here to serve you?"

The doctor jumped up and, giving no thought to what he was doing, swung with all his strength and punched the assistant in the face. He did not do this with forethought but felt great satisfaction from it: That his fist hit the mark, and that a person who was a God-fearing pillar of society, a self-respecting family man, could have lurched, bounced up like a ball, and done this. He sat down on the stool. He had a powerful urge to hit him once more, but, seeing the disturbed faces of the nurses surrounding the disgusting face of the assistant, he ceased feeling satisfied, waved his hand, and left the ward.

On the outside, entering the hospital, he met Nadezhda Osipovna, an unmarried woman of about twenty-seven, with a pale, jaundiced face and loose, flowing hair. Her pink cotton skirt was very narrow at the bottom so that her steps were small and quick. Her skirt rustled, her shoulders twitched with every step, and her head moved as if she were humming a tune reflecting happy thoughts.

What a nymph! thought the doctor, recalling that in the hospital they teased the midwife, calling her a nymph, and he felt better for the thought. He then cut short this small-stepping, self-confident, smart woman.

"Where have you been?" he shouted upon approaching her. "Why aren't you in the hospital? Temperatures have not been recorded, everything is a mess, the assistant is drunk, and you've slept until twelve o'clock! . . . Please find yourself another position! You're no longer needed here!"

Arriving at his apartment, the doctor pulled off his white hospital coat and the towel which he had used as a belt, threw them angrily into a corner, and stomped around the room.

"God, what people, what people!" he muttered. "They're not assistants but obstacles blocking my work! I haven't the strength to go on! I can't! I quit!"

His heart was beating rapidly, he was trembling and wanted

to cry. In order to relieve himself of these sensations, he calmed himself with self-righteous thoughts and justifications of his actions, especially the punching of the assistant. The worst thing, he thought, was that the assistant was given the job in the hospital not on his merits as the others, but through the intercession of his aunt, who was the nanny in the house of the chairman from the district council. (It irked him to look at this influential aunt when she came to the hospital for medical care and pulled rank as if she were in her own home, demanding attention out of turn.) The assistant was poorly prepared, knew very little, and had absolutely no understanding that he knew very little. He was rarely sober, impertinent, slovenly, took bribes from the patients, and secretly sold the district's medicines. Everyone knew he had a practice on the side, and covertly treated the diseases contracted by the young landowners when they needed some kind of special medication. It might have been tolerable if he were an ordinary charlatan, there were many of these, but this charlatan thinks he knows it all and in secret operates accordingly. Without the doctor's knowledge he would bleed patients with leeches, would present himself at operations with unscrubbed hands, poked into wounds with an unsterile probe—this in itself was enough to recognize how deeply and maliciously he despised the doctor's medical procedures with their scientific basis and pedantry.

Waiting until his fingers had stopped trembling, the doctor sat down at his desk and wrote a letter to the chairman of the council: "Most respected Lev Trofimovich! If when you receive this your council does not dismiss the assistant, Smirnovski, and does not give me the right to select my assistant, then I will feel obliged to leave (not without regret, of course), and beg you no longer to consider me the doctor of N—— Hospital, and will attend to finding someone to take my place. Regards to Lyubova Fedorovna and Yus. Respectfully, G. Ovchinnikov." Rereading this letter, he found that it was too brief and not cold enough. The regards to Lyubova Fedorovna and Yus (the name they used to tease the younger son of the chairman) in an official business letter was, at the least, inappropriate.

Why the hell include Yus? the doctor thought, tore up the letter, and began to plan another.

Dear Sir . . . , he thought, sitting down by the open window and looking at a duck with ducklings, which, waddling and stumbling, were hurrying along the road bound for the pond. One of the ducklings picked up some kind of gut, moved on, and let out a sorrowful shriek. A second one ran to him, pulled out the piece of gut, and they moved on. . . . At a distance in the surrounding shade along the fence where young linden trees were sprouting on the grass, Darya, the cook, wandered and was picking up sorrel for a green soup. . . . Voices could be heard. . . . The driver, Zot, with a bridle in his hand, and the muzhik, Manuilo, a hospital orderly who had a dirty apron, were standing near the barn talking and laughing about something.

They must be talking about how I socked the assistant . . . , thought the doctor. Today everyone in the district will hear about my scandalous behavior. . . . And so: "Dear Sir! If your council will not dismiss . . ."

The doctor knew very well that the council would not under any circumstances exchange a doctor for an assistant, and would quickly agree not to have a single assistant in the whole district than to lose such an excellent man as Doctor Ovchinnikov. It was probable that as soon as Lev Trofimovich received the letter he would trot over to him in his troika and begin with: "What have you dreamed up, old chap? Jesus Christ, dear fellow, what big deal is this? What for? What's the matter? Where is he? Bring him here, the rascal! We'll get rid of him! He must be dismissed! Another day shouldn't go by with this rascal around!" He would then dine with the doctor, and after dinner would flop down on his back on the crimson couch, close his eyes, and snore. After a good nap he would have his fill of tea, and insist that the doctor spend the night at his home. The whole story would end with the assistant remaining in the hospital, and the doctor would not resign.

Deep in his heart the doctor really did not want such an outcome. What he wanted was to have the assistant's aunt be triumphant and that the council, regardless of his courteous service for the last eight years, would accept his resignation without discussion and even with some satisfaction. He thought over about how he would leave the hospital, to which he was accustomed, how he would write a letter to the newspaper "Doctor," and how his colleagues would be sympathetic. . . .

The nymph appeared on the road. Walking with small steps and her skirt rustling, she came up to the window and asked him:

"Grigory Ivanich, are you going to attend to the patients yourself, or will you simply give orders?"

But her eyes said: "You were burned up, and now that you've calmed down, you're ashamed, but I'm tactful and won't take notice of that."

"Thanks, I'll be there presently," said the doctor.

He again put on his white coat, tied the towel around his waist, and went to the hospital.

It wasn't right to leave after I hit him . . . , he thought on the way. As it turned out, it was as if I were disconcerted or frightened . . . a schoolboy's trick. . . . It's awful!

It seemed to him that as he entered the ward the patients would be uncomfortable in his presence, and he himself would feel guilty, but when he did go in the patients were lying peacefully on the beds and hardly noticed him. The face of the tubercular Gerasim expressed perfect indifference as if to say: "He was making you trouble and you gave him a little lesson. . . . Without that, old man, it became impossible."

The doctor lanced two abscesses on the crimson arm and bandaged it, then went to the women's section where he operated on the eyes of a peasant woman. The nymph followed him throughout and helped him just as if nothing had happened and everything was as it should be. After he made the rounds of the wards, he began to receive the outpatients. In the small admissions office the window was wide open. One only had to sit on the sill and lean over a little in order to see the new grass about two feet away. The night before there had been a powerful thunderstorm, so the grass was a little crushed and glossy. The path, which led to the ravine and was not far from the window, seemed scrubbed. The apothecary dishes dug in around its edges also appeared scrubbed, playing in the sun and forming dazzling bright beams. Beyond the path young fir trees pressed close together dressed in elegant green wraps, and behind them stood birches with their paper-white trunks, and the endless blue sky could be seen through the slight fluttering of the green leaves caused by the wind. When you glanced out the window, the starlings hopping on the path turned their stupid beaks toward the window as if trying to decide: are we to be frightened or not? And, deciding to be frightened, one after another with a merry shriek flew up to the highest branches of the birches, as if making fun of the doctor who could not fly. . . .

Penetrating the strong smell of iodine, the freshness and aroma of the spring day could be felt. . . . It was wonderful to breathe! "Anna Spirdonova!" the doctor called out.

A young peasant woman wearing a red dress entered the reception room and stopped to say a short prayer before the icon.

"What hurts you?" asked the doctor.

With a suspicious look at the door through which she had entered and at the door leading to the pharmacy, she moved closer to the doctor and whispered:

"I haven't any children!"

"Who hasn't signed up yet?" called out the nymph from the apothecary. "Come over here and sign up!"

He's already using it, the brute, thought the doctor while examining the woman. He forced me to fight for the first time in my life. Never in my born days have I fought.

Anna Spirdonova left. After she left came an old man with a serious ailment, then a peasant woman with three mangy children, and the work piled up. The assistant didn't show up. Behind the door to the apothecary the nymph gaily chattered, her clothes rustled, and the utensils tinkled. She did everything the same way: this job, or if she walked into the receiving room in order to help during an operation, or to pick up prescriptions—as if everything was as it should be.

Upon hearing the voice of the midwife, he thought, She's glad that I socked the assistant. She and the assistant have gotten along like a cat with a dog, and she'll celebrate if they dismiss him. And the nurse is probably glad, too. . . . What a nuisance!

The receiving room was in full swing and it appeared to him that the midwife and the nurses, and even the patients, were deliberately trying to appear indifferent. It was as if they understood that he was ashamed and distressed, but from sensitivity did not show that they knew anything. He, on the other hand, wanting to show that he was not ashamed, called out angrily:

"You, over there! Close the door, there's a draft!"

But he was ashamed and felt wretched. After seeing forty-five patients, he was slow to leave the hospital. The midwife, on the other hand, was hurrying to leave for her apartment where, no doubt, she would put on a bright red kerchief, a cigarette between her lips, and a flower in her loose, flowing hair. She was rushing somewhere out of the courtyard either to a case or to visit someone. The starlings, as before, were making a racket and chasing after beetles. The doctor looked around and thought that among all these levelheaded, unruffled lives, like two defective keys of the piano that were singled out as not suitable, there were two lives: the assistant's and his. The assistant, no doubt, was in bed in order to sleep it off, but no way could he sleep away the thought that he was guilty, that he had been abused, and had been dismissed from his job. His situation was anxiety-ridden. The doctor himself had never before socked anyone, and felt as if he had lost his innocence forever. He no longer blamed the assistant and justified himself, but only was perplexed: how could this have happened, that he, a decorous person, never even having struck a dog, had hit him? Arriving at his apartment, he lay down on the couch in his study and, turning to its back, began to ruminate in this manner:

He's a bad person, unsuitable for this work; for the three years he's been working here, I've been stewing about it, but that does not excuse my action—which in no way can be justified. I took advantage of the privilege of the strong. He's my subordinate, he was guilty because he was drunk, but I'm his supervisor, and am correct and sober. . . . This in itself declares me stronger. Also, I hit him in public, a public which considers me an authority, and in this way gave them an abominable example. . . .

The doctor was called to his dinner. . . . He ate a few spoonfuls of cabbage soup and, getting up from the table, once more lay down on the couch.

What's to be done now? he continued to muse. One must give him satisfaction as soon as possible. . . . But in what way? As a pragmatic person he will consider a duel stupid, or he doesn't understand what a duel means. Suppose I apologize to him in the same ward where I hit him before the nurses and patients, the apology would satisfy only me, but not him. He's a stupid man and would take my apology as cowardice and fear, and would complain about me to the authorities. At the same time, my apology would put an end to hospital discipline. Offer him money? No, that would be immoral and resemble bribery. Suppose that I now turn the decision over to our immediate authority, that is, our board. . . . They could reprimand or dismiss me. . . . However, they won't do that, and they'll not be at ease involving themselves in the internal matters of the hospital which, incidentally, they have no right to do. . . .

About three hours after dinner, the doctor walked to the pond to bathe and thought:

Why shouldn't I be able to behave like others do in similar circumstances? He can take me to court. It goes without saying I'm guilty. I won't be able to justify myself and the justice of the peace can arrest me. The victim is given satisfaction in this way, and those who consider themselves authorities will see that I am in the wrong.

This idea made him smile. He felt happier and began to think that the question was settled in an amicable way, and a more just way could not be.

That's it, excellent! he thought, while lying in the water and observing how a school of small gold carp scurried away from him. . . . Even though I'm charged. . . . This would be more satisfactory for him. Our working relationship is already damaged and after this scandalous affair one of us will find it impossible to remain in the hospital . . .

In the evening he ordered that his carriage be harnessed so that he could go to an army officer's to play cards. As he stood in the center of his study with his hat and coat on and pulling on his gloves, the front door creaked open, and someone entered noiselessly into the foyer.

"Who's there?" called out the doctor.

"It's me, sir . . . ," the enterer answered softly.

The doctor's heart stood still and he really felt a chill from shame and an incomprehensible fear. The assistant, Mihail Zaharich (for it was he), coughed quietly and timorously entered the study. Remaining silent for a few moments, he then spoke in a flat, apologetic voice:

"Forgive me, Grigory Ivanich!"

The doctor was taken aback and did not know what to say. He understood that the assistant had come to grovel and beg forgiveness not from Christian humility and not, in spite of that, in order to crush his abuser, but simply from the calculation: "I'll restrain myself, apologize, and on the off chance, I won't be dismissed and be deprived of earning a living. . . ." What could be more demeaning to a human being's dignity?

"Forgive me . . . ," repeated the assistant.

"Look here . . . ," said the doctor, trying not to meet his eyes, and not yet knowing what to say. "Look here. . . . I offended you and . . . and I must bear the responsibility for my action . . . that is, to give you satisfaction. . . . You don't know anything about duels. . . . In any case, I don't want to duel with you. I offended you and you . . . you can take me to court and complain. . . . But we both cannot remain working in the hospital. . . . One of us, you or I, must leave!" (Dear God! Am I saying this! thought the horrified doctor. How idiotic, how idiotic!) "Briefly, submit a petition. Whatever happens we cannot continue to work together! . . . It's either you or I. . . . Tomorrow you must go to court!"

The assistant looked up at the doctor and from his dark, sullen eyes flashed frank contempt. He had always considered the doctor impractical, a whimsical youth, and now scorned him for his unsteadiness, for his incomprehensible choice of words. . . .

"I'll go to court," he said in a sullen and malicious tone.

"That's right. Take me to court!"

"What do you think? Do you think I won't do it? I'll go to court. . . . You had no right to strike me. You should be ashamed! Only drunken peasants use their fists, and you're educated. . . ."

All of the doctor's detestation for this man arose unexpectedly in his breast, and in a strange voice he declared: "Get out of here!"

The assistant hesitatingly moved (it was as if he wanted to say more), then went into the foyer where he stopped to think something over. Having thought it over, he resolutely left. . . .

"How stupid, how stupid!" grumbled the doctor after the assistant left. "How stupid and vulgar!"

He felt that he had conducted himself like an inexperienced youth, and he now realized that his suggestion to go to court was not very smart and would not settle the question but only complicate it.

How stupid! he thought while sitting in the carriage and later when playing cards at the army administrator's house. Is it true that my education is so deficient, and I know so little about life that I can't solve this simple problem? Well now, what's to be done?

The next morning the doctor saw how the wife of the assistant sat in a carriage as if ready to go somewhere, and he thought: She's going to the aunt. Let her go!

The hospital got along without the assistant. A report to the board had to be written, but the doctor could not think of how it should be written. He was now thinking of saying in the letter: "I ask you to dismiss the assistant, even though he is innocent and I'm the guilty one." He wanted to put it this way so that it would not sound stupid or deplorable. A respectable person could do nothing else.

Within several days the doctor was informed that the assistant had gone to Lev Trofimovich. The chairman hadn't permitted the assistant to say a word but had stamped his feet and sent him away, shouting: "I know you! Get out! I don't want to listen to anything you have to say!" From Lev Trofimovich the assistant went to the board and there gave a slanderous statement in which he did not mention what had gone on and did not ask for anything for himself. He informed the board that the doctor had several times made malicious remarks about the board in his presence, that he didn't do his work, had an illegal private practice, and so forth. Hearing of this, the doctor laughed and thought: What a fool! but he did feel a pang of conscience and regret that the assistant was behaving foolishly. The more defenseless and weak one was, the greater the folly that such a person commits in his defense!

Exactly a week after the slanderous statement, the doctor received a summons from the district court.

This is really stupid . . . , he thought as he signed the receipt. You can't imagine anything more stupid.

On the dismal, quiet morning when he was to go to court, he was no longer ashamed, but vexed and irritated. He was angry with himself and with the assistant, and with the situation. . . .

"I'm going to go ahead and say to the court: 'All of you go to hell! You're all asses and know-nothings!' " he fumed.

Approaching the court chambers, he saw on the threshold three of his nurses who had been subpoenaed as witnesses, and the nymph. Upon seeing the nurses and the lively midwife, who impatiently shifted from one foot to the other when she saw the main character of the forthcoming procedure, and even brightened with pleasure, the angry doctor had the urge to descend upon them, attack, and stun with: "Who permitted you to leave the hospital? Please, get yourselves back there this minute!" but restrained himself and, trying to appear calm, pushed through the crowd of muzhiks to the chamber. The chamber was empty, and the judge's watch chain hung on the back of the armchair. The doctor went into the court recorder's room. There he saw a young man with an emaciated face, in a Kolemenski jacket with bulging pockets—it was the court recorder. The assistant was sitting at the table and, not having anything else to do, was leafing through the court's inquiries. The court recorder rose when the doctor entered; the assistant was disconcerted and also rose.

"Has Alexander Arkipovich arrived?" asked the embarrassed doctor.

"Not yet. He's still at home," answered the court reporter.

The chamber was in one of the cottages of the district judge's country estate and the judge himself lived in the big house. The doctor left the chamber and headed for the house. Alexander Arkipovich was standing by the samovar in the dining room. He had no vest or jacket on, and his shirt was unbuttoned. Holding a teapot with both hands, he was pouring himself a glass of tea that was as dark as coffee. Upon seeing his guest, he quickly got another glass and filled it and without a word of greeting asked:

"With or without sugar?"

He had served in the cavalry long ago. He had already chosen to serve for many years as an active State Councillor but had not thrown out his army uniform or his army habits. He had a long mustache such as worn by the chief of police, trousers with cuffs, and all his actions and words were in the style of the military. When he spoke, he threw back his head a little, and garnished his words with a juicy, general-like "Mneheheh . . . ," moved his shoulders, and used his eyes expressively. When he greeted anyone or offered a cigarette, he shuffled the soles of his feet, and walked carefully so that his spurs would only jingle softly, as if every sound made by his spurs was unbearably painful. Offering a chair by the tea to the doctor, he looked at his large chest and at his stomach, gave a deep sigh, and said:

"Nn. Yes-s. . . . Maybe I should offer you some mneheh . . . vodka and a snack? Mne-eh?"

"No thanks, I'm full."

They both knew that they couldn't avoid talking about the hospital scandal, and it was awkward for both. The doctor remained silent. The judge, with a graceful movement of his hand, caught a mosquito which had bitten his chest, attentively looked it over on all sides, and then let it go. He then sighed deeply, raised his eyes at the doctor, and asked in a measured tone:

"Listen, why don't you sack him?"

The doctor caught a sympathetic note in his voice; instantly he was sorry for himself and felt worn out and broken up from the fracas and the last week's emotional excesses. He rose from the table with the exasperated look of someone who had reached the end of his patience, and, frowning irritably, shrugged his shoulders and replied:

"Sack him! By God, that's how you'd settle it. . . . It's

amazing how you figure everything! Is it possible for me to sack him? You sit here and think that I'm the boss in the hospital and do whatever I please! Amazing how you settle everything! Can I sack the assistant when his aunt is the nanny at Lev Trofimich's, and if Lev Trofimich needs such informers and lackeys like this Zaharich? What can I do if the council places us, the doctors, without a safety net, and, at every step a stumbling block? The hell with them, I'm quitting and that's that! I'm through!"

"Now, now, now. . . . You, my dear fellow, attach too much importance to this, so to speak . . ."

"The chief tries in every way to declare all of us nihilists, spies on us, and slights us as if we were his clerks. Where does he get the right to come to the hospital in my absence and question the nurses and patients? Isn't that insulting? And this crackpot of yours, Semyon Aleksyeich, who only messes around and does not believe in medical treatment, because he is healthy and fit like a bull, publicly and to our faces calls us freeloaders and begrudges us a piece of bread! The hell with him! I work from morning till night, no rest, I'm more needed here than all these crackpots, the holy men, the reformers, and other clowns put together! I've lost my health on the job, and instead of thanking me, begrudge me a piece of bread! I humbly thank you! And everyone considers it his right to poke his nose in what is none of his business, in order to instruct and control! That member of your board, Kamchatski, at a meeting of the District Council gave the doctors a dressing-down because the hospitals throw out too much potassium iodide, and he recommended that we be more prudent in prescribing cocaine! What does he understand, I ask you? What business is it of his? Why doesn't he teach you how to make decisions?"

"But . . . but you know, my dear man, he's a boor and a groveler. . . . You shouldn't pay any attention to him. . . ."

"He may be a cad and a toady, however, you've selected this windbag for the board, and allow him to poke his nose in everything! You're smiling! In your opinion all this is trivia, foolishness, but all the same these trifles are many and complicate life, just as a grain of sand can develop into a mountain! I can't take it anymore! I just don't have the strength, Alexander Arkipich! It won't be long before, believe me, I won't just sock mugs, but will begin to shoot people! You must understand that it's not just provocation, but the nervous system. I'm a human being the same as yourself. . . ."

The doctor's eyes had become full of tears and his voice shook. He turned around and stood facing the window. Silence filled the air.

"Hm—yes-s, you're the most esteemed . . . ," mumbled the judge, apparently meditating. "On the other hand, if one adjudicates in cold blood, then . . . (the judge caught a mosquito and, intensely screwing his eyes, squeezed it and threw it in the wastebasket) then, you can see, there is no reason to get rid of him. You get rid of him and in his place you'll get another just like him, or I'm sorry to say, still worse. Take a hundred different men and you won't find a good one. . . . They're all scoundrels. (The judge smoothed his sleeves under his arms and slowly lit a cigarette.) It's necessary to get along with this kind of rot. I must tell you that, currently, honest and sober workers upon whom one can depend can only be found at the extremes of society, among the intelligentsia and the muzhiks—and only there. It can be said that you can find an honest doctor, a superior pedagogue, an upright ploughman or a blacksmith, but the average individual, if you want to express it in this way, those who are part of the general population who have not become intellectuals, make up a hopeless group! For this reason it is exceedingly difficult to find an honest and sober assistant, a clerk, a salesman, and so forth. Exceedingly difficult! I served in the Justice Department during the time of this tsar, and in the whole period of my service I didn't once have an honest and sober clerk, even though I dismissed them in my time in huge numbers. Most people have no moral discipline, and I'm not talking now of principles, so to speak. . . ."

Why is he saying this? thought the doctor. We aren't talking about what needs to be talked about.

"In fact, as recently as last Friday," continued the judge, "my Dyuzhinski, you can picture this for yourself, pulled just such a trick. He invited some drunks in the evening, who the

hell knows from where, and they caroused all night in the
chambers. How do you like that? I don't have anything against
drinking. Go to hell, drink, but why bring strangers into the
chambers? Really, judge for yourself, to steal legal documents,
to take notes, and the like—takes only a minute to do! And
what do you think of this? After the orgy I had to check everything for two days to see if anything was missing. . . . Well,
what do you do with a vulture? Dismiss him? Okay. . . . But
how do you guarantee the next one won't be worse?"

"All right, but how dismiss him?" remarked the doctor. "It's
easy to dismiss someone with talk. . . . How do you dismiss him
and deprive him of his piece of bread, if you know that he has
a family, that he's hungry? Where will he and his family go?"

What the devil am I saying, thought the doctor, and it
seemed strange to him that he could in no way consolidate his
concentration on a single, definite thought or on some kind of
feeling. It's because I'm shallow and don't know how to think
about anything.

"The average person, as you've described him, is hopeless,"
he continued. "We turn him out, curse him, beat his body, but
it really is necessary to put ourselves in his place. He is neither
a muzhik nor a gentleman, neither fish nor meat. His past is
bitter, and presently he has only twenty-five rubles a month, a
hungry family, and is under someone's commands. In the future
he will also only have the same twenty-five rubles and a dependent existence, even if he served for a hundred years. He is uneducated, has no property, he never reads or goes to church, he
doesn't hear us because we never permit him close to us. He
lives from day to day in his way without hope of anything
better, eats sparingly, fears that he is just about to be evicted
from his assigned one-room apartment and doesn't know where
he will put his children. So, in this situation, tell me, why not
drink, steal? Where do you apply principles in this case!"

It seems to me that we're deciding social problems, he
thought. Lord, how awkward! Why all this?

Bells were heard. Someone had entered the courtyard and
had at first stopped at the chambers and then at the entrance
to the main house.

"The chairman himself has come," said the judge, looking out the window. "Well, you're in for it!"

"Let's get it over quickly, please . . . ," requested the doctor. "If it's possible, give my case precedence. Really, I don't have time."

"Fine, fine. . . . Only I still don't know, old man, if this falls under my jurisdiction. Your relations with your assistant, one can say, are on the job and you smeared him while performing your duties. However, I'm uncertain. I'll have to ask Lev Trofimovich."

They could hear hasty footsteps and heavy breathing and Lev Trofimovich, a gray and bald old man with a long beard and red eyelids, appeared in the doorway.

"My compliments . . . ," he said, taking a deep breath. "Phew, my dear fellows! Judge, order some kvass for me. I'm half-dead. . . ."

He dropped into an armchair, but in no time quickly jumped up and approached the doctor and, angrily goggling at him, emitted in a piercing tenor voice:

"I'm very, extraordinarily, grateful to you, Grigory Ivanich! I'm obliged, I thank you! If I live to the end of time, I'll never forget it! But friends don't behave this way! It was convenient, but it wasn't good judgment on your part! Why didn't you let me know? Who do you think I am? Who? An enemy or a stranger? Am I your enemy? Have I ever denied you anything? Ah?"

Eyes staring and fingers shaking, the chairman drank his kvass, quickly wiped his lips, and continued:

"I'm very, very grateful to you! Why didn't you let me know? If you had any true sense of who I am, you would have come to me and as a friend said: 'Dear man, Lev Trofimich, the situation is such and such . . . the story such, and so forth. . . .' " I would have settled it for you in a minute, and there wouldn't be this scandalous affair. . . . This fool, as if crazy, gads about the district, slanders and gossips with peasant women, and you, it's a shame to say, excuse the expression, started the devil knows what, induced this fool to go to court! Shame, for shame! Unadulterated shame! Everyone is asking me what it's all about, how and what, and I, the chairman, know nothing about it—what's going on there. You don't need me! I'm very, very grateful to you, Grigory Ivanich!"

The chairman bowed so low that he actually flushed from top to bottom, then went over to the window and called out:

"Zhigalov, tell Mihail Zakarich to come here! Tell him to come here immediately! It's not good!" he said, moving away from the window. "Even my wife will be offended, but no matter, I believe that I've already decided in your favor. You, gentlemen, have already thought about it! You strive to handle this intelligently, even in a principled way, with all kinds of twists and turns, but only one thing will result from all this: it will muddy the water."

"You will proceed irrationally and what will be the result?" asked the doctor.

"What will be the result? The result will be that if I hadn't come here immediately, you would have covered yourself and us with shame. . . . Fortunate for you that I'm here!"

The assistant arrived and stood on the threshold. The chairman went up to him, and putting his hands in his pockets, coughed and demanded:

"Apologize to the doctor now!"

The doctor blushed and left the room.

"You can see the doctor doesn't want your apology!" continued the chairman. "He doesn't want your repentance with words but with deeds. Do you give your word from this day you will lead an obedient and sober life?"

"I give my word . . . ," declared the assistant in a morose, deep voice.

"Take a look at yourself! G-o-d preserve you! I'd give you the sack in a minute! If I hear of anything else, don't ask for mercy. . . . Now, go home. . . ."

For the assistant, who had resigned himself to his bad luck, this turn of affairs was an unexpected surprise. He even blanched from pleasure. Whatever it was that he wanted to say, he said nothing, but extended his hand, smiled dully, and left.

"That's all there is to it!" said the chairman. "And you don't need a court."

He took a deep breath as if he had just completed a very

difficult and important duty, glanced at the samovar and the glasses, rubbed his hands together, and said:

"Blessed are the peacemakers. . . . Pour me a glass, Sasha. But, maybe you might order me something to bite on. . . . Well, and a little vodka. . . ."

"Good Lord, this is impossible!" said the doctor, entering the dining room, still flushed and wringing his hands. "This . . . this is a comedy! It's lousy! I can't bear it. It would be twenty times better to be taken to court than to settle problems in such a vaudevillian manner. I can't take it!"

"What do you want?" snapped the chairman at him. "Do you want him dismissed? If you wish, I'll dismiss him. . . ."

"No, not dismissal. . . . I don't know what I want, but, Lord, to conduct life in this way. . . . Ah, my God! It's intolerable!"

The doctor nervously fussed around and looked for his hat, and finding it, dropped into the armchair from exhaustion.

"It's nasty!" he repeated.

"My dear fellow," said the judge quietly. "I don't understand you fully, that is to say. . . . You know you are guilty in this case! This is the end of the nineteenth century and to sock someone—that, to some extent, as you wish, is not the question. . . . He's a scoundrel, b-u-t you will agree, you didn't act prudently. . . ."

"Of course!" agreed the chairman.

The whiskey and snacks were served. When offered, the doctor mechanically drank a glassful and ate a radish. When he returned to his office in the hospital, his thoughts were as hazy as cloud-covered grass on an autumn morning.

Is it really true, he thought, that during the last week there had been so much distress, vacillation in one's mind and words, only so that it would end so absurdly and ugly? How stupid! How stupid!

He was ashamed that he had brought in outsiders to settle his personal problem; ashamed of what he had said to those people; of the vodka which he had drunk only because of the custom to drink and to live a useless life; ashamed of what he considered his imperceptive, shallow mind. . . . Returning to the hospital, he at once began his rounds of the wards. The assistant walked alongside, stepping softly like a cat, and answering softly to questions put to him. . . . And the assistant, and the nymph, and the nurses outwardly gave no sign that anything untoward had occurred, and that all was fine. And the doctor, himself, did his best to appear indifferent. He gave orders, got annoyed, anguished with the patients, but in his brain swarmed:

"Stupid, stupid, stupid . . ."

1888

CHRONICLE OF A
COMMERCIAL ENTERPRISE

Andrei Andreyevich Sidorov inherited four thousand rubles from his mother and decided to open a bookstore with the money. There was only a marginal demand for such a store. The town was steeped in ignorance and prejudice. Only the aged used the bathhouse; the officials simply played cards and guzzled vodka; the women gossiped; the young men had no ideals; the young women did nothing the livelong day but dream of marriage and eat buckwheat pancakes. The husbands beat their wives, and pigs roamed in the streets.

It needs stimulating ideas, better ideas! thought Andrei Andreyevich. Ideas!

After renting premises for a store, he drove to Moscow and brought back from there many old and new authors and many textbooks, and displayed them all invitingly on shelves. For the first three weeks there were no buyers. Andrei Andreyevich sat behind the counter, read Mihailovski, and tried to think honorably. When, by chance, it entered his head, for example, that it wouldn't be a bad idea to give it all up as useless, he put a stop to these thoughts with: Ah, how nasty! Every morning when the shop opened, a young peasant girl with a kerchief on her head and leather galoshes on bare feet would run in out of the cold and say:

"Give me two kopecks worth of vinegar!"

And Andrei Andreyevich would scornfully reply:

"You've entered the wrong door, Ma'am!"

When any of his neighbors came in he assumed an important and inscrutable appearance, would bring down from the most inaccessible shelf the third volume of Pisarev, blow off the dust, and act as if there were someone in the shop to whom he did not want to show it, and he would say:

"Yes, my good man. . . . I'll show you this piece, not that one. . . . Yes. . . . Here, my good man, I must remark in a word, that it's such writing that you won't be able to put it down until you've read it through. . . . No doubt." Or,

"Look it over brother. It won't burn you!"

After the shop had been open for three weeks, the first customer arrived. He was a stocky, gray-haired gentleman with long sideburns. He had on a cap with a red band and by all appearances was a landowner. Unfortunately, he wanted the second volume of Vernacular Words, which was not in stock.

"Do you carry slate pencils?"

"No, I don't."

"Came in vain. . . . Sad. I didn't want to have to go to the fair for such trivia. . . ."

That's right, thought Andrei Andreyevich when the customer left. It wouldn't be useless to carry slate pencils. In this province it's not possible to narrowly specialize, and one must sell everything that pertains to enlightenment, and therefore, one way or another to further it.

He wrote to Moscow, and within a month pens, penholders, pencils, notebooks, slates, and other school supplies were displayed in the window of his shop. Gradually, boys and girls came to his shop, and it even happened that one day he netted a ruble and forty kopecks. Once the girl in the leather galoshes rushed into his shop. He had already opened his mouth to tell her that she had come in the wrong door, when she screeched:

"Give me a kopeck's worth of paper and seven kopecks' worth of stamps!"

After this, Andrei Andreyevich began to carry postal and special issue stamps and, besides these, accounting paper. Within eight months (counting from the day the shop was opened) a lady came in to buy pens.

"Do you carry knapsacks?" she asked.

"Too bad, Madame, I don't"

"Oh, what a pity! In that case, show me what kind of dolls you have, but give me a cheap price."

"Madame, I don't carry dolls either!" said Andrei Andreyevich glumly.

He thought about this for some time, and then wrote to Moscow, and soon his store displayed knapsacks, dolls, drums, sabers, accordions, balls, and all kinds of toys.

"It's all trivia!" he remarked to his buddies. "Just wait, I'll handle schoolbooks and educational games! It must be understood that the educational section will be based on what are unanimously called the finest scientific publications. . . ."

He sent for gymnastic weights, croquet, backgammon, children's billiards, children's garden tools, and several dozen of very well-thought-out educational toys. Later, the residents, to their great satisfaction when passing by his shop, saw two bicycles displayed: one large and the other a little smaller. The business grew nicely. It was especially good before Christmas when Andrei Andreyevich announced in his store window that he had for sale decorations for Christmas trees.

"I'm going to bring in hygienic goods while I'm at it," he told his buddies, rubbing his hands. "Just wait until I go to Moscow! My shop will have filters and every kind of scientific improvements that'll blow your minds, that is to say. Science, old man, must not be ignored. No way!"

Having made a lot of money, he went to Moscow and for cash and on credit bought a variety of goods for five thousand rubles. He bought filters, first-class desk lamps, guitars, hygienic underpants for children, and pacifiers, and purses, and a zoological collection. Besides these, he bought five-hundred rubles' worth of first-class china, and was pleased he had bought such beautiful things that would help develop fine taste and soften customs and improve morals. Returning home from Moscow, he busied himself

with placing his new purchases on the shelves and in the what-
nots. It so happened when he climbed to clear the top shelf, there
was some kind of rattling and ten volumes of Mihailovski fell one
after the other from the shelf. One of the volumes hit him on the
head, and the rest fell on the lamps and broke two of the globes.

"Well, anyhow, they . . . are heavy books!" muttered Andrei Andreyevich, scratching his head.

He collected all the books, tied them together with some
sturdy twine, and hid them under the counter. About two days
after this incident, he learned that his neighbor, a grocer, was
arrested and sentenced for torturing his nephew and that the
shop would be for sale. Andrei Andreyevich was delighted and
declared that he wanted to buy it. It wasn't long before a door
was cut through between both shops and they were united as
one, and were full of merchandise. When customers walked
into the second half of the shop, from habit they would ask for
tea, sugar and kerosene. It didn't take Andrei Andreyevich
long to think about dealing in grocery goods.

At the present time he is the most prominent merchant in
our town. He sells dinnerware, tobacco, tar, soap, thick bagels,
paint, haberdashery and chandlery, guns, hides, and hams. At
the auction he came away with a lease on a cellar, and it is said
he is getting ready to open up a family bathhouse with private
rooms. Concerning the books which had been lying on the
shelves, including the third volume of Pisarev, they had long
ago been sold for one ruble and five kopecks a pood.*

At name-day celebrations and at weddings, his former buddies, whom Andrei Andreyevich now jokingly calls "Ameri-
cans," engage in conversations with him about progress, literature, and other highbrow subjects.

"Have you, Andrei Andreyevich, read the latest edition of
the *European Herald*?" they ask him.

"No, no I haven't . . ." he answers, frowning and playing
with his heavy watch chain. "It doesn't concern us. We're
better off tending to our own business."

1892

---

*thirty-six pounds

At a Country Estate

The floor over which Pavel Ilich Rashevich was softly walking was covered by heavy Ukrainian rugs. His body was casting a long shadow on the wall and the ceiling. Mayer, his guest, having completed his duties as a court investigator, sat on the Turkish divan with one leg tucked under, and was smoking and listening. The clock indicated that it was already eleven o'clock. Sounds of the dining-room table being set could be heard from the room adjacent to the study.

"It might be desirable," remarked Rashevich, "from the point of view of fraternity, equality, etcetera, that the swineherd, Mitka, is just such a person as Goethe or Frederick the Great, but if your position is based on knowledge, if you have the courage to look the facts straight in the eye, it will become evident to you that having noble blood—is not a prejudice or an old wives' tale. Noble blood, my dear sir, has a natural historical justification, and to deny it, in my opinion, is as strange as to deny that a deer has antlers. One must consider the facts! You—are a lawyer and haven't had a go at other areas of knowledge besides the humanities, so you can still labor under the illusion of equality, fraternity, etcetera. But I—an incorrigible

Darwinian—for me such words as 'breeding,' 'aristocracy,' 'noble blood'—are not empty expressions."

Rashevich was excited and spoke with feeling. His eyes shone, his pince-nez would not stay on his nose; he nervously shrugged his shoulders, blinked, and at the word "Darwinian" nattily looked at himself in the mirror and with both hands smoothed his gray beard. He was dressed in a very short, threadbare jacket and narrow trousers. His rapid movements, sprightliness, and this too-tight-and-too-short jacket did not become him. It seemed that his large, longhaired, handsome head, which reminded one of a bishop or a venerable poet, was set upon his body as upon a tall, slender, pretentious youth. When he stood with his legs spread apart, the long shadow resembled a pair of scissors.

More than anything else he liked to talk, and it always seemed to him that he was saying something new and original. In the presence of Mayer he felt unusually animated and mentally stimulated. He was fond of the court investigator and derived inspiration from his youth, health, fine manners, reliability, and, most important his heartfelt regard for Rashevich and for his family. By and large people did not like Rashevich, stayed away from him, and, as he knew, talked about him; said that he had sent his wife to her grave with his talk, and behind his back called him a misanthrope and a repulsive individual—that is, a toad. Only Mayer, a new and unprejudiced person, came often to his home and eagerly remarked somewhere that Rashevich and his daughters were the only people in the district at whose home he felt warmth and as if he were with relatives. Rashevich also liked him because he was a young man who could be considered a good match for Zhenya, his oldest daughter.

So now, happy with his thoughts and the sound of his voice, and observing with satisfaction the handsomely trimmed hair, the moderately stocky figure, and the pleasant demeanor of Mayer, Rashevich dreamed about how to set up his Zhenya with such an excellent man and how his problems with the estate could be transferred to his son-in-law. Nasty troubles! The last two payments of the interest on his loans had not been paid to the bank, and a variety of arrears and fines had added up to more than two thousand rubles!

"There is no doubt in my mind," Rashevich, all the more excited, continued to muse, "that if some kind of Richard the Lion-Hearted or Frederich Barbarossa,* let us suppose, who is brave and magnanimous, passed these qualities on to his son together with the convolutions and bumps of the brain, and if the bravery and magnanimity are sheltered by his upbringing and application, and if he marries a princess, who is also brave and magnanimous, these qualities will be inherited by the grandchild, and so forth, while this isn't apparent to the naked eye and is not organic, that is to say, in the flesh and blood. Thanks to strict conjugal choice, noble families instinctively protected themselves from disparate marriages. Smart young people didn't marry the devil knows whom, and superior mental qualities were passed on from generation to generation without blemishes, sheltered, and with the passage of time were perfected by exercise and moved to an even higher level. Nature obliges us to maintain that which is desirable in human beings and is in accordance with historical natural law. The advisable conduct throughout the ages required to assiduously keep apart the refined noble blood from the crude of the hoi polloi.

"Oh yes, my fine fellow! It wasn't the great unwashed or the cook's son that gave us literature, science, art, law, understanding of the meaning of honor, duty. . . . All these human characteristics were exclusively the obligations of the aristocrats, and in this manner from the point of view of the natural law, the wretched Sobakevich, only because he was a blue blood, was more useful and above the best merchant even if the latter had built fifteen museums. Whatever you might wish! And if I don't offer my hand to the unwashed or the cook's son, and don't have them sit down at the table with me, in this way I do a better job of protecting the world's environment and fulfilling one of the most important plans of mother nature that is leading us to perfection. . . ."

Rashevich stopped talking, groomed his beard with both hands; his shadow also stopped on the wall, resembling scissors.

---

*king of Prussia (1713–1740)

"Take our Mother Russia," he continued, putting his hands in his pockets and leaning back on his heels and then forward on his toes. "Who are her best people? Take our first-class artists, literary writers, composers. . . . Who are they? These are the achievements, my dear man, of the aristocracy. Pushkin, Gogol, Lermontov, Turgenev, Goncharov, Tolstoy—weren't the children of a church reader!"

"Goncharov was a merchant," remarked Mayer.

"So what! The exception only proves the rule. And as to the genius of Goncharov, one can argue powerfully. Well, let's leave out names and return to facts. What would you say, for example, my dear sir, about this eloquent fact: When the unwashed swarmed here—where they had not been permitted before—in the realms of high society, in science, in literature, in the district councils, in the courts, you can note that nature herself intervened for a higher level of human law, and was the first to declare war against this horde. Really, as soon as the unwashed were out of their element they began to sour, wither, get crazy, and degenerate. Nowhere can you meet such neurotics, psychological cripples, consumptives, and every kind of slovenliness, as among these poor devils. They perish like flies in the autumn. If it weren't that we were rescued from degeneracy, not a stone upon a stone would have been left long ago of our civilization—the unwashed would have destroyed it all. Tell me, do me the kindness: What, up to this time, has been the benefit of this incursion? What did the unwashed bring with them?"

Rashevich made a secretive, frightened face and continued:

"Our science and literature has never been at such a low level as now! Today's generation, my dear sir, has neither ideas nor idealists, and all their action is intrinsically this: How best to fleece the other guy and to strip him of his last shirt. Those of the current generation who pretend to be foremost and honorable people can be bought off for one ruble. The contemporary intellectual is only notable for the fact that when you're speaking with him you'd better keep a tight grip on your wallet or he'll fleece you."

Rashevich winked and laughed.

"Really, he'll pick your pocket!" he declared gleefully in an undertone. "And morals? What kind of morals?" Rashevich glanced at the door. "Currently it's not even amazing when a wife takes everything from a husband and leaves him—but that's nothing! Today, brother, twelve-year-old little girls seek lovers and all these amateur theatricals and literary evenings are devised only to make it possible to nab the rich kulak and be supported by him. . . . Mothers sell their daughters, and ask a man candidly what price would be given for a wife, and can even haggle about it, dear man. . . ."

Mayer, having been quiet and motionless, suddenly arose from the divan and looked at his watch.

"Sorry, Pavel Ilich," he said, "but it's time for me to go home."

But Pavel Ilich, who was not yet finished with what he wanted to say, put his arm around him and forced him back on the divan, and swore he wouldn't let him leave without supper. And Mayer sat and listened again, but was already looking at Rashevich with amazement and uneasiness, as if he had just now begun to understand him. Red spots were breaking out on his face. And when the maid finally entered and announced that her mistress was inviting them to supper, he sighed lightly and led the way out of the study.

In the adjacent room Rashevich's daughters, Zhenya and Iraida, twenty-four and twenty-two years old, were sitting at the table. Both had dark eyes, were very pale, and of the same height. Zhenya's hair was let down, but Iraida had hers piled up high. It appeared that for the first time in their lives, they had each just had a glass of bitter liqueur, and that they had drunk it accidentally, and both were confused and giggling.

"Stop being silly, girls," ordered Rashevich.

Zhenya and Iraida spoke in French with each other, but spoke Russian with their father. Interrupting each other and blending their Russian speech with French, they began to rapidly tell how just at this time in August of the previous year they had left for the teachers' college and how delightful it had been. Now they didn't go anywhere and they lived on the estate without leaving all summer and winter. How boring it was!

"Stop being silly, girls," repeated Rashevich.

He wanted to be the only one talking. When others were speaking in his presence he experienced a feeling not unlike jealousy.

"That's how it is, my dear fellow," he began again, looking fondly at the investigator. It's out of kindness and simplicity, and from the fear that we might be suspected of backwardness, that we fraternize, excuse me, with all kinds of trash, advocate brotherhood and equality with the kulaks and the tavern-keepers. If we wanted to think about it we would realize to what extent our liberality has transgressed. What we have done is causing our civilization to hang by a hair. My dear fellow! That which our ancestors achieved over the ages will not be achieved today or tomorrow, and will be destroyed by these new Huns. . . ."

After supper they all went into the drawing room. Zhenya and Iraida lit the candles on the piano and brought out some sheet music . . . but their father continued to talk. It was impossible to know when he would stop. They looked with anguish and exasperation at their egotistical father for whom, it was apparent, the satisfaction from babbling on and showing off his wit was dearer and more important than the happiness of his daughters. Mayer—the only young person who came to their home, came—they knew this—because he enjoyed their pretty, feminine company. But, the indefatigable old man took possession of him and didn't let him escape for one moment.

"Just as the Western knights fended off the Mongols, so we, while it's still not too late, must unite and attack the enemy quickly," continued Rashevich in the tone of a prophet, raising his right arm. "Allow that I approach the unwashed not as Pavel Ilich, but as the terrible and powerful Richard the Lion-Hearted. We would stop handling them with kid gloves; we've had it up to here! Allow that we all agree that if one of the unwashed came too close to us, we'd hurl directly at his mug the disdainful words 'Buzz off! You don't belong here!' Right in his ugly mug!" continued Rashevich with relish, poking himself with his bent finger. "Right in his ugly mug! Right in his ugly mug!"

"I couldn't do that," remarked Mayer, turning away.

"Why not?" Rashevich asked briskly, expecting an interesting and long argument. "Why not?"

"Because I, myself, am a petty bourgeois."

Having said this, Mayer flushed, and even his neck swelled and tears glistened in his eye.

"My father was a simple worker," he added in a gruff, curt voice, "but I don't see anything stupid about that."

Rashevich became terribly confused, stunned, and as if having immediately recognized his mistake, looked at Mayer in embarrassment and did not know what to say. Zhenya and Iraida blushed and focused their attention upon the sheet music. They were ashamed of their tactless father. A moment of silence went by and the situation became unbearably disgraceful, when suddenly, as if painfully strained and irrelevant, the following ringing words were heard:

"Yes, I'm a petty bourgeois and proud of it."

After this Mayer, stumbling awkwardly against the furniture, excused himself and hastily walked to the entrance even though his horses had not been brought out.

"It's going to be a dark ride tonight," babbled Rashevich, going after him. "The moon comes out late now."

They both stood on the porch in the twilight and waited for the horses to be brought.

"There's a falling star . . . ," exclaimed Mayer, muffling himself in his overcoat.

"Many stars fall in August."

When the horses were delivered, Rashevich looked attentively at the sky and said with a sigh:

"It's a scene worthy of the pen of Flammarion.* . . ."

After accompanying his guest he strolled about the garden, his hands gesturing in the twilight, not wanting to believe that such a strange, stupid misunderstanding had just occurred. He felt ashamed and vexed with himself. In the first place, it was the epitome of carelessness and tactlessness to raise this cursed subject about the upper classes, not knowing beforehand with whom he was talking. Something similar had already happened

---

*French astronomer and writer (1842–1925)

earlier, when he had begun to bash the Germans, and later dis-
covered that all those present were—Germans. In the second
place, he felt that Mayer would never again come to his house.
These intellectuals who arise from the common people were
oversensitive, stubborn, and rancorous.

"Too bad, too bad . . . ," muttered Rashevich, spitting in
disgust. He felt uncouth and nasty, as if he had eaten soap.
"Ugh, it's too bad!"

From the window facing the garden it could be seen that in
the drawing room around the piano, Zhenya, with her hair
falling, very pale, looking frightened, was saying something
very rapidly. . . . Iraida was pacing the room and appeared deep
in thought. Then she, too, said something rapidly and her face
expressed indignation. They both seemed to speak at once.
Not a single word could be heard but Rashevich guessed what
they were talking about. Zhenya, probably, was grumbling that
her father with his talk had driven off from the home all decent
people and today had taken away from them the only acquaintance who might even have been a suitor. Now there wouldn't
be a place in the whole district where the poor young man
could relax. But Iraida, judging by the way she raised her hands
in despair, was probably talking about their boring life and her
lost youth. . . .

Upon going to his room, Rashevich sat on the bed and
slowly began to undress. He was depressed and tormented by
the same sensation of having eaten soap. He was ashamed.
Having undressed, he looked at his long, veiny old man's legs
and recalled that on his estate they had nicknamed him "Toad"
and that after every long conversation he was ashamed.
Somehow that which started out softly, courteously, with good
intentions, calling himself an old student, an idealist, a Don
Quixote, concluded in this fatal way. Not even aware of it, he
gradually crossed into abuse and slander. And the most amazing
thing of all, he criticized education, art, and morals in the most
sincere way, even though he hadn't read a book in the last
twenty years, or traveled any farther than the provincial town,
and in truth knew nothing about what was going on in the
whole wide world. If he sat down to write something, even a

congratulatory note, this letter, too, resulted in abusive language. And this was strange because he really was a feeling, tearful person. Was there an evil spirit lodged in him, who hated and slandered without his being conscious of it?

"It's not right," he sighed as he lay under the bed covers. "It's not right!"

The daughters also were not sleeping. They heard boisterous laughter and cries as if someone were being chased. This made Zhenya hysterical. It did not take long for Iraida to sob. A barefoot maid ran up and down the corridor several times. . . .

"What a messy business, Lord . . . ," muttered Rashevich, sighing and turning from side to side. "It's not right!"

In his sleep a nightmare crushed him. He dreamt that he was a lone, naked, tall giraffe, standing in the middle of the room, his finger poking at something before him and saying: "In his ugly mug! In his ugly mug! In his ugly mug!"

He awoke frightened and immediately thought of the misunderstanding with Mayer, and that, of course, Mayer would never come again. He remembered that he had to pay the interest owed to the bank, to find husbands for his daughters, that they had to eat and drink, and about the onset of illness, old age, unpleasantness, that winter would soon arrive and that there wasn't enough wood. . . .

It was already ten o'clock in the morning. Rashevich dressed slowly, drank his tea and ate two large chunks of bread and butter. His daughters did not join him. They were avoiding him and this hurt him. He went into his study and lay down on the divan. Later he sat at the desk and began to write his daughters a letter. His hand shook, and his eyes itched. He wrote that he was already old, no one needed him and no one loved him, and begged his daughters to forget about him, and when he died, to bury him in a plain pine coffin without ceremony, or to send his corpse to Kharkov to the anatomy laboratory. He felt that all of his connecting tissues gasped with malice and hypocrisy, but he could not stop and continued to write, write. . . .

"Toad!" suddenly could be heard from the adjacent room.

It was the voice of the older daughter, an indignant, hissing voice. "Toad!"

"Toad!" like an echo, repeated the younger daughter. "Toad!"

1894

FEAR:
A TALE TOLD BY
ONE OF MY FRIENDS

Dmitri Petrovich Silin graduated from the university and took a job in Petersburg, but when he was thirty he quit his job and assumed the work of a gentleman farmer. He did a good job, but all the same, it seemed to me that he was a misfit, and that it would be better if he returned to Petersburg. When he met me at the gate or in the driveway, overheated, covered with dust, fagged out by his work, and later after dinner nodding in the need to sleep, and his wife led him to his bed like a child, or when, overcoming his need to sleep, he began in his soft, sensitive, almost pleading voice to lay out his good thoughts, I didn't see a good administrator, or even an agronomist, but only a tortured individual. It was clear to me that he didn't want to be any kind of administrator, but needed to get through the day—and thank God.

I liked to be at his estate, and it so happened that I would be a guest for a day, or two, or three. I liked his house, his grounds, his huge fruit orchard, and the stream, and his philosophizing, which was a little listless and florid, but lucid. I must have liked him too, but I can't say this convincingly, since even now I can't sort out my feelings at that time. He was smart, well intentioned, not at all dull, and an earnest human being. However, I recall when he confided in me his innermost secrets and called our relationship friendship it unpleasantly annoyed me, and I felt awkward. His friendship had something uncomfortable, irksome about it, and I would gladly have preferred a more ordinary friendly association.

The trouble was that I found his wife, Maria Sergeyevna, extraordinarily attractive. I wasn't in love with her, but I found her face, her voice, the way she walked all very pleasing, and yearned to see her when a long time elapsed between my visits. At that time, in my mind's eye I did not picture anyone so gladly as this young, beautiful, and elegant woman. I had no intentions whatsoever toward her, not even dreams, but for some reason, every time when we two were left alone, I remembered that her husband considered me his friend and felt ill at ease. When she played my favorite compositions on the piano or told me something interesting, I listened contentedly, and at those times thoughts entered my head that she loved her husband, and that she, too, considered me a friend. And my mood would change and I became languid, clumsy, and bored. She would note this change and would usually say:

"You are bored without your friend. He must be called from the fields."

And when Dmitri Petrovich arrived, she said:

"Well, your friend has arrived now. Rejoice."

Things went on this way for a half-year.

Once, one July Sunday, Dmitri Petrovich and I, having nothing to do, drove to the larger village of Klushino in order to buy some hors d'oeuvres for supper. While we were walking around the shops, the sun disappeared and it became windy. This wind is one which, probably, I will never forget in my life. Having purchased cheese that looked like soap, and a petrified sausage, which smelled of wood tar, we went to a tavern to get some beer. Our coachman had gone to the blacksmith to have a horse shod, and we had told him that we would wait for him near the church. We were walking, talking, and laughing about our purchases.

Behind us quietly, and with the suspicious appearance of a

spy, followed a man who in our environs had a rather strange nickname: Forty Torments. This Forty Torments was no other than Gavrila Sevrov, or simply Gavrishka, who had worked for me as a butler for a short time, and who had been fired because of drunkenness. He had worked for Dmitri Petrovich, too, and was fired for the same sin. He was a fierce drunkard, and in general he had always indulged in depravity. His father had been a priest and his mother of the gentry, which means that by birth he belonged to the privileged class, but when I would look at his emaciated, respectable, constantly perspiring face, with his red beard already showing signs of gray, and at his pitiful, torn jacket and red shirt hanging out of his trousers, I couldn't find a trace of anything that in our community we called privilege. He declared himself an educated man and spoke of how he had been a student at a theological school, where he never graduated, and where he was expelled for smoking. After this he sang in a bishop's choir and lived for two years in a monastery where he again was thrown out, not for smoking this time but for "weakness." He covered on foot two provinces, submitted a petition for something at an ecclesiastical court, and was arraigned in a variety of places four times before the court. Finally he settled in our district and worked as a butler, a woodsman, in kennels, and as a church warden. He got married to a widow who was a traveling cook. He then sank into a bachelor's life and became so accustomed to live in filth and squabbles with her that he himself began to speak with disbelief in his privileged heritage, as if it were some kind of myth. At the time this was being written, he knocked around without a job, hiring himself out as a horse veterinarian and a hunter, and his wife had disappeared who knows where.

From the tavern we went to the church and sat in the front entranceway and waited for the coachman. Forty Torments stepped a little away and raised his hand to his mouth in order to politely cough into it, when it was necessary.

It was already dark. The air was fragrant with the evening dampness, and the moon was beginning to rise. In the clear, starry sky there were only two clouds immediately above us. One was large and the other a bit smaller. They were so alike that they looked like mother and daughter and moved in tandem in the direction that the evening sunset directed them.

"What a marvelous day," said Dmitri Petrovich.

"Not unusual," agreed Forty Torments and politely coughed behind his hand. "How come, Dmitri Petrovich, that you thought of coming here today?" he asked in his ingratiating voice, obviously trying to start a conversation.

Dmitri Petrovich didn't answer. Forty Torments sighed deeply and continued to speak softly, not looking at us:

"I suffer alone for the reason that I must answer to Almighty God. That is, of course, since I'm an incompetent, a wastrel of a person, but believe it, I have a conscience: If you're destitute, you're worse off than a dog. . . . Excuse me, Dmitri Petrovich!"

Silin paid no attention to him, and, holding his head up with his fists, was deep in thought about something. The church stood at the end of the street on a high bluff and through the slots of the fence could be seen the river, the flooded plains on this side, and a bright, crimson flame from a campfire, around which moved dark figures of people and horses. There were more fires at some distance away: it was not a large village. . . . There was singing over there.

Upon the river and on some of the floodplain the fog was lifting. High narrow clumps of mist, thick and white like milk, hovered over the river, overshadowing the reflection of the stars and clinging to the willows. They were changing their appearance momentarily and it seemed that some were embracing, others were bowing, and a third were lifting their arms toward the heavens with wide priestly sleeves, as if praying. . . . They probably led Dmitri Petrovich to think about ghosts and the dead, because he turned to me and asked, gruesomely smiling:

"Tell me, my dear, why whenever we want to tell about something frightful, veiled, and fantastic, we derive our material from supernatural phantoms and spooks and not from the world itself?"

"What we don't understand frightens us."

"Do you really understand what life is all about? Tell me:

Do you really understand life more than you understand the netherworld?"

Dmitri Petrovich sat down so close to me that I could feel his breathing on my cheek. In the evening twilight his pale, lean face seemed even paler, and his dark beard—darker than soot. His eyes were sad, sincere, and looked a little frightened as if he were getting ready to tell me something fearful. He looked into my eyes and continued in his usual pleading voice:

"Our life and our afterlife both are similarly not understood, and fearful. He who is afraid of ghosts must also be afraid of me, and of those fires, and of heaven, since all that which is dreamed up is no less unfathomable and fantastic than that which is found in the real world. Prince Hamlet didn't kill himself because he was afraid of those visions, which it is possible would visit him after death. I admire his remarkable monologue, but frankly, he has never touched my inner being. I admit to you as a friend, never in a minute of depression have I imagined the hour of my death. My fantasy has contrived a thousand of the most dismal visions and I have succeeded in driving myself into torturous ecstasy, producing nightmares, and I say to you that these things did not seem frightening. The otherworld is frightening, but so is life. I, my good man, don't understand and am afraid of life. I don't know, perhaps I'm sick or I'm out of my mind. A normal, healthy person it appears understands everything he sees and hears, and I have lost this 'appears' and from day to day I poison myself with fear. It is a disease—I suffer from agoraphobia. So there it is and I'm sick because I fear life. When I lie on the grass and look for a long time at a gnat which had just been born yesterday and understands nothing, it appears to me that its life consists of constant fear, and I see this same thing in myself."

"What is it that you find so frightening?" I asked.

"I'm afraid of everything. I wasn't born profound and interested myself very little in such questions as the afterlife, the fate of humanity, and generally was rarely transported to heavenly heights. What is chiefly terrible for me is the ordinariness which none of us can conceal. I am unable to distinguish which of my transgressions involve truth and which are lies and this bothers me. I am aware that the circumstances of life and one's upbringing bind one in a tight circle of lies; that my whole life is none other than a daily anxiety to be able to fool myself and other people without noting this, and it is awful to think that until the day I die I won't even know why I did what I did. I took a job in Petersburg and became frightened, then returned here to take over agricultural responsibilities, and also became frightened. . . . I observe that we know little and therefore err every day, are dishonest, smear others, use up others' inheritance, use up our talents on nonsense—which we don't need. This messes up our lives, and this is frightening to me because I don't know what it's all about, and for whom it is necessary.

"I, my dear, don't understand people and am afraid of them. I find it terrible to look at the muzhiks. I don't know what the higher purpose is for their suffering and why they exist. If the purpose of life is the pursuit of happiness, they are superfluous, unnecessary beings; if the purpose and meaning of existence is bound in poverty and hopeless ignorance, I can't understand why this kind of torture is necessary. I don't understand anything or anybody. Please take a look and try to understand that individual!" remarked Dmitri Petrovich, pointing to Forty Torments. "Figure him out!"

Noting that we were both looking at him, Forty Torments politely coughed into his fists and said:

"I was a loyal servant when I worked for kind gentry but the chief reason for my downfall—was alcoholic drink. If I were now treated with respect, an unhappy human being, and you hired me, I would kiss an icon in gratitude. I have determined to keep my word!"

The church sexton went by and looked at us inquisitively and started to pull the bell cord. The bell, slowly and deliberately, sharply disturbed the evening silence, and rang out ten o'clock.

"However it's ten o'clock already!" noted Dmitri Petrovich. "It's time for us to get going. Yes, my dear," he sighed, "if you only knew how I fear my ordinary, everyday thoughts about life, which really should not be anything to fear. In order not to think I divert myself with work and try to numb myself in order to have a good night's sleep. My children, my wife—for others this is not unusual but for me it is extremely difficult, my dear!"

He pressed his face with his hands, let out a groan, and laughed.

"If I could tell you what a fool's game my life has been!" he said. "Everyone tells me: you have such a lovely wife, and you yourself are a wonderful family man. They think that I am very happy and are envious of me. Well, I will tell you confidentially: My happy family life—is another painful mystery to me and I am afraid of it."

A tense smile made his pale face become ugly. He put his arm around my waist and continued in an undertone:

"You are my sincere friend, I believe you and deeply respect you. Friendship is sent to us from heaven so we can be relieved of secrets which are strangling us. Allow me to make use of your friendly disposition toward me and tell you the whole truth. My family life, which appears delightful, is the greatest source of my unhappiness and my greatest fear. I married strangely and stupidly. I must tell you that I loved Masha madly and courted her for two years. I proposed to her five times and she rejected me because she was completely indifferent toward me. The sixth time, when I, madly in love, fell on my knees before her and begged for her hand, as if out of charity, she agreed. . . . She said to me: 'I don't love you, but I will be true to you. . . . ' I accepted such a condition and was ecstatic. I understood then what that meant, but now, I swear to God, I don't understand. 'I don't love you, but I will be true to you'—what does that mean? It is mist, twilight. . . . I love her now just as fiercely as the first day of our marriage, but she, it seems to me, is as indifferent as before, and probably is glad when I leave the house. I don't know with certainty whether she does or doesn't love me, but we do live together under one roof; we sleep together, have children, and our property is owned jointly. . . . What does all this mean? What does it achieve? What does this mean to you, my dear? It's cruel torture! That's why I don't understand anything in our relationship. I hate this in her, in myself, and in both of us together. Everything in my head is muddled. I torture myself and become dull, and, as if in spite, she becomes

more attractive every day. She becomes even more wonderful.
. . . As I see her, her hair is remarkable, and her smile is unlike
that of any other woman. I love her and I know that my love
is hopeless. A hopeless love for a woman with whom you've
already had two children! Really, isn't that more terrible than
a fantasy?"

He was in such a state that he would have gone on for even
a longer time, but fortunately the voice of the coachman was
heard. Our horses arrived. We got into the carriage and Forty
Torments, removing his cap, and with an expression as if he
had been waiting for the opportunity for a long time to come
close to our very worthy figures, settled us both in it.

"Dmitri Petrovich, permit me to come to your home," he
spoke out, blinking his eyes with his head bowed and turned to
one side. "Show mercy! I'm starving!"

"Well, all right," said Silin. "Come. We'll give you three
days and then see."

"I hear you!" exclaimed a joyful Forty Torments. "I'll come
today."

It was about six versts to their home. Dmitri Petrovich, satisfied that he had finally spoken out before his friend, had his
arm around me the whole way, and with warmth and not with
fear he spiritedly told me that if everything in his family had
been flourishing, he would have returned to Petersburg and
continued his education. The trend that had influenced some
young talented people to come to the village had a grievous
effect. There's plenty of rice and wheat in Russia, he declared,
but not enough cultured people. It is necessary that gifted,
healthy youth spends its time studying the arts and politics:
Any other kind of behavior results in improvidence. He enjoyed his philosophizing and expressed disappointment that
we would be separated on the following morning because he
had to go away on business relating to the forests he owned.

I found it awkward and saddening that I had somehow
deceived another human being. But at the same time it felt
pleasant. I looked at the huge crimson moon that was rising
and pictured for myself a tall, elegant blonde, fair face, always
proper, giving off a special fragrance something like musk, and

for some reason it was a happy thought that she did not love her husband.

We sat down to dinner as soon as we arrived at the house. Maria Sergeyevna, laughing, served us the delicacies we had purchased, and I found that her hair was really remarkable and that her smile was unlike any other woman's. I followed her, and I wanted to see in her every movement and look that she did not love her husband, and it seemed to me that I did see this.

Dmitri Petrovich soon began to struggle with the need to sleep. After dinner he sat with us for about ten minutes and then said:

"If you don't mind, ladies and gentlemen, I must get up at three o'clock tomorrow morning. Allow me to be excused."

He affectionately kissed his wife, firmly shook my hand, and got a promise from me that without fail I would come the next week. In order not to oversleep, he went to bed in the added wing.

Maria Sergeyevna went to bed late, as they do in Petersburg. For some reason, I was glad for this.

"And so?" I began when we were left alone. "And so, be so kind as to play something."

I didn't want to listen to music, but I didn't know how to start a conversation. She sat down at the piano and played, but I can't remember what. I sat nearby, looked at her plump white hands, and tried to read something in her cold, inscrutable face. However, she smiled about something and turned to me.

"You are bored without your friend," she said.

I laughed.

"Friendship requires only monthly visits, but I come here more often, at least every week."

Having said this, I stood up and in my agitation paced back and forth. She rose also and went over to the fireplace.

"What is it you want to say?" she asked, lifting her large, bright eyes upon me.

I did not reply.

"You haven't spoken the truth," she continued thoughtfully. "You are here only because of Dmitri Petrovich. I, too, am happy about this. Such friendships are rarely seen nowadays."

Ugh! I thought and not knowing what to say, asked her: "Would you like to walk in the garden?"

"No."

I went out on the terrace. My head felt itchy and I shivered from inner turmoil. I already knew that our conversation would be inconsequential, and that we would not be able to say anything that made sense to each other, but unquestionably there would occur during this night that which I hadn't even dared to dream. If not tonight, then never.

"What wonderful weather!" I loudly exclaimed.

"It is decidedly all the same for me," I heard her answer.

I went into the drawing room. Maria Sergeyevna stood by the fireside as previously, with her hands behind her back, thinking of something and not looking at me.

"Why is it decidedly indifferent for you?" I asked.

"Because I'm bored. You're only bored when your friend isn't here, but I'm always bored. However, that's not interesting for you."

I sat down at the piano and picked out a few chords, waiting to see what she would say.

"Please, don't bother to be courteous," she said, looking at me angrily and as if she were getting ready to cry from aggravation. "If you want to go to bed, leave. Don't think that just because you're Dmitri Petrovich's friend that you're obligated to be bored by his wife. I don't want to victimize you. Please, do leave."

Of course, I didn't leave. She walked out on the terrace, and I remained in the drawing room and for about five minutes turned over a few pages of sheet music. Then I walked onto the terrace. We stood alongside each other in the shadow of the awning, while below us the steps were lit by the light of the moon. Across the flowering bushes and the yellow sand stretched lanes of dark shadows from the trees.

"I, too, must leave tomorrow," I said.

"Of course, if my husband is not at home, it will be impossible for you to remain here," she remarked laughingly. "I can imagine how unhappy you would be if you were in love with me! But wait, what if I threw myself around your neck. . . . I would see with what fright you would run away from me. It would be interesting."

Her words and pale face appeared angry, but her eyes were full of tenderness, passionate love. I already looked at this beautiful creation as my own property, and here for the first time I noticed her golden eyebrows, marvelous eyebrows such as I had never seen before. The thought that I could now hold her close, caress her, and touch her remarkable hair suddenly presented itself to me so miraculously that I laughed and closed my eyes.

"In any case, it's time to go to bed. . . . Good night," I heard her say.

"It's not good night for me," I said, laughing and following her into the drawing room. "I'll curse this night if it's going to be peaceful."

Taking hold of her hand I accompanied her to the door. I saw by her face that she understood me and was glad that I understood her, too.

I went to my room. On the table by the books lay Dmitri Petrovich's cap and it reminded me of his friendship. I picked up my cane and went out into the garden. The mist was already forming clouds over the trees and bushes, embracing them, and the same tall and narrow apparitions that I had noted previously floated over the river. How unfortunate that I could not speak with them!

In the unusually clear atmosphere, every leaf, every reed could be seen—it all smiled at me in the quiet, half-awake, and passing by the green benches, I remembered the words from one of Shakespeare's plays: "How sweet sleeps the light of the moon on the bench!"

In the garden was a hillock. I went up to it and sat down. I was bothered by a fascinating feeling. I knew that it was likely that today I was going to embrace her, press myself next to her lush body, kiss her golden eyebrows. I did not want to believe that I was teasing myself and that it was too bad that she didn't torture me a bit longer, but gave in to me so easily.

But then I heard some unexpected heavy footsteps. On the path a man of medium build could be seen and I immediately recognized Forty Torments. He sat down on the bench and sighed loudly, then crossed himself three times and lay down. But within a minute he got up and lay down on his other side. The mosquitoes and the dampness of the night kept him from sleeping.

"Oh, life!" he emitted. "Unhappy, bitter life!"

Looking at his emaciated, curled body and listening to his hoarse breathing, I remembered another unhappy, bitter life which had been confessed to me today. I shuddered and feared for my state of bliss. I came down from the hillock and went into the house.

Life, in his opinion, is terrifying, I thought. Don't waste time being polite with it, take hold of it before it crushes you; take whatever you can from her.

Maria Sergeyevna was on the terrace. Without saying a word I embraced her and began to greedily kiss her brows, her eyelids, her neck. . . .

In my room she told me that she had loved me for a long time, more than a year. She swore her love for me, cried, begged that I take her away with me. I led her to the window in order to look at her face by moonlight and she seemed like a marvelous dream to me. I hastily held her close in order to confirm the reality. It had been a long time since I had experienced such ecstasy. But at the same time, somewhere deep in my being, I felt a kind of awkwardness, and I was uncomfortable. There was something objectionable and difficult in her love, just as in the friendship of Dmitri Petrovich. It was a much bigger and serious affair with tears and vows than I wanted. I did not want anything so intense—not tears, not vows, and no talk of the future. It was enough that this moonlit night flashed through our lives like a bright meteor—and disappeared.

Exactly at three o'clock she left my room and when I, standing in the doorway, watched her leave, at the end of the corridor Dmitri Petrovich suddenly appeared. Meeting him, she stepped aside and allowed him to pass, and her whole figure spelled hate and aversion. He smiled somehow strangely, coughed, and came into my room.

"I left my cap here yesterday," he said, not looking at me.

He found it and put it on using both hands, then looked at

my embarrassed face, at my slippers, and remarked, not in a voice I knew but in some kind of strange, husky voice:

"You can be assured that I was stamped from birth not to understand anything, If you understand something then . . . I congratulate you. My eyes have seen nothing."

And he left, coughing a great deal. Later I saw through the window how he harnessed the horses himself near the stable. His hands shook in his hurry as he looked back at the house: truly, it was fearful for him. He then sat in the small carriage and with a weird look on his face, as if he were afraid of being pursued, he whipped the horses on.

A little later I drove off, too. The sun had already risen, and yesterday's mist had settled sadly on the bushes and knolls. Forty Torments sat on a coach box and had already succeeded to get a drink somewhere and was muttering some drunken nonsense.

"I'm a free man!" he yelled at the horses. "Hey you, raspberries to you! I'm of good lineage, a respectable citizen, if you want to know!"

Dmitri Petrovich's fear, which I could not get out of my head, had invaded me. I thought of what had happened and understood nothing. I looked at the crows and I felt it strange and scary that they were flying around.

Why did I do that? I asked myself with wonder and with regret. Why did it turn out the way it did and not differently? For whom and for what was it necessary that she should love me sincerely, and that he should show up at my room for his cap? Why was the cap there?

That same day I left for Petersburg and never again saw Dmitri Petrovich and his wife. I've heard that they continue to live together.

1892

IT WAS SHE!

"Tell one of your stories, Peter Ivanovich!" exclaimed the young girls.

The colonel curled his gray mustache, hemmed, and began: "It was 1843 when our regiment was stationed at Tshenstohova.* It's necessary to note, dear young ladies, that winter in that year was fierce. There wasn't a single day when the sentries' noses weren't frozen or the roads weren't covered with snow by a blizzard. We had a hard frost from the end of October until April. You also might be reminded that at that time I didn't react like an old, soot-covered Turkish pipe, as now, but was, you can imagine, but a robust lad, the very picture of glowing good health—in a word, a handsome man. I was a dandy like a peacock, squandered money right and left, and curling my mustache unlike any other ensign on earth.

"All I had to do was to bat an eye, jingle my spurs, twirl my mustache—and the proudest beauty turned into an obedient lamb. I was greedy where women were concerned, like a spider for flies, and if, my dear young ladies, I would try to enumerate

---

*city in south central Poland

236

the Polish and Jewish women who literally hung on my neck, I dare say the arithmetic would be impossible. . . . Add to all this that I was a colonel's adjutant, was an excellent dancer of the mazurka, and was married to a superior woman, may her soul rest in peace. You can't imagine what a madcap I was. If in the district an amorous liaison was going on, if someone pulled out an orthodox Jew's fringes, or beat the mug of a Polish gentleman, it was known that it was the act of the ensign Vivyertov.

"In the capacity of adjutant I had to roam about a large area of the district. I was sent to buy oats or hay, and sell defective horses to the Jews and the Polish gentlemen, but more than anything else, dear young ladies, in the course of duty I would ride at a gallop for a rendezvous with a little Polish lady or to rich landowners to play cards. . . .

"One Christmas Eve, as I now recall, I was on my way from Tshenstohova to the village Shevyelki, where I had been sent to pick up some service supplies. The weather, I assure you, was unbearable. . . . There was an angry crackling frost, such that even the horses wheezed, and I and my driver turned into two icicles in a half hour. . . . It was still possible to cope with the frost, come what may, but picture this, halfway there the storm got worse. A white shroud whirled around, muffled up like the devil himself before morning services, the wind groaned as if his wife had been taken away from him, the road disappeared. . . . It took no more than ten minutes for the driver, myself, and the horses to be completely covered by snow.

" 'Your excellency, we've left the road!' exclaimed the driver.

" 'The hell you say! Why, you blockhead, didn't you keep your eyes open? Well go straight ahead, we'll probably stumble into some kind of dwelling!' I proclaimed.

"Well, we rode on, and the storm whirled and whirled, and just at midnight our horses turned in at the gates of an estate. As I recall now, it was that of Count Boyadlovski, a rich Pole. Poles and Jews are all the same to me, like horseradish after dinner, but, to tell the truth, the gentry are hospitable people and there aren't any warmer women than the Polish ladies. . . .

"They let us in. . . . The Count Boyadlovski himself was

living in Paris at the time, and his steward, Kazimir Kaptsinski, received us. If I remember correctly, not an hour passed before I sat in the steward's cottage, gushed over his wife, drank and played cards. Having won five gold coins, and having had enough to drink, I excused myself in order to go to bed. They didn't have a room for me in the steward's cottage so they settled me in a room in the count's mansion.

" 'Are you afraid of ghosts?' asked the steward, leading me into a small room that was near a huge, empty, dark, and cold ballroom.

" 'Do you really have ghosts here?' I asked, as a remote echo reverberated my words and steps.

" 'I don't know,' answered the Pole, beginning to laugh. 'But it seems to me that this place is the most suitable place for ghosts and evil spirits.'

"I gave my tie a good tug, and I was drunk, dead drunk, but I admit that at these words I felt chilled. The devil will affirm that you'd prefer a hundred Circassians to one ghost! But I had no choice, undressed, and lay down. . . . My candle barely lit the walls, but on the walls, picture this for yourselves, were portraits of ancestors—one more terrible than the other—old weapons, hunter's trophies, and other phantasmagoria. . . . The silence was that of a morgue and the only sound came from the next room where mice rustled, and the old dry furniture creaked. And behind the window something infernal was going on. . . . The wind was conducting a funeral service, the bent trees were howling and weeping; some kind of deviltry was going on. It must have been the shutters, plaintively creaking and banging against the window frame. Add to this that my head was spinning. Along with my head all else was spinning. . . . When I closed my eyes, it seemed to me that my bed was floating over the empty house and was playing leapfrog with the spirits. In order to temper my panic, I doused the candle since the dark, empty room would be less frightening. . . ."

The three young girls listening to the colonel moved closer to the storyteller, staring at him.

"Well," continued the colonel, "since I was trying to sleep, sleep escaped me. It seemed to me that bandits were lying in wait behind the window, that whispers could be heard, that someone was touching my back—in general, the deviltry went on, the kind that's known to any one who at sometime has experienced nervous tension. Well, you can imagine, between the ghoulishness and the chaotic noise, I clearly distinguished a sound that resembled the shuffling of slippers. I heard—what would you think?—I heard someone approaching my door, cough, and open it. . . .

" 'Who's there?' I asked, sitting up.

" 'It's me. . . . Don't be afraid!' answered a woman's voice.

"I went toward the door. . . . A few seconds passed and I felt two woman's hands, soft like eiderdown, placed on my shoulders.

" 'I love you. . . . You mean more than life to me,' said a musical feminine voice.

"Warm breathing stroked my cheeks. . . . I forgot about the storm, about the spooks, about everything else in the world, and put my arms around her waist . . . and what a waist! Nature cannot produce such a waist except by special order, once in ten years. . . . Slender, perfectly formed, warm, ephemeral, like the breathing of an infant in arms! I couldn't restrain myself and embraced her energetically. . . . Our lips met in long, drawn-out kisses, and . . . I swear to all the women in the world, I'll never forget those kisses 'til the day I die."

The colonel grew silent, drank half a glass of water and continued, lowering his voice:

"On the following day when I looked out the window, I saw that the storm had increased in intensity. . . . There was no possibility of leaving. The whole day was spent at the steward's, playing cards and drinking. In the evening I was again settled in the vacant house, and exactly at midnight I again embraced the familiar waist. . . . Oh yes, young ladies, if it weren't that I was in love, I would have died from boredom. I'm sorry to say, I could have become an inveterate drunkard."

The colonel took a deep breath, arose, and silently walked around the drawing room.

"Well . . . go on. What happened?" asked one of the young ladies, holding her breath in expectation.

"But . . . who was this woman?" asked the befuddled young ladies.

"It's obvious who!"

"We don't understand any of it. . . ."

"It was my wife!"

All three of the young ladies arose as if something had stung them.

"That's. . . . How is that possible?" they asked.

"Ah, good lord, what's impossible about that?" asked the colonel with annoyance in his voice and shrugging his shoulders. "Really I, it seems to me, expressed myself clearly enough! I was traveling to Shevyelki with my wife. . . . She was spending the night in the empty house in the next room. . . . That's crystal clear!"

"Mmm . . . ," murmured the young ladies, dropping their arms in disappointment. "The beginning of your story was great but the ending, God. . . . Your wife. . . . Sorry, but that's uninteresting and . . . not even very smart."

"That's strange! That means that you preferred that it wouldn't be my wife but some kind of strange woman! Ah, young ladies, young ladies! If you want that kind of situation now, what will you say when you get married?"

The young ladies became embarrassed and silent. They pouted, frowned, and, being thoroughly disappointed, began to yawn audibly. . . . They had no appetite at suppertime, played with their bread, and remained silent.

"No, that's even . . . unconscionable!" declared one of them who could not refrain from saying something. "Why even tell the story if that's the end? It's not a good story. . . . It's even primitive!"

"The beginning was so enticing and . . . it was suddenly changed . . . ," added another young lady. "You just made fun of us and nothing else."

"Now, now, now . . . I was joking . . . ," said the colonel. "Don't be angry, young ladies, I was joking. It wasn't my wife, but the steward's wife. . . ."

"Really?!"

The young ladies immediately became lively and their eyes

sparkled. . . . They moved closer to the colonel, filled his wine glass, and showered him with questions. Their boredom disappeared, and their supper was soon consumed as they ate with gusto.

1886

THE PRELIMINARY EXAMINATION

"The geography teacher, Galkin, has it in for me, and believe me, I'll fail the exam he'll give me today," said Efrim Zakarich Fendrikov, nervously rubbing his hands and perspiring. He was a graying, bearded man with a respectable bald spot and a solid paunch and was a candidate from the postal district K——. "I won't pass. . . . It's as if God himself anointed him. . . . He's mad at me for some trivia. . . . He approached me once with a written order and pushed his way toward me before others waiting to see me so that I would handle his mail first and that of others after that. I'm not able to do that. . . . Even though you're from the educated class you must observe the rules and wait your turn. I did remind him courteously, 'Please wait your turn, dear sir.' He became angry and from that time opposes me like some kind of Saul. "He gave my small son, Yegorushka, a one, the worst possible grade, and calls me a variety of names around town. Once I was going by Kuktin's tavern and he leaned out the window with a billiard stick and yelled in a drunken stew so that the whole square could hear him: 'Gentlemen, take a look: a formerly needed stamp is passing by!' "

Pivomedov, a teacher of Russian, who was standing in the entrance of K—— District College together with Fendrikov and smoking a cigarette, condescendingly shrugged his shoulders and comforted him:

"Don't get so worked up. There is no precedent here where they cut anyone down. It's all pro forma!"

Fendrikov calmed down, but not for long. Galkin came though the foyer. He was young, with a thin, somewhat ragged beard, in canvas britches and a new, blue frock coat. He looked sternly at Fendrikov and went on his way.

After that it was announced that the inspector had arrived. Fendrikov got cold feet and waited with the same apprehension that anyone who has been examined for the first time knows well. The state examiner of the college, Hamov, hurried across the foyer. After him hurried Zimiyezhalov, the law professor, in a kamilavka* and wearing a cross on his chest. Several other professors followed after them.

Akanov, the inspector of public schools, greeted all profusely, exclaimed his displeasure with the dust, and then entered the college. Within five minutes all were ready for the examinations.

Two priests who wanted to be village teachers were tested. One passed, the other failed. The one who failed blew his nose in a red handkerchief, stood a moment, thought about it, and left. Two unsupervised administrators of the third order were examined. Then Fendrikov's time came.

"Where are you working?" asked the inspector, turning in his direction.

"I'm the receiver of mail at the local postal department, your honor," he replied, straightening up and trying to hide his shaking hands. "I've been there for twenty-one years, your honor, and now I've asked to be considered for a promotion to the rank of college registrar, for which I am willing to take the examination for first-class ranking."

"Fine. . . . Take this dictation."

Pivomedov stood up, coughed, and began to dictate in a

---

*high headdress worn by orthodox priests

thick, penetrating basso voice, trying to trip up the examinee, who wouldn't be able to write what was being expressed, something like "Cold water calms the crusty esophagus," and other tongue twisters.

But no matter how Pivomedov schemed, the dictation was successfully taken down. The future college registrar made a few small errors, and leaned more in the direction of the elegance of his handwriting than on his grammar. He misspelled "extraordinary" and instead of "better" wrote "blooper," and when he heard "new field" a smile appeared on the face of the inspector as he wrote "new underground," but all the same, these were not big mistakes.

"Dictation results were satisfactory," declared the inspector.

"May I be so audacious as to inform your honors," said the emboldened Fendrikov, giving a side-glance at his enemy, Galkin, "may I be so audacious as to tell you that I studied geometry from Davidov's text, had studied with the nephew of Varsonov when he came for his holidays from Troitse-Sergiyevska, also at the Vivanski Seminary. I also learned surveying and stereometry. . . . Everything as it should be. . . ."

"Stereometry is irrelevant here."

"Isn't relevant? I worked on it for a month. . . . What a waste!" exclaimed Fendrikov.

"Well, we'll put geometry aside for the time being. Let's turn to the knowledge you've acquired as a chief of a postal service, which no doubt you know intimately. Geography—that's a postal subject."

All the professors smiled politely. Fendrikov did not agree with them that geography was a subject for the postal workers (nothing about this had been written in the postal regulations, nor in orders relating to them), but out of politeness said: "Precisely." He coughed nervously and fearfully awaited the questions. His enemy, Galkin, leaned back in his chair, and, not looking at him, asked—dragging it out:

"Eh . . . tell me, what kind of government do they have in Turkey?"

"It's known as some kind of . . . Turkish . . ."

"Hm! . . . Turkish. . . . That's understood. They have a constitutional government. And what do you know about the tributaries of the Ganges?"

"I did learn Smirnov's geography, but if you'll excuse me, I didn't learn very much. . . . The Ganges is a river in India . . . which flows into the ocean."

"I'm not asking you that. What are the branches of the Ganges? You don't know? And where does the Araks flow? You don't know that too? Strange. . . . What province is Zhitomir in?"

"The eighteenth tract, Local 121."

A cold sweat arose on Fendrikov's brow. His eyes blinked and he swallowed so loudly that it seemed he had swallowed his tongue.

"As if before God himself, your honors," he grumbled. "Even the archbishop can confirm . . . I served for twenty-one years, and now this I will too. . . . I'll swear eternally to God . . ."

"All right, we'll put geography aside. What have you prepared for arithmetic?"

"But I didn't count on arithmetic. . . . Even the bishop can confirm it. . . . I'll swear eternally to God. . . . I studied all of Pokrov and . . . this makes no sense. . . . My knowledge is a little rusty. Be so kind, your excellency. Let me be thankful and swear to God eternally."

It was apparent that his tears were ready to fall.

"I've been a responsible and honest servant. . . . I perform my religious duties every year. . . . Even the bishop can confirm this. . . . Be generous, your excellency."

"You haven't prepared anything?"

"I prepared everything, but I don't remember anything. I'll be sixty soon, your excellency. What can I learn? Be kind!"

"We've already ordered your new visored cap . . . ," said Zmiezhalov, the archpriest, and then laughed.

"Fine, we're finished!" declared the inspector.

Within a half-hour Fendrikov was on his way to the Kuktin Tavern with the teachers to drink tea and celebrate. His face shone, his eyes were glistening happily, but he was constantly scratching the back of his neck because he was befuddled by some kind of thought.

"What a pity!" he muttered. "Really what stupidity on my part!"

"What do you mean?" asked Pivomedov.

"Why did I study stereometry if it's not part of the program? I spent a whole month over it. Sat at it for nothing. What a shame!"

1884

A MAN BOUND BY
A COCOON

At the very edge of the village of Mironosits, a couple of
hunters who were too late for the hunt settled for the night
in a barn owned by the village elder, Prokofiya. There were
only two of them: Ivan Ivanich, a veterinarian, and Burkin, a
high school teacher. Ivan Ivanich had a rather strange, hyphen-
ated last name, Chimsha-Himalayski,* which didn't become
him, and in the whole province he was simply known by his first
name and his patronymic. He lived near the town on a breeding
farm for thoroughbreds and had come to hunt and indulge in
some fresh air. The high school teacher, Burkin, was a guest
every summer of the Count P—— and he felt completely at
home in this locality where everybody knew him.

They did not feel like sleeping. Ivan Ivanich, a tall, thin,
aging man with a long, drooping mustache, sat outside the
entrance smoking a pipe. The moonlight shone brightly upon
him. Burkin lay inside on the hay and was hidden by the darkness.

They were telling stories. Among other things they talked
about the elder's wife, Mavra, who was a healthy and intelligent

---

*"High-minded"

247

woman but who had never been outside the village in which she was born, had never seen a town or a railroad, and for the last ten years sat behind the stove and only went out at night. "That's not all that remarkable!" declared Burkin. "People whose nature is similar and are like a hermit crab or a snail and withdraw into their shells are not rare. It could be that it is a form of atavism, reverting to that time when man's ancestor was not gregarious and lived alone in his den, or possibly it is just another aspect of the human character—who knows? I'm not a scientist and it is not my business to be concerned with such questions. I only want to say that this type of person, such as Mavra, is not unique. I don't have to seek very far to give you an example.

"About two months ago one Belikov died in our town. He was a teacher of Greek and was my colleague. You must have heard of him. The outstanding thing about him was that he always, even when the weather was wonderful, had on galoshes, carried an umbrella, and wore a warm, quilted coat. The umbrella was always in its cover, his watch was in a gray chamois case, and when he took out his penknife to sharpen a pencil, it, too, was in a case. His face, in the same manner, was also encased as he constantly hid it in his turned-up collar. He wore dark glasses, a knitted sweater, covered his ears with quilted muffs filled with cotton wool, and when he took a cab he ordered that it be enclosed. In a word, it could be observed that this man had a persistent and irresistible need to surround himself with covering, to create for himself, so to say, a cocoon, which would isolate and protect him from external intrusions. Reality irritated him, frightened him, put him in a tizzy, and probably in order to justify his timidity and his aversion to the present, he always praised the past and that which had never occurred. The ancient tongues that he taught were for him, in truth, the galoshes and umbrella, where he hid himself from an active life.

" 'Oh, how sonorous, how beautiful is the Greek language!' he would exclaim with a benign expression on his face. And as if to emphasize the exactness of his words, he would narrow his eyes and, lifting a finger, would proclaim: 'Anthropos!'*

---

*"Man!"

"Belikov also tried to hide his thoughts in a wrapper. Government regulations and newspaper articles in which something was forbidden were the only writings he considered clear. When a curfew was issued after nine o'clock for high school students or an article forbade making love, this was clear and definite for him: it was forbidden—and that was that. But when something was sanctioned or permitted, he always harbored an element of doubt and said that it was incomplete and vague. When a dramatic circle or a reading room or a tea house was permitted, he would shake his head and say quietly, 'It is, of course, all very well and sometimes good, but sometimes bad comes of it; let's hope that only good comes of it.'

"Any type of violation, deviation, or departure from the law made him gloomy even though it would appear to be no concern of his. If a colleague were late for prayers, or if there was gossip about some student pranks, or if a female staffer was seen out late at night with an officer, he would become very agitated and always commented that one could never know what might come of it. At faculty meetings we felt intimidated by his cautiousness, his suspiciousness, and his simple, rigid understanding with regard to any unruly conduct of the high school boys and girls. Noise in the classroom became worthy of extreme statements: 'Oh, if this should get to the administrators, you don't know what might happen.' 'And in the second class Petrov should be expelled, and in the fourth, Yegorov should also be thrown out.' And what else? With his sighs, his dreariness, his dark glasses on his pale, small face—you know his small face was like a polecat's—he intimidated all of us and we gave in, and lowered the conduct grades of Petrov and Yegorov, pulled them out of class and confined them, and finally expelled both Petrov and Yegorov.

"He had the strangest habit—to visit us in our apartments. He would arrive, sit silently, and look around as if he were spying. He would sit in this way for an hour or two and then leave. He called this 'conducting good relations with his colleagues' and apparently it was very difficult for him to call on us, but did so because he felt it was a requirement of his position. We, the teachers, were afraid of him. Just imagine, we, the faculty, are thoughtful, extremely respectable, brought up on Turgenev and Shchedrin, but this person always wearing galoshes and carrying an umbrella somehow took over the whole school for fifteen years! Not just the school, but the whole town! Our ladies stopped performing plays in their homes on Saturdays because they were afraid he'd find out. And the clergy refrained from eating meat and playing cards when he was around. The effect upon the town of a man like Belikov for the last ten to fifteen years was to be fearful of everything. We were afraid to raise our voices, to send letters, to make acquaintances, to read books, afraid to help the poor, to teach reading and writing. . . ."

Ivan Ivanich, wanting to say something, coughed, and after lighting his pipe and looking up at the moon, spoke in a measure tone:

"Yes. They were thoughtful, respectable, read Shchedrin and Turgenev and Buckle* and so forth, but were intimidated, put up with it. . . . That's the way it is."

"Belikov and I lived in the same house," continued Burkin, "on the same floor and our doors faced each other, so we often met. I knew his domestic habits. At home it was the same story: his dressing gown, nightcap, blinds, bolts, a whole batch of restrictions and prohibitions, and 'Oh, you don't know what might come of it!' He couldn't eat Lenten food and meat was forbidden; so that people wouldn't say he didn't fast, he ate perch fried in butter—not a Lenten dish but you couldn't say it was meat. He didn't have a female servant because he was afraid for his reputation and engaged a cook, one Afanasiya, who was about sixty, a drunk, and an idiot, who at one time served in the army as an orderly and could throw something together. This Afanasiya usually stood by the door with folded arms, and with deep sighs always muttered one and the same thing:

" 'There's too many of *them* around here already!'

"Belikov's bedroom was small, like a box, and his bed had curtains. When he lay down to sleep, he covered his head; it would be hot, stuffy, and the wind made the closed door rattle,

---

*an English liberal historian and sociologist (1821–1862)

and the stove hummed; loud sighs could be heard from the kitchen and they were ominous. . . .

"And he found it terrifying under the covers. He imagined what might happen, that Afanasiya would knife him, that robbers would break in, so he had nightmares all night long. In the morning when we walked together to the school, he was dull and pale and it was obvious that the crowded school toward which he walked was terrifying. His whole being was full of aversion and as a person who by nature was a loner, he found it difficult to walk along with me.

" 'It's really very noisy in the classrooms,' he would say, trying to rationalize his anxiety. 'I've never seen anything like it.'

"And this teacher of Greek, this man who had wrapped himself in a cocoon, incredible as it may seem, almost got married."

Ivan Ivanich gave a quick glance around the barn and said: "You're joking!"

"Yes, strange as it may seem, he really almost got married. A new history and geography teacher had been assigned to our school, a Ukrainian whose name was Mihail Savich Kovalenko. He didn't arrive alone, but with his sister, Varenka. He was tall, swarthy, with enormous hands, and you could even tell from his face that his voice was deep. It actually sounded as if it came out of a barrel. Boom-boom-boom! Varenka wasn't that young, but about thirty, and also was tall, well-stacked, with dark eyebrows and red cheeks—simply put, not a young girl but a sweet dish, spaced-out, and loud. She was always singing Ukrainian songs and laughing. At the slightest suggestion her ringing laughter would peal out: Ha-ha-ha!

"Our first significant acquaintance with the Kovalenkos, as I recall, happened at a name-day party at the principal's house. Among the reserved, strained, and dull pedagogues who even attend name-day parties as an obligation, suddenly there appeared a new Aphrodite, arising out of the foam of the sea: walking with arms akimbo, laughing, singing, dancing. . . . She sang with feeling 'The winds are blowing,' and still another Ukrainian melody, and more. And we were all enchanted—all, even Belikov. He sat down beside us and said, smiling good-naturedly:

" 'The Little Russian language in its softness and pleasant sonority reminds me of ancient Greek.'

"This flattered her and she began to tell him with feeling and persuasiveness that in the Gadyachski district where she came from, they owned a farm where her dear little mother lived, and where they grew fantastic pears, melons, and pumpkins! In the Ukraine they called pumpkins 'tabaki,' while in Russian, taverns are called 'kabaki'; and in their home they made borscht with tomatoes and eggplant 'so delicious, so delicious, that it's simply—astonishing!'

"We listened, kept listening, and suddenly the same thought dawned upon all of us.

" 'Wouldn't it be great if we could get these two to marry?' whispered the principal's wife to me.

"For some reason we all remembered that Belikov was a bachelor and it now seemed strange that we didn't note this before. This vital detail of his life had never entered into our observations previously. How did he conduct himself with women generally? How did he handle such an essential question? Earlier this did not concern us. It could be we even had thought that a man who in all kinds of weather wore galoshes and who slept behind bed-curtains could not fall in love.

" 'He's already past forty and she's thirty . . . ,' the principal's wife expanded her thought. 'It seems to me she'd be interested in him.'

"What useless rubbish is created out of boredom in our provinces! And this because what is necessary is not done at all. So, why did we suddenly find it desirable to marry off this Belikov, whom we couldn't imagine married? The principal's wife, the superintendent's wife, and our faculty women became livelier and better looking, as if they had been given a new purpose in life. The principal's wife purchased a box in the theater and we see—in her box sits a shining, happy Varenka fanning herself, and beside her is Belikov, a short, curled-up man, looking as if he had been dragged out of his house with pliers. I give an evening soiree and the ladies insist that without fail I invite Belikov and Varenka. Briefly, the wheels were set in motion.

"It was obvious that Varenka was not averse to the thought of marriage. Living with her brother was not a very happy situation, and we knew that they argued and abused each other for days on end. Picture this: Kovalenko is walking on the street, a tall, healthy, lanky fellow in an embroidered shirt; a lock of hair which has fallen from under his cap lies on his forehead. He carries a bundle of books in one hand and a stout walking stick in the other. Behind him walks his sister, also carrying books.

" 'All the same, Mihailik, you haven't read that!' she argues loudly. 'I say to you, I swear that you haven't read it at all!'

" 'But I say to you that I've read it!' shouts Kovalenko, stomping his walking stick against the sidewalk.

" 'My God, Minchik! What are you getting so hot about? We're only talking about principles.'

" 'But I repeat, I read it!' shouts Kovalenko even louder.

"At home if there were an outsider present, it was certain there would be a skirmish. She must have been sick of this kind of life really, and would have liked to have a home of her own. And she probably considered her age. There was little time to be choosy and even a teacher of Greek would have been satisfactory. Besides, for the majority of our young ladies, it was important to marry, and it made little difference to them whom they married. Be that as it may, Varenka did indicate to our Belikov that she was favorably inclined.

"And Belikov? He began to visit Kovalenko just as he did us. He would arrive, sit down, and keep his mouth shut. He remains silent and Varenka sings to him 'The winds are blowing,' or looks at him intensely with her dark eyes, or suddenly laughs merrily:

" 'Ha-ha-ha!'

"In matters of love, especially where marriage is concerned, suggestion plays a big part. All of us—colleagues and ladies—began to persuade Belikov that he should marry and that nothing was more important for him than to marry. All of us complimented him, assumed airs of authority, spoke a variety of platitudes like 'marriage is a serious step.' As to Varenka, we noted that she was not bad-looking, was interesting, and was the daughter of a district councillor and owned a farm, but most important, she was the first woman who was kind and affectionate with him. His head was turned, and he decided that he really should marry."

"At that point you should have taken his galoshes and umbrella away from him," remarked Ivan Ivanich.

"Keep in mind that that was not possible. He put a photograph of Varenka on his desk, often came to me to talk about Varenka and about family life, and how serious a step it was to marry. He was often at the Kovalenkos, but his way of life did not change very much. On the contrary, the decision to marry had a somewhat sickly effect upon him. He lost weight, lost color, and it appeared he retreated further into his shell.

" 'I like Varvara Savishna,' he told me with a weak distorted smile. 'I know that every person needs to marry, but . . . all the same, this has really come about too quickly. . . . One should take time to think it over.'

" 'What's there to think over?' I replied. 'Get married, that's all there is to it.'

" 'No.' he said. 'Marriage—is a serious step and one must first weigh the forthcoming duties and responsibilities . . . so that later something might not come of it. This disturbs me so, I have sleepless nights now. And, I admit, I'm afraid. She and her brother have an odd way of reasoning; they argue, you know, so strangely, and she is impetuous. You get married and then anything can happen, both good and bad.'

"And he didn't propose and procrastinated, to the great annoyance of the principal's wife and all our ladies. He constantly weighed the forthcoming duties and responsibilities, and meanwhile went out every day with Varenka—perhaps thinking that good manners required this; and he would come to me to talk about family life. Most probably, he would have finally proposed and ultimately entered into one of those unnecessary, stupid marriages—thousands of which are performed in our country out of boredom—if it weren't for the fact that suddenly there occurred a *Kolossalische Scandal.** It must be

---

*Russian academics like to use German expressions. This means simply a "colossal scandal."

told that Varenka's brother, Kovalenko, despised Belikov from the time he first met him and could not endure him.

" 'I can't understand,' he said to us, shrugging his shoulders, 'I don't understand how you can stomach this informer, this vile ugly thug. Ugh, gentlemen, how can you continue to live here! The atmosphere is stifling, filthy. Are you really pedagogues, teachers? You're bureaucrats. We don't have a cathedral of knowledge here, but a church directorate that has the sour smell of a police station. No, brothers, I won't be here long and will leave for my farm to catch crayfish and to teach Ukrainians. I'll leave, and you'll stay here with your Judas—he's damnable!'

"Or he would laugh, laugh until the tears flowed, sometimes with a deep tone, sometimes shrilly, and, spreading his arms wide, would ask me:

" 'Why does he come to my house? What does he want? He just sits and stares.'

"He even gave Belikov a nickname. He was the 'slick spider.' And, you must understand, we avoided speaking with him about the fact that his sister was aiming to marry the 'slick spider.' When the principal's wife once alluded to him that it would be nice for his sister to marry a steady person, respected by everyone, such as Belikov, he frowned and said:

" 'It's none of my business. Let her marry a snake if she wants to. I don't like to interfere in what's not any business of mine.'

"Now listen to what followed. Some cutup drew a cartoon: Belikov is walking along in his galoshes with his trousers tucked in them and under his umbrella with Varenka on his arm. Below was the caption: 'Anthropos in love.' He captured the resemblances remarkably. It was obviously not the accomplishment of a single night's work. All the teachers in both the boys' and girls' high schools and in the seminary, and the bureaucrats received copies. Belikov received one, too. The cartoon made a very grim impression upon him.

"He and I were walking out of the house together. It was the first day of May, a Sunday, and we were all, teachers and students, gathering on the campus to walk as a group to a grove outside the town. As we came out together I noted that his face looked bitter and gloomier than a thundercloud.

" 'There are ugly, malicious people!' he exclaimed, his lips trembling.

"I couldn't help being sorry for him. We're walking along together, and picture this: here comes Kovalenko on a bicycle and behind him is Varenka, also on a bicycle. She looks flushed, her eyes fixed forward, but obviously enjoying herself and exuberant.

" 'We'll go on ahead of you!' she shouted. 'It's such wonderful weather, so wonderful that it's awesome!'

"And then they both disappeared in the distance. Belikov's grim face blanched and he seemed to become numb. He stopped short and stared at me. . . .

" 'Tell me, what's going on?' he asked. 'Are my eyes hoodwinking me? Do respectable school teachers and women ride bicycles?'

" 'What's improper about that?' I asked. 'It's healthy to ride bicycles.'

" 'How is it possible?' he shrieked, agitated by my nonchalance. 'What are you saying?!'

"He was so affected that he didn't want to go any further and returned home.

"On the following day he kept constantly rubbing his hands and nervously wincing. It was obvious that he wasn't well. For the first time during his tenure he left school early. He ate no dinner. Before evening set in he dressed warmly even though it was summer weather outdoors and headed for the Kovalenkos. Varenka was not at home and only the brother was there.

" 'Please sit down,' said Kovalenko coldly, with a frown on his face. He was sleepy-looking, for he had just taken a nap after dinner and was in a bad mood.

"Belikov sat silent for about ten minutes and then began:

" 'I've come here in order to relieve my soul. It's very difficult for me. Some lampoonist has drawn in a laughable way a picture of me and one other person who is close to both of us. I consider it my duty to assure you that I had nothing to do with it. . . . I gave no grounds for such malice—on the contrary, I have always conducted myself as an entirely respectable man.'

"Kovalenko sat, his face angry and dark, and remained silent. Belikov waited a bit and then continued in a soft, plaintive voice:

" 'I have something else to say to you. I have been teaching for a long time and you are just a novice. I consider it my duty, as an older colleague, to put you on your guard. You ride a bicycle and that's not at all proper for an educator of the young.'

" 'Why so?' asked Kovalenko in his deep voice.

" 'Is it really necessary to explain, Mihail Savich? Isn't it self-evident? If a teacher rides a bicycle, what remains for the student to do? The only thing left is to stand on their heads! If it isn't explicitly permitted by the principal, then it shouldn't be done. I was horrified yesterday! When I saw your sister, my eyes became bleary. A lady on a bicycle—that's awful!'

" 'What is it you want?'

" 'All I want to do—is warn you, Mihail Savich. You—a young man with your future ahead of you—must always conduct yourself conservatively, and you are so careless and don't think of the consequences. Oh, so careless! You wear an embroidered shirt, are constantly seen on the street carrying miscellaneous books, and now on a bicycle. When the principal hears that you and your sister ride bicycles, and the trustee hears of it. . . . What will come of it?'

" 'That my sister and I ride bicycles is nobody's business!' declared Kovalenko turning red. 'Anyone who will meddle in my domestic and family affairs can go to a cur's hell!'

"Belikov grew pale and rose.

" 'Since you speak to me in this way, I can't go on,' he said. 'And I beg you never to express yourself in this way in my presence about the administration. You must conduct yourself with respect toward the powers that be.'

" 'What have I said that's offensive about the administration?' asked Kovalenko, looking at him angrily. 'Please leave me in peace. I'm a respectable person and with a gentleman like you I have no desire to carry on a conversation. I detest spies.'

"Belikov nervously fussed, got up, and quickly put on his coat, and his face displayed horror. This was really the first time in his life that he had been spoken to so rudely.

" 'You can say whatever you want,' he said walking out of the entryway onto the landing of the staircase. 'I must warn you: someone could have heard us and in order that our conversation is not misinterpreted and something come of it, I must inform the principal of the content of our conversation . . . of the important parts I feel obliged to do so.'

" 'Inform him? Leave and make your damn report!'

"Kovalenko took hold of Belikov's collar from the rear and shoved him. Belikov rolled down to the bottom of the stairway, his galoshes clopping noisily. It was a steep stairway but he reached the bottom unhurt. He got up and felt his nose: were his glasses intact? As he was rolling down the stairs, Varenka entered with two other ladies. He stood at the bottom and stared—and for Belikov this was the most dreadful circumstance of all. It would have been better for him to break his neck, both of his legs, than to appear ridiculous. Now the whole town would hear of it, it would get to the principal and the trustee—ah, what would come of it! The wag would draw another cartoon and it would all end up in his having to retire. . . .

"When he stood up, Varenka recognized him and seeing his laughable face, wrinkled coat, galoshes, and not comprehending what had happened, she assumed that he had stumbled and could not restrain herself and her laughter could be heard throughout the house.

" 'Ha-ha-ha!'

"And this booming, buoyant laughter put an end to everything—to the expected marriage and to Belikov's existence on earth. He couldn't hear what Varenka said and could see nothing. Upon returning to his quarters, he took Varenka's photograph from his desk, lay down in his bed, and never got up again.

"About three days later Afanasiya came to me and asked that a doctor be called, for something was wrong with his master. I went across to Belikov's place. He lay behind the bed-curtains, covered with blankets, and made no sound. His answers to questioning were only yes and no—and nothing else. He lay there, and Afanasiya fussed around, glum and frowning, sighing deeply and reeking of liquor, smelling like a barroom.

"Within a month Belikov died. We all attended the funeral, that is to say, everyone connected with both the high school and the seminary. Now, as he lay in the casket, his expression was mild, pleasant, even happy, as if he were glad that he finally was lying in a case which he would never have to leave. He had reached his ideal situation! And, as if in honor of his funeral, the weather was gloomy and raining, and we all wore galoshes and carried umbrellas. Varenka was also at the funeral and when the casket was let down into the grave, she cried. I noted that Ukrainian women can only cry or laugh—they have no temperate moods.

"I must admit that it is very satisfying to bury people like Belikov. When returning from the cemetery, we were modest in our expressions and our body language. No one wanted to broadcast this feeling of satisfaction. It was a feeling resembling one which we had experienced a long time ago in childhood when the adults were going out, and we ran about the yard for an hour or two enjoying complete freedom! Even a hint, even a weak hope of its possibility, gives the spirit wings. Isn't that true?

"We returned from the cemetery in good humor. However, a week didn't go by when our lives fell into the previous pattern—as gloomy, tiresome, and useless, where nothing is expressly forbidden but on the other hand, not fully allowed. There was no improvement. Although Belikov was buried, how many other such men were there whose lives were restrained by a rigid set of rules that bound them like a cocoon. How many more of them will there still be!"

"That's the way it is," said Ivan Ivanich, lighting his pipe.

"How many more of them will there still be!" repeated Burkin.

The high school teacher came out of the barn. He was a short, stout man, perfectly bald, and with a black beard that almost reached his waist. Two dogs came out with him.

"What a beautiful moon!" he exclaimed, looking up at the sky.

It was already midnight. The whole village could be seen

on the right, and the long street stretched far—at least for five versts. Everything had subsided into a quiet, deep sleep; not a move, nor a sound, and it seemed improbable that nature could be so still. If on a moonlit night you see a wide village street with its huts, its haystacks, sleepy weeping willows, the same peace rests in your soul. Hidden by the night's shadows from toil, trouble, and grief, the street in its serenity appears meek, sad, beautiful, and as if the stars are looking down upon it kindly and tenderly, and that there is no more evil on the earth and all is well. On the left at the edge of the village begin the fields. They could be seen stretching out to the horizon and the whole span was drenched by the moonlight and there was the same stillness and silence.

"Yes, that's the way it is," repeated Ivan Ivanich. "Perhaps because we live in town, in oppressive, crowded conditions, write useless treatises, play cards—perhaps we, too, live confined in a cocoon? Or, that we spend our lives among contentious idlers and their silly, indolent wives, say, and listen to a variety of nonsense—isn't that the same thing as a cocoon? If you wish I'll tell you a very informative story."

"No, it's time to sleep." said Burkin. "Tomorrow's another day!"

They both went back into the barn and lay down on the hay. They were already covered and half asleep when suddenly they heard light footsteps: tup, tup. . . . Someone was walking near the barn. Walking and stopping a moment and then walking again: tup, tup . . . the dogs growled.

"That's Mavra ambling around," remarked Burkin.

The footsteps died away.

"To see and to hear how they lie," commented Ivan Ivanich, turning on his side, "and to be called a fool for tolerating these lies; to be insulted, demeaned, not to dare to openly state that you are on the side of the honorable and free, and to lie to oneself, to smile, and all this for a piece of bread and a warm bed; to be some kind of petty official whose price is cheap—no, you can't continue to live that way."

"Well, that's a different opera, Ivan Ivanich," said the teacher. "Let's sleep."

And in about ten minutes Burkin was asleep. But Ivan Ivanich tossed from side to side and then got up and went outside again. He sat down by the door and lit his pipe.

1898

HE COULDN'T REMEMBER!

He had once been an adroit lieutenant, a dancer, and a ladies' man, but now he was overweight, short of breath, already paralyzed twice; the landowner, Ivan Prokhorich Gauptvakhtov,* worn-out and tormented by shopping for his wife, entered a music store to buy sheet music.

"Greetings!" he exclaimed as he entered the store. "Permit me . . ."

The small German behind the counter extended his neck and registered a questioning smile on his face.

"What can I do for you?"

"Allow me. . . . It's terribly warm! You can't do anything in this climate! Allow me. . . . Hmmm. . . . I—eh. . . . Hm. . . . Allow me. . . . I've forgotten what I want!"

"Try to remember!"

Gauptvakhtov placed his upper lip over his lower one, wrinkled his ample brow into deep furrows, raised his eyes, and indulged in intense thought.

"I can't remember! Such a, forgive me Lord, such a devilish

---

*Gayptvakhta is the military guardhouse in old Russia. Chekhov is making fun of an old soldier who has retired to the equivalent in his private life.

memory! It's . . . it's. . . . Allow me. . . . Hm. . . . I can't remember!

"I told her: Write it down! But no. . . . Why didn't she write it down? I can't remember everything. . . . Maybe you can deduce it yourself? It's a piece from abroad. It's played very loud. . . . Yes?"

"We have many pieces like that you know, that . . ."

"Well, yes. . . . That's understandable! Hm. . . . Hm. . . . Let me try to remember. . . . Well, what can it be?

"I can't go home without the music—my daughter, Nadya, will chew me out; when she plays without the music it's clumsy. . . . she makes mistakes! Even when she has the music, I admit, I would like to accidentally pour kerosene over it in order that the noise would disappear. I'd throw it behind the highboy. . . . I don't like women's screams! I was ordered to buy. . . . Well, yes. . . . Pff. . . . What an important-looking cat you have!" And Gauptvakhtov stared at a huge gray cat that had jumped on to the counter. . . . The cat purred and stretched luxuriously.

"He's magnificent. . . . He's a Siberian scoundrel! . . . A purebred, a rascal. Male or female?"

"A male."

"Why are you staring? You ugly mug! Fool! Tiger! Are you a mouser? Meow, meow? What a hellish memory! You fat rascal! Is it possible to get a kitten from you?"

"No. . . . Hm . . ."

"I'd take one. . . . My wife has a passion for this kind—cats!. . . . What's to be done now? I knew it all the way here and now I've forgotten. . . . My memory is gone, that's it! I've gotten old, my time is up. . . . I'll die soon. . . . She plays so loud, with emphasis, with grandeur. . . . Allow me. . . . Kgm. . . . Maybe I can sing it . . ."

"Sing it . . . *oder* . . . *oder* . . . or whistle it! . . ."

"It's a sin to whistle indoors. . . . One Sedelnikov whistled in our house, whistled and whistled . . . and overdid it. . . . Are you German or French?"

"German."

"To—to, I think it's something like that. . . . It's good you're not a Frenchman. . . . I don't like Frenchmen. . . . Khryu,

khryu, khryu. . . . That's awful! During the war they ate mice.
. . . He whistled in his shop from morning 'til night and blew all
his groceries up the chimney! He owes everybody now. . . .
And he owes me two hundred rubles. . . . I did mutter under my
nose sometimes. . . . Hm. . . . Allow me. . . . I'll sing it. . . .
Wait, it'll come to me. Now. . . . Kgm. . . . I have a cough. . . .
My throat is raspy. . . ."

Gauptvakhtov snapped his fingers three times, closed his
eyes, and sang falsetto:

"Ta-ta-ti-ta—tam. . . . Ho-ho-ho. . . . I'm a tenor. . . . At
home best of all I sing descant. . . . Allow me. . . . Tri-ra-ra. . . .
Kgrrm.. . . . Something's stuck in my teeth. . . . T-phew! A seed.
. . . O-ta-a-auu. . . . Kgrrm. . . . I must have caught cold. I drank
cold beer at the stock exchange. . . . Tru-ru-ry. . . . It's like that
in the upper register. . . . and then, understand, down, down. . . .
Approaches the bottom and then takes off on a high note, like
being shattered . . . ta-ta-ti . . . ruuu. Do you get it? At this point
the base picks it up: gu-gu-gu-tutu. . . . Get it?"

"No, I don't. . . ."

The cat looks in amazement at Gauptvakhtov, probably
grins, and lazily jumps off the counter.

"You don't get it? Too bad. . . . Anyhow, I didn't sing it
perfectly. . . . I've forgotten it entirely. What a pain!"

"Play it on the piano. . . . Do you play?"

"No, I don't. . . . I did play a little on the violin, on one
string, and that's all. . . . It was foolish. . . . I wasn't taught. . . .
My brother, Nazar, plays. . . . He was given lessons. . . . From
the Frenchman, Rokat, it's possible you know of him; he was
taught by Benedict Frantsich. He was such a funny little
Frenchman. . . . We would call him Bonaparte to tease him. . . .
He would become furious. . . . 'I,' he would say, 'am not Bonaparte. . . . I am a French republican.' To tell the truth, he had
a republican mug. . . . Totally like a dog's. . . . My dead parents
never taught me anything. . . . My grandfather used to say, they
called you Ivan, and you are Ivan, and because of this you're
like your grandfather in everything: and in war a lousy soldier!
Blow it up! Softness, brother . . . brother. . . . I, brother . . . I,
brother, won't allow you to be soft! My grandfather ate horse-

flesh at one time, and you, too, will eat some! Put a saddle under your head instead of a pillow!.... I have to go home now! I'll be chewed out! To arrive without the music is forbidden.... In any case, goodbye! I'm sorry to have inconvenienced you! ... How much is that piano?"

"Eight hundred rubles!"

"Phew-phew-phew.... Good heavens! That means: buy yourself a piano and go without trousers! Ha-ha-ha! Eight hundred rub ... les!!! You know what's good for you! Goodbye! *Sprechen sie! Geben sie!** You know I had dinner with a German once.... After dinner I asked a gentleman, also a German, how to say in German: 'I'm most humbly grateful for your hospitality'? And he told me ... he told me.... Allow me.... And said, '*Ich liebe dich, von ganzen gerzen!*' What does that mean?"

"I ... I love you," translated the German, remaining behind the counter, "from my whole heart!"

"Well, that's so! I went up to the daughter of my host, and simply said that.... She was embarrassed ... but she didn't get hysterical.... Commission unaccomplished! Goodbye! When the head is stupid even the feet hurt.... Having a poor memory makes for trouble: I'll be back many times! Be well!"

Gauptvakhtov opened the door gingerly, went out into the street, and put on his hat after taking a few steps.

He swore at his memory and became thoughtful....

His thoughts centered around his arrival at home, how he would be met by his wife, his daughter, the little ones.... His wife would examine his purchases, reproach him, call him some kind of animal—a donkey or a mule.... The little ones would attack the sweets and begin frantically to spoil their already upset stomachs.... Nadya, in a blue gown with a rose-colored tie, comes to meet him and asks: "Did you buy the music?" Hearing, "No," she castigates her old father, shuts herself up in her small room, howls, and doesn't come out to eat her dinner. ... Later she leaves her room and her face is tear-swollen, and, brokenhearted, she sits down at the piano ... begins to play something mournful, hums something, gulps tears.... By

---

*His crude German: "Tell me! Give it to me!"

evening Nadya becomes more cheerful, and finally, sighing deeply for the last time, plays the beloved: ta-ta-ti-ta-ta. . . .

Gauptvakhtov slaps his forehead and like a madman hurriedly returned to the music shop.

"Ta-ta-ti-ta-ta, that's it!" He sang out as he rushed into the shop. "I remembered!! It's like this! Ta-ta-ti-ta-ta!"

"Ah. . . . Well, now I know. That's Liszt's rhapsody, number two. . . . Hungarian. . . ."

"Yes, yes, yes. . . . Liszt, Liszt! God-given, Liszt! Number two! Yes, yes, yes. . . . My dear fellow! That's it! You're a kindred spirit!"

"It's difficult to sing Liszt. . . . Was it somehow spontaneous or forced?"

"Somehow! Only the number two, Liszt! He's sharp that Liszt! Ta-ta-ti-ta. . . . Ha-ha-ha! It took a lot of effort to remember! Precisely!"

The German took the sheet music down from the shelf, wrapped it along with a large catalogue and other information, and handed the package to the ecstatic Gauptvakhtov. Gauptvakhtov paid him eighty-five kopecks and left the shop whistling.

1882

ROTHSCHILD'S VIOLIN

It was a small town, worse than a village, and only old people lived there who died so rarely that it was even a nuisance. There weren't many people in the clinic or behind bars, and very few coffins were needed. In a word, business was bad. If Yakov Ivanov were a coffin maker in a large town in the province, then truly, he would have owned a nice house and he would have been called Yakov Matveich; here he was even simply called Yakov, and for some reason he was given the nickname, Bronza. He lived on the border of poverty like an unskilled muzhik, in a small old hut where there was only one room, and this room was shared with him by his wife, Marfa, a stove, a double bed, coffins, a joiner's bench, and all the other things necessary for existence.

Yakov made fine, solid coffins. For the muzhiks and the gentry he made them to his own measurement and never made a mistake. There were no people anywhere who were taller and sturdier than he, even behind bars, even though he was already seventy years old. For the nobility and for women he constructed according to size and needed a metal measuring rod for this. Orders for a child's coffin he took very unwillingly and made them without measurement, finding the work contemptible, and every time, when he was paid for his work, he said:

"I must confess I don't like to spend my time on nonsense."

Besides his craft, he did have a small income from playing the violin. At weddings in town, a Jewish orchestra was hired whose conductor was a tinsmith, Moisay Ilich Shakhkes, who kept half of the take for himself. Since Yakov was a fine violinist and played Russian songs especially well, Shakhkes sometimes asked him to play with the orchestra and paid him fifty kopecks a day, not counting the tips from the guests. When Bronza sat in the orchestra, even before playing, he began to sweat and his face flushed. It was hot, the garlic smell was oppressive, the violin screeched, and at his right ear the bass croaked, and on his left—the flute cried out. It was played by a red-headed, emaciated man with a whole network of red and blue veins on his face, having the name of the rich man Rothschild. This damn Jew had the nerve to play the most happy music in a plaintive way. Without any kind of apparent reason, Yakov little by little developed a hatred and contempt toward Jews and especially toward Rothschild. He began to find fault with him, abuse him verbally, and even wanted to beat him. Rothschild was insulted and said, looking at him angrily:

"If I didn't respect you for your talent, I would have you thrown out the window."

After this Rothschild wept. Because of this occurrence, Bronza was not invited to play with the orchestra very often, and only in extreme emergency when no one else was available.

Yakov was never in so bad a mood as when he had to continually suffer income loss. For example, on Sundays and holidays it was a sin to work. Monday—was a difficult day, and in this way around two hundred days a year he had to sit involuntarily with his hands folded. And really, what a loss of income! If someone in town got married and didn't hire musicians, or Shakhkes didn't ask Yakov to play, that also was considered a loss of income. The police inspector was sick for two years and was withering away. Yakov waited impatiently for his death, but then the inspector went to the county seat to be cured and died there. Here was another loss, not less than ten rubles since the coffin would have been expensive and lined with silk brocade. The thoughts of the losses bothered Yakov mainly during the night. He kept the violin by his side on the bed and when some kind of idiocy lodged in his head, he plucked the strings. The sounds of the violin filled the darkness, and he relaxed.

On the sixth of May last year, Marfa suddenly was taken ill. The old woman had difficulty breathing, drank a great deal of water, was staggering, but all the same, in the morning got the stove going and even went to get water. Toward evening she lay down. Yakov played the violin all day. When it got dark, he took out a little account book and from boredom began to do sums. They came to thousands of rubles. It disturbed him so that he threw the accounts on the floor and tramped on them. Later he picked them up and for a long time smacked his lips and took deep, strained breaths. His face became crimson and wet with perspiration. He was thinking, how, if these lost thousands of rubles had been put in the bank, the interest in a year would have been at least—forty rubles. That meant that these forty rubles were also a loss. In a word, no matter which way you turned, there were losses and nothing else.

"Yakov!" his wife called out unexpectedly. "I'm dying!"

He turned to look at his wife. Her face looked red, unusually bright and elated. Bronza, who was accustomed to see her face pale, shy, and gloomy, became confused. It looked as if she were happy now that she was dying and finally leaving forever this hut, these coffins, leaving Yakov. . . . She stared at the ceiling and moved her lips, and her expression was joyful, as if she saw death as her savior and was whispering with him.

It was already getting light, and in the window the rising sun could be seen. Looking at the old woman, for some reason Yakov recalled that never in her whole lifetime with him had he caressed her, had sympathy for her, not once had he even thought of buying her a kerchief, or to bring her something sweet from the weddings, but had only shouted at her, blamed her for her losses, punched. True, he didn't really beat her, but he did frighten her and she always froze with fear. Yes, he didn't allow her to drink tea because even without that the expenses were high, and so she only drank hot water. And he understood why her face was so strange and radiant and he felt weird.

Waiting until morning, he got a horse from a neighbor and drove Marfa to the clinic. There weren't many patients so it happened that he only had to wait three hours. It was his good fortune that the doctor himself was ill and the patients were being seen by his assistant, Maksim Nikolaich, an old man whom everybody in the town praised, and that even though he was a lush and cheeky, he knew more than the doctor.

"Good health to you," said Yakov in greeting, obsequiously polite, and leading the old woman into the office. "Excuse me for disturbing you, Maksim Nikolaich, with my trivial troubles. My wife, as you can see, has taken ill. She is my life's companion, as the saying goes, excuse me for the expression. . . ."

Wrinkling his gray eyebrows and stroking his sideburns, the doctor's assistant examined the old woman, while she sat on a stool, humped over, skinny, sharp-nosed, open-mouthed, her profile looking like a bird's that wanted to drink.

"H . . . m, yes. . . . Thus . . . ," slowly repeated the assistant and sighed. "It's the flu, and probably there's high fever. Typhus is going around town. So what's to be done? She's lived a long time, thank God. . . . How old is she?"

"Sixty-nine, Maksim Nikolaich."

"So? The old woman has lived her life. It's time to die."

"That, of course, you can honestly see, Maksim Nikolaich," said Yakov, smiling knowingly. "And I sincerely thank you for your kindness, but allow me to say even an insect wants to live."

"You ask for a great deal," exclaimed the doctor's assistant in such a tone as if the life or death of the old woman depended upon him. "Well, so, kind sir, you will put cold compresses on her head and give her these pills two times a day. So, for now, goodbye."

From the look on his face, Yakov could see that things were so bad that no pills would help. It was clear to him that Marfa would die soon, any day now. He gently touched the assistant's elbow, winked, and said in an undertone:

"Right, Maksim Nikolaich, I'll put on the cupping-glasses."

"There is no time, no time, dear sir. Take your old woman, and go with God. Goodbye."

"Be so kind," begged Yakov. "You yourself know that if she had a bellyache or any kind of internal problems, then pills and powders would be okay, but she has chills! The first thing to do for chills—leeching blood, Maksim Nikolaich."

But the doctor's assistant had already called for the next patient, and a peasant woman with a young boy walked into the office.

"Begone, begone . . . ," he said to Yakov, frowning. "There's nothing to gain by clouding the issue."

"In such a case at least place leeches! Prayer is the last resort!"

The assistant blew up and exclaimed:

"Tell me! Dunderhead. . . ."

Yakov's temper also flared and he flushed all over, but he did not say a word. He took Marfa by the arm and led her out of the office. It wasn't until they were settled in the wagon and with a sour and sneering look at the clinic he said:

"They've settled you here, you artists! For the rich you'd place leeches, but for a poor person you can't even spare one leech. Tyrants!"

When they arrived home, Marfa, entering the hut, stood about ten minutes holding onto the stove. It seemed to her that if she lay down, that Yakov would begin to talk about losses and scold her because she was always lying down and not wanting to work. Because he could think of nothing else, Yakov looked at her and remembered that tomorrow was the holy day of Blessed Ioanna, and the day after tomorrow was the Nikolaya, the miracle man, and after that was Sunday, and then Monday—a difficult day. Four days when it would be impossible to work, and, certainly, Marfa would die on one of those days. It meant that he would have to make the coffin today. He took out his metal measuring rod and went up to the old woman and measured her. After this she lay down, and he crossed himself and began to make the coffin.

When this work was finished, Bronza put on his glasses and wrote in his little account book:

"Marfa Ivanova's coffin—2 rubles 40 kopecks."

And he sighed. The old woman lay quietly the whole time

with her eyes closed. In the evening when it became dark, she suddenly called the old man.

"Remember, Yakov?" she said looking at him happily. "Remember, fifty years ago God gave us a child with curly blonde hair? We were all sitting by the stream and singing . . . under the willow." And, smiling bitterly, she added: "The little girl died."

Yakov tried to remember, but no way could he recall either the child or the willow.

"That's just your imagination," he said.

The priest came and performed the last rites over her. Later Marfa began to speak incoherently, and toward morning died.

The old neighboring women washed and dressed her, and laid her in the coffin. In order not to have to pay for an extra deacon, Yakov, himself, read from the psalter. They didn't charge him for the grave as the cemetery's overseer was a god-parent. Four muzhiks out of respect carried the coffin to the grave without pay. Old people, some beggars, and two retarded individuals considered saintly walked behind the coffin, and the people who met the procession crossed themselves. Yakov was satisfied that everything went according to the church's dictates, and cheaply, and no one had his feelings hurt. Bidding Marfa farewell for the last time, he stroked the coffin and thought: "Good job!"

But when he returned from the cemetery, depression gripped him. He felt sick: his breathing became difficult and hot, his legs became weak, and he couldn't get enough to drink. His head became filled with all kinds of miscellaneous thoughts. Once again he remembered that never in his life had he once had sympathy for Marfa, had never caressed her. They had lived together for fifty-two years in one hut, a long, long time, but as things turned out, in all this time he had never once thought of her, paid no attention to her, as if she had been a cat or a dog. And every day she had kept the fire going, cooked and baked, brought in the water, chopped wood, slept in one bed with him, and when he came home drunk from the weddings, she hung up his violin on the wall with great care, and put him to bed. All this without saying a word, with a shy, concerned look.

Smiling and bowing, Rothschild came toward Yakov. "I've been looking for you, uncle!" he said. "Moisay Ilich sends his regards and wants you to come to see him immediately, if you can."

Yakov was not up to this. He wanted to cry.

"Leave me alone!" he said and walked away.

"Is this really possible?" Rothschild was confused and ran before him. "Moisay Ilich will be insulted! He wants you right away!"

Yakov found it bothersome that Rothschild was having difficulty breathing from walking so fast, was blinking his eyes, and that he had so many red freckles. And he found it disgusting to look at his green jacket with the dark lapels, and at his whole fragile, delicate figure.

"Why are you following me, garlic head?" screamed Yakov. "Get out of the way!"

Rothschild became angry and also screamed:

"You, you, if you please, quiet down, or you'll find yourself flying over the fence."

"Get out of my sight!" raved Yakov and threw himself with his fists upon Rothschild. "There's no living with you wretches!"

Rothschild paled from fear. He sat down and covered his head with his hands, as if to shield it from blows, and then jumped up and ran away as fast as he could. As he ran, he leaped, threw up his hands, and you could see how his long, emaciated frame quivered. The little boys were glad of the opportunity to run after him with derogatory cries of "Kike! Kike!" The dogs also barked and ran after him. Someone laughed and then whistled, and the dogs' barking got louder and more harmonious. . . . Subsequently, a dog must have nipped Rothschild for an awful, painful scream was heard.

Yakov walked across a pasture, then along the edge of town where he ambled along without a destination, and the little boys yelled: "Here comes Bronza! Here comes Bronza!" He reached the river. He heard the screeching of snipes, the quacking of ducks. The sun was very hot and the water sparkled so brilliantly that it hurt the eyes to look at it. Yakov followed

the path down to the bank and saw a red-cheeked lady come
out of the bathhouse and had malicious thoughts about her:
"That's for you, you wet slob!" Not far from the bathhouse
young boys were catching crabs for meat; seeing him, they
started nastily calling out: "Bronza! Bronza!" And now, here
was an old willow with a huge hollow and a crow's nest in it.
. . . Suddenly in Yakov's memory, as if alive, there arose a young
child with curly, blonde hair, and the willow was the one Marfa
spoke about. Yes, it was the same willow—green, silent, melancholy. . . . How it had aged, poor thing!

He sat under the willow and began to think about the past.
On this bank, where it was now flooded by spring rains, at that
time there had stood a large birch forest; and on this barren
mountain that could be seen on the horizon, there had been a
very old pine forest. Barges had roved along the river. Now, it
was all even and smooth, and on the bank there stood only a
small birch, young and elegant, like a young gentlewoman,
and on the river there were only ducks and geese, which did
not in any way resemble moving barges. It seemed, in contrast
to his previous observation, there were even fewer geese. Yakov
closed his eyes, and in his imagination, one after another, enormous flocks of white geese were rising up out of the water.

It puzzled him, how it happened that for the last forty or fifty
years of his life he had not once been on the river, and possibly
he had been, but had paid no attention to it? It was a good-sized
river, alive with fish. One could catch enough fish to sell to the
merchants, the managers for the cafeteria at the station, and
then put the money in the bank. One could go by boat from one
estate to the other and play the violin, and all kinds of people
would pay him for it. It would have been possible to transport
loads on the barges—that would have been better than making
coffins. Finally, it would have been possible to breed geese,
slaughter them, and in the winter take them to Moscow. The
down from just one would probably bring in about ten rubles. But
he had been asleep and he hadn't done anything. What losses!
Oh, what losses! If only he could have done all these things
together—catch fish, play the violin, load the barges, and
slaughter the geese, he would have accumulated real capital!

But he hadn't even dreamt of all this, and he had led a useless life, without satisfaction in anything, all in vain, not even for some snuff. The future had nothing left for him, and to look back—there was nothing besides losses, so terrible that one got the willies thinking about them. How was a person to live so that he could avoid these casualties and losses? He asked himself, why did they fell the birch and pine forests? Why is the common pasture unused? Why don't people always do what's necessary? Why did he, Yakov, spend his whole life using invectives, digging, using his fists, abusing his wife, and why did he find it necessary recently to insult and frighten Rothschild? Why don't people mind their own business and leave others alone? What losses there are from this kind of life! Such terrible losses! If there weren't any hate or malice, people would reap tremendous benefits from each other.

In the evening and during the night he fancied he saw the child; the willow; the fish; the slaughtered ducks; and Marfa, her profile like a bird's who wants a drink; and the pale, pitiful face of Rothschild; and all other kinds of mugs arose from all sides, and he grumbled about losses. He rolled from side to side and got out of bed five times to play his violin.

In the morning he could hardly get out of bed. He went to the clinic. Here Maksim Nikolaich told him to put cold compresses on his head, gave him some powders, and from the expression on his face and the tone of his voice, Yakov perceived that things looked bad and no powders would help. Arriving at home, he reasoned that death would be good for something: he wouldn't have to eat, or drink, or pay taxes, or insult people, and since a person lies in his grave not for one year, but for hundreds, thousands of years, if you calculate accurately the benefits would be tremendous. A person's life yields—losses, but death—benefits. Such considerations, of course, are honest, but all the same they hurt and cause bitterness; why is there such a crazy arrangement that life, which is given only once to a person, comes without benefits?

Death would have been welcome, but when he got home he saw his violin and it gripped his heart and he became depressed. He couldn't take his violin to his grave, and it would become an orphan and the same thing would happen to it as happened to the birch and pine forests. Everything on this earth perishes and will perish! Yakov went out of the hut and sat on the threshold holding his violin close to his chest. Thinking of the lost, wasted life, he played the violin instinctively, not even knowing what he was playing, and it sounded mournful and moving, and tears ran down his cheeks. The deeper his thoughts, the more sorrowfully sang the violin.

The iron lock on the gate clicked several times and Rothschild appeared at the gate. He boldly crossed halfway into the yard, but when he saw Yakov, he stopped at once, scrunched up, and it must have been from fright, made signs with his fingers as if he wanted to show what time it was.

"Come closer, it's okay," said Yakov kindly, and beckoned to him. "Come closer!"

Looking as if he didn't believe it, and with obvious fear, Rothschild approached but kept his distance.

"But you, be merciful, don't beat me!" he said, cowering. "Moisay Ilich has sent me again. He said don't be afraid, go again to Yakov and tell him we can't get along without him. The wedding is on Wednesday. . . . Yes-s! Mr. Shapavalov is giving his daughter in marriage to an excellent man. It will be an extravagant wedding, phew—phew!" added Rothschild, winking with one eye.

"I can't," uttered Yakov, breathing heavily. "I'm sick, brother."

And once again he began to play, and the tears streamed from his eyes down onto the violin. Rothschild listened attentively, standing by his side with his hands folded on his chest. The frightened, bewildered expression gradually left his face and changed into a doleful and suffering one. He closed his eyes, and as if experiencing a tortuous ecstasy, whispered: "*Vox celestis*."* And tears slowly ran down his cheeks and wet his green jacket.

After this, Yakov spent a whole day lying down and suffering. When in the evening the priest came, and during con-

---

*"Voice of heaven"

fession asked him if he recalled any special sin, he strained his feeble memory, recalled again the unhappy face of Marfa, and Rothschild's desperate shriek when the dog bit him, and he said in a barely audible voice:

"Give my violin to Rothschild."

"Good, I'll do so," answered the priest.

So now the question is asked: where did Rothschild get such a fine violin? Did he buy it or did he steal it, or can it be that it fell to him from someone who owed him money? He has for a long time given up playing the flute and now only plays the violin. From under his chin come such yearning sounds as in the past had come from the flute. When he tries to repeat what Yakov had played when sitting on the threshold of his hut, something so eerie and suffering comes out that those who hear it weep, and he himself toward the conclusion closes his eyes and says: "*Voxxx. . . .*" And this new piece so pleases the town that the merchants and officials vie with each other to have him play for them over and over again.

1889

THE CHIEF ELDER

In one of the dirty taverns in a small town in District N the chief elder, Shelma,* sits at a table eating a rich gruel. After three spoonfuls he takes what he calls his "last drink."

"That's the way, my good man, the difficult village business is carried on!" he says to the tavern-keeper, buttoning himself up under the table, because this business, too, had become unbuttoned. "Dealings with the peasant are political and even a Bismarck would have a hard time. In order to conduct them, you have to have a unique wisdom, a knack for it. Why do the muzhiks like me? Why do they cling to me like flies? Why? What's the reason that I eat my gruel with butter, and the other advocates without butter? Because I have a head that's savvy and that's a gift."

Shelma, puffing, drinks up and then with dignity stretches his dirty neck. Not only the neck is dirty on this man. His hands, shirt, pants, napkin, ears . . . were all dirty.

"I'm not educated. Why lie? I never finished school, don't put on the airs of an educated man, but brother, I can immod-

---

*"Knave"

278

estly say that I can tell you about all kinds of decisions that if you examine millions of others, you wouldn't find another such an advocate. That is not to say I handle the business of piling up wealth, and won't take on Sarru Bekker, but if there's a peasant's property involved, then no kind of defense, no kind of lawyers . . . no one is able to defeat me. Really. I'm the only one who can solve the peasants' problems, and no one else can. Even if you were a Lomonosov, or a Beethoven, if you don't have my knack, don't try it. For example, take the case of the elder from Replovska. Have you heard about this?"

"No, I haven't."

"A big political scam! If you tried to spit on it you'd miss it, but I didn't. It was, brother mine, not far from the Moscow bell factory. At this factory, dear man, our Replovski muzhik, Yev-dokim Petrov, works as a senior craftsman. He's been working there for twenty years. According to his passport he is, of course, a muzhik, he should wear bast shoes, a peasant's short jacket, but he doesn't carry himself like a muzhik. He's had fine manners and polish for twenty years. He dressed, you know, in a knitted outfit, wore rings on his fingers, a gold chain across his whole paunch—don't come near him! He's not really a muzhik. I should think so, brother mine! About one and a half thousand for a salary, an apartment, grub, hobnobs with the masters, so he doesn't go to bars. His whole appearance, you know, is the kind that (the "big shot" drinks up) is impressive. But this Yevdokim Petrov dreamed up the idea of visiting his birthplace, that's our Replov. He yearned to do this for a long time. Life at the bell factory was sweet as honey, the old craftsman had no need to be bored, but, you know, he was drawn by the vague memories of his fatherland. Even if you go away to America, settle there, and have hundreds of rubles up to you neck, you'll still be drawn back to your hometown bar. So—he asked his master for a week's leave and left. He arrived in Replov. The first thing he did was to go to his relatives.

" 'This is where I tended my father's herd, this is where I slept, and so on. . . .' In a word, memories of his childhood were awakened. Well, this was not enough. He had to brag: 'Take a look, brothers! I was a peasant just like you, but with work and sweat I acquired status, am rich, and eat well. Work hard, as they say, and you too . . .' The lumbering peasants listened at first and praised what he said, but later thought: 'That's the way it is, dear man, all that you say is worthy and even wonderful, only what sense does it make for you to say this to us? You've been living here with us for a week, and you haven't given us anything. . . .' They sent a deputy bailiff to speak to him. . . .

" 'Yevdokim, give me a hundred rubles.'

" 'What's that all about?'

" 'To treat the village to vodka. . . . The whole village wants to drink to your health and have a good time. . . .'

"Now Yevdokim was a proper, God-fearing man. He didn't drink vodka, or smoke, and objected to others doing so.

" 'For vodka,' he says, 'I won't pay.'

" 'How come! By what right? Aren't you one of us?'

" 'What does "one of you" mean? I don't owe anything . . . all is as it should be. Why should I pay?'

"And so on, and so on. . . . Yevdokim held his position and the people theirs. The people became angry. You know how dumb they are! You can't talk sense with them. They wanted to party, and if you tried to explain to them two times ten in different words, even if shot out of a cannon, they wouldn't get it. They want to drink and that's it! True, it's a bother: a rich fellow-townsman and suddenly he acts as if he doesn't have a shirt to his name or bread to eat! They had to think up a way to wrest the hundred rubles from Yevdokim. All the people tried to dream up something, but they could come up with nothing. They paced their huts and could only think of threatening him: We'll let you have it and I'll take care of you! But he sat at home and didn't give a damn. 'I'm clean,' he thinks, 'before God and before the law, and before the world, so what have I to fear? I'm as free as a bird!' Okay. The muzhiks, seeing that he's not going to give the money, were turning a deaf ear, began to figure out how to clip this free bird's disrespectful wings. Since they weren't smart enough, they sent for me.

"I go to Replov. 'So and so,' they say, 'Denis Semyenich, he won't hand over any money! Dream up a scheme!' What's that, brother mine? It's impossible to think up anything; it's all plain to see, Yevdokim's rights are in his favor. No lawyer can think up a scheme if he worked on it for three years. . . . The devil himself can't hook onto his money."

The honcho drinks up and winks.

"But I did find a way to snare it! Yes, sir! You can't guess what I thought up! If you lived forever, you wouldn't be able to guess! I told them: 'Boys, elect him to your village council.' Now listen to this. They took an elder's badge to Yevdokim. He laughed. 'You're joking,' he says. 'I don't want to be one of your elders.'

" 'We're not joking!'

" 'But I refuse! I'm leaving tomorrow!'

" 'No you can't. You don't have the right. According to the law, an elder can't give up his seat.'

" 'So I,' says Yevdokim, 'refuse the post.'

" 'You don't have the right. An elder has to keep the post for three years and only the courts can release him. Once you're elected, neither you nor we . . . no one can release you!'

"Yevdokim let out a howl. He ran as if he were on fire to the district chief. The clerk and he reviewed all the laws.

" 'According to this and that law, you can't retire sooner than three years! Serve the three years and then leave.'

" 'Spend three years here? It's impossible for me to stay another month! When I'm gone, for my master it's like losing his own hands! His losses are in the thousands! And besides the factory, I have a home, a family.'

"And so on. A month goes by. Yevdokim has already promised the people, not a hundred rubles, but three hundred, if only he could be released. They would really have been happy to take the money, but it was too late to do anything. Yevdokim goes to the permanent member of the council.

" 'This is the situation, your excellency. Because of my circumstances at home, I cannot serve here. Please, for God's sake, get me out of this.' 'I don't have the right. There are no legal reasons for the release. You, in the first place, are not sick, and in the second place, there are no shameful circumstances for the release. You must serve.'

"I have to tell you that they poke into everything over there. The district chief or the village elder are no small change in the state government. They're more esteemed and really more important than any office drudge who is pushed around as if he were a lackey. Who's there to listen to Yevdokim in his knitted suit? He begs the permanent member in the name of Jesus Christ."

" 'I don't have the right,' says the member. 'If you don't believe it, ask the district office. They'll tell you the same thing. Not just me, but even the governor can't release you. The verdict of the community's meeting, if the rules aren't broken, is not subject to appeal.'

"Yevdokim goes to the chief, from the chief to the district bailiff. He covered the whole district, and they all said the same thing: 'You have to serve. We have no authority in this situation.' What's to be done? He's getting letter after letter from the factory, dispatch after dispatch. Yevdokim was advised by a relative to send for me. So, he—can you believe it?—he didn't send for me but rushed to me himself. When he arrived, not saying a word, he presses a ten-ruble note into my hand. I was, he says, his only hope.

" 'How's about it?' I say. 'If you wish, I can liberate you for a hundred rubles.'

"I took the hundred rubles and took care of the problem."

"How?" asked the bartender.

"Try to guess. The solution was simple. The solution to the puzzle was in the law itself."

Shelma comes closer to the bartender and, laughing loudly, whispers in his ear:

"I advised him to steal something and to be taken before the court. Where was the hitch? In the beginning, brother, he was bowled over. How could he steal? 'This way,' I said, 'steal from me this here empty wallet, and you'll be incarcerated for a month and a half.' At first he balked: he was worried about his good name and so forth. 'Is your good name your distinction? You have a work record, don't you? You'll spend a month and a half behind bars, this business will be finished, and you'll then have the shameful circumstance, and they'll remove your badge!' This guy thought it over, waved his hand in the air, and stole my wallet. He's already done his time, and prays for me in thanks. That, brother, is wisdom! If you searched the entire globe you wouldn't find politics like those in the dealings of peasants, and if anyone knows how to settle with them, it's me. There isn't anyone who can turn things around as I can. Yes, siree."

The schemer orders another bottle of vodka and begins another tall tale—about how the Replov muzhiks saturate outsiders' standing crops.

1885

THE CRITIC

A venerable aged father (of the theater), old and bent over, with a crooked chin and crimson nose, met with an old friend, who was a journalist, in the cafeteria of one of the privately owned theaters. After the customary greetings, questions, and sighs, the venerable father proposed that they have a little drink.

"How much is it?" asked the journalist, wrinkling his brow.

"No matter, let's have a drink. I, brother, don't drink by myself, and they give us actors a discount here—almost half—even if you don't want to, you'll drink. Let's go."

The friends approach the bar and have a drink.

"I've seen enough of your theaters. They're okay; but nothing to talk about," grumbles the venerable father, sardonically smiling. "*Merci*, I didn't expect it. But it's a capital city, the center for the arts! It's shameful to observe."

"Were you at the Alexandria?" asks the journalist.

The venerable father scornfully waves his hand and smirks. His crimson nose wrinkles and gives out a mocking sound.

"I was there!" he answers, as if reluctantly.

"So? Did you like it?"

"Yes, I liked the building. The theater is fine on the outside; I won't dispute that, but as far as the artists are concerned—well, excuse me. It may be that they are excellent people, geniuses, Diderots,* but from my point of view they are murderers of art and nothing more. If it were in my power, I would banish them from Petersburg. Who's the boss?"

"Potyekin."

"Hm . . . Potyekin. What kind of entrepreneur is he? Nothing unusual, no showmanship, no voice. An entrepreneur or a director who is good has to have vision, solidity, inspiration, so that the whole troupe senses it. The troupe has to be ruled with an iron hand, that's how!"

The venerable father stretches a clenched fist before himself, and emits from his lips a sound like sizzling butter in a frying pan.

"That's how! And you wonder how? Our brotherhood of actors, especially the young ones, must not be given a free hand. It's imperative that the actor understands and feels what kind of human being he's projecting. If the director is too familiar with the actor, pats him on the head, the actor will walk all over the director. The late Sava Trifonich, maybe you remember him, was a hail-fellow-well-met, as if everyone was on the same level, but where art was concerned, he—was thunder and lightning! It happened that he either fined you or shamed you before the audience, or dressed you down so that for three days afterward you were in the dumps. Can Potyekin get away with that? He has neither the strength nor the genuine voice. He's not a tragedian or a philosopher. The worst squeaker from Fortinbras't retinue wouldn't be daunted by him. Anyhow, let's have another drink, okay?"

"How much does it cost?" asks the frowning journalist.

"Forgive me, but to drink at this time of night it doesn't matter . . . our brotherhood gets a discount—it would be a sin not to have a drink."

The buddies drink up.

"All the same, if you discuss it dispassionately, our troupe

---

*eighteenth-century French encyclopedist
†reference from Shakespeare's *Hamlet*

is excellent," says the journalist while nibbling on some red cabbage.

"The troupe? Hm. . . . Excellent, you don't say. . . . No, brother, good actors in Russia today have disappeared! Not a single one is left!"

"You don't mean it—not a single one! Maybe not in all Russia, but even here in Petersburg, we can find good actors! Take for example, Svobodin. . . ."

"Svo-bo-din?" remarks the venerable father, who in horror steps back and throws up his hands. "That's an actor? Have the fear of the lord in you, if that's an actor. He's a dilettante!"

"But all the same . . ."

"What's all the same? If it were in my power, I would chase your Svobodin out of Petersburg! Can he really perform, huh? Can he really? He's cold, dried up, not an iota of sensitivity, monotonous, expressionless. . . . Nah, let's have another drink! I can't stand it! It's stifling!"

"No, brother, spare me. . . . I can't drink any more!"

"It's on me! The brotherhood is given a discount—even a dead man can drink to that! Others pay a ten spot and we only pay a five. It's dirt cheap! Cheaper than mushrooms."

The old pals drink up, while the journalist shakes his head, croaks as if he had decided to give up life in the pursuit of truth.

"He performs without heart, simply brain!" continues the venerable father. "The genuine actor performs with his nervous system and every fiber, while that guy comes off like a textbook or written instruction. . . . And later, the same thing. He plays every role identically! No matter what kind of sauce you serve with a pike, it's still a pike! That's the way it is, brother. . . . Put him in a melodrama or a tragedy, and you'll see what he is. . . . A comedy can be pulled off by anybody, but not melodrama or tragedy! Why don't they put on melodramas? They're afraid! They can't cast it! Your actor doesn't know how to dress, how to project, or how to strike a pose."

"Hold on, I find this all incredible. . . . If Svobodin has no talent, then besides him we have Sazonov, Dalmatov; we had Petipa; and in Moscow there is Kiselevcki, Gradov-Sokolov; and in the province there is Andreev-Byrlak. . . ."

"Listen, I speak seriously with you, and you're making jokes," said the offended venerable father. "If, in your opinion all of these are artists, then we can't have a conversation. Are these really actors? They are perfect mediocrities! Caricatures and exaggeration, whining and nothing more! If I had the power, I'd deny them entrance to the theater at the point of a gun. They bother my soul so much that I'm ready to fight a duel with them! For pity's sake, are these really actors? When they have to die on stage, they pull such faces that in an outlying district they split their sides with laughter. The other day it was proposed that I acquaint myself with Varlamov—not for anything!"

The venerable father angrily stares at the journalist, makes an indignant gesture, and in the tone of a scornful tragedian says:

"As you wish, but I'm going to have another drink!"

"Ugh . . . but why? You've had enough to drink!"

"Why are you complaining? I get a discount! I don't drink alone, and if you won't drink . . ."

The old friends have a drink and for a minute look dully at each other, trying to recall the subject of their conversation. . . .

"Of course, everybody has his point of view," grumbles the journalist, "but one has to be very partial and prejudiced in order not to agree that, for example, Goreva . . ."

"They exaggerate!" interrupted the venerable father, "A lump of ice! A talented fish! Tsirlick-manirlick! She does have a little talent, I won't dispute that, but there's no fire, no power—there isn't any, you can perceive this, no pepper! That's the way she acts! A serving of pistachio ice cream! Lemonade! When she performs, if you have a decent, perceptive audience, they settle into their mustaches and beards from cold! And in general, in Russia there are no genuine actresses. . . . None! There's not even a trace anywhere. And if someone has a little talent, it quickly degenerates, and is lost because of today's directors. . . . And there are no actors. . . . For example, take your Pisarev. . . . What kind of talent does he have?

The venerable father steps back and in amazement stares at the journalist.

"What kind of talent does he have?! Is he really an actor?

No, tell me in good conscience: Is he really an actor? Can you
really put him on the stage? He screams with some kind of
wild voice, stamps his feet, waves his arms without a purpose.
. . . He shouldn't be portraying people, but ichthyosauruses and
mammoths from before the flood. . . . Yes!"
     The venerable father bangs his fist on the table and yells:
"Yes!"
     "Now, now . . . quiet down," says the journalist, trying to
calm him. "It's embarrassing; everybody is looking. . . ."
     "It's impossible, brother mine! It's not acting, not art! It
means the loss, the slaughter of art! Take a look at Savin. . . .
What kind of talent does he have? No talent—only, by God,
affected liveliness and playfulness that shouldn't be allowed on
the serious stage! You look at it and simply put, do you understand, you're horrified: Where are we? Where are we heading?
What are we striving for? Art is dis-a-ppear-ing!"
     The old buddies became silent, understanding each other,
probably, without saying more, and approach the bar to have
another drink.
     "You . . . you're too ha-ard . . . ," stutters the journalist.
     "I can't say anything different! I'm a classicist. I did Hamlet
and it is imperative for me that this sacred art remains art. . . . I'm
an old man. . . . In comparison, they're all lit-tle b-oys. . . . Yes. . . .
They've destroyed Russian art. Take, for example, Moscow's
Fedotov or Yermolov. . . . They're arranging a celebration but
what's been done that's worthwhile for art? What? They've simply
corrupted the public taste! Or, let's take the praise of Moscow's
Lenski and Ivanov-Kozelski. . . . What kind of talent do they
have? Affected. . . . And their interpretation, my God! You know
that for that it's not enough to want to perform, but you have to
have a gift, the spark! How about a last drink, okay!"
     "But we just had a dr-r-ink!"
     "Nah! All the same . . . it's my treat. . . . We of the broth-
erhood get a discount, it won't be too much. . . ."
     The old buddies have another drink. They already sense
that it's much more comfortable sitting than standing, and sit
down at a table.
     "Or take the rest of them . . . ," grumbles the venerable

father. The only thing they are is a misfortune and a disgrace for the human species. . . . Others who aren't even twenty years old are already corrupted to the marrow of their bones. . . . A person who is young, healthy, handsome, but strives to play some kind of Svistyulkin or Pishtalochkin, would find it easier and would even please people in the outlying districts, if he would try a classical role, and that never even enters into his dreams. In our time, brother, every actor played Hamlet. . . . I remember, in Smolensk, the deceased prompter, Vasha, played Richelieu's knight when the actor got sick. . . . Art was looked at with earnestness, not like today. . . . We worked at it. . . . On the holidays we did *King Lear* in the morning and in the evening *The Cavaliers* with such draconian energy that the theater shook with applause. . . ."

"No, even now we do come upon fine actors. For example, in Moscow you have Korsha Davidov—my compliments to him! Have you seen him? A giant! Co-los-sal!"

"Psss. . . . Nevertheless, it's unimportant . . . a useful actor. . . . Only, brother, he has no poise, no training. . . . He needs a good manager who would see to it that he got genuine teaching—ah, what an actor would come out of it! But now he's colorless. . . . That's neither here nor there. . . . It seems to me that even he has no talent. He's been bl-o-wn up, made a big deal of. Bar-r-tender! Give us two clean glasses! Step lively!"

The venerable father mutters yet for a long time. He takes advantage of the bar's discount until the crimson color from his nose spread over his whole face and until the journalist could no longer close his left eye. As formerly, his face was stern and constrained by a sardonic smile, his voice flat like a voice from the grave, and his eyes looked with implacable anger. But suddenly the face, the neck, and even the fists of the venerable father lit up and he smiled more blissfully and indulgently, blowing up like down; winking an eye mysteriously, he leaned over to the journalist's ear and whispered:

"If it were possible to smoke out your Alexander Potyechkin and his whole cast—phew!! Then to select a new, more genuine, uncorrupted cast, and to seek in Ryazanyaks and Kazanyaks a director who would know how to rule with an iron hand."

The venerable father gulps and continues, dreamily looking at the journalist.

"I could put on *The Death of Ugolino* and *Velizarya* and warm up a new production of a diabolical *Othello*, or produce a more draconian *Mail Robbery*. You'd then see what a full house I'd have! You would see what it means to have real performances and talents!"

1887

THE DESERTED SLAVE

"Our little river wiggled around like a snake, that is to say it zigzagged around. . . . It rushed by the fields in curves, rising and falling as if giving itself airs. When it so happened that you were up on a hilltop and looked down, you could see it as if it were in the palm of your hand. During the day it was like a mirror, but at night, it was like quicksilver. Reeds stand tall on its shores and spy on the water. . . . Beauty! Over here canes, over there a basket willow and pussy willows. . . ."

That was how Nikifor Filimonich, sitting at a table and drinking beer at a local bar, described what he had seen. He spoke with warmth and enthusiasm. . . . His wrinkled, shaven face and brown neck quivered convulsively every time he emphasized some especially poetic place in his tale. Pretty sixteen-year-old Tanya, a medical nurse, listened to him. Leaning her breast on the counter and supporting her head with her fists, she was dumbstruck, pale, and unblinkingly soaked in every word.

Nikifor Filimonich was in the bar every evening and talked with Tanya. He was fond of her because she was an orphan, and for the gentle sweetness that flooded her pale, enraptured face.

And if he liked someone, he revealed to them all the secrets of his past. He generally began his conversation in the same way —with a description of a rural scene. From nature he would move to the hunt, and from the hunt—to the personality of his deceased master, Prince Svintsov.

"A remarkable human being!" he would declare about the prince. "Not only was he renowned for his wealth and enormous holdings of land, but for his character. He was a regular Don Juan."

"What is a Don Juan?"

"That indicates that women found him irresistible and so he was a Don Juan. And, he really liked me. The barriers set up by the female sex were no problem for him. Yes, sir. . . . When he lived in Moscow, we had grand quarters taking up almost an entire upper floor which had been set aside for our use. In Petersburg we had an important liaison with the Baroness Von Tusick and other affairs from which a child resulted. This same baroness lost her fortune gambling and wanted to kill herself, but the Prince did not permit her to end her life. She was so beautiful, so young. . . . She spent a year with him and then died. . . . How women adored him, little Tanya! How they loved him! They couldn't live without him!"

"Was he very handsome?"

"How can I put it? . . . He was mature and not handsome. . . . You, too, would have been attractive to him, little Tanya. . . . He liked your thin, pale type. . . . Don't be embarrassed. Why be embarrassed? I've never lied in my whole life and I'm not lying now. . . ."

Then Nikifor Filimonich took to describing the carriages, the horses, the smart clothing. . . . In all these he was a good judge. Later he began to list the wine.

"There is wine that costs twenty-five rubles per bottle. Drink a glass of this wine, and your stomach reacts in such a way that you could die from joy. . . ."

More than anything else Tanya liked his descriptions of moonlit nights. . . . In the summer a sensational orgy on the grass, among the flowers; and in the winter—in the sleighs with warm lap robes, in sleighs that shot ahead like lightning.

"The sleighs fly and it seems to you that the moon is also in flight. . . . Wondrous!"

Nikifor Filimonich spoke for a long time in this manner. He only stopped when the young lad lit the lamp over the door and carried in the tavern's door sign.

One winter evening Nikifor Filimonich lay drunk by a fence and caught pneumonia. They took him to the hospital. He was in the hospital for a month and when he returned to the bar, his avid listener was not there. She had disappeared.

About a year and a half later he was in Moscow walking along Tverskoy Boulevard and hawking used summer clothing. He ran into his beloved Tanya. She, powdered, dressed to kill, in a hat and enticingly turned-up skirts, walked arm in arm with a gentleman in a high hat, and for some reason was laughing loudly. . . . The old man looked at her, recognized her, and followed her with his eyes, and slowly removed his cap. Tenderness suffused his face and in his eyes tears sparkled.

"Well, God bless her . . . ," he whispered. "She's beautiful."

And, putting his cap on, he quietly laughed.

1883

THE WAGER

I

It was a dark, autumn night. An old banker was pacing up and down in his study recalling how fifteen years ago, in the fall, he had been giving an evening affair. There were many clever people, and interesting conversations were conducted. Among other things, capital punishment was discussed. The guests were mainly scientists and journalists; the majority were against capital punishment. They considered this type of punishment barbaric, unsuitable for Christian countries, and immoral. In the opinion of several of them, in the place of capital punishment it followed that life imprisonment be substituted everywhere.

"I don't agree with you," remarked the host. "I haven't tried out either capital punishment or a life sentence, but if one could judge a priori, then, my preference would be capital punishment as more moral and humane. Capital punishment kills at once, while a life sentence does it slowly. Which execution is more humane? The one that kills you in a few minutes or the one that drags it out over many years?"

"Both of these methods are immoral," noted one of the

guests, "because they both have the same goal—to take away life. The state—is not God. It does not have the right to take away that which it cannot return even if it wanted to."

Among the guests was a lawyer, a young man of about twenty-five. When he was asked his opinion, he replied:

"Both capital punishment and a life sentence are equally immoral, but if it were proposed to me to choose between a death sentence and imprisonment for life, then, of course, I would choose the latter. No matter what kind of life it is, it is better than none."

A lively argument arose. The banker, who had previously been quieter and more reserved, suddenly became agitated, struck his fist on the table, and shouted in the direction of the young lawyer:

"That's a lie! I'll wager two million that you wouldn't last five years in solitary confinement."

"If you're serious," answered the young lawyer, "I'll take on your wager that I couldn't survive five years, but I'll make it fifteen years."

"Fifteen years? You're on!" shouted the banker. "Gentlemen, I'm good for two million!"

"Agreed! You put up the millions and I my freedom!" declared the young lawyer.

So this wild, thoughtless wager was set!! The banker, not knowing how many millions he was worth, being self-indulgent and frivolous, was ecstatic over the wager. At dinner he joked with the young lawyer and said:

"Come to your senses, young man, while it's still not too late. Two million is nothing to me, but you are risking the loss of three or four of the best years of your life. I say three or four because you won't last any longer. Also, don't forget, poor man, that voluntary incarceration is infinitely more difficult to bear than involuntary. The thought that you have the right to freedom every minute of the day and night will poison your entire existence in the cell. I'm sorry for you!"

And now as he paced the room, the banker recalled all this and asked himself:

"What was this wager all about? What use was it for the

young lawyer to lose fifteen years of his life and I to throw away two million? Would this demonstrate to people that capital punishment is worse or better than life sentencing? No, no. . . . That's stuff and nonsense. On my side it was the fancy of a wealthy person, but on the side of the young lawyer—simple greed for money. . . ."

He reminisced further about what happened after the evening just described. It was decided that the lawyer would carry out his incarceration under the surveillance of the watchman, in one of the cottages in the banker's garden. It was agreed that for fifteen years he would be deprived of the right to cross the threshold of the cottage, to see anyone, hear a human voice, or to receive letters and newspapers. He would be permitted to have a musical instrument, read books, write letters, drink wine, and smoke. According to the conditions, the only contact he could have with the outside world was to be mute and through a small window which had been set in the wall for just this purpose. Everything that he needed—books, sheet music, wine, and other things—he could receive only by writing a request indicating the amount, and only through the window. The agreement stipulated all the details and trivia, making the confinement relentlessly solitary, and obligating the young lawyer to remain exactly fifteen years, from twelve o'clock of the fourteenth of November, 1870, to twelve o'clock on the fourteenth of November, 1885. The slightest attempt on the part of the young lawyer to violate the conditions, if but for two minutes before the end of the term, would free the banker from the obligation to pay the two million.

In the first year of the confinement the young lawyer, as much as could be deduced from his short notes, suffered a great deal from loneliness and boredom. The sounds of the piano were heard constantly day and night from his cottage! He rejected wine and tobacco. Wine, he wrote, awakens desires, and desires— were the primary enemies of the prisoner; there was nothing more depressing than to drink good wine and not to see anyone. Tobacco would foul the air in the room. The books he had sent in during the first year were mainly light works: novels with complicated love affairs, fantastic tales, comedies, and so forth.

In the second year, the music died down in the cottage and the young lawyer only asked for classics. In the fifth year music was again heard, and the prisoner asked for wine. Those who looked after him through the window said that all year he only ate, drank, and lay on the bed, yawned a great deal, and angrily talked to himself. He read no books. Sometimes at night he would sit down to write, wrote for a long time and in the morning tore up what he wrote into tiny bits. He could often be heard crying.

In the second half of the sixth year the prisoner diligently studied languages, philosophy, and history. He was so zealous in this pursuit that the banker had difficulty getting the books. In the following four years about six hundred volumes were ordered at his request. During the period of this passion, the banker received, among other things from the prisoner, this letter:

"My dear jailer! I write you these lines in six languages. Show them to people who are versed in them. Ask these people to read what I wrote. If they can't find a single error, I beg you to order that a shot be fired in the garden. This shot will tell me that my efforts have not been in vain. Throughout the ages and countries, geniuses have spoken in different tongues, but the same flame burned in them. Oh, if you could only know what transcendent happiness my soul is experiencing now that I can understand these languages!"

The wish of the prisoner was fulfilled. The banker ordered two shots be fired in the garden.

Subsequently after the tenth year, the lawyer sat motionless at the table, and read only the Gospels. It seemed strange to the banker that a man who took four years to read through six hundred books of wisdom spent a year reading one not incomprehensible and not massive volume. The Gospels were replaced by the history of religion and divinity.

During the last two years of the incarceration, the prisoner read a great deal but indiscriminately. He would tackle the natural sciences and then request Byron or Shakespeare. He would at one and the same time want chemistry and medieval texts and novels, and some kind of philosophical or theological treatise. His reading resembled swimming in a sea among debris from shipwrecks and, wanting to save his life, would desperately hang onto one piece of debris after another!

II

The banker recalled all of this and thought:

"Tomorrow at twelve o'clock he will receive his freedom. According to the conditions, I will have to pay him two million. If I pay him, I will lose everything I have: I will be completely ruined. . . ."

Fifteen years ago he had no idea how many millions he was worth, but now he was afraid to ask himself which was greater—his money or his debts? He had recklessly gambled in the stock market, impetuously took speculative risks from which he could not release himself even in old age, which little by little led to the failure of his dealings. The fearless, presumptuous, arrogant, rich man became an average banker, trembling at every rise and fall in the value of his currency.

"That damn wager!" muttered the old man, grasping his head in desperation. "Why didn't this man die? He's only forty years old. He'll take all I have left, get married, will have a happy life, gamble in stocks, and I, a beggar, will look in envy and every day hear from him one statement: 'I'm obliged to you for my happiness, let me help you!' No, that's too much! There is only one way to be saved from bankruptcy and ignominy— the death of this man!"

The clock struck three o'clock in the morning. The banker listened for sounds: all were asleep in the house, and the only thing that could be heard was the moaning of the shivering trees. Trying not to be heard, he took from his fireproof safe the key that would open the door which had not been opened for fifteen years, put on his coat, and went out of the house.

It was cold and dark in the garden. Rain was falling. A sharp, damp, howling wind blew through the garden and gave no peace to the trees. The banker strained his eyes, but he could see neither the ground nor the white statues that were there, nor the cottage, nor the trees. Finally reaching the spot where he thought the cottage was, he twice called out to the guard. There was no answer. It was evident that the guard had found shelter from the foul weather, and was sleeping at this time somewhere in the kitchen or the conservatory.

If I'm capable of fulfilling my intentions, thought the old man, the suspicion will immediately fall upon the guard.

He felt the steps and door and entered the foyer of the cottage. He then groped his way to the small antechamber and lit a match. Not a soul was there. There was someone's unmade bed, and in the corner in the stove a fire was dying out. The seals on the door leading to the prisoner's room were unbroken.

When the match died out, the old man, shaking with trepidation, looked into the small window.

In the prisoner's room a candle flickered dimly. The prisoner was sitting at the table. Only his back, the hair on his head, and the back of his hands were visible. Open books lay on the table, on the two chairs, and on the floor near the table.

Five minutes went by and the prisoner had not made a single move. The fifteen-year incarceration had taught him how to remain immobile. The banker knocked at the window but the prisoner did not make a move to answer the knock. The banker then carefully removed the seals from the door and put the key into the damp keyhole. The rusty lock made a squeaky sound and the door creaked as it opened. The banker waited for the sound of surprise and footsteps, but three minutes passed and it was silent behind the door as before. He decided to enter the room.

Sitting at the table sat a human being who did not resemble ordinary human beings. It was a skeleton covered by skin, with long, femininelike curly hair and a shaggy beard. His face was jaundiced, the shade of clay, his cheeks were sunken, his back was long and narrow, and the hand that held up his hairy head was so delicate and thin that it made the banker feel creepy to look at it. His hair was already graying, and, looking at the aged, emaciated face, no one would be able to confirm that this man was only forty. He was sleeping. . . . Before his lowered head, a sheet of paper lay on the table on which something was written in a minute handwriting.

What a pitiful man! thought the banker. He sleeps and

probably sees millions in his sleep! I need only to pick up this half-dead creature, throw him on the bed, lightly smother him with a pillow, and the most knowledgeable expert wouldn't find evidence of a violent death. However, before I do this, I'll read what he has written. . . .

The banker took the sheet of paper from the table and read the following:

"Tomorrow at twelve o'clock I will receive freedom and the right to associate with human beings. But, before I leave this room and see the sun, I consider it necessary to say a few words. With a clear conscience and before the all-seeing God, I inform you that I despise freedom, and life, and health, and all that which in your books are called the world's blessings.

"I diligently studied life on earth for fifteen years. It is true, I saw neither the earth nor people, but from your books I drank fragrant wine, sang songs, pursued deer and wild boar in forests, made love to women. . . . Beautiful women, ethereal like clouds, created by the magic of your poetic geniuses, who visited me at night and whispered wonderful tales to me from which my head reeled. From your books I reached the heights of Elbrus and Montblanc, and saw from there how in the morning the sun rose and how in the evening it flooded with crimson gold the sky, and the ocean, and the mountain peaks. I saw from here, how over me clouds cut across and how lightning flashed. I saw green fields, woods, rivers, lakes, towns. I heard the singing of sirens, played the shepherds' pipes, and felt the wings of marvelous devils flying toward me to converse about God. . . . I threw myself into bottomless pits in your books, created miracles, murdered, burned towns, propagated new religions, conquered whole realms. . . .

"Your books gave me wisdom. All that was for ages divined by the tireless human mind was deposited into my skull in one small lump. I know that I'm wiser than all of you.

"And I disdain your books, disdain the riches of the world, and its wisdom. It's all inconsequential, perishable, transparent, and fraudulent like a mirage. Allow that you are proud, wise, and wonderful, but death will render all equal on the face of the earth with burrowing mice; and your ancestors, your history, your immortal geniuses will freeze or burn along with the terrestrial globe.

"You have lost your senses and your way. You accept lies as truth and ugliness as beauty. You would be amazed if, in consequence of some kind of circumstances, in place of apples and oranges on trees, frogs and lizards grew, or if roses began to smell like horse's sweat. I am not amazed that you have exchanged heaven for earth. I don't want to understand you.

"In order to show you that I disdain all which you live for, I refuse the two million, about which I, at one time, had dreamed as paradise and which I now despise. In order to deprive myself of the right to them, I will leave here five hours before the agreed time and in this way will violate the agreement. . . ."

After reading this, the banker put the sheet down on the table, kissed the weird man's head, wept, and left the cottage. Never before, even after having lost millions in the stock exchange, had he felt such contempt for himself as now. Arriving at the house, he lay down on his bed, but the emotional upheaval and tears did not let him sleep. . . .

The next morning the pale guards hurried in and informed him that they saw how the man living in the cottage climbed through he window into the garden, went to the gates, and then went on until he was out of sight. The banker went along with the servants directly to the cottage and verified the escape of his prisoner. So as not to arouse unnecessary gossip, he took the sheet of paper from the table without a remark and upon returning to his house locked it in his fireproof safe.

1889

NAMELESS

In the fifth century, as now, the sun rose every morning and every evening lay down to sleep. In the morning when the first rays were kissed with dew, the earth awoke, the air was filled with sounds of joy, ecstasy, and praise, but in the evening the same earth became still and sank into the stern darkness. Day looked like day, and night looked like night. Now and then storm clouds raced overhead and thunder roared angrily; or you gaped at a falling star; or a pale monk raced inside and told his brothers that he had seen a tiger near the monastery—and that's all, and then day again resembled day, and night, night.

The monks worked and prayed to God, and their Father Superior played on the organ, wrote Latin verses, and composed music. This amazing old man was endowed with unusual talent. He played on the organ with such skill that even the old monks, who in their old age were hard of hearing, couldn't keep back their tears when the sounds of the organ carried from his cell. When he spoke even of something very ordinary, for example, of the trees, the wild beasts, or of the sea, it was impossible to listen to him without smiling or without tears. It seemed that there were strings in his soul that sang out just as the organ did. If he were angry or consumed by ecstasy, or began to speak of something terrible and great, passionate inspiration seized him, tears streamed from his sparkling eyes, his face became flushed, his voice thundered, and the monks, upon hearing him, felt that his inspired words bound them together. In such magnificent, miraculous minutes, his power had no limits, and if he had told those old monks to jump in the sea, all, to the very last one, would rush with exhilaration to fulfill his wish.

His music, his voice, and the verses with which he praised the Lord, heaven, and earth were the source of continual joy for the monks. It so happened that the monotonous life caused them to become weary of the countryside, of the flowers, the coming of spring, of the fall. The sound of the sea dulled their hearing and the singing of the birds became unpleasant for them, and the talents of the Father Superior were like bread, which they needed every day.

Ten years passed, and every day was like every other day, every night like every other night. Other than the wild birds and beasts, no one ever showed up around the monastery. The nearest human settlement was a long distance away, and in order to come to the monastery, one would have to cover about a hundred versts of desert. The only ones who crossed the desert were those who disdained life, rejected it, and came to the monastery to bury themselves.

It was because of this that the monks were amazed one night when a person knocked on their gates who was from town and was the most ordinary of sinners who loved life. Without asking the Father Superior for his blessing and prayers, this person wanted to be given food and wine. When asked how he had come to the desert from the town, he told a long hunting story. He had gone on a hunting trip, drank too much, and lost his way. At the proposal that he enter the monastery and save his soul, he replied with a smile, saying: "I'm not one of you."

After having eaten and drunk his fill, he contemplated the monks who had served him, shook his head reproachfully, and said:

"You monks do nothing. The only thing you know how to

do is eat and drink. Is that really how souls are saved? Consider this: as you now sit here in peace, eat, drink, and dream of bliss, your fellow men are lost and going to hell. Take a look at what's going on in town! Some are dying from hunger and others don't know what to do with their gold and sink into depravity and are lost like flies stuck in honey. The people have neither faith nor integrity! Whose business is it to save them? Whose business is it to preach? Me, who's drunk from morning 'til night? Is it really that a peaceful spirit, a loving heart, and a belief in God were given you in order that you could sit here within four walls and do nothing?"

The drunken words of the townsman were impudent and unpleasant, but affected the Father Superior in a strange way. The old man scrutinized his monks, grew pale, and said:

"Brothers, he really speaks the truth! Indeed, these poor people because of foolishness and weakness are sunk in vice and paganism, but we don't stir as if it is not our concern. Why don't I go and remind them of Christ, of whom they've forgotten?"

The words of the townsman had captivated the Father Superior. On the next day he took his staff, parted with his brothers, and left for the town. And the monks were left without music, without his words and verses.

A month went by, then another, and still the Father Superior did not return. Finally, after the third month had gone by, the familiar sounds of his staff were heard. The monks rushed to meet him and showered him with questions. He, however, instead of being delighted, cried bitterly and did not say a word. The monks noticed that he had aged greatly and had lost weight, that his face looked exhausted and expressed deep sorrow, and when he cried he looked like a person whose innocence had been outraged.

The monks also cried and anxiously began to ask why he was crying, why his face was grief-stricken. He spoke not a word and shut himself in his cell. He secluded himself for seven days, ate nothing, drank nothing, did not play the organ, and wept. When the monks knocked on his door and begged him to come out and share his grief with them, he was profoundly silent.

He finally came out. Gathering the monks around him, his face tearstained and with an expression that was pained and indignant, he began to recount what had happened to him during the last three months. When he described his trip from the monastery to the town, his voice was calm and his eyes smiled. On the road, he exclaimed, the birds sang to him, the branches rustled, and sweet, innocent hopes excited his soul. He walked and felt like a soldier who goes to battle convinced he would be victorious. Dreaming as he walked, he composed verses and hymns, never thinking of how the trip might end.

When he began to speak about the town and its people, his voice shook, his eyes began to flash, and he was consumed by anger. Never in his life had he seen, or even imagined, that which he met going on in the town. For the first time in his life, in his old age, it was only here that he saw and understood how powerful the devil was, how exceedingly evil, and how weak, fainthearted, and worthless were the people.

By an unfortunate coincidence the first house that he entered was a whorehouse. Some fifty-odd people, having a lot of money, were eating and drinking great quantities of wine. Drunk from wine, they sang and boldly said terrible, repulsive words, which one could not repeat for fear of God's wrath. They were completely unrestrained; were bold, gay, unafraid of God, the devil, death; and said and did whatever they wished, and proceeded to go wherever their lust led them. The wine, like amber covered by gold sparkles, was agonizingly sweet and fragrant, and because of this, all those who drank it smiled benignly and asked for more. The smile of the person who drank it was reflected in the wine, and when they drank it, it sparkled gleefully, as if it knew the devilish charm harbored in its sweetness.

The Father Superior, all the more incensed and weeping from anger, continued to describe what he had seen. On the table among those feasting, he said, stood a half-naked whore. It is difficult to picture oneself or to find in nature something more beautiful and fascinating. This vile creature, young, long-haired, swarthy, with black eyes and with full lips, shameless and naked, bared her teeth, which were white like snow, and smiled, as if she wanted to say: "Take a look at my nakedness, at my beauty!" Silk and brocade in beautiful folds fell from her shoulders, but her beauty could not be hidden by the cloth, but like the burgeoning green of the earth in the spring, greedily burst through the folds of the cloth. The naked woman drank wine, sang, and surrendered herself to anyone who desired her.

The Father Superior continued, angrily shaking his fists, describing horse races, bullfights, theaters, the work of a master artist who painted and sculpted naked women. He spoke emotionally, beautifully, and sonorously, as if he were playing on invisible strings. The monks were stunned, greedily taking in his words, and gasping from ecstasy. . . . Having described all the charms of the devil, the beauty of evil, and the fascinating grace of the loathsome feminine body, the old man cursed the devil, turned around, and hid himself behind the door of his cell.

On the next morning when he came out of his cell, there wasn't a single monk left in the monastery. They had all sprinted to town.

1888

A Tale Told by a Senior Gardner

In the greenhouse belonging to the Count N—— a flower sale was in process. There were not many customers: only myself, the owner of the estate next to mine, and a young merchant who dealt in forests. While the laborers carried out our fabulous purchases and were putting them into the wagons, we sat at the entrance to the greenhouse and conversed about many things. It is extraordinarily pleasant on a warm April morning to sit in a garden, to hear the birds sing, and to see how flowers are being carried out into the open air and leaning toward the sun.

The gardener, Mihail Karlovich, directed the placing of the plants. He was a respectable-looking old man with a clean-shaven face, wearing a woolen vest and no jacket. He was silent the whole time, but was listening to our conversation, as if waiting to see if we had anything new to say. He was a wise, very fine person who was esteemed by all. For some reason he was considered a German, even though his father was a Swede and his mother Russian, and he attended the Russian Orthodox church. He spoke Russian, Swedish, and German, read a great deal in all three languages, and nothing gave him more pleasure than to be given some kind of new book to read, or to discuss with him, for example, Ibsen.

He had a weakness, but it was harmless. He called himself the senior gardener, even though there were no younger ones. His facial expression was unusually grand and haughty. He did not permit controversy and loved to be listened to attentively and seriously.

"That youngster, I propose, is an awful scoundrel," said my neighbor, pointing at a laborer with a swarthy, Gypsy face, who had driven by us with a barrel of water. "Last week he had been accused in town of stealing but was acquitted. They decided he was a mental case, but meanwhile, take a look at his hideous mug. He's not sick. Lately in Russia they are often acquitting scoundrels, declaring they are sick. The obvious effect of these acquittals is indulgence and pandering, and will lead to no good. It demoralizes the general public, who sense that justice has been diminished for everyone, and all are becoming accustomed to seeing vice unpunished. You know that today we can unabashedly quote Shakespeare: 'In our evil, depraved time, the virtuous must beg pardon of the vicious.'"*

"That's certainly true," agreed the merchant. "Because the courts are so generously acquitting, murders and arsons have greatly increased. Ask the muzhiks."

The gardener, Mihail Karlovich, turned to us and said:

"As far as I'm concerned, gentlemen, I always meet verdicts of not guilty with joy. I don't fear for morality and justice when not guilty is declared, but on the contrary, feel content. Even when my conscience tells me that in acquitting the criminal the judges and courts would have more faith in the *human being* than in the evidence, that is material evidence and words, then certainly isn't the *faith in the human being* itself on the same level as other common observations? It is easy to believe in God. The inquisitors, and Byron, and Arakcheyev believed in God. But, you must believe in the human being! This belief

---

*Hamlet, act 3, scene 4, lines 153–54:

"For in the fatness of these pursy times
Virtue itself of vice must pardon beg."

can only be achieved by a few. Those who understand and are sensitive Christians.

"That's an admirable thought," I remarked.

"It's not a new thought. I recall a legend I heard on this subject very long ago. A very nice legend," said the gardener and then smiled. "My dead grandmother told it to me, the mother of my father, a wonderful old woman. She told it in Swedish, so it doesn't come out in Russian so well—not like a classic Russian tale."

Well, we begged him to tell it to us and not be constrained by the clumsiness of the Russian translation. He, very pleased, slowly lit his pipe, looked angrily at the laborers, and then began:

"There lived in one small town an aging, lonely, and ugly gentleman whose last name was Thomsen or Wilsen—but that makes no difference. The matter doesn't involve the proper name. He had a noble profession: he healed people. He was always morose and unsociable, and spoke only when it was necessary in his professional work. He never visited anyone, and did not extend recognition to anyone by more than a silent nod, and lived as modestly as a hermit. The fact is that he was a scientist, and at this time scientists were not looked upon as ordinary people. They spent day and night in contemplation, in reading books, and treating the sick. All else was considered trivial and they didn't have the time for superfluous words. The people of the town understood this very well, and did their best not to bore him with greetings and empty chatter. They were very happy that God had finally sent them a person who knew how to treat their illnesses and were proud that in their town lived such a remarkable person.

" 'He knows everything,' they said of him.

"But this was not enough. It was necessary also to say: 'He loves everybody!' In this learned person's breast there beat a wonderful, angelic heart. Even though the residents of the town were not related to him, he loved them as if they were his children and did not deny them even his life. Although he was consumptive and coughed a great deal, when he was called to a patient he forgot his own sickness and did not spare himself.

Breathing heavily, he climbed the hills no matter how high. He ignored heat and cold, scorned hunger and thirst. He would not take money for his services, and stranger still—when a patient died, he walked with the relatives behind the coffin and cried.

"It was not long before he became so necessary to the town, that the residents wondered how they had ever been able to get along without him. Their gratitude knew no bounds. The adults and the children, the good and the bad, the honorable and the knavish—in a word, everybody respected him and recognized his worth. In the town and its outskirts there wasn't a person who would have permitted himself to do him some harm, or even to think of it. When he left his lodgings he never locked his doors or windows, with complete faith that there was no robber who would decide to harm him. Often during his duties as a doctor visiting patients it was necessary to cross forests and mountains where hungry bandits gathered, but he never felt himself in danger. One time during the night when he was returning from seeing a patient, some bandits in the forest attacked him, but upon recognizing him, they respectfully removed their hats and asked him if he would like something to eat. When he replied that he was full, they gave him a warm coat and accompanied him to the town, happy that fate had given them an opportunity to return some kindness to this charitable person.

"Well, to continue, it was understandable, recounted my grandmother, that even the horses, cows, and dogs knew him, and when meeting him showed their pleasure.

"It seemed that this person, who by his saintliness had shielded himself from everything evil, whose good deeds were valued even by bandits and animals, one beautiful morning was found murdered. Bloody, with a pierced skull, he lay in a ravine with his pale face exhibiting amazement. Yes, not fear, but amazement was frozen on his face when he saw his murderer before him.

"You can now imagine the grief that enveloped the people of the town and the outskirts. Full of remorse, not believing their eyes, they asked themselves: Who could have murdered this man? The judges who conducted the investigation and examined the corpse of the doctor put it this way: 'We have here all the signs of a murder, but since there can not be such an evil human being who could have killed our doctor, it is obvious that it was not a murder, and on the basis of all the evidence it appears that it simply must have been an accident. It is necessary to assume that in the darkness the doctor fell into the ravine and died from the fatal injury.'

"The whole town agreed with this opinion. They buried the doctor and shortly thereafter no one even spoke of the possibility of a violent death. The existence of an individual so base and vile as to kill the doctor seemed inconceivable. Villainy also has its limits. Isn't that so?

"Well, suddenly, you can picture to yourself an event that did lead to the murderer. It was seen how one good-for-nothing, already having been tried many times and known for his degenerate living, sold a snuffbox and a watch that had belonged to the doctor in order to buy a drink in one of the bars. When he was caught he became agitated and obviously lied. His room was searched and under his bed was found a shirt with bloody sleeves and the doctor's lancet in a gold casing. What other evidence was needed? They put the criminal behind bars. The townspeople were outraged, but at the same time said:

" 'Unbelievable! This can't be so! There must be some mistake. It does happen that material evidence does not always reveal the truth!'

"In court the killer persisted in pleading not guilty. Everyone spoke against him and it was not difficult to be convinced of his guilt—as easy as it was to know that earth's soil was black, but the judges almost went out of their minds: For the tenth time they weighed every bit of evidence, questioned the witnesses' credibility, became flustered, drank a lot of water. . . . They started early in the morning and quit late in the evening.

" 'Guilty!' declared the chief justice, turning toward the killer. 'The court has judged you guilty of murdering the doctor and has sentenced you to . . .'

"The chief justice wanted to say: 'sentenced you to death,' but he threw down the sheet of paper upon which the judgment was written, wiped the cold sweat from his face, and cried out:

" 'No! If I am making an unjust verdict, let God punish me, but, I swear, he's not guilty! I cannot erase from my mind thoughts that it is impossible to find a man who would dare to kill our friend, the doctor! No man could stoop so low!'

" 'True, there cannot be such a person,' agreed the other judges.

" 'There can't be,' cried the crowd. 'Let him go free!'

"They released the murderer to depart to the four corners of the earth, and no one upbraided the judge for injustice. My grandmother said that God, too, with the same faith in mankind, forgave the sins of all the townspeople. God rejoices when man believes that he was created in His image. He grieves when man's true worth is forgotten and human beings are judged more harshly than dogs. Allowing that the sentence of not guilty would bring future harm to the townspeople, it would be made up by, you must admit, the salutary effect this faith would have. Faith truly never dies. It nurtures in us generous feelings and always awakens love and respect for every human being. Everyone! And that's important."

Mihail Karlovich was finished. My neighbor wanted to say something to him, but the old gardener made a gesture, letting us know that he wanted no discussion, and went toward the wagons, and with an expression of self-righteous importance on his face, involved himself in the arrangement of the plants.

1894

A Tedious Tale (From the Notes of an Old Man)

I

In Russia there is a highly respected Professor Nikolai Stepanovich who is what you may call a counselor and associate; he has so many Russian and foreign medals that when he wears them, students honor him as they would the church's iconostasis. His acquaintances are only people of the upper classes in the best sense of the term. For the last twenty-five to thirty years, at least, there hasn't been a famous scientist in Russia with whom he hasn't been well acquainted. At this time he doesn't carry on a friendship with anyone, but if one speaks of the past, there's a long list of his renowned friends ending with such names as Pirogov, Kaveling, and the poet Nekrasov—all of whom had felt the most sincere and warm friendship with him. He is a member of all the Russian and three foreign universities. And so on and so forth. All this and more which could be added, constitute that which is said about my name.

My name is well known. Every literate person in Russia knows it and abroad my lectures are announced with encomiums: famous and distinguished. It belongs to those few fortunate names which to inveigh against or to take in vain in public or in print would be considered a sign of bad taste. That's as it should be. My name is tightly bound to the knowledge of a remarkable person who was inestimably gifted and unquestionably useful. I'm a workaholic and have the endurance of an ox, and that's important, but what's more important, I'm talented. Along with this it can be said I'm polite, modest, and a nice guy. I've never buried my nose in books nor dabbled in politics, never sought popularity by indulging in polemics with the ignorant, or made after-dinner speeches, or speeches at the funerals of friends. . . . My scholarly name hasn't a single blemish and there is no need to grumble about it. It is a fortunate name.

Carrying this name, that means me, is a person sixty-two years old, bald, with dentures, and an incurable tic. As brilliant and illustrious as my name is, that's how dreary and ugly I, myself, am. My head and hands tremble from weakness. My neck, like one of Turgenev's heroines, resembles the neck of a double bass; my chest is sunken and my back is narrow. When I speak or lecture I curl my lips; when I smile—my whole face is covered with ghastly, senile wrinkles. Nothing is impressive in my sorry appearance except when at times my nervous tic aggravates me, then I have a unique look which those who observe it must have the drastic, disturbing thought: "It's obvious this person's days are numbered."

I continue to be as competent a lecturer as previously. As before, I can hold the attention of the listeners for two hours. My enthusiasm, well-planned presentation, and the humor interspersed almost cover up the deficiencies of my voice, which is dry, harsh, and with the intonation resembling that of a canting hypocrite. But my writing is poor. That piece of my brain which directs writing ability refuses to function. My memory has weakened, my thoughts are not sufficiently coordinated, and when I put them down on paper, it always seems to me that I've lost the flair I had for consistency. The construction is monotonous and my vocabulary is limited and irresolute. I often write something different from what I had in mind, and when I come to the conclusion, I can't remember the beginning. I often forget ordinary words, and I always have to spend a lot of energy eliminating superfluous material and unnecessary parenthetical remarks. These and other things are clear evidence of a decline in my mental acumen. And it is manifest that the simpler the topic, the more agonizing is the effort. When I'm writing a scholarly paper I feel freer and wiser than when writing a congratulatory letter or a memo. One more thing: it is easier for me to write in German or English than in Russian.

With regard to my present way of life, the most important matter is to free myself of insomnia from which I have suffered lately. If I were asked: What is now the most important and fundamental feature of your existence? I would answer: insomnia.

As it had been my custom previously, exactly at midnight I undress and lie down to sleep. I fall asleep quickly but between one and two o'clock I wake up and it is as if I have never slept. I get out of bed and light the lamp. I pace the room for an hour or two and look at pictures and photographs that I have seen many times. When I've had enough of pacing, I sit down at my desk. I sit motionless, my mind is a blank, and I crave nothing. If there is a book lying before me, I thoughtlessly move it closer and read it mechanically. One night not long ago, I read a whole novel in this way. It had a strange title: *What Was It the Swallow Was Singing?* Or if in order to occupy my mind, I give myself the task to count to a thousand, or to picture the face of one of my colleagues and try to recall: In what year and under what conditions did he become a member of academia?

I like to listen for night sounds. Two rooms away my daughter is saying something feverishly in her sleep. My wife, holding a candle, walks in the hallway and without fail drops a box of matches. A warped chest squeaks or a lamp burner unexpectedly buzzes—and all these sounds, for some reason, excite me.

If you don't sleep at night—you are constantly conscious that this is abnormal. I impatiently await the morning and the daytime when I have the right to be awake. The time before

the rooster crows is full of anguish. The rooster is my first
courier of good news. As soon as he crows I know that within
an hour the butler will awake and, coughing irritably, come
upstairs for something. After these sounds, little by little light
begins to creep in from behind the window, and the sound of
voices on the street can be heard. . . .

My day begins with the entrance of my wife. She comes in
her nightgown, uncombed but washed, smelling of flower-
scented cologne, and as if she has come in casually, always asks
the same question:

"Excuse me, I'll only be a minute. . . . You didn't sleep
again?"

After this she douses the lamp, sits down near the desk, and
begins to talk. I'm not prescient but I can predict what the
topic will be. It is the same every morning. Usually after concerned questions about my health, she will change the subject
to that of our son who is an officer in the army and stationed
in Warsaw. After the twentieth of each month we send him
fifty rubles—and this is the chief topic of our conversation.

"This is difficult for us, of course," my wife says and sighs,
"but until he can finally stand on his two feet, we have to help
him. He's young and abroad, and his pay is pathetic. . . . However, if you so wish, next month we'll not send him fifty but
forty rubles. What do you think?"

Daily experience could have convinced my wife that frequent discussions about expenses in no way reduced them, but
experience is not recognized by my wife; and every morning she
repeats exactly the same facts about our officer son, that bread
had become cheaper, thank God, and the price of sugar had
gone up by two kopecks—and all this as if she is informing me
of news.

I listen, mechanically assent, and perhaps, because I haven't
slept all night, strange, unrelated thoughts possess me. I observe
my wife with amazement, like a child. In wonder I ask myself:
is this old, fat, clumsy woman whose anxiety about trivia and
fear of poverty is expressed in her vacant face which is constantly clouded by thoughts of debts and necessities, knowing
only how to talk about expenses and smiling only when some-

thing becomes cheaper—is it really true that this woman had once been the slender Varya whom I had loved passionately for her fine, clear mind, her pure heart, her beauty, and as Othello had loved Desdemona, for her "appreciation" of my profession? Is she really the same Varya who had borne me a son?

With great effort I look into the face of this sodden, lumbering old woman and try to find in her my Varya, but the only thing remaining of her past was the concern about my health, and my salary is referred to as "our salary," my cap—our cap. It is painful for me to look at her, and in order to calm her down a little, I allow her to go on about what is desirable to do and even remain silent when she judges people unjustly, or scolds me for doing my job and not publishing textbooks.

Our conversation always ends the same way. My wife suddenly remembers that I haven't had my tea and is startled by the fact.

"What am I thinking about?" she says, getting up. "The samovar has been on the table long ago and here I am chattering. Good Lord, how forgetful I've become!"

She moves quickly but stops at the door in order to say:

"We haven't paid Yegor's wages for five months. Are you aware of that? We shouldn't let debts to the servants mount up. I've said this over and over again! It's easier to pay ten rubles a month than to have to pay fifty—for five months!"

From outside the door, she again stops and says:

"For me, our poor Liza is the saddest case. She attends the conservatory, is constantly in the company of the best people, but is dressed like God knows what. I'd be ashamed to show myself on the street in her coat. If she were someone else, that wouldn't matter, but everyone knows that her father is a distinguished professor, a Privy Councillor!"

So, after needling me about my notoriety and rank, she finally leaves. That is how my day begins. What follows is no better.

As I drink tea, my daughter Liza enters in her coat and cap and with sheet music ready to leave for the conservatory. She is twenty-two years old. She looks younger, is self-confident, and looks a little like my wife when she was young. She gently kisses my forehead and hand and says:

"Good morning, Daddy. Are you feeling well?"

When she was little she loved ice cream, and I often took her to the ice cream shop. Ice cream was more wonderful than anything else for her. If she wanted to pay me a compliment, she would say: "You, Daddy, are ice-creamy." One of her little fingers she called pistachio, another was plum, a third was raspberry, and so on. When she would come to greet me in the morning, I would usually put her on my knees and kissing her little fingers would say:

"Plum . . . pistachio . . . lemon. . . ."

And now, with nostalgia, I kiss Liza's fingers and mutter: "Pistachio . . . plum . . . lemon . . . ," but it doesn't come out right. "I'm cold, like the ice cream, and I'm ashamed. When my daughter comes to my study and kisses my forehead, I wince, as if a bee were stinging me, force myself to smile, and turn my face away. Since the advent of my insomnia my brain has been pounded by the question: my daughter often sees how I, an old, renowned person, painfully flushes from the fact that I need a valet. She sees how anxiety about small debts makes it impossible for me to work and for hours to pace up and down and to think. Why didn't she, not even once, come to me secretly without her mother's knowledge and whisper: "Father, here's my watch, my bracelets, earrings, dresses. . . . Pawn it all, you need the money . . ."? Why didn't she, seeing how her mother and I tried to hide our poverty from everyone, why didn't she refuse the expensive satisfaction of studying music? I wouldn't take her watch, her bracelets, any of her sacrifices, Lord preserve me from this—this I don't need.

At the same time I'm reminded of my son the Warsaw officer. He's a smart, honest, and sober human being. But that's not the point. I think that if I had an aging father, and if I knew that he had moments when he was ashamed of his poverty, I'd give up my officer's commission to someone else and get myself a real job. Similar thoughts about my children poison my psyche. What is their purpose? Only a narrow, embittered man can hold a grudge against ordinary people because they have no courage. But enough of this.

At a quarter to ten I must go and lecture to my beloved students. I get dressed and go out on the road which I have known for thirty years. The road has its own history for me. Here is the large, gray house with an apothecary. At one time a tiny house where they sold port beer stood over there. In there I conceived my dissertation topic and wrote my first love letter to Varya. I wrote with a pencil the title "Historia Morbi"* on a scrap of paper. Here's the grocery shop. It was once run by a short Jew who sold me cigarettes on credit, and later run by a fat peasant woman who loved students because "every one of them was a mother's son." Now a red-haired merchant, a very indifferent person, sits there drinking tea out of a tin pot. And over here are the dismal, broken-down gates to the university. A bored yardman in a sheepskin coat sweeps the snow with a broom. Such gates cannot make a sound impression upon a callow youth, arriving from the provinces and for whom the cathedral of learning is a true temple. It is my opinion that one of the most important reasons for the long history of Russian pessimism is the existence of the generally dilapidated university buildings, the dark corridors, the walls covered with soot, the insufficient lighting, the cheerless appearance of the stairs, clothes racks, and benches. Our garden is over here. Since my days as a student it has not changed—neither better nor worse. I disliked it. It would be infinitely wiser if in the place of the consumptive linden trees, yellow acacias and rarely pruned lilacs, tall pines and healthy oaks stood. A student, whose mood in the main reacts to his environment, must at every step see before him where he is studying only that which is tall, strong, and elegant. . . . Protect him, dear God, from scrawny trees, broken windows, gray walls, and doors covered with torn wallpaper.

When I approach my own entrance the door is thrown open and I am met by my old servant, who is my own age and my namesake, Nikolai, the butler. Letting me in he grunts and says:

"It's freezing out, your excellency!"

If my fur coat is wet, then:

"It's raining, your excellency!"

*"History of Diseases"

After this he rushes in front of me to open the doors as I go along. In my study he carefully helps me out of my coat and at the same time he succeeds in informing me about some university news. Thanks to the friendly relations that exist among the university valets and guards, he knows all that is going on in the four faculties, in the chancellery, in the rector's office, and in the library. What he doesn't know! If we have a bad day, for example, the resignation of a rector or a deacon, then I hear how he, after conversing with the young guards, names the candidates and also tells me who the minister will not confirm, who he will dismiss; then he goes into fantastic details about some mysterious papers received by the chancellor, or about supposedly secret talks between the minister and a trustee, and so forth. If you leave out these details, he's almost always generally proved right. His characterizations of the candidates though very original are fairly accurate. If you need to know in what year someone defended his dissertation, got a job, retired, or died, ask this old soldier. He has a voluminous memory and not only can tell you the year, the month, and the day, but can give you the special circumstances under which anything occurred. Only someone who is devoted to his subject can retain such information. He is a custodian of university traditions and legends. His predecessors have provided him with many tales about university life, and he has added to this abundance many that he has collected during his own service, and, if you wish, he can tell you many short and long stories. He can tell about unusual eccentrics; he knows *everything*. He can tell you about numerous martyrs and victims in the pursuit of knowledge. Good always triumphs over evil, the weak defeat the strong, the wise overcome the stupid, the modest subdue the proud, the young leave the old behind. . . .

All these legends and cock-and-bull stories needn't be taken literally at face value, but after you've filtered them out, you will have left our fine traditions and the names of our distinguished scholars acknowledged by everyone.

The public only knows the anecdotes about the absentminded old professor, and a couple of sharp one-liners attributed to Gruberu, to myself, or to Babukin. This doesn't say much for an educated community. If they truly appreciated scholarship, scientists, and students as much as Nikolai, its literature would have long ago included epic poetry, chronicles, and legends which it does not now include, I'm sorry to say.

Having given me the news, Nikolai puts on a stern mien, and we begin to discuss the business of the day. If at that time an outsider would hear how easily Nikolai used technical terms, he would very likely think that this was a scientist masquerading as an old soldier. It can be said, by the way, that the erudition of university maintenance staff is highly exaggerated. It is true that Nikolai knows more than a hundred Latin terms, knows how to assemble a skeleton, sometimes can prepare a specimen, amuse students with long scientific citations, but, for example, the elementary theory of the circulation of the blood is for him as obscure today as it was twenty years ago.

At a desk in the office, hunched over a book or specimen, sits my dissector, Peter Ignatyevich, a hardworking, modest, but untalented man, thirty-five years old, already bald and with a paunch. He works from morning 'til night, reads voluminously, and has an excellent memory of all he reads—and in this endeavor he's worth his weight in gold. With respect to other things—he's like a cart horse, or, in other words, a scholarly blockhead. The characteristics of a drudge distinguishing him from someone with talent are: his horizons are limited and narrowly confined to his specialty; outside his own field he's as naive as a baby. I recall going into the office one morning and declaring:

"Imagine what has happened! They say Skobelev* has died."

Nikolai made the sign of the cross, but Peter Ignatyevich asked:

"Who was Skobelev?"

Another time—this was somewhat earlier—I informed him that Professor Perov had died. Dear Peter Ignatyevich responded:

"What was his field?"

It seems that if Patti herself sang by his very ear, if the

---

*a famous Russian general of that period

Chinese hordes invaded Russia, or if there were an earthquake, he wouldn't move a muscle and would continue unperturbed to look with squinting eyes into his microscope. Simply stated, Hecuba was none of his business. I'd pay a great deal to see how this dried-up old stick sleeps with his wife.

Another of his traits is his fanatical belief in the infallibility of science and particularly the work of the Germans. He has faith in himself, in his concoctions, knows the value of life, and has none of the doubt and disillusions that make the hair of more talented men turn gray. The slavish deference to authority makes it unnecessary for him to think for himself. His rigidity makes it impossible to argue with him. It's impossible to argue with a man who has a firm conviction that the super-science is medicine—that the best people are doctors—the best traditions, medical. Of the malpractice of medical practitioners in the past only one tradition, that of wearing a white tie, remains. For the scientist and even the more generally educated person, there is no separation of scholarly traditions into medical, judicial, etcetera, but for Peter Ignatyevich it is difficult to agree that this is true, and he is ready to argue with you 'til doomsday.

His future is obvious to me. During his whole life he will prepare several hundred experiments of unusual purity, write up very excellent dry reports, and a dozen or so conscientious translations, but will never produce a single original breakthrough. To do this one must be able to fantasize, be an innovator, make intelligent guesses, but Peter Ignatyevich has none of these qualities. Briefly, he's not a master of science but a laborer.

Peter Ignatyevich, Nikolai, and I are conversing in an undertone. We're a little uneasy. It is an odd sensation that you get when from behind the door the buzzing from the lecture hall sounds like the booming of the sea. This has been going on for thirty years but I'm still not immune to it and experience it every morning. I nervously button my jacket, ask Nikolai unnecessary questions, become irritated. . . . It appears like cowardice, but it's not cowardice, but something else which I cannot name or describe.

For no reason at all I look at the clock and say:
"How's about it? It's time to go."

And we march in this order: first goes Nikolai carrying the experiments or charts, I'm next, and following me, with his head modestly lowered, shuffles the cart horse. Or, if when needed, a corpse is carried on a cot before us, and then comes Nikolai, and so on. When I enter the lecture hall, the students rise, then are seated, and the sealike hum suddenly quiets down. Stillness sets in.

I know what I'm going to lecture about, but I don't know exactly how I'll proceed, what I'll begin with, or what I'll conclude with. I don't have a single phrase ready in my head. But all I have to do is take a look at the packed lecture hall (it's in the style of an amphitheater) and spontaneously start with the stereotypical: "The last lecture stopped at . . ." and out comes a long succession of sentences that rush out from my inner being and—the game's on! I speak swiftly, enthusiastically, and it appears that there isn't anything powerful enough to interrupt the flow of my words. In order to be a decent lecturer, that is, one who is not boring and is of value to the listeners, it is necessary not only to be talented but to have a special ease and experience. One must have complete confidence in one's abilities to present the subject one is lecturing about, must know those to whom one is lecturing, and know the subject. Besides that, it's necessary to have your wits about you, be vigilant, and not for a second lose sight of your thesis.

When a good conductor interprets a composer's composition, he performs twenty things at once: follows the score, waves his baton, pays attention to the singers, cues the timpani or the French horns, and so on. It is the same when I lecture. There are before me one hundred and fifty faces, each one unique, and three hundred eyes staring at me. My purpose—is to conquer this many-headed hydra. If every minute when I'm lecturing I have a clear picture of the degree of attention and the depth of comprehension, then I'm completely in control.

My other adversary is myself. This—the infinite variety of forms, phenomena, and laws, and the great number of qualifications attached to my own and others' thoughts. It is necessary to be on the alert every minute in order to select from the mass of material the most important and relevant elements at the same time as my words flow; to present my thoughts in such a way that the hydra can understand and be stimulated. I must be constantly vigilant that every thought is in the proper sequence—not as they accumulate in my head—so that I paint an accurate picture of what I wish to portray. I also try to lecture in the style of fine literature and to keep my definitions brief and to the point, and my sentences as simple and elegant as possible. I have only one hour and forty minutes, so I must keep a check of every minute that goes by. There is little time to do the work. At one and the same time I must be both scientist and pedagogue, and orator, and it's bad news if the orator takes over from the scientist and the pedagogue, or vice versa.

If after a quarter or a half-hour of lecturing you notice that some students are looking at the ceiling or at Peter Ignatyevich, and that one is fishing for his handkerchief, another the same thing, a third is smiling to himself . . . these are indicators that attention is waning. Something must be done. Taking the first opportunity, I tell a joke. One hundred and fifty people grin broadly, eyes shine, for a little while the sound of the sea is heard . . . I laugh, too. Attention is resumed and I can continue.

There is no sport, no diversion, no game that gives me more pleasure than lecturing. It is only when I'm lecturing that I can lose myself completely. I can understand the inspiration that poets experience, for it must be similar. I think that Hercules after his most exciting feats did not feel such a sweet exhaustion as I do after every lecture.

But that's all in the past. When I lecture now I go through torture. A half-hour doesn't pass when I begin to feel my legs giving out under me and my back collapsing. I sit down in the armchair, but I'm not accustomed to lecturing from a sitting position. My mouth gets dry, my voice grows hoarse, my head spins. . . . In order to hide my condition from the students I take a drink of water, cough, blow my nose frequently—as if I had a head cold which was bothering me. I tell unsuitable jokes and finally cut the lecture short. But more important than this is that I feel ashamed.

My conscience and my brain tell me that the best thing which I can do now—is to give my final lecture to the youngsters, say good-bye, give them my best wishes, and leave the podium to a more capable younger man. But as God is my witness, I don't have the courage to do what my conscience dictates. Unfortunately, I'm neither a philosopher nor a theologian. I know very well that I'll live no more than a half-year. It would appear that I should now pursue questions about the mystery of the afterlife, and of those ghosts which invade my sepulchral sleep. Whatever may be the reason, I don't have the heart to consider these questions, although my mind recognizes their importance. As true as it was some twenty or thirty years ago, the only thing which interests me is scientific knowledge. When my last bit of breath leaves me, I will still believe that learning— is the most important, the most beautiful, and the most vital necessity in man's existence, and that it has always been and always will be the greatest manifestation of love, and is the only way to have control over nature and oneself. This belief may be naive and inaccurate in its assumptions, but I can't be criticized for this. It's impossible to dispossess myself of it.

In any case this is not important. I only beg indulgence for my failings and to understand that I am more interested in the fate of the marrow of the bones than in the purpose of the universe. To wrench me from the faculty and my students is tantamount to nailing a man in his coffin before his death.

Along with the insomnia and the consequent struggle with the loss of strength, something strange is happening to me. In the midst of giving a lecture, I feel tears rising in my throat, and I have a terrible, hysterical desire to stretch out my arms and yell complaints. I want to shout that I, a well-known authority, have unfairly been sentenced to death by fate, that in approximately six months someone else will take over that lecture hall. I want to shout that I've been poisoned. Thoughts which I've never had before have tainted the last days of my life and sting my brain like mosquitos. My condition now seems so awful that I wish that my audience would become appalled, leave panic-stricken from their seats, and with desperate cries head for the exit.

It's not easy to live this way.

II

After the lecture I go home and work. I read the journals, a dissertation, or prepare the next lecture. Sometimes I write something. I do get interrupted when it's necessary to receive guests.

The doorbell rings. A colleague has come to talk about his work. He comes into my study with hat and cane in hand, and approaching me points both toward me and says:

"Only for a minute of your time, only a minute! Don't get up friend! Only a few words!"

Our first concern is to show each other our most deferent courtesy and our pleasure at seeing each other. I make him take a seat and he insists I sit down, too. At the same time we are stroking each others' waists, touching buttons, and it looks like we are acting toward each other as if we were afraid of getting burned. We both laugh though nothing funny has been said. After we both are seated, we lean toward each other and begin to speak in soft voices. As if we were not sympathetic toward each other, we can't refrain from embellishing our words in the Chinese fashion: "As you have so correctly remarked" or "As I have already had the honor to tell you." We laugh at each other's puns even if they are bad ones. Having finished our business, my colleague gets up abruptly and, waving his hat in the direction of my work, begins to make his departure. Once again we touch each other and laugh. I accompany him to the entrance, I help him into his coat, but he wants to refrain from accepting this great honor. Then, as Yegor opens the door, my friend warns me of catching cold as I give the appearance of being ready to escort him into the street. And when I finally return to the study, my face retains a smile, probably from passivity.

In a short while the doorbell rings again. Someone has entered the foyer, takes a long time to relieve himself of his overcoat, and is coughing. Yegor announces a student. I tell him to ask him in. A good-looking young man enters shortly after. It's been a year since we've been on easy terms: he gave terrible answers when I examined him and I gave him a failing grade. I had about seven such youths yearly whom I, as expressed by students, nudged out or flunked. Those who don't pass an examination because of incompetence or illness usually bear their cross patiently and don't try to bargain with me. The ones who bargain and come to my house are the optimists, uninhibited temperaments, for whom the taking of tests makes them lose their appetites and cuts into their regular enjoyment of the opera. The first type I'm easy with, the second I fail throughout the year.

"Please sit down," I tell my guest. "What is it you wish?"

"Excuse me, professor, for disturbing you," he begins, hesitating and not meeting my eyes. "I wouldn't have dared to disturb you, if it weren't for . . . I've taken your exam five times now and . . . and I've been flunked. I beg you to be so kind as to give me a passing grade, because . . ."

The argument which every sluggard uses is always the same: they receive excellent grades in every subject but mine, and it is even more remarkable because they have spent more time on my subject and know it very well. They fail for some incomprehensible reason.

"I'm sorry, friend," I tell my guest. "I can't pass you. Study your lecture notes again and come back. Then we'll see."

There's a pause. I have the desire to torture this student because he likes his beer and the opera more than knowledge and I say with a sigh:

"In my opinion, the best thing you can do is to quit medical school. If you are incapable of passing examinations, then obviously, you have neither the desire nor the vocation for being a doctor."

The optimist pulls a long face.

"Excuse me, professor," he smirks, "but in my opinion that would be at the least, strange. I've been studying for five years, and suddenly to quit!"

"Well, yes! It's better to give up five years than to spend the rest of one's life doing what one doesn't like."

But, instantly I feel sorry for him and hasten to say:

"However, who knows? So, apply yourself a bit more and then return."

"When?" dully asks the sluggard.

"When you wish. It can be tomorrow."

In his fine eyes I can read: "I can come back but you know this jerk will flunk me again!"

"Of course," I add, "you won't know any more even if you take the examination with me fifteen times, but it will help to train your character. So give thanks for that."

Silence descends. I get up and wait for my guest to leave, but he stands, looks out the window, tugs on his beard, and thinks. It's getting boring.

The voice of this confident youth is pleasant, mellifluous, his bright eyes are mocking, and his handsome face is a little worn-looking from too much beer-drinking and spending long periods of time on his couch. He obviously could tell me many interesting anecdotes from the opera, about his love affairs, about a friend he is close to, but, unfortunately to speak of these things is not done—as much as I might like to hear them.

"Professor! I give you my word of honor that if you pass me, that I . . ."

As soon as he emitted "word of honor" I waved my hand and sat down at my desk. The student hesitates for another minute and then says despondently:

"In that case, good-bye. . . . Excuse me."

"Good-bye, my friend. Be well."

He enters the hall indecisively, slowly dons his overcoat, and goes out into the street. He, no doubt, ponders what has occurred, but doesn't think of anything new besides calling me that "old devil." He goes to a cheap restaurant to drink beer and eat his dinner, then goes home to sleep it off. Rest in peace, you honorable laborer!

The doorbell rings a third time. A young doctor enters wearing a new black suit, gold-rimmed glasses, and, of course, a white tie. He introduces himself. I ask him to sit down and ask what I can do for him. Not without some trepidation the young priest of science begins to tell me that in the current year he had passed his doctoral examination and the only thing left to do was his dissertation. He wished to work with me and to have me as his dissertation supervisor; and he would be most obliged to me if I would give him a topic for the dissertation.

"I'd be happy to help you, friend," I say, "but let's begin by agreeing as to what is understood as a dissertation. A dissertation is to be the original work of the candidate. Isn't that correct? A thesis written on someone else's topic and under someone else's supervision has another name—"

The candidate does not respond. I lose patience and leap from my chair.

"Why do you all come to me?" I cry out angrily. "Do I have a shop here? I'm not a merchant selling topics! For the thousandth time I beg you all to leave me in peace! Excuse me for my rudeness, but I've finally had too much!"

The doctoral candidate keeps quiet and flushes about his cheekbones. His face reflects a deep respect for my distinguished reputation and scholarship, but I can see in his eyes that he despises my voice, my sad physique, and nervous gesticulation. In my anger I presented myself as some kind of eccentric.

"This is not a shop for topics!" I explode angrily. "What an amazing business! Why don't you want to be independent? Why is freedom so repulsive to you?"

I say a great deal while he remains silent. In the end, little by little, I quiet down and, needless to say, I give in to his request. The candidate gets his topic from me, which isn't worth a dime, writes under my supervision a worthless dissertation, participates with dignity in a public defense, and receives an academic degree for which he has no need.

The doorbell can ring continually but I limit myself here to four. When the fourth bell rings, I hear familiar steps, the rustle of skirts, a voice I like. . . .

Eighteen years ago a comrade of mine, an oculist, died and left a seven-year-old daughter, Katya, and sixty thousand rubles. I was named her guardian in his will. Katya lived with my family for ten years, then left for college and lived with us only during the summer months when classes were not held. I didn't have any time to involve myself in her upbringing, and only rarely looked after her, so I can't say much about her childhood.

My earliest memory of her which I cherish is—the unusual trustfulness with which she entered my home, allowed doctors to treat her, and which always shone on her small face. It so happened that at times she would sit apart from others, with a bandaged cheek, and stare at something with persistent attention. At such times, she observes how I write or turn over the pages of books, or how my wife bustles around, or how the cook in the kitchen peels the potatoes, or how the dog plays; her eyes always expressed without fail only one thing, namely: "Everything which is done on earth is wonderful and wise." She was curious and liked to speak with me. She would sit opposite me at my desk, follow my movements, and ask questions. She found it interesting to know what I was reading, what I was doing at the university, whether I feared the corpses, and what I did with my salary.

"Are the students in the university impudent?" she asks.

"They are impudent, my dear."

"Do you make them get on their knees?"

"I do."

She thought it was funny that students were naughty and that I would force them to get on their knees, and she would laugh. She was a meek, patient, and good child. Not infrequently I happened to notice how something was taken from her, how she was punished without cause, or her curiosity was disparaged. At these times, along with the constant look of trust on her face, sadness was intermingled—and only that. I didn't know how to take her part and when I saw the sadness, the only thing that I wanted to do was to hold her close and like an old nanny to say: "My dear little orphan!"

I also recall that she liked to be well dressed and to spray herself with perfume. In this she took after me. I also like beautiful clothes and fine perfumes.

I am sorry that I didn't have the time or the desire to observe the beginning and development of the passion which overtook Katya when she was fourteen or fifteen. I'm speaking of her passionate love for the theater. When she came to us during her vacations and lived with us, there wasn't anything that she spoke about with such satisfaction and with such

warmth as of plays and actors. She wearied us with her inces-
sant chatter about the theater. My wife and children did not
listen to her. I was the only one who didn't have the courage
not to give her my attention. When she wanted to share her
enthusiasm, she would come to me in my study and with a
pleading voice would say:

"Nikolai Stepanich, permit me to discuss the theater with
you!"

I would point to the clock and say:

"I give you a half-hour. Begin."

Later she began to bring dozens of photos of actors and
actresses with her—which she treated as icons; then she performed several times in amateur theatrical productions, and
finally, when she graduated, she told me that she was born to
be an actress.

I never analyzed Katya's fascination for the theater. In my
opinion, if the play is worthwhile, in order for it to get the
desired attention, you don't have to bother with actors: One
can satisfy oneself by reading. If the play is a dud, no performance will improve it.

In my youth I often attended the theater and now, once or
twice a year, my family books a loge and takes me in order to
"be refreshed." That, of course, is not sufficient to have the
right to make a judgment about the theater, but I do have
something to say about it. In my opinion the theater is no
better than it was thirty or forty years ago. You still can't get a
glass of clean water in the corridors or the foyer. The ushers still
touch you for a two-bit tip when they take your coat, which
must be worn in the winter. Music is still played during the
intermission, adding another sensation to that of the play itself,
which is new and uncalled for. As in the past the men go to the
bar during the intermission for an alcoholic drink. If no
progress can be seen in the little things, it would be folly to look
for it in the important ones. When the actor is bound from
head to toe by theatrical traditions and prejudices, if he tries to
give a simple, ordinary soliloquy, "To be or not to be," for some
reason he can't do it without sputtering and with his whole
body convulsing. Or when I'm supposed to be convinced that

Chatski—who spends a lot of time talking with fools and loves a foolish girl—is a very wise person and that *Woe from Wit** is not a boring play, and on the stage is the same old routine that bored me forty years ago when I was treated to classical howling and breast-beating. Every time I leave the theater I'm more conservative than when I entered.

You can persuade a sentimental and trustful rabble that the theater in reality is a school, but you won't snare with this ploy the individual who is acquainted with a genuine school. I don't know what will happen in fifty or a hundred years, but under present conditions the theater is only entertainment. But this entertainment is too costly for it to continue. It takes from the nation thousands of young, healthy, and talented men and women who, if they had not devoted themselves to the theater, could have been doctors, agronomists, teachers, officials. From the public are taken the evening hours—the best time for intellectual activity and comradely conversation. This is not to mention the monetary cost and those moral losses that the audiences bear when they see on the stage murder, adultery, or slander erroneously interpreted.

Katya was of an entirely different opinion. She assured me that the theater, even in its present state, was superior to the lecture hall, superior to books, and superior to everything else in the world. The theater was a force that incorporated within itself all the arts, and the actors—were missionaries. No other art and no other areas of knowledge could impact the human soul as effectively as the stage. It was not without reason that an actor of average notability achieves a much greater popularity in the country than the best scholar or artist, and that no public service could give as much happiness and satisfaction as performance on the stage.

So, on one very beautiful day Katya joined a theatrical company and left for Ufa, taking with her a lot of money, a pile of jaunty clothes, and an aristocratic attitude toward the venture.

Her first letters from the road were amazing. I read them

---

*a satirical Russian comedy acclaimed as one of the best Russian plays of the nineteenth century and was simply dumbfounded as to how these small sheets of paper could embody so much youth, purity of heart, saintly naivete, and combine with it keen, sensible criticism that would not put to shame a smart male brain. She didn't just describe but glorified the Volga, nature, the towns which she visited, her comrades, her own successes and failures. Every stroke of her pen breathed the same trustfulness that I had become accustomed to seeing on her face—all was written full of grammatical errors and almost no punctuation marks.

A half-year had barely passed when I received an ecstatic letter that could be considered poetic. It began with the words: "I'm in love." A photo was pasted alongside these words showing a young man with a shaven face, wearing a broad-brimmed hat, and with a plaid blanket thrown casually over his shoulders. The letters following this one were just as splendid, but did begin to show punctuation, the grammar became correct, and they had a strong masculine scent. Katya began to write about the advisability of building a large theater somewhere on the Volga. This could be achieved by creating a stock company that would attract large merchants and the steamship owners. It would be a source of huge sums of money, the take enormous, and the actors could perform as members of a partnership. . . . It could be that all this was worthy, but it seemed to me that this kind of mental concoction was distinctly the product of a male's brain.

Be this as it may, all seemed to be going on well for almost two years. Katya loved, believed in what she was doing, and was happy. But then I began to note the signs symptomatic of depression. It began with complaints by Katya about her colleagues—this is the first and most ominous symptom. If a young scholar or writer begins his work by being bitter against other scholars or writers, it indicates that he's burned-out and is not able to do the work. Katya wrote to me that her coworkers didn't attend rehearsals and never knew their parts. By performing inane plays and in the way they were staged could be seen in all of them a disrespect for the public. In the interests of box office receipts, which was the only thing they talked about, dramatic actresses lowered themselves and sang in

musical comedies, and tragedians sang satirical couplets about
philandering husbands and the pregnancies of unfaithful wives,
and so forth. How the theater continued to be attended in the
provinces was a wonder, or how long it could continue in such
a shallow and rotten vein.

In reply I sent Katya, I admit, a very long and boring letter.
Among other things I wrote her: "I often have conversations
with old actors, excellent people, who consider me good company. In my talks with them I have been able to understand
that their work is controlled not only by their individual intel-
ligence and freedom, but just as much by society's mood and
style of life. The best of them were able to perform in tragedies,
and in operettas, in Parisian farces, and in fairy tales. To all of
them it seemed that they had chosen the right path and that
they have been of use. The cause of the decline must be sought
not in the actors but deeper, in the art itself and the way society
reacts to it."

This letter only annoyed Katya. She answered me:

"We're singing two different operas. . . . I didn't write you
about well-born people, who were on your level, but of a band
of foxes who have nothing in common with nobility. This herd
of anarchists took to the stage because no other place would
accept them, and call themselves artists only because they are
brazen. Not a bit of talent, but lots of bungling effort, drunkenness, intrigues, slanders. I can't express how bitter I feel that
the art which I loved so much has fallen into the hands of
people I hate. I'm bitter that better people see this evil only
from a distance. They don't want to come any closer and
instead write me stuffy platitudes and moral lessons which
nobody wants to hear . . ." and so on in the same manner.

After a short time I received this letter:

"I have been inhumanely deceived. I don't want to go on
living. Do what you want with my money. I have loved you like
a father and my only friend. Forgive me."

It appeared that even *he* belonged to the "herd of anarchists." Subsequently from a few hints I deduced that she had
attempted suicide. Katya, apparently, had tried to poison herself. She must have been seriously ill later since the next letter

I received from her was from Yalta where she evidently had been sent by her doctors. The next letter requested that I send her a thousand rubles as soon as possible and ended in this way: "Please excuse the gloomy nature of this letter. I buried my child yesterday." After living in the Crimea for about a year, she returned home.

Her travels encompassed about four years, and during these four years it must be recognized that I played an unseen and incomprehensible role. When earlier she had revealed to me that she was going to be an actress, and when she wrote me that she was in love, when she periodically became extravagant and I would be asked to send her thousands of rubles or two rubles, when she spoke of her intention to die, and later about the death of her child, at every instance I became flustered and the only way I was involved in her fate was that I thought about it a great deal and wrote her long, boring letters which I ought not to have written. That was how I took the place of her father and loved her like a daughter!

⊠　　⊠　　⊠

Katya now lives about one-and-a-half versts from me. She has rented a five-room apartment and furnished it comfortably and in her own distinctive taste. If one took it upon oneself to describe her furniture, the dominating mood of the scene would be indolence. For a languid body—soft couches, soft stools for the lazy feet—rugs for lazy observation—faded, wan, or luster-less flowers; for the indolent spirit—a profusion of cheap fans on the walls and small pictures in which originality of technique prevails over its content, a surplus of little tables and shelves that are absolutely unnecessary, and hangings of no value, shapeless rags in the place of curtains. . . . All this, together with the frightfully gaudy flowers, symmetry, and spaciousness, apart from the languid spirit, still show natural good taste. Katya lies around on a couch most days and reads novels and short stories. She leaves the apartment only once a day in the afternoon in order to visit me.

I work and Katya sits on the divan nearby, silent and huddled in a shawl as if she were cold. It may be that I find her sympathetic or that I had become accustomed to her frequent visits when she was a little girl; her presence does not interfere with my concentration. Once in a while I ask her something mechanically and she answers curtly; or in order to take a breather, I turn to her and see how she thoughtfully looks over one of the medical journals or the newspaper. It is at such times that I note that her face no longer has the former expression of innocence. The expression is now cold, nonchalant, absentminded, like that of passengers awaiting a train. She is dressed beautifully and simply as in the past, but without concern. It's apparent that her clothing and hairdo show the effects of constant reclining for days on end on the couches and rocking chairs. And she is not curious as she was previously. She doesn't ask me questions. It is as if she had already experienced everything and didn't expect to hear anything new.

As four o'clock is approaching one can hear activity beginning in the dining room and in the drawing room. Liza has returned from the conservatory and has brought a friend with her. You can hear how they are playing the piano, testing their voices, and laughing. Yegor is setting the table in the dining room and rattling dishes.

"Farewell," says Katya. "I won't go in to your family today. Make my apologies. I don't have the time. Come to my place."

When I accompany her to the foyer, she looks me over from head to foot and in a vexed voice says:

"You're getting thinner! Why don't you see a doctor? I'll go to Sergei Fedorovich and ask him to see you. Let him examine you."

"It's not necessary, Katya."

"I don't understand what your family sees! All's well, indeed."

She puts on her fur coat crossly, and at the same time her loosely put together hairdo falls apart and several hairpins fall on the floor. As earlier, she straightens it out carelessly. She roughly tucks in fallen strands under her hat, and leaves.

When I enter the dining room my wife asks me:

"Was Katya with you just now? Why didn't she come in to see us? It's somewhat peculiar. . . ."

"Mama!" reproachfully exclaims Liza. "If she doesn't want to, forget it. We don't have to get on our knees to her."

"Say what you want but it's contemptuous. She was in the study for three hours and didn't think of us. Anyway, it's her choice."

Varya and Liza both dislike Katya. I don't understand their animosity. Probably, you have to be a woman to understand it. I'd stake my life on it that out of the one hundred and fifty young men I see almost daily in the lecture hall, and the hundred old men whom I meet with every week, it would be difficult to find one who could understand this dislike and repugnance for Katya's past—that is, her pregnancy out of wedlock and her illegitimate child. At the same time I can in no way recall a single woman or young girl that I'm acquainted with who wouldn't consciously or instinctively entertain such feelings. And it isn't because a woman is more virtuous and purer than a man; virtue and purity aren't very different from vice, if they're not free of malicious feelings. I interpret this as simply the backwardness of women. The doleful feeling of compassion and pangs of conscience that the contemporary man experiences when he sees such calamity—say more to me about culture and moral maturity than dislike and repugnance. The contemporary woman is just as tearful and her heart is as crude as in the Middle Ages. In my opinion, those who campaign for educating her just as you do men are on the right track.

My wife doesn't like Katya also because she has been an actress, for her thanklessness, for her arrogance, for her eccentricity, and for all those numerous improprieties that one woman can always find in another.

Besides my family and myself, dinner includes several of my daughter's girlfriends and Alexander Adolphovich Gnekker, Liza's admirer and pretender for her hand. This young blond is not more than thirty, of average height, very sturdy, broad-shouldered, with chestnut-colored sideburns around his ears, and with tinted mustachios that give his full, smooth face a playful expression. He wore a very short jacket, a colorful vest, checked trousers—very wide at the top and very narrow at the bottom—and yellow boots without heels. He had bulging, goggly eyes, a tie resembling the neck of a crawfish, and, it seems to me, everything about this young man gives off the scent of crab soup. He's in our house every day, but no one in my family knows what his profession is, where he went to school, and by what means he lives. He isn't a musician or a poet, can neither sing nor play, sells someone pianos somewhere, is often at the conservatory, is acquainted with all the celebrities, and takes charge at concerts. He criticizes performances with great authority and I have noticed that most people agree with him.

Wealthy people always have hangers-on around them, as do academics and artists. It seems that there isn't anywhere on earth where artists or academics are free of the presence of "foreign bodies" of Mr. Gnekker's type. I'm not a musician and it's possible I'm mistaken in my opinion of Gnekker, when after all, I know very little about him. But his air of authority and the dignified way that he stands by the piano and listens when someone plays or sings appear suspicious to me.

You can be a hundred times over a gentleman or have a high professional rank, but if you have a daughter, there's no way you can escape this kind of philistinism that is often brought into your home, coming along with it courtship, proposals, and marriage. I, for example, cannot in any way be reconciled to the reverent expression that exhibits itself on my wife's face every time Gnekker is in our house. I can't be reconciled to the bottles of Chateau Lafite port and sherry which are put on the table solely for the purpose of convincing him that our life is luxurious and sophisticated. And I can't stand Liza's jerky laughter, which she learned in the observatory, and the way she squints her eyes when men are around. But most important, I'll never understand why every day my home is invaded by, and dines with us, a human being who is perfectly alien to my habits, to my teaching, to my way of life, and in no way resembles people I like. My wife and the servants covertly whisper that "he is a suitor" but I still can't understand his presence. He awakens in me such bewilderment as if a Zulu were seated by me. And it also seems strange to me that my daughter, whom I had become accustomed to thinking of as my child, loves this tie, these eyes, these puffy cheeks. . . .

In the past I enjoyed dinner or was indifferent about it, but now it arouses nothing in me but boredom and irritation. From the time that I became a full professor and became a dean of the faculty, my family found it necessary to change drastically our style of dining. In place of the simple dishes that I had been used to when I was a student and a doctor, now they feed me bouillon in which floats some kind of icicles, and there are leaf buds in the Madeira. The rank of general and notoriety have deprived me forever of a bowl of cabbage soup, tasty pies, goose stuffed with apples, and bream with porridge. They took away from me the maid, Agasha, a talkative and humorous old woman, and in her place I'm being served by Yegor, a dull and supercilious young fellow, with a white napkin laid over his right arm. The times between dishes are short, but they seem excessively long because there is nothing to fill them. No longer was there the former gaiety, uninhibited conversations, jokes, laughter, mutual kindnesses, and that delight which the children stirred in my wife and myself when we got together in the dining room. For me, a working person, dining was a time of relaxation and socializing, but for my wife and the children who did not work, it's true, it was short, but bright and happy. They knew that for at least a half-hour I belonged not to education, or to students, but to them alone and no one else. No longer can I get a little tipsy from a glass of wine, no Agasha, no bream with porridge, none of the uproar that accompanied the petty misdemeanors during dinner such as kittens squabbling with the dog under the table or a bandaid from Katya's cheek falling into the soup tureen.

It's not in good taste to describe literally the current dinner. On my wife's face is solemnity, an affected air of importance, and her customary expression of vexation. She fusses over the dishes and remarks: "I can see that you find the roast unappetizing. . . . Tell me: you really don't like it?" And I must answer: "You're getting disturbed for no reason, my dear. The roast is very good." And she will reply: "You always intercede for me, Nikolai Stepanich, and never tell the truth. Why does Alexander Adolphovich eat so little?" The rest of the dinner continues in this way. Liza laughs sporadically and squints her eyes. I look at both of them and it is only now at dinner that it becomes perfectly clear that the domestic life of both had long since ceased to be part of my life. I have a feeling that I no longer am part of a genuine family, and now dine with guests and not with a true wife and do not see the real Liza. A sharp change occurred in both of them. I missed the long process during which this change occurred, and it wasn't wise of me not to comprehend this. Why did this change occur? I don't know. It might be the trouble is that my wife and daughter are not endowed with the same convictions as I am. I was accustomed from childhood to take a stand on the basis of my convictions and thereby acquired enough strength to do so. Everyday catastrophes such as fame, a general's rank, the transition from living comfortably within one's means, acquaintance with bigwigs, and so forth, really hardly touched me, and I remained whole and undefiled; but the weak, not toughened wife and Liza were overwhelmed by this as if a snowdrift had inundated them.

The ladies and Gnekker converse about fugues, counterpoint, of singers and pianists, of Bach and Brahms, and my wife, fearing that she will be scorned as a musical ignoramus, smiles benignly and babbles: "That's charming. . . . Isn't it? Inform me. . . ." Gnekker eats voraciously, cracks jokes, and condescendingly listens to the observations of the ladies. Once in a while he reveals a desire to speak in his poor French, and then for some reason finds it necessary to address me as *votre excellence*.

And I'm glum. It's obvious that I inhibit them and they inhibit me. In earlier times I was never curt with signs of class antagonism, but now I'm bothered by anything which appears in this manner. I try to find in Gnekker only stupid characteristics, and find them easily and suffer torments that as a suitor for my daughter sits a person outside my class. His presence irritates me in yet another regard. Usually, when I'm alone or if it happens that I'm in the company of people I like, I never think of my achievements, or if I do, I find them minuscule, as if it were only yesterday that I became a scientist. In the presence of people like Gnekker my accomplishments appear so superior to me that they rise above the clouds and in their height can hardly be noticed by Gnekker.

After dinner I go to my study, light my pipe, the only one for the day; it is a survivor from my past, a dirty habit of smoking from morning 'til night. While I'm smoking my wife enters and sits down. She wants to speak with me. Just as in the morning, I know beforehand what our conversation is going to be about. "We must have a serious talk, Nikolai Stepanich," she begins. "With reference to Liza. . . . Why won't you pay attention?"

"That is?"

"You give the appearance that you don't notice anything, and that's not right. It can't be treated lightly. . . . Gnekker is going to declare his intentions. . . . What will you say?"

"That he's a stupid man, I can't say, because I don't know him, but that I don't like him, I've already told you a thousand times."

"But you can't do that . . . it's impossible."

She gets up and walks around, disturbed.

"It's impossible to treat a serious step this way . . . ," she says. "When the question is the happiness of our daughter, one must cast aside what's personal. I know you don't like him. . . . All right. . . . If we reject him now, thwart everything, how will you guarantee that Liza won't refuse to forgive us for the rest of her life? Who knows how many suitors are out there, and it could happen that there won't be another one. . . . He loves Liza very much, and apparently she finds him desirable. . . . Of course, he hasn't made a definite proposal, but what's to be done? God willing, in time he'll propose. He comes from a good family and is rich."

"How do you know this?"

"He said so. His father has a large home in Kharkov and an estate in the outlying area. In a word, Nikolai Stepanich, you must take a trip to Kharkov."

"What for?"

"You'll learn everything there. . . . You have colleagues there and they'll be able to help you. . . . I would go myself but I'm a woman. I can't. . . ."

"I'm not going to Kharkov," I say gloomily.

My wife became frightened and her face became distorted with anguish.

"For God's sake, Nikolai Stepanich!" she pleaded, sobbing.

"For God's sake, take this load from my back! I'm suffering under it!"

It became painful for me to look at her.

"All right, Varya," I say to her kindly. "If you wish, it will happen. I'll go to Kharkov and do what you want."

She wipes her eyes with her handkerchief and retires to her room to cry. I remain alone.

A little later a light is brought in. Shadows lie on the floor and on the walls from the armchairs and the lampshade that begin to bore me, and it seems to me that night has come and my cursed insomnia is beginning. I lie down in bed, later get up and walk around the room, then lie down again. . . . Usually after dinner and before evening, my nervous exacerbation reaches its highest level. Without any reason I begin to weep and cover my head with the pillow. At this time I'm afraid that someone might come in, afraid of unexpected death, ashamed of my tears, and in general my soul senses something unbearable. I feel that soon I won't see the lamp, or the books, or the shadows on the floor, or hear the sound of voices that can be heard from the drawing room. An unseen and not understood power is dragging me from my study. . . . I jump up, hastily dress, and, cautiously, so as not to be noticed by anyone in the house, I go out into the street. Where shall I go?

The answer to this question had already been settled for some time in my brain: to Katya's.

III

Usually she is lying on the Turkish divan or is sitting on the small couch and reading something. Upon seeing me she lazily raises her head, sits up, and stretches her hand toward me.

"You're always lying around," I say, hesitating a little and taking a rest. "That's bad. You'd do better to involve yourself in something."

"What?"

"You'd do better, I repeat, to involve yourself in something."

"With what? A woman can only do unskilled work or be an actress."

"So what? If it's impossible to be a worker, be an actress."

Silence.

"You could get married," I said, half-jokingly.

"There's no one for me to marry. And, no reason for it."

"You can't continue to live the way you do."

"Without a husband? Big deal! If I were willing, there'd be men around."

"That, Katya, is ugly."

"What's ugly?"

"That which you just said."

Noting that I was disturbed, and wanting to smooth over the offensive impression, Katya says:

"Come. Let's go in here."

She leads me into a small, very cozy room and says, pointing to the desk:

"See. . . . I got this ready for you. You can work here. Come every day and bring work with you. All they do at home is disturb you. Will you work here? Do you want to?"

In order not to hurt her with a refusal, I said I would work there and that I found the room attractive. . . . After this we both sat down in the cozy little room and talked.

The warm, pleasant situation and the presence of a sympathetic human being does not, as previously, awaken in me a feeling of contentment, but a powerful urge to complain and fret. Why I don't know, but it seems that if I express my discontent and complain, it would feel better.

"It's a bad business, my dear!" I begin with a sigh. "Very bad. . . ."

"What is?"

"It's like this, my friend. The best and most holy right of kings—is the right to pardon. And I've always considered myself in the position of a king and made use of this right in an unlimited way. I've never been judgmental, was indulgent, gladly forgave all on both the right and the left. Where others protested and were indignant, I only gave advice and tried to persuade. All my life I have only tried to make my existence tolerable for my family, for the students, for friends, for the servants. This kind of behavior toward people, I know, guided all who came in contact with me. But now I'm no longer king. In me there exists now something that is only fit for slaves. Day and night my head is swarming with angry thoughts, and in my soul feelings such as I had never had before are weaving for themselves a nest. I hate, and I despise, declare worthless, become enraged and frightened. I have become an immoderately severe taskmaster, irritable, unkind, suspicious. Even that which previously had given me cause to make a superfluous pun and to laugh good-naturedly now creates in me a kind of depression. Even my logic has changed. Formerly I only scorned money, but now I have malicious feelings not toward money but toward the wealthy, as if they were sinners. Formerly, I fervently hated violence and tyranny, but now I hate those who act violently as if they alone are guilty. But aren't we guilty, too, who don't improve each other's characters? What does this mean? If new thoughts and new feelings are derived from changes in convictions, where can these changes come from? Has the world become worse and I better, or was I blind earlier and indifferent? If this change occurred because society has declined both physically and mentally—I lose weight every day and am ill—my condition is pitiful: This makes my new thoughts abnormal, unhealthy, and I must be ashamed of them and consider them demeaning. . . ."

"Sickness is neither here nor there," Katya interrupts me. "Your eyes have simply been opened; and nothing else. You saw what you could not see before, and what you did not want to notice. That is why, more than anything else, you must break with your family and leave."

"What you're saying is disgraceful."

"You don't love them, so why twist your soul with pretending to love them? And what kind of a family do you have? They're low-class. When they die no one will notice their absence on the following day."

Katya despises my wife and daughter as much as they hate her. It is not good form in our day to talk of the right of people to despise each other. But from Katya's point of view one has such a right, and she has the right to despise my wife and daughter just as they have to hate her.

"Nonentities!" she repeats. "Have you eaten today? Have they forgotten to call you to the dining room? Do they still remember that you exist?"

"Katya," I address her sternly, "please be quiet."

"Do you think I enjoy saying this about them? I would be happy not to know them at all. Listen to me, my dear: chuck it all and leave. Go abroad. The sooner the better."

"What nonsense! And the university?"

"The university, too. What good is it to you? It's of no use to you. You've been lecturing for thirty years and where are your students? How many of your students are renowned? Count them! If you put together all those doctors who exploit the ignorant and earn hundreds of thousands, you don't have to be talented and have your heart in the right place. You're superfluous."

"Dear God, how sharp you are!" I was appalled. "How sharp! If you don't stop it, I'll leave! I don't know how to answer your cutting remarks!"

The maid enters and calls us to tea. Sitting by the samovar, the conversation, thank God, changes. Later, as I had earlier complained, I wanted to give vent to another of my senile weaknesses—recollections. I tell Katya of my past and with great amazement describe details that were still intact in my memory which I had not suspected. And she listens fondly to me, with pride and with bated breath. I especially liked to describe to her the time when I studied in the seminary, and how I dreamed of entering the university.

"It would be that I was strolling in the seminary's garden . . . ," I told her. "From some distant tavern the wind carried the sounds of the crude playing of an accordion and singing, or a troika with its bells ringing passes the seminary's gate, and it was enough for happiness to suddenly fill not only my breast, but my stomach, my legs, my arms. . . . You hear the accordion or the waning peel of the bells and you imagine yourself a doctor and paint pictures for yourself—one better than the other. And so, you see, my dreams came true. I

346   Stories of Men

achieved more than I dared to dream. For thirty years I was a beloved professor, had wonderful comrades, was the recipient of honorable distinction. I loved and married because of passionate love, and had children. Simply said, if I look back, all my life presents itself to me as a beautiful composition put together in a talented way. The only thing left for me to do is not to ruin the finale. For that it is necessary for me to die like a man. If death is indeed perilous, then it must be met as is fitting for a teacher, a scholar, and a citizen of a Christian country: boldly and with a peaceful soul. But I'm spoiling this finale. I'm drowning, I run to you for help, and you give me the warmth that I need."

But then the doorbell rang. Katya and I both recognize it and remark:

"That must be Mihail Fedorovich."

Within a minute my colleague, Mihail Fedorovich, a philologist, enters. He is tall, about fifty years old, with bushy gray hair, black eyebrows, and clean-shaven. He is a fine fellow and a great comrade. He is from an old patrician family, well-off, and talented, and plays an important part in our literary and educational history. He is smart, gifted and well educated, but not without eccentricity. Up to a certain point we're all strange and a bit odd, but his eccentricity is somewhat exceptional and threatening to his acquaintances. Among the latter I know a good many who do not recognize his many good qualities because of his eccentricity.

As he entered, he slowly slipped off his gloves and said in a velvet basso:

"Greetings. Having tea? That's just what I need. It's devilishly cold outside."

He then sat down at the table and helped himself to a glass and immediately began talking. The main characteristic of his style of speaking is continual humor, a mix of philosophy and buffoonery, reminiscent of Shakespeare's grave diggers. He always speaks of serious matters but never in a serious manner. His criticisms are always sharp, nit-picking, but thanks to his gentle, even jocular tone, it somehow comes out in a fashion that does not grate on the ears, and you soon get used to it.

Every night he brings with him some five or six anecdotes from university life and usually starts out by telling them as soon as he sits down at the table.

"Oh, Lord," he sighs, ridiculously wiggling his black eyebrows. "What clowns inhabit this earth!"

"Who?" asks Katya.

"I had just left the lecture hall and met on the stairs that old idiot, our NN. . . . He was walking, as is his custom, with his equine chin protruding forward and is looking for someone to complain to about his migraine headache, his wife, and his students who don't want to be present when he lectures. Well, I think, he saw me—now I'm a goner, the jig's up. . . ."

And so on in the same vein. Or he might begin in this way:

"I went to our ZZ's public lecture yesterday. I'm amazed that our alma mater—the less said the better—decides to show the public such a booby and patented dunce as this ZZ. For pity's sake, you couldn't find another fool like this in all of Europe even if you put everything you had into it! He lectures, as you can imagine, as if he's sucking on a gumdrop: syu-syu-syu. . . . He panics, his paper is poorly thought out, the points drag on with the speed of an overseer of a monastery on a bicycle, but most important, no way can you figure out what he wants to say. The boredom is overwhelming. The flies buzz. The boredom is equal to that which we suffer during the annual ceremony in the university auditorium when the traditional oration is given, damn it."

And then an immediate sharp change:

"Three years ago, Nikolai Stepanich, I remember it was my turn to give the oration. It was hot, close, my uniform was too tight under the arms—it was deadly! I read for a half-hour, an hour and a half, two hours. . . . Well, I thought, thank God, only ten more pages left. It was impossible to read four pages, so I decided to skip them. That meant only six would be left. But, imagine this scene; I take a glance at the front row and see a top-echelon chief wearing all his ribbons, and an archbishop. They were bored stiff; they stared in order to keep awake and tried to decipher what I was saying and appear attentive to show that they understood my lecture and found it pleasing. Well, I think, if you like it, it's yours! So I went ahead and read the four pages."

When he remarks about anything, as can be observed in most derisive people, only his eyes and brows smile. It's not that there is hate in his eyes, nor malice of any kind, but perspicuity and that special foxy slyness that can be noticed only by perceptive individuals. Speaking of his eyes, there is still another uniqueness. When he takes a glass from Katya, or listens to what she has to say, or follows her with his eyes when she leaves the room for something, I see in his glance that which is gentle, entreating, artless. . . .

The maid removes the samovar and places on the table some fruit, a large piece of cheese, and a bottle of Crimean champagne—a rather poor wine that Katya acquired a taste for while living in the Crimea. Mihail Fedorovich takes two decks of cards from the curio cabinet and spreads out a game of patience. Although he believes that some of the games require astuteness and concentration, he nevertheless doesn't stop talking in order not to be distracted while setting up the cards. Katya assiduously follows his cards and without words helps him by facial movements. She drinks no more than two glasses of wine during the whole evening; I drink four glasses; what's left is drunk by Mihail Fedorovich, who can drink a great deal and never gets drunk.

During the patience we discuss a variety of questions authoritatively. These concern that which we honor more than anything else, that is, science.

"Science, thank God, has had its day," says Mihail Fedorovich in a restrained voice. "Its song has been sung. Yes-s. Mankind already feels the need to replace it with something else. It arose from the soil of prejudices, was fed by prejudices, and consists now of the quintessence of superstitions like the old wives' tales known as: alchemy, metaphysics, and philosophy. And, moreover, what has it given to mankind? There isn't much difference between the learned European scientists and the unscientific Chinese. The Chinese were unscientific, but what did they lose?"

"Flies aren't aware of any scientific knowledge," I comment, "so what?"

"It's nothing to be angry about, Nikolai Stepanich. I only

say this between the two of us. . . . I'm more careful than you think, and wouldn't say that in public, Lord preserve me! The masses live according to prejudices that science and the arts are above agriculture, commerce, and industry. Our class is fed by these prejudices and I'm not about to disturb that. Lord preserve me!"

When the patience is over, he goes after the young.

"Our public is degenerate today," sighs Mihail Fedorovice. "I'm not talking about ideals anymore; if they'd only know how to work and think efficiently! To be precise: 'I have a dismal opinion of our generation.' "*

"Yes, terribly degenerate," agrees Katya. "Tell me, has there been at least one remarkable event in the last five to ten years?"

"I don't know what is true in other professions, but in mine, I can't think of anything."

"I've seen in my time many students, actors, and your young scientists. . . . What of it? Not once did I manage to meet a hero or a talent, or even simply an interesting person. All were dull, untalented, and full of pretensions."

All these conversations about the decline in our culture always make an impression upon me as if I had eavesdropped accidentally upon a nasty conversation about my daughter. I find it vexing to hear unfounded accusations built on such old, trite generalizations, such bugbears about cultural decline, lack of ideals or reverence for the marvelous past. Every accusation, even if expressed in the presence of women, must be formulated with the possibility of knowing something for certain, otherwise it is not an accusation but an empty, malicious piece of gossip unworthy of respectable individuals.

I'm an old man, have worked for thirty years, but have not noticed either degenerateness or the absence of ideals, and do not find that it is any worse today than in the past. My doorkeeper, Nikolai, who from experience has his own opinion of this, says that today's students are no better and no worse than in the past.

If I were asked what I didn't like about my current students,

*Lermontov

I would not answer and hold off for a time, but when I did, I would attempt more detailed certainty. I know their deficiencies and therefore don't have to deal in the fuzzy area of generalities. I don't like the fact that they smoke, that they need to drink liquor, and that they marry late; that they are happy-go-lucky and often indifferent to the extent that they tolerate in their midst the starving, and don't pay their debts to society for the student assistance they receive. They don't learn new languages and their Russian is poor. Just last evening one of my colleagues, a hygienist, complained to me that he has to take twice as much time to lecture because their knowledge of physics is meager and they are completely ignorant of meteorology. They readily give opinions about the latest writers, even those who are far from the best, but are perfectly indifferent about the classics such as Shakespeare, Marcus Aurelius, Epictetus, or Pascal. And this inability to distinguish between what is more or less important reflects their lack of practical experience. The difficult questions have more or less a social character (for example, immigration), and they make decisions from secondary information and not by way of scientific research and personal experiments, even though the latter means is available to them and is the primary purpose of their appointment. They eagerly accept positions as interns, assistants, laboratory technicians, even if not qualified, and are ready to remain such until they are forty, even though independence, the sense of freedom, and personal initiative in scientific scholarship are needed as much as in industry or commerce. I have students and an audience but no assistants or successors, and because I like them and am touched by them, I am not proud of them. And so on, and so on. . . .

Similar deficiencies, and there are many of them, can only give rise to pessimism or an abusive attitude in a fainthearted or weak person. They all have an opportunistic, transient character and their behavior is completely dependent upon their environment. It wouldn't be too bad if after ten years they would disappear or give up their positions to others, perhaps with new limitations. It's not possible to get along without them and they, too, in their turn, will alarm the fainthearted. Students' sins are revealed to me often, but this grief is nothing in comparison with the delight I've had for thirty years from speaking with students, lecturing to them, and I really am pleased with their activities when I compare them with people outside their circles.

Mihail Fedorovich reviles, Katya listens, and they both don't notice what a deep ravine they are gradually being dragged into by what seems to be an innocent diversion like criticizing their neighbors. They do not sense how such talk develops into mockery and humiliation, and how both of them are beginning to slander in the process.

"I ran into an extremely funny situation," says Mihail Fedorovich. "I went to our Yegor Petrovich yesterday and met there one of these nerdy students—one of your third-year medics. His face was the kind . . . known as good natured with profundity stamped on his brow. We had a conversation. 'Things are in bad shape, young man,' I say. 'I read that a German—I can't remember his name—extracted from a human brain a new alkaloid—idiotine.' What do you think was his reaction? He believed me and even his face expressed esteem: i.e., one of us, you know!

"The other day I went to the theater. I found my seat and in front of me in the next row sat two men: one 'of ours' and the other apparently a lawyer. The medic was disheveled and dead drunk. He has no idea of what is going on on the stage. He dozes and his head nods. But, whenever an actor begins to raise his voice or has a loud soliloquy, my medic shudders, pokes his neighbor, and asks: 'What's he saying? Is it no-o-ble?' 'It's noble,' answers the lawyer. 'Bravo!' yells the medic. 'No-o-ble! Bravo!' This drunken blockhead came to the theater not to appreciate art but to find nobility. He needs nobility."

Katya listens and laughs. Her laugh is somehow strange: she breathes in and out quickly and in a regular rhythm—as if she were playing an accordion and only her nostrils are laughing. I'm disturbed, but do not know what to say. My temper being sorely tried, I lose patience, jump up, and shout: "Shut up! Why do you sit here like two toads and poison the air with your breathing? Enough!"

And, not waiting for them to finish their bad-mouthing, I get ready to go home. And it's time: it's eleven o'clock.

"I'm going to stay awhile," says Mihail Fedorovich. "May I, Yekaterina Vladimirovna?"

"You have my permission," answers Katya.

"*Bene.** In that case, order another bottle of champagne."

They both accompany me with candles to the entry, and as I put on my fur coat Mihail Fedorovich says:

"You've gotten frightfully thin lately and you've aged, Nikolai Stepanovich. What's up? Are you ailing?"

"Yes, I have a minor ailment."

"And you're not doing anything about it . . . ," Katya gloomily chimes in.

"Why don't you take care of it? How can that be? God takes care of the one who takes care of himself, dear man. My regards to your family and apologize to them for my absence. I'll drop in in a few days to say good-bye before I go abroad. Without fail! I'll be leaving next week."

I leave Katya's aggravated, alarmed by the talk about my health, and dissatisfied with myself. I ask myself: Really, can't you go to one of your colleagues for advice? At the same time I picture my colleague listening to my heart and poking around, then he leaves me and stands by the window deep in thought. He will then turn to me, tries not to let me see the truth on his face, says with an unconcerned voice: "While I don't see anything in particular, all the same, comrade, I would advise you to cut down on your work. . . ." And that will deprive me of all hope.

Who doesn't have hope? Now, when I make my own diagnosis and treat myself, I'm optimistic at times and know that I'm being deceived by my own ignorance. My measure of albumin and sugar is inaccurate—wrong about my heartbeat, too, and other signs that I've observed in the mornings. With the intensity of a hypochondriac I peruse the therapeutic texts and daily change my medication. It seems to me that I will happen upon something palliative. It's all of little use. Whether the sky is covered with storm clouds or is bright with stars and the moon, I gaze at it always with the thought that I will soon die. It would seem that at such times my thoughts would be profound like the

---

*Italian for "fine." He likes to show off his erudition.

sky, enlightened, startling. . . . But no! I think only of myself, of my wife, of Liza, Gnekker, of the students, and, in general, about people. My thoughts are unpleasant, petty, crafty even with myself, and at such times my worldview can be expressed by the words of the renowned Arakcheyev* in one of his letters: "Everything that is good in this world cannot exist without its opposite, and always there is more evil than good." That's vile and states there's nothing to live for and that the sixty-two years I have already lived have been wasted. I curb such thoughts and convince myself that they are incidental, momentary, and superficial, but at the same time I think:

If so, why am I drawn every evening to those two toads?

And I swear to myself that I will never go to Katya's again, although I know that on the next day I will go.

I pull the bell at my own door and then go up the stairs. I sense that I no longer have a family or a desire to return to it. It is clear that new Arakcheyevian thoughts are part of me and not incidental, and not temporary, but have dominated my whole being. With a pained conscience, depressed, lazy, barely able to move my limbs as if I had put on a hundred pounds, I lie down in my bed and soon fall asleep.

But later—insomnia. . . .

IV

Summer arrives and my life changes.

One beautiful morning Liza comes into my study and says with a jocular tone:

"Come, your excellency. Everything is ready."

They take my excellency out to the street, put me in a cab, and we go off. From nothing else to do, I read signs from the right to the left. The word "tavern" becomes "nrevat." That would be a good baronial name: Baroness Nrevat. Further on

---

*Russian soldier and statesman who was counselor and friend to Alexander I. He was a stern disciplinarian and instituted hygienic reforms in the army, which created for him both enemies and friends.

I'm driven by a field near a cemetery, which doesn't make an impression upon me even though it won't be long before I'm lying there. We ride through a forest and by another field. Nothing of interest. After a two-hour ride they lead my excellency to the ground floor of a cottage and settle him in a small, very cheerful room with blue wallpaper.

As before, my nights continue to be sleepless, but instead of getting up in the morning and listening to my wife, I stay in bed. Not sleeping, I endure half-forgotten sleeplessness, knowing that I'm not sleeping but am dreaming. At noon I get out of bed. Out of habit I sit at my desk but no longer work, but distract myself with French novels in yellow paperbacks that Katya sends to me. Of course it would be more patriotic to read Russian writers, but I admit I'm not especially attracted to them. Except for a few old writers, today's literature does not appear to be literature to me. In its way it's a handicraft industry, existing only to stimulate interest in it by those who are reluctant to make use of its productions. The best of these craftsmen's work cannot be called notable, and it is impossible to praise them without a *but*. This holds true for all the literary novelties I've read in the last ten to fifteen years: not a single notable work, and you can't avoid the *but*. It's smart, in good taste, *but* without talent; or talented, in good taste, *but* not smart, or finally—talented, smart, *but* not in good taste.

I'm not saying that the French books are talented, smart, and in good taste. They, too, dissatisfy me. But they're not as boring as the Russian, and it isn't a rarity to find in them an important component of creativity—a sense of personal freedom that Russian writers do not have. I don't know of a single Russian novel in which the author from the first page doesn't strive to entangle himself in all kinds of conditions and contracts with his conscience. One is afraid to write anything about the naked body, another binds his arms and legs in psychological analysis, a third must have "a warm regard for humanity," a fourth for no purpose at all covers whole pages describing nature in order not to be suspected of bias. . . . One wants to be recognized in his works as a low-class urbanite, and another doubtless of the rural gentry, and so on. They have deliberateness, prudence, cunning, but there is neither freedom nor courage to write as one might wish and, consequently, there is no creativity either. All this has to do with what is called refined literature. As to serious Russian articles, for example, about sociology, about art, etcetera, then I don't read them simply from diffidence. In my childhood and youth for some reason I was afraid of doormen and theater ushers, and this fear remains with me to this day. It is said that only that which is not understood seems fearful. But, really, it is difficult to understand why doormen and ushers are so important, arrogant, and sublimely rude. When I read serious articles I feel exactly the same kind of vague fear. The inordinate self-importance, the wanton air of a general, the familiar reference to strange authors, the ability to pour from one empty pitcher to another in a dignified way—I don't understand any of this. It's all terrible and lacks the modesty and calm gentlemanly tone I've become accustomed to in our doctor's publications, and that of naturalists. Not just articles but translations that serious Russians write or edit. The conceited, presumptuous, copious remarks from the translator disturb my concentration. The question marks and *sic* in brackets generously distributed by the translator throughout the article or book present to me an encroachment upon the author's person and upon the independence of the reader.

I was invited once as an expert in a circuit court. During a break one of my fellow experts directed my attention to the rude approach of the prosecutor toward the accused, among whom were two intelligent women. In answer to my colleague I noted that this behavior was no more rude, it seemed to me, than that which was carried on between the authors of serious articles. Really, this behavior is so repulsive that one can only speak of it with a heavy feeling. The person-to-person relations of these writers and those they criticize are carried on excessively politely regardless of their merit—or quite the reverse and slight them far more boldly than I do in these notes and thoughts about my future son-in-law, Gnekker. Accusations of irresponsibility, shady intentions, and even criminal acts make up the usual outstanding features of serious articles. That is how

356   Stories of Men

the young doctors like to express themselves in their articles, *ultima ratio!** The morals of the younger generation of writers must be affected by such carrying-on. It is because of this I am not surprised that the latest literary innovations acquired in the last ten to fifteen years have been heroes who drink a lot of vodka and heroines who are not chaste.

I read the French books and at times look out the open window. I can see the tops of the pointed stakes of the garden fence, several scraggly trees, and beyond the fence, the road, fields, and a wide strip of coniferous forest. I often enjoy seeing a boy and a girl, both fair-haired and ragged, clamber on the fence and laugh at my bald head. In their bright eyes I read: "Get moving, baldy!" They are just about the only people who know nothing or care nothing about my rank.

I don't have visitors every day. I'll mention only the visits of Nikolai and Peter Ignatyevich. Nikolai usually comes on holidays, as if it's about work, but more than that—just so we can see each other. He comes very drunk, which he never is in the winter.

"What's new?" I ask as I meet him in the hallway.

"Your excellency!" he exclaims, pressing his hand to his heart and looking at me with the ecstasy of a lover. "Your excellency! May God strike me dead! Let lightning kill me on this spot! *Gaudeamus igitur yuvenestus!*"†

And he greedily kisses my shoulders, sleeves, and buttons.

"Is everything well with you ?" I ask him. . . .

"Your excellency! As God is my witness . . ."

He continues to swear without any reason, bores me very quickly, so I send him to the kitchen where they will give him something to eat.

Peter Ignatyevich comes during holidays in order to learn from me and to share thoughts. He usually sits by my desk, modest, lean, sober-minded, doesn't cross his legs or put his elbows on the desk. And all the time in a quiet, calm voice, smoothly and scholarly, tells me an assortment of news that he

---

*the final argument
†In drunken Latin: "Let us be joyful while we are young!"

considers interesting and savory. The news items all resemble one another and are of this type: A Frenchman made a discovery—a German exposed him, proving that the discovery was made in 1870 by an American, while another German finessed them both, proving that both made fools of themselves by mistaking globules of air under the microscope for a suspicious pigment. Peter Ignatyevich even tries to confuse me, going on at length, in great detail, as if defending a dissertation, giving a long list of references that he had made use of, striving not to make mistakes in the names or the issues of the journals. Instead of giving the common abbreviated recognized name, he insists on stating it fully. When he stays for dinner, while eating, he tells the same spicy stories, which bore the other diners to death. If Gnekker and Liza lead the conversation about fugues and counterpoint, about Brahms or Bach, he modestly casts his eyes down and withdraws. He is ashamed that in the presence of such serious people as myself and him, they speak about such trivialities.

In my present mood, five minutes are enough for him to leave me cold, since when I see and listen to him, that's how much time it takes to make it an eternity for me. I dislike the poor devil. I shrivel from his quiet monotonous voice and bookish expression, and his anecdotes numb my brain. . . . He entertains toward me the highest regard and speaks only in order to comfort me, but I repay him by staring as if I wanted to hypnotize him and think: "Leave, leave, leave. . . ." But he doesn't submit to this mental prodding and sits, sits, sits. . . .

While he sits in my house, no way can I dispense with the thought: It's very possible that when I die, they will appoint him to my position. My pathetic lecture hall appears to me as an oasis in which the streams have dried out. Peter Ignatyevich and I become antagonistic, silent, gloomy, as if he is guilty of similar thoughts, and not I alone. When as usual he extols German scientists, I no longer playfully and good-naturedly chide him, as previously, but mutter grumpily:

"Your Germans are asses. . . ."

It resembles the situation when the late Professor Nikita Krilov was swimming with Pirogov in Revel and got angry at the water because it was cold, and he exploded: "These Germans are scoundrels!" I conduct myself stupidly with Peter Ignatyevich, and it is only after he leaves and I look out the window and see his gray head disappearing behind the fence that I want to call him and say: "Forgive me, dear man!"

Dinner at our house is even more boring than during the winter. The same Gnekker whom I now dislike and despise dines with us almost every day. In the past I had tolerated his presence and held my tongue. Now I address him sharply and my wife and Liza blush. Carried away by my animus, I often say plain nonsense and I haven't a clue as to why I say what I do. It happened once that after staring with contempt at Gnekker, for no reason at all the following came out of my mouth:

"Eagles can swoop down to the level of chickens,
But chickens can never reach the lofty clouds!"

And the saddest thing of all is that the chicken-Gnekker appears much more intelligent than the eagle-professor. Knowing that my wife and daughter are on his side, he uses this tactic: He answers my caustic remarks with a condescending silence (the old boy is going balmy—why carry on a conversation with him?), or good-naturedly kids me. You have to be flabbergasted by the extent a person can be cut down! Under these circumstances and during every meal I dream about how Gnekker is proved to be an adventurer, how Liza and my wife will learn their mistake, and how I will tease them—and similar irascible dreams at a time when I already have one foot in the grave!

Misunderstandings now arise of which I had in the past only a sneaking suspicion. Even though I'm ashamed, I will write about one that occurred one day after dinner.

I was sitting in my study smoking a pipe. As usual, my wife enters and begins to talk about how pleasant it would be while it is still warm and there is free time, to drive to Kharkov and to make inquiries there about Gnekker's background.

"All right, I'll go," I agreed.

My wife, satisfied with my response, gets up and goes to the door, but then turns back and says:

"I have one more request. I know you'll get angry, but I'm obliged to warn you. . . . Forgive me, Nikolai Stepanich, but our acquaintances and neighbors are talking about your frequent visits to Katya. She's smart, educated, and I don't dispute that it is compatible for you to spend time with her, but at your age and your social position, somehow, you know, it's strange that you find her society so satisfying. . . . Incidentally, her reputation is such that . . ."

Blood shoots up into my brain, sparks dart from my eyes, I jump up, and, grasping my head, stamping my feet, I scream in a strange voice:

"Leave me alone! Leave me alone! Leave!"

Doubtless, my face was terrible, my voice strange, because my wife suddenly pales and loudly screams in a voice that is also not her own—a desperate voice. Hearing our screaming, Liza and Gnekker run in, followed by Yegor. . . .

"Leave me alone!" I scream. "Get out! Leave me alone!"

My legs gave out under me and seemed nonexistent; I felt that I was falling and someone tried to hold me up; I heard someone weeping and then succumbed into a dead faint that stretched out for several hours.

Now about Katya. She is in my study every day before evening, and therefore, of course, the neighbors and acquaintances cannot fail to notice this. She comes and stays for a minute or so and then takes me out for a drive. She has her own horse and new small carriage, which she bought this summer. Generally, she lives in a grand style: she rented an expensive single cottage with a large garden and moved all her city furniture into it; she had two maids, a coachman. . . . I have often asked her:

"Katya, what are you going to live on when you run through all of your father's money?"

"We'll see then," she answers.

"This money, my dear, was a very serious matter with him. It was earned by a good man's honorable labor."

"You've already told me about that. I know."

First we ride across fields and then through the coniferous forest that could be seen from my window. As before, the natural world appears beautiful to me even though a demon whispers to me that these pines and spruces, the birds, and the white clouds in the sky will not miss me when I die in three or four months. Katya likes to take the reins and it gives me pleasure that the weather is fine and that I am sitting beside her. She is in a good mood and doesn't make any sharp remarks.

"You're a remarkable man, Nikolai Stepanich," she says. "You're an uncommon specimen and the actor that could play you doesn't exist. But me, for example, or Mihail Fedorovich, even a bad actor could play us. And I'm envious of you, terribly envious! What am I to make of myself? What?"

She hesitates for a moment and then asks me:

"Nikolai Stepanich, am I reprehensible? Am I?"

"Yes," I answer.

"Hm. . . . What am I to do?"

What can I say to her? It's easy to say "work," or "give your property to the poor," or "know thyself," and because it is easy to say these things, I don't know what to tell her.

The therapists, my colleagues, when they are teaching, advise: "Treat every case as unique." Listening to such counsel one is convinced that the average model, which is recommended in textbooks, is perfectly useless in a specific situation. This is also true for moral problems.

But I must say something and I do:

"You have, my dear, too much free time. You must involve yourself in something. Really, why don't you become an actress again if that is your calling?"

"I can't."

"The tone of your voice and your manner are those of a victim. I don't like that, my dear. You alone are guilty. Remember, that from the beginning you acted as if you were angry with everyone and with the social mores, but you didn't do anything to improve the situation. You didn't hold your ground but caved in. You were victimized by your own weakness. Well, of course, you were young and inexperienced then, but now things can be different. It's true, do something! You will work, serve your sacred art. . . ."

"Don't be subtle, Nikolai Stepanich," interrupts Katya. "Let's agree once and for all: we will speak about actors, actresses, writers, but we'll make no comments about art. You are a wonderful, rare human being, but you don't know enough about art to be able to criticize it intelligently. You have no feeling or ear for art. You've been working all your life and have never acquired such a feeling. In general . . . I don't like conversations about art!" she continues in an agitated tone. "I don't like them! And art has already been debased, so thank you!"

"Who has debased it?"

"It's been debased by drunkenness, by the newspapers with their offhand treatment, and by the theorizing of the intelligentsia."

"What has theorizing to do with it?"

"It's very apropos. If one theorizes about art it means he has no comprehension of it."

In order to keep the remarks from becoming sharper, I hurry to change the subject and then keep quiet. It is only when we leave the forest, and ride toward Katya's cottage, that I return to the former topic and ask:

"You haven't answered my question: Why don't you want to return to the stage?"

"Nikolai Stepanich, that, finally, is cruel!" she exclaimed and flushed at the same time. "Do you want me to tell you the plain truth? All right, if that . . . if that will please you! I don't have any talent! There's no talent but . . . a great deal of false pride! That's all!"

Making this admission, she turns her face away from me, and in order to hide her trembling hands, holds the reins tightly.

Approaching her cottage, we can already see Mihail Fedorovich from afar. He is strutting around the fence, impatiently waiting for us.

"Mihail Fedorovich again!" exclaims Katya, annoyed. "Take him away from me, please! He's boring and all dried-up. . . . Oh, bother him!"

Mihail Fedorovich was to have gone abroad long ago, but every week he postpones his departure. Lately there has been some kind of a change in him: his cheeks are sunken, he gets tipsy from wine, which had never happened before, and his black eyebrows have begun to get gray. When our buggy stops at the gate, he doesn't hide his pleasure or his impatience. He fussily helps Katya and me, hastens to ply us with questions, laughs, rubs his hands together, and the modest, simple pleading which I had noted previously only in his eyes now floods his face. He is ecstatic and at the same time is ashamed of his delight, ashamed of this habit of being at Katya's every evening; and he needs to justify his arrival in an obviously awkward way such as: "I had to come this way on business and so, I thought, I'll drop in for a minute."

The three of us go inside. First we have tea, then the familiar two decks of cards, large piece of cheese, fruit, and the bottle of Crimean champagne. The topics of conversation are not new either. They are the same as during the winter. They touch upon the university, the students, literature, and the theater. The air is thicker, more suffocating with malice, and poisoned now not by two toads, as in the winter, but by all three. Besides the velvet baritone laughter and boisterous giggling resembling an accordion, the maid who hears us hears another, more unpleasant rattling laugh like that of a vaudeville performer's imitation of a general's: heh-heh-heh. . . .

V

There are terrible summer nights with thunder and lightning, rain and wind, that the peasants call "sparrow nights." I personally experienced one of these sparrow nights. . . .

I awoke in the middle of the night and jumped out of bed. For some reason it seemed to me that I was about to die. Why? There wasn't a single sensation in my body that would indicate the imminence of death, but I was gripped by a fear such as if I were seeing the glow from an ominous fire.

I quickly lit a lamp, drank some water directly from the decanter, and then hastened to the open window. The weather outside was splendid. The air was redolent with the fragrance of hay and something else just as pleasant. I could see the pointed tops of the garden fence; the sleepy, scraggly trees near the

It's all nonsense . . . , I think. It is the influence of one organism upon another. My extreme nervousness has infected my wife, Liza, the dog, and that's it. . . . Such transference explains foreboding, foresight. . . .

When a little later I returned to my room in order to write a prescription for Liza, I no longer thought of my imminent death, but was heavyhearted, irked, even sorry that I hadn't died suddenly. I stood motionless in the middle of the room for a long time considering what to prescribe for Liza. The groans from the room above had stopped and I decided not to prescribe anything, but all the same I remained standing. . . .

The silence is deadly, a silence so powerful that as one writer put it, it caused ringing in the ears. Time drags. The rays of the moonlight upon the windowsill are unchanged, as if trapped there. . . . The dawn is still a long time in arriving.

But the gate in the fence creaks and someone is sneaking in, and breaks off a branch from one of the emaciated trees, and cautiously knocks on my window with it.

"Nikolai Stepanich!" I hear whispered. . . . "Nikolai Stepanich!"

I open the window and it seems to me that I'm dreaming: under the window, pressed against the wall, is a woman in black clothing. The bright moon shines on her and her huge eyes are staring at me. Her face is pale, austere, made to appear spectral, marmoreal by the moonlight. Her chin is trembling.

"It's me . . . ," she says. "It's me . . . Katya!"

By moonlight all women's eyes appear larger and darker, figures appear taller, and faces paler. I truly did not recognize her in the first instance.

"What's your problem?"

"Forgive me," she says. "Life had suddenly become intolerable for me. . . . I could not bear it and came here. . . . There was a light in your window and . . . and I decided to give a gentle knock. . . . Excuse me. . . . Oh, if you only knew how painful it was for me! What are you doing now?"

"Nothing. . . . I can't sleep."

"I had some kind of premonition. Anyhow, it was silly."

Her eyebrows were raised, tears made her eyes brilliant, her whole face was shining as if lit up and had on it the look of trustfulness such as I knew in the past and which I had not seen for a long time.

"Nikolai Stepanich!" she exclaimed in a pleading voice, stretching both her arms toward me. "My dearest, I beg you . . . plead with you. . . . If you don't disdain my friendship and respect for you, agree to my request!"

"What is it?"

"Take my money away from me!"

"Well, well, you've really dreamed something up! What do I want with your money?"

"You can go somewhere to get your health back. You need to get help. Will you take it? Yes? Darling, yes?"

She avidly scrutinizes my face and repeats:

"Yes? You'll take it?"

"No, my dear, I won't . . . ," I tell her. "Thank you."

She turns her back to me and hangs her head. I must have refused her offer in such a manner that further talk about money was impossible.

"Go home to bed," I tell her. "We'll be together tomorrow."

"Does this mean that you don't consider me your friend?" she asks despondently.

"I didn't say that. But your money is useless to me."

"Forgive me . . . ," she said, lowering her voice a whole octave. "I know what you mean. . . . You don't want to be obligated to anyone such as myself . . . a rejected actress. . . . However, farewell. . . ."

And she left so quickly that I didn't succeed in saying good-bye.

VI

I'm in Kharkov.

It would be beyond my power and useless to struggle with my recent condition, so I decided that my last days should be irreproachable in the formalities at least. Even if I've been wrong in my dealings with my family, which I acknowledge without reservations, I would try to do what is asked of me. It is asked that I go to Kharkov, so I'll go to Kharkov. Moreover, lately, I've become so indifferent toward everything that it is all the same to me whether I go to Kharkov, to Paris, or to Berdichev.

I arrived here about twelve o'clock and took a room at a hotel close to the cathedral. On the train I was jolted, subjected to drafts, and now I sit on the bed with my head in my hands and await spasms. I should go today to visit professors I know, but I have neither the desire nor the strength.

The hallway caretaker, who is old, enters and asks if my bed has been made up. I keep him for a few minutes and ask him a few questions relating to Gnekker—that is why I am here. The old lackey says he was born in Kharkov, knows the town like the five fingers on his hand, but doesn't know of a single house that carries the name, Gnekker. I ask about the estate, too—the answer is the same.

The clock in the hallway chimes one o'clock, then two, then three. . . . While I await death the last months of my life seem much longer than any in my whole life. Never before have I been so resigned to having time drag as now. If, in the past, I had to wait at a railway station for a train, or sit monitoring an exam, a quarter of an hour seemed an eternity; now I can sit motionless on my bed all night long and be perfectly indifferent about the fact that tomorrow night would be just as long and lusterless, and the next night too. . . .

Out in the hallway the clock strikes five o'clock, six, seven. . . . It is becoming dark.

I have a dull pain in my cheek—my tic is acting up. In order to absorb myself in thought, I revert to my past approach before I became apathetic and ask:

"Why do I, an eminent person, a high-ranking counselor, sit in this small hotel room, on this bed with someone else's gray blankets? Why do I stare at the cheap metal washbasin and listen to the chiming of the wretched clock in the hallway? Is this really appropriate for a person of my renown and my high rank?" I answer myself with an ironical smile. My naivete is laughable, such as when I was young and exaggerated the importance of renown, and the unique status which notables were assigned. I'm distinguished, my name is uttered with rev-

erence, my portrait was in *The Field* and in *The World Illustrated.*
My biography is even in a German publication—and so what?
Here I am sitting alone in a strange town, on a strange bed, rub-
bing my aching cheek with my palm. . . .

Family unpleasantness, unsympathetic creditors, the vulgarity of the workers on the railroad, the inefficiency of the passport system, the costly and unhealthy food in the buffet, the general ignorance and crudeness of relationships—all this and many
other things that are too many to list concern me no less than
any other resident who is unknown outside his own neighborhood. What makes my situation unique? Let us grant that I'm
renowned a thousand times over, a hero that my country is proud
of. The newspapers run bulletins on the state of my health, my
mail is already packed with sympathetic notes from my colleagues, my students, and the public, but all this doesn't prevent
my dying in a strange bed, melancholy and completely alone. . . .
No one, of course, is to blame, but, I'm a sinner, and I don't like
being a celebrity. It seems to me that I'm being taken for a fool.
I fall soundly asleep about ten o'clock in spite of the tic, and
would have slept a long time but for the fact that I was awakened. About an hour later there was a loud knock at the door.

"Who's there?"

"Telegram for you!"

"They could have waited until tomorrow," I angrily remark
as I take the telegram from the delivery boy. "I won't be able to
fall asleep again."

"Excuse me, sir. Your light was on and I thought you
weren't sleeping."

I open the telegram and look for the name of the sender
before reading it: it's from my wife. What does she want?

GNEKKER AND LIZA WERE MARRIED SECRETLY YES-
TERDAY.
    COME HOME.

I read this message and am momentarily alarmed. It is not
what Gnekker and Liza did that frightens me, but my indifferent
reaction to the news of their marriage. It is said that philoso-

phers and genuinely wise men are dispassionate. That is false. Indifference—reflects a paralysis of one's spirit before death.

I lie down again and begin to think things over. What kind of thoughts should I have? It appears that I've already thought about everything and there is nothing that could now stimulate my thoughts.

When it becomes light, I sit on the bed with my arms about my knees, and having nothing to do, I try to explain myself. "Know thyself"—is a wonderful and useful maxim, but it's too bad that the ancient sages didn't indicate how to do this, how to carry out this advice.

When in the past I desired to understand someone or myself, I didn't concentrate on the transgressions where all is relative, but on what results were desired. Tell me what you want and I'll tell you who you are.

And now I examine myself: What do I want?

I want that our wives, children, friends, and students not love us for what we are recognized, not for our brands and labels, but as ordinary people. What else? I'd like to have helpers and heirs. I would like to sleep for a hundred years and awake to at least cast a cursory eye upon how science had changed. I'd like to live another ten years. . . . What else?

Nothing more. I ponder, rack my brains for a long time, but arrive at nothing new. And no matter what I thought of and where my thoughts drifted, it was clear to me that there was nothing of significance in my desires and that they were lacking something very crucial. In my partiality for science, in my desire to live, in this sitting on an alien bed, and in the striving to know myself, in all my thoughts, feelings, and knowledge, no matter how I put it all together, there is nothing that would bind similarities to make a generalization. Every sensation and every thought exists in me in isolation. In all my opinions about science, the theater, literature, students, and in all the pictures drawn by my imagination, not even the most skilled analyst could detect that which could be called a general concept, or the God of a live human being.

But if one doesn't have this, then one has nothing.

In this destitute situation it was sufficient for a serious illness, a fear of death, the impact of circumstances, and people to capsize and scatter away in bits my former outlook—everything that gave pleasure and meaning to my life. There's nothing amazing about this—that I have tainted the last months of my life with thoughts and feelings worthy of a slave or a barbarian, and that I am apathetic and ignore the coming of dawn. When a person has nothing that maintains his aloofness to external influences, then it is true that even a good cold will make him lose his equilibrium and see an owl in every bird and to hear a dog's howl in every sound. His pessimism or optimism, whatever he thinks is serious or petty, these have meaning only as symptoms and nothing more.

I'm defeated. And if that is the case, there's no point in continuing to ponder or discuss. I will sit quietly and wait for what will be.

In the morning the hallway servant brings me tea and the local newspaper. I read mechanically the news on the front page, the leading article, extracts from other papers and journals, and the list of events of the day. . . . Among other things in the list I find the following: "Yesterday our well-known scientist, the distinguished Professor Nikolai Stepanich, arrived in Kharkov by express train and is staying in such and such a hotel."

Prominent names obviously have a life of their own, having nothing to do with the one who bears them. My name is now serenely making the rounds in Kharkov. In three months it will be engraved in gold letters on my tombstone as the sun itself—and will go on when I'm covered with moss. . . .

There is a light knock on the door. Someone wants me.

"Who's there? Come in!"

The door opens and I step back in surprise and hasten to wrap my dressing gown around me. Before me stands Katya.

"Greetings," she says, winded from climbing the stairs. "You didn't expect me? I, too . . . I also have arrived here."

She sits down and continues, stammering and not looking at me:

"Why don't you say hello? I arrived here. . . . Today. I learned that you were here in this hotel so I came to see you."

"I'm very happy to see you," I say, shrugging my shoulders,

"but I'm surprised. . . . It's as if you dropped out of the sky. Why are you here?"

"Why am I here? Just like that . . . I simply decided and came."

Silence.

She suddenly gets up and impetuously approaches me.

"Nikolai Stepanich!" she exclaims, blanches, and clasps her bosom. "Nikolai Stepanich! I can't continue to live this way! I can't! For God's sake, tell me quickly, this very minute: What shall I do? Tell me, what shall I do?"

"What can I say?" I ask in bewilderment. "I can't say anything."

"Tell me, I beg you!" she goes on, gasping, and her whole body trembling. "I swear to you that I can't go on living like this! I can't take it anymore!"

She drops into a chair and begins to sob. Her head is thrown back, she is wringing her hands and stamping her feet. Her hat has fallen from her head and is dangling from the elastic, and her hair is disheveled.

"Help me! Help me!" she pleads. "I can't go on like this!"

She takes a handkerchief out of her expensive handbag and at the same time pulls out several letters that fall from her lap unto the floor. I pick them up and notice Mihail Fedorovich's handwriting and cannot help reading part of a word: "passion——."

"There's nothing I can say to you, Katya," I declare.

"Help me!" she sobs, grabbing my hand and kissing it. "You are my real father, my only friend! You are truly wise, educated, have lived a long time! You have been a teacher! Tell me: What am I to do?"

"Truly, Katya: I don't know. . . ."

I became upset, disconcerted, shaken by her sobbing, and could feel my legs caving under me.

"Let's have breakfast, Katya," I suggest, trying to smile. "Tears can come later!"

And then I immediately add softly:

"I'm on my last legs, Katya. . . ."

"One word from you would be enough, just one word!" she pleads, her hands outstretched. "What am I to do?"

"You're acting a little demented . . . ," I sputter. "I don't understand you at all! Such a smart young woman and suddenly—well, I never! Too many tears. . . ."

Silence descends. Katya straightens her hair, puts on her hat, crumples up the letters and shoves them into her handbag—all of this slowly and silently. Her face, her breast, and her gloves are wet with tears, but the expression on her face is now parched, bitter. . . . I look at her and am ashamed because I am happier than she. It is only now that death is imminent and I have reached the sunset of my thoughts that I realize that I do not have what my philosopher colleagues refer to as a general concept. But this poor beggar has never known and will never know a haven all of her life, all of her life!

"Let's have breakfast, Katya," I say.

"No, thank you," she answers coldly.

Another minute passes in silence.

"I don't like Kharkov," I comment. "It's so gray. It's a dismal town."

"Yes, perhaps . . . it is ugly. . . . I'm not staying long. . . . I'm just passing through. I'm leaving today."

"Where to?"

"The Crimea . . . more precisely, to the Caucasus."

"Oh. For how long?"

"I don't know."

Katya gets up, smiles coldly, not looking directly at me, and extends her hand.

I want to ask her: "Does this mean you won't be at my funeral?" But she is not looking at me, her hand is cold, as if a stranger's. I say nothing while accompanying her to the door. She is now leaving me, walking down the long corridor without looking back. She knows I am watching her go, and certainly, she will look back when she reaches the turn.

No, she does not look back. The black gown flashes by for the last time, the sound of her steps gradually disappears. . . .

Farewell, my precious!

1889